The Magic Ship

Nothing in this novel is pure invention.

The Magic Ship

SANDRA PARETTI

translated from the German by
RUTH HEIN

Down East Books
Camden, Maine

ISBN 0-89272-463-3

5   4   3   2   1

Designed by Alice E. Devine
Printed and bound at Capital City Press, Inc., Montpelier, Vermont

Down East Books
P.O. Box 679, Camden, Maine 04843
Book Orders: 1-800-766-1670

Library of Congress Cataloging-in-Publication Data

Paretti, Sandra. (1935 [?]–1994)
    [Zauberschiff. English]
    The magic ship / Sandra Paretti : translated from the German by
Ruth Hein.
        p.   cm.
    ISBN 0-89272-463-3 (pbk.)
    1. Kronprinzessin Cecilie (Ship)—Fiction. 2. Bar Harbor
(Me.)—
History—Fiction. I. Hein, Ruth. II. Title.
PT2676.A67Z2413 1999
833'.914—dc21   98-46393

Friday, July 31, 1914

THE LINER, She's a Lady.

—*Rudyard Kipling*

*T*he resplendent ship moved shining through the night; she held to an eastward course, heading for the precise point where the world was darkest. The moon, almost full, hung above starboard.

The constant sinking and rising of the bow could barely be felt on the bridge; the ship seemed to be cutting, not through water, but through night and eternity. The sea parted of itself, as if the ship were merely a mirage of the night, no more real than her own reflection on the black surface of the water—both ships magical in their sparkling glitter.

No lights were burning on the bridge of the *Kronprinzessin Cecilie;* a muted semidarkness surrounded the illuminated instrument table. The man standing at the wall of windows, looking out over the forward part of the ship and the bow, was a giant. His captain's cap nearly touched the ceiling. Appropriate to the cooler temperatures prevailing at this latitude, he wore the uniform of navy-blue wool. The jacket stretched taut across his back. A few brightly colored flakes of confetti were spinkled on his left shoulder.

The arrival in the first European port, and with it the traditional Captain's Dinner, was yet to come; but the shipboard store that carried the articles indispensable to the festivities—confetti, streamers, paper hats—had already begun to put them on sale, and one of the ladies at the captain's table had been unable to wait for the following day.

Besides Charles Pollak, the captain, five other men were on the bridge. All had known Pollak for a long time, and the glances they exchanged behind his back expressed astonishment, a certain unease. It was almost eleven o'clock; there was no reason for the captain to be on the bridge at this hour. The course of the ship had been set for the night, as had the speed. There was nothing for him to do here. Why, then, should he leave the dining saloon, when usually he was only too fond of prolonging the dinner hour with the ladies at his table until long after midnight?

Many captains of the larger transatlantic liners plying the North Atlantic routes considered the social aspect of their jobs a burden. Not Charles Pollak. Though the ship he commanded was not the swiftest or the most luxurious, the *Cecilie* was indisputably one of the most popular on the golden route of the North Atlantic. The passengers adored him, this walrus-moustached giant, especially the Americans. When they made their bookings in the New York office of North German Lloyd, they did not ask for the ship herself, the double-screwed liner *Kronprinzessin Cecilie*—the name was, in any case, unpronounceable to American tongues. They simply asked, "When is Captain Pollak sailing for Europe?" Some passengers had been loyal to him for twenty years and had traveled with him on all his ships. To them he was Papa Pollak or quite simply Charlie.

He was one of the best and most experienced captains on the North Atlantic. He had brought off miracles recorded in the manuals of seafaring. If the occasion demanded, he stayed on the bridge for forty-eight hours. At a dinner party he exhibited the same tenacity, and it was no simple matter to pry him loose once he had arrived at dessert and his favorite coffee liqueur. This preference was strange in a man such as Pollak. He could consume glass after glass of it, cheerfully leaning back in his chair at the captain's table in the large and splendid first-class dining saloon—coffee liqueur alternating with dishes of strawberry ice. Why had he abandoned his position tonight?

None of the men on the bridge knew him better than Pommerenke, his personal steward, his "tiger," as they were called at sea. The two men had been together for thirty years, twenty-six of them in the employ of Lloyd; Pommerenke therefore sensed even more than the others the tension emanating from the oversize figure. Pollak had not spoken a word since coming on the bridge. He was still standing in the same spot, the tips of his black shoes on the polished teak, his heels on the red runner. The confetti on the captain's left shoulder upset Pommerenke more than anything else; he was superstitious, and the bits of colored paper, scattered too quickly and prematurely, aroused dour premonitions in him. His hands itched to reach out and brush them away.

He came a step closer. "Coffee?" he asked.

A dark brown special brew was always kept ready on the bridge for Pollak. He seldom refused the offer. But this time the captain seemed not even to have heard the question.

"The telescope," he said, holding out one hand. Pommerenke observed him as he lifted the glass with both hands and adjusted it to his eyes. But what was there to see out there in the darkness, impenetrable even to the fine lens?

"Anyone . . . coffee?" Pommerenke asked cheerfully.

The men standing by the instruments—oddly resembling each other in the weak illumination from below—exchanged glances, but none replied in the affirmative. The silence remained, broken only by the normal sounds of the ship—the soft sighing as the hull rose and fell, the barely perceptible swish of the rudder, the thud of the engines, the distant music occasionally rising from the lounge.

They were therefore all the more startled by the sound of steps approaching along the passageway and the roll of the iron door being raised at the side of the bridge. Simoni, the *Cecilie's* wireless operator, hesitated when he caught sight of the silent figures. Pollak lowered the telescope; he had heard the wireless operator approaching, and in the lens before him, which worked like a dark mirror, he could see Simoni's shape. But he did not turn around. Pommerenke had the absurd impression that the captain's back was growing even broader and more unapproachable.

Simoni stood still, nervously staring at the white paper in his hand. He rarely came on the bridge; generally he used a messenger to bring up incoming cables, and while the silence around him lasted, he wished that he had done so now rather than yielding to the temptation to run the errand himself. When he spoke at last, his voice sounded less alarmed than apologetic. "A message for the captain." He avoided addressing the large, silent shape directly. "Urgent and confidential."

Slowly Pollak turned, and that gesture alone was enough to persuade the men that their gloomy thoughts were mere crotchets.

Even when the captain was serious, as he was now, his features radiated optimism. Most of all it was his eyes—merry eyes, wreathed in a multitude of little crinkles, in which an amused smile always seemed to nestle. He returned the telescope to the third officer and took the paper from the wireless operator's hand; he did not bother to glance at it, as if wholly indifferent to its contents.

"I'll have that coffee now," he said. "I hope it's strong enough, Pommerenke." He pronounced his *s*'s like a man from the North Sea region.

"Thick and hot as hell, Captain," came Pommerenke's answer. "Coffee for anyone else?" His voice and his features expressed relief. Three men spoke up simultaneously, and the aroma of coffee permeated the bridge. Simoni still stood rooted to the spot, his eyes turned expectantly on Pollak. The coded text of the cable troubled him; that was why he had delivered it in person. But when no response was forthcoming even now, when Pollak turned and moved toward the door at the back, the wireless operator also left the bridge. And although he was reassured that he had obviously overestimated the importance of the message, he came near to feeling something like disappointment.

Pollak had opened the door to the navigation room. He had to stoop to enter. The *Cecilie* had not been built for him; he had taken over the ship only three years ago, replacing a captain over whom he towered by a foot.

Pollak switched on the lamp over the table where the navigational charts were spread out. Pommerenke, who had followed him, set down a second cup of coffee. The cable, a yellow strip glued to the white sheet, caught the light of the lamp, but Pommerenke made no attempt to decipher the message. Rather, he raked the paper with a hostile glance.

"May I?" Now that they were alone, he could no longer resist, and he swept the confetti off Pollak's shoulder.

"American ladies . . ." Pollak smiled. "At sixty they're still teenagers."

"Gloria Lindsay has a long way to go before she's sixty."

"You're right, as always. But where is it written that the captain may ask only older women to share his table?" He was glad of the chance to make a remark that betrayed nothing of his true mood; it was always difficult to keep his feelings from Pommerenke. Of course, the advantage was that Pollak never needed to tell his tiger when he wished to be left alone. Even now Pommerenke understood and withdrew.

Charles Pollak was unaccustomed to ambivalence; he hated the condition, and whenever possible he put a stop to it as quickly as possible. A ship and a man had to be in good working order—that was the rule by which he lived.

He smoothed out the paper, weighing down the curled corner. The coded text was brief, readable at a glance:

ERHARD ILL WITH COLITIS, SIEGFRIED.

Although he had some idea of the decoded meaning, he found the words ridiculous. The code book had been handed to him three days ago in New York, shortly before they left port. It had been a strange moment when the bearer, a naval attaché of the German embassy, placed the sealed envelope in Pollak's hand. In spite of widespread rumors about the imminent outbreak of war in Europe, Pollak found the pomp with which it was done exaggerated, and after the envelope had been tucked away in the safe, he forgot all about it; he told himself to forget. . . .

Even when he sailed from Bremerhaven, setting a westward course for New York on July 15, he had resolved to ignore the talk about impending war. Like many captains, he was apolitical. Certainly he was a German. But his real country was the sea; his actual home was his ship; and his proper nationality was the shipping company whose emblem—an anchor and key—he wore in his lapel. War was not good for shipping, not good for Lloyd, not good for anyone.

With every day that passed, with each additional sea mile that *Cecilie* put between herself and Europe, the thoughts of war had actually grown dimmer, and in New York they had at last disappeared altogether. Some obscure Austrian successor to the throne had been assassinated along with his consort in some out-of-the-way place in the Balkans. In New York, with more than three thousand miles of Atlantic separating them from Europe, the event provoked at most a smile.

A further event had helped to dispel Pollak's worries. In Bremerhaven they had counted on the *Cecilie's* traveling back empty; the reverse was the case. Impervious to all the talk, the Americans had booked their summer trips to Europe. Pollak had done something he rarely did: he had asked the chief purser for the passenger list. It contained the familiar names that recurred every summer. He still had the full complement of the faithful following that crossed the Atlantic on his ship year after year.

The passenger list for the first class read like a *Who's Who* of the top ten thousand: the son of a president, senators, bankers, and the flower of the fair sex—the cream of wealthy widows and marriageable daughters of the leading families, who placed great value on a son-in-law with a European title. None of them believed in the coming of war. They set out as always on the Grand Tour: shopping in the Place Vendôme and the Faubourge St.-Honoré; an audience with the German Kaiser in Potsdam; a cruise up the Rhine; a visit to Bayreuth. The obligatory program also included the Train Bleu from Paris to the Riviera, the Louvre, the Prado, a boat ride through the Blue Grotto, a climb up Mount Etna, a donkey ride to Amalfi, feeding the pigeons in the Piazza San Marco in Venice, scratching one's name into the Spanish Steps in Rome, and brunch at the Hofbräuhaus in Munich, among other musts.

The *Cecilie* carried over twelve hundred passengers. The first- and second-class accommodations were fully booked. When a cabin had been required at the last minute for the two New York bankers accompanying the transport of gold bullion, Pollak voluntarily gave up his captain's quarters, camping out in the navigation room for the length of the crossing.

The gold! Eleven million dollars in gold coins for English and French banks. In addition, three million in silver. Pollak thought of it even as he continued to stare at the coded cable.

It might well be that a few American ladies—tanned beauties from Kentucky and peach-skinned debutantes from Kansas—had a mistaken view of the situation. But hard-boiled New York bankers? Would the two largest American banks entrust forty-four million marks in gold and silver to a German ship if they feared that the transport would never reach Europe? Never before had one of his ships carried such a valuable cargo. In New York the fact had reassured him, but now the memory of the stacks of gold bars in the specie room of the *Cecilie* added to his concern.

He rose to his feet. In spite of his size, his movements were light, almost elegant. The letter combination of the safe was known only to him and to the chief purser. He twisted the dial to one letter after another, E—D—J—E—D, working slowly and carefully. He broke the seal on the envelope and returned to the chart table with the gray folder. Once more he hesitated, as if there were still time to alter events. The signature on the cable—Siegfried—meant that the message had been sent by the directors of North German Lloyd.

He opened the gray notebook and looked for the code, wrote the solution on the edge of the white sheet. Deciphered, the message read:

> WAR WITH FRANCE, ENGLAND, AND
> RUSSIA IMMINENT. TURN BACK.

Who had invented the codes? Right now the question was absurd, but it was the only clear thought Pollak could cling to. His cup of coffee stood on the table untouched.

He pulled over the charts on which the *Cecilie*'s course was plotted. Her position was thirty degrees west, north of the Azores, almost sixteen hundred sea miles from New York, roughly fourteen hundred sea miles from the first European port they were scheduled to reach by late Sunday. He shut the code book and locked it in the safe together with the cable.

Outwardly he appeared calm when he returned to the bridge. He knew that he owed the men an explanation, and he realized that they were waiting for it. Why did he not simply tell them what there was to tell, using the plain words they were accustomed to hearing from him? *We are at war.* Why not?

He had never been afraid of responsibility. On the contrary, to be absolute ruler of a piece of universe that bowed to his laws was something he took for granted. It had always been so and would remain so for as long as he commanded a ship. He was fifty-four years old now, and just as he sometimes thought back to his early years as a captain, he also tried at times to imagine what life would be like when he was no longer going to sea but living as a retired old gentleman. As much as he liked to dwell on the first thought, the second filled him with terror—and it was just such terror that had been triggered by the news of the outbreak of war. This single sensation had possession of him at the moment. It was not the thought of war—here, in the middle of the Atlantic, abstract, inconceivable. If he was capable of thought at all, he held one idea alone: *They'll take your ship away from you.* He was not ready for decisions and orders.

He opened the door leading to the deck and stepped to the parapet. The air was calm, ruffled only by the airstream. He looked down at the reflection of the illuminated ship in the dark water, at the rows of brightly refracted light glittering like ropes of faceted diamonds. He listened to the music from the lounge, to the voices and laughter that rang more loudly out here. He closed his eyes. He felt himself to be a part of the ship, rooted in her. His feet on the rough iron platform, his hands on the railing—they drew in everything that happened on the ship, every movement, every noise. He had come to know many ships, but he had never before felt as connected as he did with *her*, as if the ship and he were in fact one body.

Nothing seemed more important in these minutes than to assess his relationship to his vessel; only in this way could he come to terms with himself. Although his was not a split personality, Pollak was not quite as uncomplicated as most people believed. Under the soft shell he was a hard, ambitious man. When he had commanded the *Kaiser Wilhelm der Grosse* and the *Kaiser Wilhelm II*, he was captain of the swiftest ships on the North Atlantic route. Both ships had sported the coveted Blue Riband until the *Mauretania*, an English vessel, had captured the speed record. Though it had happened seven years ago, he still felt a stab whenever he saw the Blue Riband fluttering from the mast of the British liner in New York harbor.

The *Cecilie* had never had a real chance to win it back, and for that reason he had at first hesitated to assume her command. He remembered clearly the day when he had seen her for the first time, at the Columbus Quay in the outer harbor of the great imperial dry-docks. It had been love at first sight. The *Cecilie* was beautiful, her proportions so harmonious that she looked graceful even tied up at the pier, where many ships looked ungainly and clumsy. He had even harbored a secret faith that she might win back the Blue Riband. But like a beautiful woman who nevertheless does not bear sons, she had not fulfilled his hopes. He had become resigned, and the joint defeat, which he and the ship had to accept, had strengthened the bond between them. He could no longer count the number of times he had crossed the Atlantic in her—more than a hundred, he was sure. She had not disappointed him in any kind of weather. What he loved in her most, and what he felt very intensely at this moment, was her soft gait, very womanly, very elegant. She was a lady through and through. Ships had souls, this he firmly believed, and the soul of his *Cecilie* was filled with feminine sweetness.

That this might be their last journey together was so inconceivable to Charles Pollak that the solution suddenly seemed very simple: he need only stop the sun from rising, and he would be able to sail his ship through the unending night. . . .

He returned to the bridge. His officers were waiting; he felt their glances, but none put a question or tried to hurry him.

"We will reduce speed," he ordered. "Fifteen knots, same course."

The officer manning the telegraph to the engine room repeated the command. Pollak's tone of voice had been quite ordinary.

The rhythm of the engines altered. Pollak went to the door through which the wireless operator had disappeared. Before opening it, he turned back once more. "Call the officers together—everyone who can be spared. I'll also need to see the chief purser, the chief engineer, and the victualler." He hesitated before continuing. "I'd like him to bring an inventory of all stores. . . . Please don't speculate, gentlemen. And not a word to any of the passengers. I want everyone assembled here in half an hour. . . . Until then, maintain the same course."

The wireless cabin was situated on the top deck. On his way Pollak took in the sounds of the orchestra playing dance music in the main lounge. The "Blue Riband Rag" . . . there was no ignoring the fact that the stewards' band was having trouble with the newfangled American beat. But the dance floor was sure to be so crowded that it would be impossible to dance properly anyway. Was Temperance C. Butler still waiting for him to return and dance with her? An old-fashioned dance, of course. On such matters Temperance C. Butler tended to be very conservative. Weren't they playing one of her favorites now?

> *Linger longer Lucy,*
> *Linger longer, Lu.*
> *How I love to linger, Lucy,*
> *Linger longer, you.*

Temperance C. Butler always hummed along with her favorite songs when she was dancing. Presumably Fred Vandermark was looking after her. No, Pollak needn't worry about the ladies he had abandoned at the captain's table as long as his second officer was with them.

Until this moment Pollak had thought only of his ship. Now he tried to imagine the passengers' response to the news. He would have liked to send Kuhn, the chief purser, to pave the way; he generally delegated unpleasant tasks to Kuhn, but this time the maneuver would surely not work. The most Kuhn could do was to select the passengers who would later be asked to come to the smoking room. The rest was up to the captain. . . .

Pollak had arrived at the wireless cabin. A square metal box, it clung to the mast that bore the antennas, completely isolated from the rest of the ship. Although the door was closed, Pollak could hear the crackle and tick of the Morse telegraph. All the doors on the ship were too low for Pollak, but this one was also extremely narrow, so that he had not only to duck his head but also to draw in his shoulders.

Simoni, in his swivel chair, looked up. When he saw the captain, he tried to assume something resembling a military posture. He straightened up, and his melancholy eyes widened. For a moment he became a well-built, handsome man; then his back curved again, his head sank forward, and he returned to being part of his instrument board; his entire body seemed to become a receiver, as if it were his secret ambition to catch the waves directly out of the air, if necessary without the instruments at his disposal.

Pollak sat down on the single chair in the cabin for no other reason than to leave more space in the cramped little room. Simoni looked at the instrument that had just begun to tick again.

"More messages from Europe?" Pollak asked.

Simoni leaned over the strip of paper. "A private cable."

"No mobilization? Cessation of diplomatic relations?" Pollak pronounced the words slowly. "No declaration of war? Nothing official? Not from anywhere?"

The wireless operator's back rounded even more. "The last few messages were rather reassuring."

Pollak was not surprised. But the information was not sufficient reason for him to feel renewed hope. He found it very natural that North German Lloyd had information unavailable to the general public. The shipping firm—his thoughts focused on it. Not on war, not on armies being mobilized at that very moment—but on North German Lloyd. He had been in its service for twenty-six years. All his loyalties belonged to it—to his ship and to Lloyd. What was good for Lloyd was good for all of Germany. "Heard anything from the *Ryndam*?" he asked. The Dutch liner had left New York for Europe on the same evening as the *Cecilie*.

"She's trailing us by about two hundred sea miles."

"Keeping to her course?"

"According to the latest radiograms, yes."

"What's it look like in New York harbor? The *Vaterland*—wasn't she supposed to sail today?" He was referring to the new 54,000-ton liner of the competition in Hamburg, at present the largest ship in the world, which was making only her fourth voyage.

Simoni hesitated. He suffered visibly from having to pass on bad news. "The sailing has been postponed, or so they say. For twenty-four hours—so far. The *Prinzessin Irene* didn't leave Hoboken either."

"And *Kronprinz Wilhelm* and the *Grosse Kurfürst*?"

The wireless operator seemed even more deeply rooted in his instrument panel. "They sailed, but the shipping company recalled them to New York. I don't have confirmation from the ships. Just the recall."

Pollak was beginning to see the picture more clearly. Previously he had thought only of himself; now he began to see the other ships on the North Atlantic, the other captains, most of them personal acquaintances. Were they facing a decision similar to the one he had to make? "How about the English and French vessels?" he asked.

"The *Mauretania* and the *Olympic* are sailing westward, toward New York. The *Olympic* will be passing us in the early morning hours."

The *Olympic*, thought Pollak. She bore some resemblance to the *Cecilie;* her four funnels were similarly raked. An idea began to take shape in his mind, but he pushed it aside. "Any English or French ships asking our position in the last couple of hours?"

Simoni looked up in surprise. "The *Savoia*. Just an hour ago they requested a report of our position." Apologetically he added, "A cousin of mine . . . he's the sparks on her."

Pollak's eyes were riveted to the floor. "No warships?"

The wireless operator ran his hand through his dark, curly hair. "The *Essex*—English cruiser. She's wiring around wildly . . . using a code."

Pollak nodded and straightened up as best he could in the low-ceilinged cabin. "Fine, Simoni," he said. "You won't be getting much sleep in the next few days. Stay with your instruments. Forget about everything else. Keep only one thing in mind—*Who wants to know our course?* Forget Europe and New York, but listen in on every English and French report. And watch out for anyone coming near our position. If anyone at all moves in on us, send me a message at once."

Once more the instrument began to tick. The narrow strip pushed its way out of the slot and curled. Simoni took one end, pulled it smooth, and leaned over it.

Pollak, standing behind him, showed impatience for the first time. "What is it?"

The ticking stopped. The unusual metallic smell in the cabin seemed to increase. "What's up?"

When Simoni turned, a strange smile illuminated his features; a remnant of his unease, his worry, was still present, but it was overlaid by another emotion. "A telegram for the second officer."

"For Vandermark?"

"Yes, Captain." The smile grew stronger, expressing the hope that the world would remain in order after all. "It's the fourth one today, sir. And that's less than the usual amount after we sail from New York. Two ladies bombarding him with wires at the same time, one from Philadelphia, one from New York. No wonder they call him Lucky Fred. You want to hear what it says?"

"Another time. Besides, I can imagine. Get it to him, and then—" Pollak's features grew stern. "Then, Simoni, close your cabin to any private cables. . . . Just be prepared. In about an hour they'll be storming your doors. Dozens of passengers will be wanting to send cables; you'll be besieged; they'll use every trick—tears, bribes, threats. You can send them to me. . . . No, let them go to the purser. All right, then, be prepared for anything. Put up a sign saying that no telegrams will be accepted, and bolt your door. Let's be quite clear on this—not a single wire leaves the ship from now on. No radiograms, nothing. From no one, and that includes the officers and the crew. Absolute radio silence, starting immediately. Understood? All right, let it be as if there were no such ship as the *Cecilie,* as if the Atlantic had swallowed us up."

"May I ask you one question? Is there going to be war, Captain?"

Pollak was silent for an instant. Then he answered. "It's here, Simoni. We are at war."

"Will we be turning back?"

Pollak lowered his head. At bottom it was this that had disturbed him about the order—not to complete a crossing was something that went against his whole nature. Every port where the *Cecilie* docked had made a byword of his punctuality. Ten minutes leeway for an Atlantic crossing was the outside delay he allowed the *Cecilie*. Why not, then, continue the crossing, omit the English and French ports, and head full steam for Bremerhaven? But it was not a matter of himself alone. He had to think of the passengers—and of the gold he carried on board. The English and French ships would be hunting him. A golden cargo worth millions . . .

"Yes, we're turning back."

"To New York?"

This, too, was a decision he had already settled. New York was out of the question. It was the course he was most likely to set, and they would be waiting to intercept him. Besides, in a few minutes, talking with his officers, he would surely be told that the ship's coal supply would not stretch for the return to New York. Newport News, then? Boston? Presumably there was not enough fuel to reach these, either. That left only the shortest route, the northernmost one. At this time of year heavy fog was certain, but as far as he was concerned, nothing could be better. . . .

"No, not New York," he said. "We'll take the northern route and become invisible. And remember . . . as of this moment, there is no such ship as the *Cecilie*."

It was almost midnight. The mood of the passengers in the main lounge was one of abandonment. No one had noticed that during the last half-hour the officers had left one by one. The twelve musicians in the stewards' band were playing a piece called "Alabama Jigger," but in their hands it became more a Sousa march than a rag. The dance floor was crowded, and the couples seemed determined to make a night of it—dervishes who did not require a band but drummed their own beat with their feet. For some, dancing was only a pretext for holding another closely entwined. But now something unusual happened. The dancers suddenly moved as if the parquet under their feet had become unsteady. All lost their footing, a couple in a deep tango dip lost their balance, the regular swaying of partners was thrown into confusion.

Now the music also changed. A singer stepped forward. "By the light of the silvery moon. . . ." His English had a Berlin accent.

Had the sea suddenly become rougher? The altered thud of the ship's engines clarified the situation; it was no longer the deep regular rhythm that had sounded almost like an additional bass instrument, but a harsh, irregular thumping. Couples began to leave the dance floor, making their way to the bar or to their tables. Some went out on deck to catch a breath of air.

It was they who were the first to notice what had happened, and their astonished exclamations ran through the ship. Then others came on deck, lured from every direction—the dining saloon, the Viennese Café, the library, the writing room, the smoking room. They joined the groups already gathered on deck pointing to the night sky.

The moon, almost full, riding in the cloudless night sky, had hung above starboard; now it had made a complete half-turn and shone down on the port side of the ship. Minutes passed before the passengers began to realize what the shift meant. The *Cecilie* had altered her course by a hundred and eighty degrees. She was no longer traveling eastward, toward Europe, but heading at full speed back to the west.

PART ONE

Chapter 1

*B*ar Harbor, on Mount Desert Island in the state of Maine, is very nearly the northernmost point of the United States, and its mountains are the highest along the Atlantic coast. Even in the heart of summer some days recall the nearness of the Arctic—but not this one. August 3, 1914, was what the natives called a typical Bar Harbor day—sunny, with cloudless skies and air clear as glass.

She had left the horse and buggy at the end of the wooded path, and now she was climbing the steps hewn into the coastal rock. From here she had a full view of the town and the bay. The water was as clear and transparent as if the sky had changed places with the bay; and the air was so clear that it altered distances and colors, even objects themselves. She could distinguish each wave driven across the surface of the water by the breeze, could see the pearly foam glistening on the crest. She could make out darned patches on the sails of the fishing skiffs, the names on the yachts, and the signs on the buoys marking the sea-lanes of the steamboats that plied between Bar Harbor and the outside world. The cliffs of Egg Rock, usually a gray mass guarding the approach to Frenchman Bay, today gave off a rosy shimmer, and the lighthouse glowed white and blue like a newly painted toy

The trees on the mountain chain—especially the poplars, firs, and spruce of Green Mountain—stood outlined against the sky as if defined by a jigsaw. Toward the east, opposite Frenchman Bay, the Schoodic peninsula, usually no more than a smudged line along the horizon, seemed close enough to touch.

A perfect summer day. Summer and Bar Harbor—the two concepts were inseparable in her mind. As far back as she could remember, she had spent her summers here, and the memories she cherished were all lovely.

She had stopped counting the steps; she knew without keeping track that there were two hundred and twenty-one before she came to the fence enclosing Uncle Sol's estate. There was a second, less wearying approach—an elevator leading straight up the cliff wall from the shore—but she could not bear the rickety cage, just big enough to hold two people, clattering in a way that frightened her. In fact the elevator ran only once a month, to haul up supplies. Uncle Sol himself had long ago ceased using it; for years he had not left his rocky fortress, and he had no intention of doing so in the future.

She had now arrived at the fence, and Uncle Sol's watchdog promptly began to bark. Inside the paling his angry yelps pursued her as she made her way to the gate. She yanked the rusty bellpull, and somewhere in the distance a soft tinkle responded. At the high wooden gate that barred any glimpse inside, she waited for the steps, for the click of a gun being cocked, for the rough, testy voice—and would have felt a sense of loss if the welcome had turned out differently. Solomon Butler, her grandmother's brother, detested all humanity.

"What is it? What's going on? This is private property." There it was, the hoarse, cross voice.

"It's me," she shouted through the gate. "Anne."

"Anne Butler?"

"What's the matter—don't you know my voice anymore?"

"To me all women's voices sound alike. Wait. . . ."

She heard him calling the dog to his side. The wooden gate was concealed among wildly proliferating bushes, and it took some time before he had undone all the locks and bolts.

The man who came into view was holding a rifle in the crook of his arm and the dog on a leash. His bare feet were tucked into sandals; the light-colored trousers were shabby and so short that they ended far above the ankles; the plaid flannel shirt, open across the chest was darned. "Well, come on in. So you're back?" His shoulders were broad, his stomach was flat, and his face was deeply tanned by the sun. Not even the snow-white hair protruding from his straw hat gave away his age. He was seventy-six.

Anne had never known him any other way than white-haired. It was a hereditary trait in the Butler family; around the age of forty their dark hair turned gray and was white within a few years. Sometimes Anne wondered whether she would be subject to the same fate. Though she had her mother's pale hair, her dusky complexion and dark eyes were a Butler heritage. Not that she was worried; at nineteen, forty was an age beyond imagining. . . .

Uncle Sol gave the dog some slack. "Don't worry. He just has to get your scent again. A year is a long time." He let the sheepdog go, and the large black-and-brown animal strolled around Anne, sniffing her shoes, her skirt.

"You see? We Butlers seem to have a special scent. He's never attacked a Butler." His dark eyes remained alert, suspicious. "I mean a genuine Butler, not just a Butler by marriage."

Had Anne ever seen her uncle smile? He could laugh out loud—laugh until he shook. But smile? "How do we Butlers smell, then?"

He shrugged his shoulders as he led the way. "Whatever it is, it's different from other people." He gave her a sidelong glance. "What's the matter with your hair?"

Her hand automatically flew to her head. "My hair?"

"It used to be longer."

"Oh, that." For the debutante ball, the major event for a young girl from one of the first families of Boston, Anne had had her long hair cut the winter before.

Uncle Sol shook his head. "Skirts get shorter and shorter, hair gets shorter and shorter. . . . what do they call your new-fangled hairdo?"

"Once it was a Gibson Girl. I've been letting it grow again for about six months now."

"It used to be even shorter?"

"A kind of pageboy." Anne's hair grew quickly, but it still took time, and at the crown of her head, above the temple, it was simply a little too short and so unmanageable that most of the time she had to wear one of the headbands from her college days.

"Green and white," he noted. "The colors of Oldfields School, aren't they?"

"Imagine you even noticing something like that."

As if he had already displayed too much interest and warmth, he muttered incomprehensibly and quickened his steps. The house toward which he was heading lay at the end of a flat meadow; from a distance it seemed to be part of the rock face before which it stood, distinguished from the gray stone only by its glittering windows. To one side of it, at the edge of the cliff, was a second building, a plain cube flaunting a high antenna from its roof. The complicated technical apparatus seemed alien, unsuitable to this otherwise wild and primeval place, and it neatly embodied the modern world from which Uncle Sol had withdrawn.

He had spent a great deal of money to make the cliff accessible and livable. The water pipes alone had consumed a small fortune. The drinking water, carried along wooden tubes from Kebo Mountain many miles away, was collected in a well at the front of the house. A pile of freshly cut wood lay by a chopping block into which an ax was stuck, and the scent of pine resin rose on the air. Apparently she had interrupted him—one of his prescriptions for a healthy life was to chop wood for an hour a day. He had dozens of such specifics for good health and longevity. They varied from month to month; chopping wood was the only one he had maintained over the years.

He hung the gun on a hook next to the front door and pointed to a roughly fashioned garden bench. "How long have you been in Bar Harbor?"

"Today's my first day."

"Did you come straight from Boston?"

"From New York. The two of us—Edith Connors and I—saw Grandmother off on the ship."

"Ah, it's that time again. Europe once a year. It's like a disease." He had sat down next to her, but now he jumped up and picked up the hatchet. Placing a log on the block, he stared at it as if it were a condemned man he had been ordered to execute.

"To hell with all females." He struck. "My darling sister . . . In every other way Temperance is a sensible sort of person, but in this one thing she takes leave of her senses. Europe! What do women see in it?" A second log splintered. "Paris, eh? Gay Paree—hip hip hooray, let's be gay. . . . A miserable bunch, those Europeans, the French most of all. Monsieur Seligman is laughing up his sleeve because he can get rid of his fake Rembrandts, and the Sèvres china service was made in Italy. But art is only the pretext. . . . The real reason for our American ladies are the Frenchies with their charm and their long swallowtails and their waxed moustaches. All those phony counts, long-haired artists, idlers, parasites . . . but they kiss the ladies' hands—if that's all there is to it."

"Uncle Sol!"

"Wee! Tray bong! I'll shut up. Temperance is my favorite sister, but I'll never understand this one quirk she has. Whenever she comes back, she has a French accent—or at least something she takes to be one."

"I'm worried about her," Anne said. "Don't you read the papers?"

"Why?"

"There's going to be a war in Europe."

"Let it come is what I say. The Germans will show those Frenchies."

"I saw Grandmother on board a week ago. It's been four days now since I heard from her. There's no more news of any kind from the ship. Nobody knows where she is. Listen, I'm really worried. I asked Alec . . . he is here, isn't he?" She looked over at the antenna above the gray house at the edge of the cliff.

At the mention of Alec's name the old man's face became even more closed. He lowered the hatchet. "And for a moment I really thought you had come to visit me. . . . Yes, he's here. What are you waiting for? Go to him."

Anne rose. "May I have a drink of water?"

"Nobody's stopping you."

She filled a cup from the well and drank it slowly, making a show of savoring every sip. "I don't know any other water that tastes so good."

He muttered, and his face brightened.

"Really. It's the best water far and wide." Living with her grandmother, Anne had learned how to get along with older people. No matter how flinty and stubborn they were, they grew soft as wax if one only touched the right chord. It was particularly simple with Uncle Sol. When the name of his son, Alec, was mentioned, he turned to stone; when his drinking water was praised, his heart melted.

"Kebo Mountain water," he said. "Unpolluted. There's no better in the whole state of Maine. Do you know that they urged me to bottle and market it? That's how people are. Turn everything into a business!" He pushed the straw hat to the back of his head. "Bar Harbor used to be paradise on earth, and what is it now? A penny arcade. Tourists, stinking automobiles, clattering motorboats. Do you ever see anybody with a sketch pad or a plant specimen box? Do you see even one person collecting shells? Man can't help himself—he has a need to destroy everything."

The complaint that Bar Harbor was not what it used to be was an essential element of Uncle Sol's nature, like his hatred of the French and the conflicts with his son, Alec. Anne accepted it without further thought. He was just a crusty old man who had withdrawn from the world and mankind, whose thoughts and feelings concentrated on only a very few subjects now. Sometimes, though, she asked herself what had become of the other man, the Uncle Sol she used to know, the New York banker. These were her first memories of him, still vivid: New York, Wall Street, that constricted gorge of a thoroughfare; a narrow building, the bank, a dusky office; and in it Uncle Sol dressed in black, white-haired even then. That man had taken the five-year-old girl by the hand and led her down to a subterranean vault to show her the piles of gold bars. The adventure had made an indelible impression on her. He had laid one of the bars into her outstretched hands. The size of a brick, it was much, much heavier. Nor had she forgotten his words: "Aren't these the most beautiful bricks in the world?"

Gold and soil—those had been Solomon Butler's profession, and even in Bar Harbor he had pursued the same interests. He had hoarded land for years and years, and then he had driven up the prices. It was his land holdings among others that made it possible for Astors and Vanderbilts, millionaires and social leaders of all sorts, to acquire estates, build impressive summer "cottages," and turn the village into a summer center. After each of these spectacular purchases prices rose even higher, and Sol Butler reaped the profits. Objectively, he had done all he could to turn the drowsy resort on the Atlantic coast into the nation's summer capital, a place where many of the leading families maintained vacation homes and which year after year attracted ever more vacationers. But obviously he had conveniently forgotten this process.

"Years ago, long before you were born, sometimes in the summer moose swam in the bay and uprooted your grandmother's garden. . . ."

Anne laughed. She was too young to let herself be infected by the old man's gloom. Probably another of his many prescriptions for good health was to complain a great deal on any one day. Her eyes traveled

across the landscape: green hills—the green of the mixed forests of
Bar Harbor composed into a symphony—the houses surrounded by
large gardens, the village itself with its many piers extending into the
water, the wide blue bay, and in it Bar Island and the Porcupines,
whose wooded crests really did make them look like the animals they
were named for.

"For me," she said, lost in the view, "it's still a paradise."

He looked at her, this time not defensively and critically but only
with melancholy. "That takes being young like you." He picked up the
hatchet, gripping the haft with both hands. He assumed a broad-
legged stance in order to increase his balance and strength; the plaid
flannel shirt whipped outside his trousers.

As Anne walked over to the radio station, her steps were mea-
sured by the sound of splintering wood.

Chapter 2

The closer she came to the edge of the cliff, the more clearly she could hear the lap of the surf rising from the sea and the cry of the seagulls nesting in the crags. Here, where the bay opened out, on a day such as this the currents of the Atlantic were clearly marked in the distance by the deeper hue of the water.

A side-wheeler was just pulling into the bay, plowing a broad wake with its two paddles. Judging by the time, it had to be the steamboat from Rockland, where the connection with Boston was made. Without a railway spur, Bar Harbor could be reached only by carriage or by water. It was still a ten-hour trip from Boston; years ago, in her childhood, the trip had taken even longer, but that was just what had made Bar Harbor special, a hideaway at the end of the world.

Alec Butler's radio station consisted of no more than a single large room; it was everything at once—living room, bedroom, and wireless room. The broad wall of windows faced southeast, giving a full view of the bay.

There, at the table with the wireless set, sat Alec Butler. Though he was wearing his earphones, he must have noticed her entrance, for he raised his hand in greeting. He scribbled something on a pad lying in front of him. Only then did he take off the earphones and turn around in his swivel chair. "Hello, Anne."

She had meant to embrace him, but now she too said, "Hello, Alec."

Greetings among the members of the Butler family were never emotional. Her grandmother was the sole exception. Temperance C. Butler was generous with hugs and kisses; Uncle Sol called her affection a "European vice," and certain circles in Boston criticized her behavior as exalted—which in no way bothered Temperance C. Butler. Quite the reverse: she had always made it a point of pride to shock the stiff, Puritan Bostonians.

Alec, Anne's second cousin, on the other hand, kept faith with the "authentic" Boston tradition; one did not make a show of one's feelings. One handled them with as much care as one did one's capital, according to the principle that what is spent cannot increase. Outwardly, too, he conformed to the image. Everything about him was scrupulously correct—his white shirt, his blue double-breasted blazer, the sharp crease in his trousers, his highly polished shoes. And although he had just removed the earphones, his dark hair lay smoothly on his head, the side part seemingly drawn with a ruler. She had never seen him any other way. Even at sixteen—he was six years her senior—he had seemed to her a complete young man; now, at twenty-five, he had already made a name for himself as a lawyer and was on the threshold of a brilliant career.

But beside the successful young man there existed another Alec Butler, one who was insecure and inhibited and who at this moment did not know what to do with his hands. "Oh, do sit down." He cleared a chair for her. "You've come alone?"

"Well, I brought the horse and buggy."

"And you brought Jenkins, I trust."

"Please, Alec, no lectures. This is Bar Harbor, not Boston."

"If you think that makes a difference."

"You'll have plenty of chances to play the watchdog. . . ." She looked at him closely, but his smooth features betrayed nothing of his feelings. That too was part of the summers in Bar Harbor—Alec's constant nearness. No matter whether she was swimming in the ocean, sailing, playing tennis, horseback riding, or dancing and flirting at the Canoe Club, Alec was always there—unobtrusive, in the background, but always at hand when she needed him.

"How did Father receive you?" he asked.

"Let's say—with his normal grouchiness. . . . Did you get my telegram?"

He gestured toward the windows out into the vastness of the

ocean. "Nothing. Not a single radiogram for days. The *Cecilie* might as well have disappeared from the face of the earth. Everyone's looking for her; I keep intercepting messages requesting her to state her position. The ether is humming with her name, but she remains silent."

Anne's glance traveled over the equipment. He had once explained to her how everything worked, and now she was annoyed with herself for not having paid more attention at the time. Alec playing at being her instructor—that was an approach she had always fended off. "What the newspapers say is contradictory."

"Because they themselves don't know. Anyway, whatever you read in the papers should be taken with a grain of salt."

The *Cecilie* had been making headlines since the first of August. The German ship had been a favorite subject with American reporters since her maiden voyage to New York. At that time, in 1907, five thousand New Yorkers had hastened to the East River to watch her arrival; and during the five days she lay at the pier in Hoboken, ten thousand visitors had gone on board to look her over. The reporters had given her the title Queen of the Seas, and she had retained it ever since. Now they had invented a new one: the Treasure Ship, because of her million-dollar cargo in gold and silver. The papers suggested the wildest suppositions—some said she was being pursued by English cruisers, that the French had captured her, that the *Cecilie* had been sighted in the Irish Sea or near the coast of Norway; still others claimed that she had long since dropped anchor in her home port. Articles about the ship dominated the front pages of the newspapers, displacing even the war in Europe, as if the fate of the *Cecilie* were the only interesting aspect of the war. Anne felt no differently; the war was distant, unimaginable, abstract. The ship, on the other hand, was real.

"I sent her a telegram a day," she said. "First only about the races. You know, the Knickerbocker Stakes. One of Grandmother's horses was entered. She wanted me to radio the outcome to her."

"Meadow Beauty?"

"Do you think something happened? A ship can't just disappear."

"If something had happened, we'd have heard. I've spent practically all of the last twenty-four hours here, ever since I arrived. No, don't worry about that. I'm sure we'll hear something today." He searched among the slips of paper on the table. "They sailed on the twenty-eighth of July. That means they've been at sea for six days. Given their coal stores, they can't stay out much longer."

Though Alec's arguments were, as always, lucid and convincing, based not on emotion but on fact, they were not powerful enough to allay her anxiety. Her fears were rooted deep inside her, going back to the terrible memory of the accident at sea that robbed her of her parents—nightmares of burning ships, never overcome even though the event lay fourteen years in the past and she had been only five years old at the time.

"Grandmother almost postponed her trip because of the races." For some reason this seemed an important fact to Anne, and she clung to it. "For the first three days Grandmother bombarded her trainer with cables."

"Meadow Beauty won the race, didn't he? Isn't that her horse?"

"Yes . . . and she doesn't even know."

"You're very fond of her, aren't you?"

She looked at him. She did not understand his question. Nor had she ever understood why there was such tension between him and his father. Since her sixth year Anne had been an orphan; she had grown up without a father or mother, but her grandmother had made up for everything, so that Anne had always felt she was living in a real family.

"Let's go outside," she said abruptly. The room was very warm, warmer than outside, for the wall of windows doubled the intensity of the sun. All the same, Anne felt suddenly chilly.

The screeching of the gulls was there again, the steady roll of the surf. The siren of the steamboat was muted in the bay; the boat herself could not be seen; she was probably just passing Egg Rock. They had sat down on the stone bench, a rocky block chiseled into shape.

"You're staying the summer?" Alec asked.

"That was the plan . . . until Grandmother comes back in October."

"And then? I mean . . . are you really going to the university?" He tried to rob the question of any weight, but he failed.

"I've enrolled."

"Veterinary medicine—insane!"

"You sang a different tune a year ago."

"To tell you the truth, I thought it was a passing whim."

"That's not exactly a compliment."

"All the girls I know think of only three things: their debut, the

Grand Tour, and—getting married. And the quicker one follows on the other, the better."

"Maybe you know the wrong girls." She laughed freely, but of course he was right. Oldfields had strict rules, and the strictest applied to young men. Young men were taboo. A student was not to meet them, was not to write letters to them, and of course was to receive none. And yet the girls with whom Anne went to Oldfields thought of little other than boys. Clothes too, but boys came first. Anne had always avoided participating in their discussions, not because she was indifferent to the subject, but simply because she preferred keeping her thoughts to herself. She would not have been Temperance C. Butler's granddaughter if she had not had very original ideas on this point and had not found the conversation of the other girls pretty silly.

"I really do believe you know the wrong girls, Alec dear."

"Maybe you're right."

Something in Alec's manner struck her as not quite right; she could not have said precisely what it was, but things between them were not as they had been. Alec and she had always been like brother and sister, except that they understood each other better than was usually the case between older brothers and younger sisters. What had happened to change their relationship? Or more correctly, which of them had changed? Was it Alec or she? She did not want change—she wanted a careless Bar Harbor summer, as before.

"Will you come to the Canoe Club with me tonight?"

Alec would not be drawn out. "You might well have changed your mind about studying. After all, it's only natural for a girl your age to be thinking of marriage."

She looked at him in surprise, trying to guess what was hidden under the remark, whether it was only a statement or whether he was speaking of himself.

"From what one hears in Boston," he continued, "you're not lacking in admirers . . . and I'm sure you've had proposals already."

"You're forgetting about Grandmother. She takes care of that department, and that's enough to make any man think twice."

"Why are you being evasive?"

"I'm not. Sure, the girls who were in school with me have nothing in their heads but to marry as soon as possible. But can you imagine it—me as a wife?"

His lips barely parted as he answered. "If we men could imagine how it is when a young girl turns into a wife, I'm afraid very few of us would marry."

For a moment she was nonplussed; then she laughed brightly. "That sounds so much like your father. I can see it now—one day you'll be stuck to this rocky fortress, just as he is, cursing all women— he says 'females,' doesn't he?"

"It's just that he didn't find out until too late. But let's change the subject."

"I didn't start it. . . . Are you planning to stay long?"

"Two or three weeks . . . until court resumes. I may have to go to Washington sometime during my vacation. The navy is interested in my wireless station."

"The navy?"

"We're closest to Europe here, and because the mountains are so high, this is the only place where you can keep in touch with Europe twenty-four hours a day."

Instinctively Anne looked around. Everything up here was as nature herself had planned it. Even the narrow paths seemed as old as the mountains.

"You can't do that to your father. Besides, he'll never agree. He'll defend his fortress with might and main."

"They won't take the trouble to ask him. When the national in- terest is at stake . . . "

"You can't be serious."

"Why not? What does an old man need with a mountain all to himself?"

Once again she was astonished at the hostility that prevailed be- tween the two men.

"What is it with the two of you?" It was the first time she had put the question so bluntly. "Why do you hate him?"

"Do I?"

"Of course."

He rose to his feet. "What were you saying about tonight? If I know you, you won't want to spend your first evening in Bar Harbor sitting home alone."

She hesitated, but she knew there was no point in pressing him further. Besides, the expectation of a cheerful evening was more im- portant to her than the problems between Alec and his father.

"Come to dinner," she suggested, "and we'll see."

"At eight?"

"On the dot of nine if you don't want White's world to collapse."

He stood before her. His tension had fled. "I hope the Canoe Club has a better band than they did last year."

"Damm's Orchestra has been playing there since the first of the month."

"I thought you just arrived today?"

"Oh, you know—the orchestra that's doing an engagement at the Canoe Club—I can get that sort of information in Boston too."

"All right, then, see you tonight." He gestured at the wireless station. "Maybe by then I'll have heard something about the *Cecilie*. . . . Anne?

"I'm . . . I'm looking forward to tonight." He turned away quickly and walked back to the wireless station.

The pile of split logs around the chopping block had grown; Uncle Sol was standing at the well, his chest bared. He must have just finished washing up, for droplets still clung to his smooth, dark skin. "You're leaving?" he asked as she came near.

Anne nodded.

"Will we see you up here again?"

"You don't really care for visitors, do you?"

He pulled on his shirt and clapped the straw hat on his head. "I make an exception for you."

"It seems today is one of your friendly days."

"I like you. You're a real Butler girl."

"And what are Butler girls like?"

His expressionless face, wholly dominated by the watchful eyes, was turned toward her, and once again she noticed the astonishing resemblance between the two of them, father and son, who hated each other so bitterly that they exchanged not one word for days on end.

"Butler girls are just the opposite of other women. Most of the others are beautiful when they're young—their beauty is nothing more than youth. Butler girls bloom late, but then they bloom for a long time."

"Thanks, Uncle. I'll do my best."

"Did you find out anything about the damned ship?"

"No, nothing."

"I wouldn't worry, not about your grandmother. Nothing's going to happen to her. I bet she's enjoying the whole thing, a great adventure. . . . Come, I'll walk you to the gate." He whistled to the dog.

"I almost forgot the most important thing," said Anne. "Jenkins told me that yesterday he saw some eagles. A pair."

The old man stopped. Wrinkling his brow, he stared at the mountains to the northwest. Then he shook his head. "It's been seven years since there were eagles in Bar Harbor. Where does Jenkins claim he saw them?"

"They were circling over Great Hill."

"Impossible. I'm telling you, we used to have whole colonies of eagles. Every summer they came down from Alaska. But those stinking cars drove them away. . . ."

"Jenkins thought they came from Alaska. He thought he recognized white ruffs."

The old man looked at her. Was he smiling? "Great Hill, did you say? That would make them the first ones in seven years. When the eagles return . . ." He did not complete the sentence, and she might have been mistaken about the smile as well.

Chapter 3

She drove along the forest path, which was narrow and so rarely
traveled that in some places it was almost entirely overgrown. The
light buggy sparkled like new; during the winters it was Jenkins' chief
activity to restore the carriages to a burning luster. Only a muffled
clatter gave away its real age. The horse, a sorrel gelding, was also on
in years and ran with an irregular gait; the noise of the hooves was
barely perceptible on the soft forest floor. It sounded more clearly
through the stillness of the woods only where rocks and roots pierced
the surface.

Wherever the trees were less dense, allowing a glimpse of sky,
Anne Butler slowed the horse's pace so that she could look for the
eagles. It was warmer in the woods than it had been on Uncle Sol's
rock, where a breeze always blew. There was the scent of ripe wood
strawberries. This was typical of Bar Harbor; nature followed a
unique calendar. Strawberries ripened in July, and lilies of the valley
often did not blossom until September. Only one thing never
changed: when the woods were lush with blueberries, summer was
over and it was time to think of leaving.

So far the path had cut deep through the woods, but now the
curves sometimes skirted the edge of the mountain, revealing the
gleaming expanse of Frenchman Bay. The sailboats that spent the day
cruising out at sea were beginning to return home, telling Anne that

it must be after four o'clock. Around five each afternoon a dead calm fell over the bay; at that time not the slightest breeze stirred, and if you were still out on the water, you were becalmed for hours in water as smooth and unruffled as glass.

The track widened; others crossed it, mostly bridle paths, but she met no one. Once an automobile approached in the opposite direction, and she led her horse to the side of the road and stopped. Though the sorrel had been "broken in to cars," as the expression went in Bar Harbor, this was his first summer in harness alone.

The horse owners of Bar Harbor had waged a long and embittered battle against the onslaught of the automobile. Shortly before the turn of the century, when the first automobile appeared in Bar Harbor, hostilities broke out. Peaceful Bar Harbor was split into two camps—the party of the horse and the automobile party. Entire families fell out over the "gasoline buggies," and neighbors stopped speaking to each other.

There could be no question as to which side the Butlers would take—Temperance C. Butler and Uncle Sol led the horse faction. Their influence and their money went far. They succeeded in obtaining state legislation banning automobiles from Mount Desert Island. For fifteen years, until early 1913, the law remained in force. Only then was the automobile party able to force a referendum. The unthinkable happened: Bar Harbor, headquarters of the horse faction, voted in favor of the automobile.

Since then Packards, Pierce-Arrows, Mercers, and of course the luxury models imported from Europe—Mercedes, Darraqs, Bugattis—rolled over the bumpy roads. The horse barns, on the other hand, were increasingly empty.

The path had come out of the woods and descended in a wide arc toward Bar Harbor. Now it was hemmed in on both sides by hedges and walls. Behind them, shielded from curious glances, lay the homes of the wealthy. Their inhabitants, with exaggerated modesty, called them cottages, even when they were built in imitation of Florentine palaces and Rhenish castles. A similar situation applied to the village itself. Officially and on the maps it bore the name of Eden, and that is what the natives called it; the summer colonists, however, possibly feeling the name to be too conspicuous and too memorable, insisted on the modest and simple older form, Bar Harbor, which increasingly prevailed. The rich in their cottages lived a life apart, withdrawn behind their hedges and walls. Their names were known; the local newspaper faithfully reported their arrivals, the names of their houseguests, their departures; but they were seen as little as were their homes, of which at best a gable, a spire, or a row of impressive chimneys was visible among the greenery.

The sorrel gelding needed little heading now. The hedge of copper beeches, the long uphill drive—a light-colored, sandy path cutting through lawns dotted with large old trees, which on a sunny day such as this formed islands of shade—were already the private property of Temperance C. Butler. There was still no sign of the residence; only a collection of outbuildings painted yellow was visible on the horizon. Anne guided the horse to the coach house, large enough for a dozen carriages—simple buggies, comfortable excursion landaus, four-in-hands for longer trips. Jenkins stood in the shade of the overhang. Over his overalls he wore a green gardener's apron, and on his head sat the knitted seaman's cap she had never seen him without.

She stopped the buggy, and he took the horse out of harness.

"How did he run?"

"He pulls to the left all the time."

Jenkins nodded. "That's a leftover from before, when he was harnessed with Carthage. He'll get better if you take him out every day."

Originally Jenkins had been employed as a gardener, but since only three horses remained of the sixteen that had once filled the stables, he had also taken on the position of coachman. Besides Jenkins, the household included a housekeeper and three maids who remained in Bar Harbor throughout the year. In the summers, when Anne's grandmother was in residence, there were several additions to the Bar Harbor staff: Benjamin White, the butler; his wife, Betty, who ruled over the kitchen; and of course Edith Connors, who had once been Anne's governess but had long since become a member of the family.

"Uncle Sol won't believe that you really saw eagles," Anne said.

"I couldn't believe it myself." Jenkins had begun to unharness the horse. "But I saw them again today over Great Hill. They must have an aerie with young ones there. They were holding fish between their claws and flying home."

"Where do you think they do their fishing?"

"Not in Frenchman Bay—there are too many people and boats.

Somewhere in the interior, maybe Lake Wood. I'll find out, don't you worry."

Anne followed as Jenkins led the horse away. Before the stables, a long building, stood Doctor Hanson's buggy. He was Bar Harbor's veterinarian.

"What does Doctor Hanson say?" she asked. "Is it serious?"

"He just got here." Jenkins opened the stable door. In spite of the empty stalls—ten to each side—the stable did not seem unused; it was simply as if all the horses happened to be out in the pasture. Names were still lettered on the black tablets, and beside each hung the colored ribbons and awards the horse had won at shows.

Doctor Hanson was busy hosing down the forelegs of the brown stallion with cold water. Swallows darted in and out through the open windows. There was a mingled smell of horse, oats, and Doctor Hanson's pipe; as Anne took it in, she remembered a saying Grandmother uttered frequently whenever speaking of Bar Harbor— "That's where my roots are." Right now Anne was in the grip of the same conviction.

"Nothing serious." Doctor Hanson spoke. "A cold hosing twice a day and a poultice at night should take care of it."

"Can he be ridden?" Anne asked.

"In about a week." He came toward her. As always he was wearing puttees and a shabby tweed suit with knickerbocker trousers. "You look wonderful. All grown up." His hand waved away the smoke of his pipe as if it were in his way as he examined her. "Miss Connors tells me you're starting your studies in the fall."

"Those are my plans."

"I only hope you'll choose a better place when you begin to practice. I hardly ever get to see horses anymore, just a lot of poodles— more and more poodles. Terrible animals. But usually in great health. The only thing Mrs. Hinkle and Mrs. Blodgett want to talk about is the artistic merit of various styles of clipping. . . . You're really still planning on veterinary medicine?"

Anne nodded silently. Somehow it made her uneasy that everyone raised this question with her in the same faintly doubting undertone reserved for any woman who marched to a slightly different drummer. She had a finely attuned ear for it, for her grandmother had gone her own way all her life. She thrived on people's shaking their heads and whispering about her. "As long as all my friends think I'm crazy, everything is all right" was one of her constant sayings. The idea made Anne smile and gave her a feeling of superiority.

"Will you have a cup of tea with us?" she asked the doctor when they stepped out of the stable into the fresh air.

He removed the pipe from his mouth, leaned down to her ear, and whispered, "I love the English, but I abhor tea."

His breath told her what he preferred to drink. There was a rumor—Maine was a "dry" state—that in the back room of his laboratory he distilled plum brandy and plied a flourishing trade in it.

He pushed his large leather satchel under the seat before climbing into his buggy. "Will your grandmother be coming here after her trip to Europe?"

"Yes," Anne answered curtly, suddenly touched again by something that did not suit this day at all.

"Meadow Beauty won the Knickerbocker, eh? She has a sixth sense for horses, does our Temperance. How much did she personally bet? I'll wager it was a bundle, if she's running true to form. Those who have, to them is given—isn't that how it goes?" Again he flapped away the pipe smoke and looked at her. "Surely you're not worried?"

"A little bit, yes. If a war—"

"Nonsense," he interrupted. "A family tragedy in the house of Hapsburg. A storm in a teacup. It will all blow over in a couple of weeks. Did you speak to the people next door?" He pointed to the neighboring property, where only a long slate-covered gable was visible, along with a couple of tall, strangely shaped chimneys. "Perhaps they know something over there."

"Why them?"

"Gloria Lindsay is a passenger on the *Cecilie* too. Before she left, she put her three kakapos in my care."

"Kakapos?"

"Yes, kakapos, owl parrots, nocturnal creatures. They're what's left of her husband's private zoo. Very delicate. There's something wrong with them all the time, and I have to nurse them back to health. They're permanent guests at my clinic. More interesting than poodles, at any rate. How about it—will you come on my rounds with me again one of these days?"

He picked up the reins, loosened the wheel brake, and shouted to the horse. The piebald's pepper-and-salt coloring exactly matched Doctor Hanson's tweed suit. He had had the animal for years, but

Anne could not recall its ever wearing blinders before. Doctor Hanson understood her expression. "There's no other way now," he said. "But at night, with the headlamps, even the blinders do no good. I've landed in the ditch twice already. And there are more and more automobiles. I don't know where it's going to end. . . ."

Chapter 4

$\mathcal{T}$hough many years had passed, the shock occasioned when Temperance C. Butler painted her house yellow was still not forgotten. A yellow house—sunflower yellow! There had never been anything like it in Bar Harbor, and even people who liked Temperance C. Butler and would have been willing to defend her found the idea crazy—in other words, typical of the Butlers.

It was one of the oldest houses—she insisted on calling it a house—in the colony of mansions, and even when it was under construction it had been the subject of much intense discussion. Temperance C. Butler had not engaged an established architect but had hired a one-time shipbuilder, someone who had only recently switched over to houses when his shipyards had gone bankrupt. In a way the house gave proof of its origins, actually bearing some resemblance to a ship: lots of wood, small windows, an extended frontage further emphasized by ample empty space. No trees, no rondelles, no beds—only broad lawns, and the house at their center, a kind of Noah's ark in a sea of green.

Temperance C. Butler spent the rest of her life filling it with the objects she acquired in her travels. Year after year hefty packing crates arrived from Europe, bringing paintings, carpets, furniture. And always she found the precise place for the tapestry from the Burgundian castle, the chandelier from Murano, the majolica figurine from Florence. The house really should have been overstuffed by now, but its capacity to absorb more seemed limitless. The objects disappeared in it as in a huge ship's hold.

From her earliest childhood Anne had spent every summer here, and as the years passed, it became her home. It was not in Boston, in the somewhat somber house, but in Bar Harbor that she had the sensation of being truly at ease.

Slowly she walked toward the house. In the course of time the sea air had altered the yellow coloring, and now in the slanting light the masonry between the wood had an amber glow. The front door opened as White, the butler, came to stand on the threshold. It was a mystery to Anne how he always managed to waylay her so exactly.

"How do you do it? Do you spend all your time standing behind the door keeping watch?"

"Something like that probably, Miss Anne. You know what I think of your gallivanting around alone in the old, rickety buggy with a horse that spends the rest of his time in the stable."

"It's up to you to convince Grandmother to buy me an automobile at long last."

"Only one person could have done that—"

"My father. Is that who you mean?"

He did not answer at once. They were standing by the front door, next to the trellised peach trees. The fruits were large, larger than in previous years, and already tinted pink. If the sun continued to shine, they would soon be ripe.

"He could get anything out of her," White said, using the soft, dreamy tone into which he fell whenever he recalled Anne's father. "The craziest whims—and he didn't have to do much pleading, either. I don't believe he ever had to beg her for anything."

"How did he do it?" Anne was curious. "He must have had a special trick."

"No, no tricks. It wasn't necessary. He was simply her favorite."

Benjamin White was the only person who felt free to speak to her about her father. Sometimes she even had the feeling that he saw himself as a kind of father figure to her. The subject was still too painful for her grandmother; of her three sons she had loved the youngest most dearly, and she had still not overcome her grief at his death.

"I never knew her to refuse him anything," White continued. "Whatever he did, she thought it was wonderful. He was a wild boy, and sometimes all Bar Harbor was agog over his escapades—those were the times when she was particularly proud of him. He was her favorite, that's all. He could do no wrong in her eyes. When I remember the first time he brought me to this house! It's almost thirty years ago, but to me it seems like yesterday. . . ."

Anne knew the story of how her father had brought White here to the house; White had told it to her over and over again. But because she never tired of hearing it, she said now, "Tell me again how it was. . . ."

"We were both fifteen years old. He was Floyd Butler, who wore a white linen suit to play golf at the Kebo Valley Club. They used to say that every square yard of grass on that place cost more than a genuine Oriental rug—not that in those days I would have known what a Persian rug is. I was his caddy; I walked alongside him for hours, carrying his golf bag, handing him his clubs. My family—it was the time when the shipyards shut down and the workers were laid off—my family lived on what I earned at the Kebo Valley Club. . . . One time your father was assigned another caddy; the club management made those decisions. After that, he insisted that your grandmother give me a permanent job. He got what he wanted. The following day I moved into a room right here in the house."

"And,"—Anne hesitated to put the question, but his open smile seemed to encourage her—"And you never regretted it? I mean. . . ."

"I know what you mean, Miss Anne. Sure, sometimes I've thought that if the times had been different, I too might have been a boatwright."

"Is that why you make model ships?"

"Yes . . . but a model is different from a real ship. I don't believe my own ships would ever have been seaworthy." His smile deepened. "I really do believe I'm born to be a butler. I liked being a caddy, I like carrying things for people. . . . No, I never regretted it. Of course, when I think . . ."

He had grown grave. His glance rested thoughtfully on her, expressing paternal concern.

"When you think *what*?" Anne asked.

"Well, one of these days you'll leave us, and then I'll have to decide where my place should be in the future—with your grandmother or—"

"What kind of talk is that? What's the matter anyway? Everyone

I've talked to today drops the same kinds of hints—Alec, Doctor Hanson, and now you. I have no intention of leaving you."

"You really don't?"

"No."

"It happens so quickly sometimes, especially here in Bar Harbor in the summer. I don't know the reason for it, but I've seen marriages being made here that never would have happened elsewhere. . . . I'll have to see to the tea now." He stepped into the shade of the overhang and opened the front door. "You'll be taking tea, won't you?" he asked.

Anne nodded. "By the way, there will be one more for dinner."

"Mr. Alec?"

"Yes. I asked him to be on time."

"Did you get any news?"

"No. And you?"

"I sent someone over to the Lindsay cottage because I thought they might know something. After all, Mrs. Lindsay is on the same ship. But not a thing . . ."

They had entered the house, crossed the hall, and were standing in the library. The open sliding doors gave a view of the adjoining rooms—the living room, the dining room, and the music room. There was no sign that as recently as two days ago the rugs had still been rolled up and the furniture covered with slipcovers and dust sheets. Everything was in the order familiar to Anne. The newspapers were laid out in their accustomed place, the faience bowl was filled with fruit, the flowers in the vases spread their scent, and outside on the terrace the white cane chairs circled the table that, as always at this time of day, held the tea tray.

"Is Miss Connors back yet?" Anne asked.

White looked at the clock on the mantel. He listened. "If I'm not mistaken a buggy just drove up. I'll check."

"White."

"Yes, Miss Anne?"

"There's really no reason why she has to know that I went out by myself."

"I'm afraid she saw you leave."

"Then I have an idea what I'm in for."

"Perhaps you underestimate Miss Connors. I think she is much more open-minded in such matters than she seems." And before Anne could ask him what he meant, the door closed behind him.

Now she too heard the noise of the carriage stopping in front of the house. The clock on the mantel showed ten minutes to five, the well-known ten minutes—to the second—that sufficed for Edith Connors to freshen up when she returned home from playing golf.

Anne stepped to the window. Edith had already alighted. The leather golf bag with the clubs stood on the ground. The man in dark clothing who had brought her was holding her hand and speaking to her intently. She shook her head and laughed. As always, she was wearing a suit of gray and brown checks, laced boots, and a kerchief on her head. To Anne it was a familiar sight.

Edith Connors was one of the people in her life whom she never really thought about, but at this instant Anne wondered what she really knew about her, about her private life. Of course Edith had always had her admirers, in Boston as well as here; Doctor Hanson, for example, and the Reverend Brinnin, who was still so persistently holding her hand out there. But what else? Edith Connors' days were one like the other: every morning on the dot of seven thirty she left the house to take a half-hour's walk before breakfast; at precisely two-thirty in the afternoon she started her game of golf, and when the clock struck ten at night she retired to her room.

The Reverend Brinnin carried her golf bag into the house. Anne heard the voices in the hall. Clearly Edith was having trouble getting rid of him, but at long last Brinnin returned to his buggy.

Anne abandoned her observation post at the window and sat down on the terrace. When the mantel clock struck the last stroke of five o'clock, Edith Connors appeared, followed by White bringing in tea.

Every sign of outdoor activity had disappeared from Edith's appearance. A stranger would not have supposed that this woman marched across a golf course for two hours every day; her complexion seemed much too delicate, much too pale. Nor could one see the governess in her. It had often happened that Edith Connors had been taken for Anne's mother. Nothing in her was obvious or loud, and yet there was something about her that attracted attention—almost a trace of bohemianism. But perhaps it was only the wealth of hazelnut-brown hair, which always appeared a little wild and unmanageable.

"How is the new course?" Anne asked when White had left the room.

"It was always good, but with the additional holes this year, it's the best one I know of. They are very close to the water, and if you're not careful, you can lose a lot of balls. But what a view! The whole bay lies before you. And on a day like today . . . well, you were out. Alone, as I noticed. I—"

"Wasn't that the Reverend Brinnin bringing you home?" Anne asked quickly.

"Yes, he just happened to come by."

"Surely he always just happens to come by? He or Doctor Hanson or Mr. Fabri . . . did I leave anyone out?"

Edith looked up, not offended, only surprised. "It's news to me that you notice such things. Besides, there's a considerable difference between my being escorted home by the Reverend Brinnin, an old friend of the family, and a nineteen-year-old girl's driving out alone, without anyone to chaperone her."

"Are you sure the Reverend Brinnin's wife feels the same way?"

"Pushy today, aren't you?" Edith slid the plate of sandwiches over to Anne, calm and kind as ever.

But was she really? Anne wondered. Nothing about her seemed strained or affected, everything was in harmony—and yet she was a woman who at forty-five had still not found a husband. Anne began to do some arithmetic. Edith Connors had joined them thirteen years ago, a woman of thirty-two. But what had her life been before then? That of a woman who had been passed over? No, surely not. But where had her life as a woman taken place, and how?

She would have liked to ask, but instead she said, "Yes, I am pushy. Today everyone's appealing to my conscience. You'd think Bar Harbor was the most dangerous place in the world—Eden just before the Fall. And all the time what goes on here is as harmless as Sunday school."

"Oh, I remember it differently." Edith leaned back in her chair. "You've fallen in love every single summer. Young Cabot—does that name mean anything to you?"

"Oh, of course I fell in love. That's part of it. But I couldn't even tell you now how he looked, this . . . what did you say his name was? Cabot? You know what Grandmother always says: just so long as my heart isn't broken at the end of the summer, everything is all right. Besides, Alec will be playing chaperone as usual."

"If you think of Alec as a chaperone . . ." Edith did not go on, for White entered with hot water to freshen up the tea.

The noise of hedge clippers rose from the garden. The long-drawn-out siren toots of the ferry, preparing for her last sailing to Rockland for the day, rang in the bay. The wind must be from the east; otherwise the siren could not be heard so clearly.

Anne watched Edith Connors as she filled the cups with tea after White had left. Whenever Anne's grandmother performed this chore, the many bangles at her wrist jingled along; the action was soundless when Edith carried it out. She wore no rings, no chains, nothing at her earlobes. She even did without the brooch that was almost a badge of office for all governesses. Her only jewelry was a watch she carried concealed in the pockets of her suits or skirts so that only a section of the chain was visible, as now on the lapel of her suit coat. Might this watch be a remnant from Edith Connors' previous life?

"By the way, why did Uncle Sol move up on top of the cliff?" Anne asked.

"He wanted to get away from people, I suppose."

"I want to know the real reason. Something must have made him the way he is now."

"Really, it's a family story, and I—"

"You've been a member of the family for a long time. So?"

"With that kind of story, there are only two people who can tell you the truth. Everything else is guesswork, gossip. . . ."

"His wife lives in France, doesn't she, with another man? She left him—isn't that how it was?"

"You see, you already know the whole story. There isn't much more I can add."

"Was it his fault? What did he do wrong to make her run away?"

"Do wrong . . . my God, Anne, that's your grandmother's philosophy. As far as she's concerned, misfortune means that somebody has done something wrong, good fortune, that he's done everything right. If it were only that simple. . . ."

Anne leaned forward. "Maybe it really is that simple. Why didn't you ever marry?" The question had been on her mind all the time, but it surprised her when she heard herself asking it now.

The napkin on Edith Connors' lap slid to the floor. She bent down for it, picked it up, and in the process, as if unintentionally, she moved her chair a little farther into the shadow cast by the awning. Anne was all the more astonished when the answer came quite unself-consciously. "Is it my turn now? When did you become interested in ancient history?"

She collected herself, as if to launch into a long story. But when she spoke, it was only to say, "The answer is very simple. I always fell in love with the wrong men."

Her candor embarrassed Anne, but curiosity made her go on probing. "Is that possible?"

"Oh, yes . . ."

Anne thought of Doctor Hanson, of the Reverend Brinnin, of the Boston gentlemen who courted Edith Connors.

"You mean all of them were married?"

"That, too . . ." said Edith.

"Even the first one?"

"You're quite different from me. You'll do it right."

"You mean that I'm like Grandmother, I won't make any mistakes?"

Edith looked at Anne with a thoughtful smile. "Perhaps. But I'm not so sure I should wish it for you. For me, in any case . . . if I hadn't made the mistakes I did, I wouldn't have had the good luck I did, either." She rose and arranged the teacups on the tray. "I've got to check on Jenkins' hedge clipping. If you don't put the brakes to him, he's likely to go too far."

Anne too stood. Many more questions were troubling her, but Edith Connors' behavior made it clear that she wished to put a stop to the conversation.

"Alec is coming to dinner," Anne said, and something like a feeling of guilt awoke in her because all this time she had not thought about the ship. "He wasn't able to find out anything about the *Cecilie*."

"I don't believe there's any reason to worry."

All of them had said the same thing, but only on Edith Connors' lips did the statement carry conviction. Anne was reminded of her last evening in New York, when she had accompanied her grandmother on board the *Cecilie*. Dinner at the Plaza Hotel before the drive downtown through the dark streets to the North River, and shortly before midnight the ferry trip to Hoboken. And then the ship herself, lying at anchor, brightly lit. On the decks, in the cabins, in the public rooms, the glow of lights everywhere; from stem to stern, along the whole length of the ship, chains of lights glittered. In the dark of night she resembled a huge, sparkling jewel—unreal, enchanted.

But even at the pier the sobering process had begun. The crush of visitors, the loud brass band, the stewards and officers arranged in a semicircle at the top of the gangway to welcome the passengers— Anne had been repelled by the hustle and bustle. And the situation had been no better on the ship itself. The heat in the corridors, the humming ventilators that brought no relief, and again and again open cabin doors revealing cheerful groups holding glasses, celebrating the sailing.

The *Cecilie* did not raise anchor until an hour after midnight, but Anne had taken her leave at once, as soon as her grandmother was on board. Though Temperance Butler's cabin was situated on the promenade deck, Anne had gotten lost on her way to the gangway. The ship had turned into a maze; over and over she found doors, corridors, stairs, but nowhere an exit, until at last an officer in a white uniform stood before her, offering his help. . . .

"What is it, Anne? What are you thinking about?"

"The ship. The last night in New York, when I took Grandmother on board. It was very strange; I had a real attack of some kind of panic. I felt afraid of all the people, the closed-in space, the idea of not being able to get off the ship once it was on the high seas. . . ."

"Your grandmother has crossed the Atlantic dozens of times, and the ships didn't used to be as comfortable as they are nowadays. The *Cecilie* is a reliable ship, believe me, and she's commanded by a first-rate captain, none better."

"But what can a captain do—"

Edith laid her arm across Anne's shoulders. The calming gesture was imbued with the same intensity that radiated from her whole being. "Your grandmother, for one, swears by Charlie Pollak."

"Charlie Pollak? Who's he?"

"That just shows how much attention you pay when your grandmother tells her stories. For seventeen years she's been sailing with him. If she were younger, you'd think that she was in love with him."

Anne laughed. "Grandmother in love! I'd like to meet the man who can make that happen. The stupid saying that all Boston women are like our two principal exports—granite and ice—really does apply to Grandmother."

A strange smile hovered in Edith Connors' eyes, which were golden brown and serious and so often seemed to look beyond the visible.

"There are men who can melt ice, you know, and Charlie Pollak is one of them. . . . I've really got to go check on Jenkins. I'm worried about the way he's clipping away out there."

Anne watched her walking across the lawn. What had she learned? If she thought about it, nothing at all. And yet she had a feeling that there had been a moment when Edith had been on the point of speaking.

Thoughtfully she returned to the table and finished her tea. The cup was very thin, almost transparent, and if you held it against the sun, every air bubble in the china became visible, every unevenness in the glaze, the point where the handle was attached. Oh, if only it were possible to hold people up to the light in the same way!

What could it have been that made Anne feel she had seen through Edith Connors for a brief moment? Something she had said—but what? On her way through the library, Anne's glance fell on a pile of books lying on a table—vacation reading Edith had brought from Boston for the months in Bar Harbor. Anne picked up one of the books. It was entitled *The Jesuit's Ring,* and according to the description on the book's wrapper, it was a story from the romantic past of Bar Harbor. Typically, it seemed to deal with the love between a Jesuit and a married woman, and it had an unhappy ending.

The lending library run by Dolly Higgins in Bar Harbor held shelf upon shelf of this sort of book. This one too would land there before the summer was over; it was a local tradition that the cottagers donated the books they had brought to the lending library. The ones that came from Edith Connors, however, were reserved by Dolly Higgins for her personal perusal first; she could always count on their being to her taste.

Chapter 5

"Now, what is this supposed to be?" Alec let go of Anne and came to a stop in the middle of the large terrace that served as a dance floor in the Canoe Club. The colorful Japanese paper lanterns gave off less light than the August moon hanging full in the sky above the bay.

"It's a Lulu Fado," Anne explained.

"Lulu Fado . . . what does that mean?"

"Presumably nothing, but does it matter? I think the orchestra is really very good, much better than last year's."

"Do I have to?"

"That's what you ask me every year. Come on, or the dance will be over before we've even begun. It's not very different from a two-step, and in the crowd no one will notice if you take a false step. Just let yourself be led. . . . Yes, that's it . . . it's going wonderfully . . . splendid. Basically you have a natural talent."

"That's what it must be."

"I really mean it."

"But whenever I look at the dance instructions they print in the newspapers, I can't understand a word."

She laughed. "Surely that's not suitable reading matter for a staid attorney."

"I'm not all that staid."

"I'll take you at your word . . . sometime or other. . . ." She closed her eyes, abandoning herself to the good feeling that came over her whenever she was dancing. Gradually it spread to Alec, making him looser and more self-assured, so that soon he stopped paying attention to his feet and, just like Anne, let the beat of the music carry him.

The clubhouse lay close to the water; a gentle breeze ruffled the lanterns, the branches of the willows growing along the shore, and the boats at their moorings. The Canoe Club was the most distinguished of the clubs of Bar Harbor, open only to members, who paid an exorbitant yearly fee entitling them to nothing more than the use of the clubhouse and grounds and the right to embroider a gold-brocaded badge on the breast pocket of their blazers.

At one time the Canoe Club had been, as its name indicated, an athletic club. Here the young people took instruction from Indians in canoeing, a pastime the young women preferred as an activity for two. Even the strictest mothers had no objection to this sort of rendezvous, because the task of keeping the narrow, handmade boats afloat rendered even the most adventurous young men harmless. But this was long since part of the past; canoeing had gone out of fashion. One thing, however, had not changed: the club was the ideal hunting ground for young girls in search of a husband. Each summer began with the great riddle, "Who with whom?" A couple who danced more than four dances in one evening made themselves suspect, and if the two young people were seen sailing together the following day. . . .

"How about sitting the next one out?" Alec asked when the band had finished the selection. Anne shook her head. A tall young man sporting a sparse little beard pushed his way over to them.

"Hello, Anne. Back again?" He bowed curtly to Alec. "Listen, you can't monopolize her all night long. Give an old friend a chance. Perhaps I'll be able to do you a favor one day. . . . Right, I knew you'd understand." The music started up again, and the young man did not hesitate for a moment to bow to Anne and place his arm around her waist.

"I've been wondering when Anne Butler would arrive."

She smiled. He was a good dancer. She tried to remember his name, but in vain. The lanterns swayed overhead, and sometimes he had to pull his head in a little so as not to bump into them. He was taller than Alec, slender and tanned, but all the young men who frequented the club were slender and tanned. Not even their clothing distinguished them one from the other. They all wore the same uniform—white trousers, navy-blue blazers with gold buttons and sporting the club badge, a silk ascot tucked into the open collars of their shirts—and everyone's hair was a little stringy from water and sun.

Anne tried to imagine his face without the wispy beard. Cabot? She must have spoken aloud, for his head suddenly turned. "Leonard Cabot? Where? To hell with him. He got in my way last year. He's very good at that—all the Cabots are."

Well, whatever the young man's name might be, he was an excellent dancer; anything else was a matter of indifference to Anne. She passionately loved to dance, forgetting herself, almost in a trance. The only drawback was that her way of dancing aroused feelings in men which she did not share. There were a couple of unmistakable signs, and when at the end of the dance her partner pulled her close while his lips touched the nape of her neck—a more difficult feat when a girl's hair was long—she resolved to be rid of him as quickly as possible. She peered searchingly across the dance floor. "Isn't that Leonard over there?" She raised her hand as if to wave.

"Cabot?" The young man let go of her hand in order to look around for his rival, and Anne made use of the moment to disappear.

She found Alec where she had expected him, at one of the tables near the ice-cream counter. A large glass goblet stood before him. "I prepared myself for a long wait. Teddy Savage is stubborn."

"So that was Teddy! Would you believe I couldn't think of his name?"

"Old Philadelphia family."

"Nothing attracts me to Philadelphia."

"Where is he now?"

"Looking for Leonard Cabot. Old Boston family."

Between them they had something like a code language that they always resorted to when they felt like allies.

"Nothing draws you to Boston?"

"Not to the Charles River." That was where the Cabots lived.

"And how do you feel about ice cream?"

"Lemon."

"Lemon, of all things."

"Just a cone to take along."

"No more dancing?"

"Too many old families."

Holding their ice-cream cones, they went down to the shore. The path led along the water. To the left were fishermen's houses, narrow and whitewashed. Moonlight caught in the glass globes of the nets suspended from poles. The tide was out; the sand flats stretched far into the bay, leaving water in only a few runnels. The east wind intermittently carried the sound of voices and laughter across from Bar Island. A few fires burned along the shore. The island, which could be reached dry-shod from Bar Harbor whenever the tide was low, was a favorite nighttime excursion point for young people, though they had to be careful not to stay too long.

"Do you remember how the high tide took us by surprise on Bar Island?" Alec asked.

She nodded silently, but her thoughts seemed far away. She stood still, staring across the bay as if searching for a particular object. Far out lay the Porcupine Islands, four of them; now, at ebb tide, they were twice as large, and their forested backs really did make them look like sea monsters keeping watch outside the bay.

The history of Bar Harbor was the history of the bay and of the ships that had taken refuge in it in earlier centuries. One of these ships, a French frigate, had even given the bay its name. Iberville's *Poli,* a pirate ship, had found it an ideal hiding place in 1692, and in the years that followed, she returned again and again, whenever Pierre Le Moyne d'Iberville found it prudent to disappear off the surface of the earth for a while. Eventually he became part of Bar Harbor, and the bay was called Frenchman Bay. But when the natives spoke of it—the old fishermen, the trappers, the woodsmen—they made it seem as though each of them had known Captain Iberville personally and that one of these mornings his ship would again drop anchor in the bay.

The wind grew stronger. It whirled up Anne's long skirt, brushing her skin. It was, or so she felt, a wind that had come from far away, holding its breath; it had made a long journey for the sole purpose of finding her. She stood very still, listening with all her senses, as if the wind were bringing her a message of great importance. . . .

"There's a late show at the Star Cinema, *The Perils of Pauline.* Pretty sentimental, I know . . ."

Alec's voice returned her to reality. "I saw all eight parts in Boston," she said. "There's no holding Edith Connors back when they show that kind of picture. Her handkerchief ends up sopping wet each time."

"While our adorable Anne is totally unmoved."

"Bringing bad luck on oneself can't move me. That's just stupidity."

"So spake the veterinary doctor Anne Butler."

"And was right, as usual."

Whenever she was ironic, Alec found her particularly pretty. Perhaps that was because he felt safe from betraying his true feelings for her only then. He had forbidden himself to call these feelings love and told himself—a Butler and a lawyer to boot—he would have to be sure. He had long since become sure of his love, but to speak of it—that was another matter altogether. Everything in good time, he kept telling himself, and felt like a sobersides as he did so. Had a sobersides ever won the fair lady? A fair lady such as Anne? When he looked around, he discovered that the biggest sobersides got the most beautiful girls. . . .

"How about going to Eagle Lake?" That too was a part of their code, one of the oldest.

"A much better idea. But it will be cold."

"I've got blankets."

"I always get terribly hungry around midnight."

"Look at the picnic hamper."

They went back to the club's parking lot. When Alec had driven his new sand-colored coupe up to the yellow house, Anne thought it racy, almost too luxurious for Alec. But now, among the other cars with their long hoods, it seemed modest if not downright old-fashioned: the short muzzle, the deep-set steering wheel, and behind the seat the strange metal box holding the plaid blankets and the covered picnic basket.

"Where is the motor?" she asked. "Under the seats?"

"Shall I roll up the roof?"

"No, leave it. I can take a blanket if I get too cold."

Alec cranked the motor before taking his place next to her on the seat. To get to the road to Eagle Lake, they had to drive all the way through Bar Harbor. Except for the houses of the natives and a couple of small old hotels, the "town" had arisen only in the last two decades. During the day it offered a colorful, lively picture, but at night, when the strangers in the hotels and boardinghouses disappeared and the streets fell silent, Anne always felt as if she were in a gold-rush town that, barely built, had been abandoned again. At such times even the large hotels with their imposing facades appeared to her only as stage sets, painted canvas, no more, ready to be carried off by the first gust of wind.

Shopwindow after shopwindow—that was Main Street. It consisted chiefly of stores. the illuminated windows displayed souvenirs, beach clothing, fishing equipment. Here and there fluttered the colorful pennants of ice-cream parlors. Many front doors sported white signs declaring *For Rent* or *Rooms Available.*

It seemed to Anne that there were more of these than in previous years. Might that have to do with the war in Europe? But then, everyone said it was only a minor private fracas, nothing to do with anyone here. The steamboat that had brought her to the island also seemed to be ferrying fewer passengers than was usual at this time of year. . . .

They had gone beyond the last houses, and soon the road was no longer paved and straight; they were driving along narrow, curving sand paths. The moon shone so brightly that the light cast by the headlamps was barely perceptible. The path gradually ascended, and the trees to the left and right of the road grew thicker. She was reminded that in the past she and Alec had always used bicycles.

Last year they had gone to Eagle Lake too. Alec had not owned a car then, and they bicycled. At the steep places they had to dismount and push them. . . .

Alec, sitting next to her, was concentrating on the road. "We should come to the turnoff any moment now." The beams of the headlights slid over the forest floor. Sometimes there was a rustle in the underbrush as a startled animal scurried into the shadow of darkness. Then the trees parted, and Eagle Lake lay before them. A large lake, it had unfortunately long since been discovered by strangers. There were bathing cabins, and the previous summer a refreshment stand had been opened.

Alec let the car roll to a halt close to the single wooden house at the shore, the private property of the Butler family. The house had a reed roof; at the landing stage before it lay a canoe painted blue and orange, shielded with a light-colored tarpaulin.

"White even had the boat refurbished," Anne noted.

Alec was standing next to her. "Shall we take the boat out on the lake?"

She looked at him with a candid smile. "We used to swim out."

The embarrassed silence that followed was something she had only met with in other young men, never in Alec. What was the matter with him?

"I'll see if there are bathing things," he said at last, but his voice did not sound natural. "Is the key kept in the same place?" he asked as he walked away.

Anne had gone closer to the shore. She knelt down and dipped her hand in the water. "It's colder than I thought," she said to him when he returned. "Let's make a fire instead. I'm getting hungry."

They looked for the old fireplace they had built together years before. Anne fetched kindling and wood from the stack under the roof of the woodshed. Alec spread a blanket on the ground and unpacked the picnic hamper. He had brought sweet potatoes, one of Anne's favorite foods—already wrapped in tinfoil.

They lit the fire and waited for the potatoes to be cooked in the glowing ashes. They spoke little, watched the embers, listened to the forest and sea noises—a rustling in the reeds, a gust of wind in the tops of the trees, the cry of a nocturnal bird of prey. At night peace still reigned here.

Even after they had eaten, they remained seated before the fire. Anne had wrapped a blanket around her shoulders. The feeling that something was different between her and Alec was still affecting her.

"Grandmother hinted that you're planning to buy a house in Boston," she said at last.

He shook his head. "She really is a marvel. Just once I'd like to see her not know something."

"It's true, then?"

"Yes."

"Why a whole house just for you?"

"It's the house where one of our ancestors lived—Augustus Butler, Wales Cottage."

"The one with the whaling fleet?"

He looked away, across the flickering fire. "Not really. He didn't own a single ship, let alone a whaling fleet."

"But—"

"No Butler ever amassed his fortune by his own hands, by hard work. All Augustus Butler had was a glorious idea, a real Butler idea. You know the stays in corsets? They're made from whalebone. These stays, they were his idea—making money out of something other people thought worthless. He bought up whalebone by the ton. . . . An accident brought me to the house. He bought it with his first earnings. I noticed it because there's an arbor made of whalebone in the front yard. The house and grounds are pretty badly run-down. No one has lived there for a long time—which of course made it available at a pretty good price."

"Augustus Butler never owned a whaling fleet? But Grandmother has a painting showing him with the crew of a whaler."

"That was his second good idea. A manufacturer of corset stays is not acceptable to Boston society, so he served up a wholly invented story to their taste."

On the other side of Eagle Lake, where the log cabins of the summer camp were massed, lights suddenly blazed. Anne moved closer to the fire as she asked, "Why do you need a house?"

Alec sat with his legs drawn up, his arms circling his knees. "The price was very good. . . ."

His evasiveness only increased Anne's curiosity. "Is there a woman?"

"Yes."

"In Boston?"

"Yes." He avoided looking at her as he answered.

"Older than you? Rich?"

"Younger."

"A Boston girl . . ." She tried to cover her surprise with mockery. "And how are they, the Boston girls?"

"Boston girls are the same as girls anywhere." He was glad that she had given an ironic twist to the conversation. "They want to get married, and when they are married, they discover that they've tied themselves to the wrong man. Some find out sooner than others. Not a single Boston woman is married to the right man, but all act as if they were."

"Your mother wasn't like that."

"She came from New York." His mocking tone sharpened. "Perhaps she wouldn't have run away from my father if she'd grown up in Boston." Until this moment they had never mentioned his mother. The subject was taboo between them. But now that it had been raised, she continued her questioning.

"She lives in Paris?"

"Yes."

"Did you ever see her again?"

"Two years ago . . . She's quite different from what I had always thought."

"Did she marry the man who"—she halted but went on at once—"who was the reason at the time?"

"She married him, and a year later she divorced him. She opened a gallery where she exhibits young, unknown painters. I suspect that she is not so much concerned with talent but that each of her 'discoveries' happens to be her lover of the moment."

"Is she happy?"

"Sometimes I think she ran away from my father for no other reason than that she had it too good. It was boring for her to be only and always happy."

"You don't hold a high opinion of women."

"I see some problems. Whatever a man does to make a woman happy, he seems always to be doing the wrong thing."

Actually the conversation should have made Anne serious, but she felt cheerful, almost exuberant. "I've no objection to your staying a bachelor."

"Are you making fun of me?"

"Not at all. I'm simply terribly selfish. Let's suppose you get married—that means I won't be seeing anything of you anymore."

Wasn't this the moment to tell her what he really felt for her? He had an urge to speak—even more, silently to take her in his arms.

A sudden noise from the water sounded like the strong beating of wings of a large nocturnal bird of prey. Then they recognized the boat moving toward them. The man, his back to them, was rowing with short, choppy strokes that roiled up the water.

"That will be Storm," Anne whispered.

The boat had almost reached the shore. The man let the oars drop into the water and straightened up.

"Put out that fire!" His voice resounded through the stillness. "Are you determined to burn down the forest?" The keel of his boat scraped the ground. "Can't you hear me? Put out the fire."

The man jumped ashore and strode toward them. He wore the uniform of a Boy Scout—short trousers, knee socks, brown shirt with knotted neckerchief, the hat with the leather band. But he was well over fifty.

"How dare you—" Recognizing them, he fell silent and came to a dead stop.

"Hello, Storm," said Anne. "How are you? How's the camp? A lot of boys this year?"

He did not answer but only stared at the fire; the expression on his face was a mixture of fascination and panic. Up close, he seemed even stranger in his childish uniform.

"We'll put out the fire according to regulations before we leave," Alec assured him.

The man's eyes never left the embers. "Didn't know it was you," he said at last. "All kinds of people hang around making fires. Once the forest starts to burn, it's too late. I just wanted to make sure. Those people picnic all over the place; they're a nuisance, and their carelessness is criminal. I can see a day when the whole place will go up in flames. . . ." He mumbled some words of leave-taking and returned to his boat. Soon they heard the splash of oars, this time slower and more deliberate.

"I'm not convinced that he's really rowing back," Anne said. "Not as long as we're here."

Alec pulled the blanket tighter around his shoulders. "We can consider ourselves lucky that he didn't rouse the whole camp."

Richard Storm ran a summer camp on the western shore of Eagle Lake for boys from ten to fifteen. The log cabins were of a spartan plainness, with wooden cots, woolen blankets, washing at the well. The program included swimming, rowing, riding, and hiking, but these were no more than annoying sidelines for Storm. In reality he cared about training the boys as his own private fire brigade. Day after day he and his troop roamed the woods around Bar Harbor to collect all the discarded bottles; he had a theory that they were the most frequent cause of forest fires. A shard could turn into a magnifying glass in the sunlight and kindle the dry grass.

Anne listened to the splashing of the oars, gradually growing fainter. I could have asked him about the eagles, she thought. It's possible that he, like Jenkins, noticed them; maybe he even knows where their nest is. . . . And then she was reminded of Uncle Sol, sitting on his cliff. It seemed that Bar Harbor attracted eccentrics, and when Alec asked, "Where to now?" she promptly answered, "To the Baroness." She was the most eccentric figure of them all.

"Isn't it very late?"

She shook her head. "Last year we held out until dawn."

"It's almost that now."

"All the better. The Baroness' log cabin has the best view of the bay."

The fire had burned down to the last few embers. They pulled the glowing ashes apart and scattered soil over them. Anne was certain that Storm had concealed himself and his boat somewhere along the shore under the branches of a willow tree, and that as soon as they left, he would return to check whether they had done a proper job of putting out the fire. They collected their belongings and carried them to the car.

They had to drive more slowly than before; the moon was already too close to the horizon to shed much light. Anne had come this way many times in daylight, but now everything seemed strange. Tightly wrapped in her blanket, she sat next to Alec and felt that they were hopelessly lost. But when the car suddenly stopped and she recognized the markings on the trunk of a spruce, she was almost disappointed, as if she had been cheated of something. There was always such a moment when she spent her first night in Bar Harbor with Alec; an expectation was never fulfilled, a hope for something wonderful was always in vain.

The forest was dark. But a few minutes later, when they stepped out of the woods onto the plateau at the top, they saw that in the east the sky was already paling to gray. Before them the day spread out at its widest. The view from this spot was so overwhelming that every summer visitor was compelled to make the long and cumbersome climb. It was equally mandatory not to leave without buying a souvenir from the Baroness.

Her log cabin stood a little to one side. A single window was lit, and Anne thought she discerned the shadow of a shape inside. It was a certainty that the cabin, built of round logs, did not consist of much more than the one room. During the day a pennant, a blue banner with a golden fleur-de-lis, fluttered from the flagstaff in front of the hut, and the outside walls were covered with souvenirs for sale. Primarily these were things made by Indians—little baskets, ponchos, snowshoes, chains, and bangles; there were also painted shells, and the Egg Rock lighthouse painted on birch bark. All these objects could be bought in the town, and more cheaply, but up here the customers were waited on by a French noblewoman.

No one seemed to know her real name. she was known simply as the Baroness, or as Baroness of Green Mountain because her cabin was located at the foot of the mountain. In spite of all the years she had lived there, she had never learned proper English. Contradictory stories about her made the rounds, but all agreed that she was a member of a noble French family that at one time had owned all of Mount Desert Island. Louis XIV himself had deeded it to her ancestors, so the story went, and she had come to America—a great-great-granddaughter of the original owners—to validate her claim. Most people considered her a harmless madwoman. The children, however, loved her because she owned a small pond in which goldfish swam; these, as she assured them, were more than three hundred years old and had come from one of the Sun King's aquariums. It was a fact—Alec had confirmed it—that the Baroness had at one time carried on lengthy lawsuits concerning ownership of the island and had become impoverished in the process.

Anne called Alec's attention to the illuminated window in the log cabin. "Apparently someone else is waiting for the sunrise," she said softly.

"I had no idea you were such an incurable romantic."

"Incurable is right. Come, let's walk to the edge."

Outcroppings of bare rock studded the ground. At the edge of the headland, where it dropped steeply for about sixty feet, a wooden fence had been erected. It was very quiet; not even the birds were stirring. The few lights of Bar Harbor, barely visible, were obscured by the gray of the sky, which grew ever more intense. Even the water in the bay was gray, the surface was ruffled. The tide was coming in swiftly. The Porcupines grew smaller by the minute and seemed to be farther and farther removed from land.

During the upward climb they had not felt the cold, but now Alec was sorry he had not brought along a blanket for Anne. "I think we should leave," he said.

"No, wait."

"It will be another half-hour before the sun rises. You'll catch cold."

"Please . . ."

A sound pierced the silence. The door of the log cabin had opened, and a gray figure stepped outside. Her steps were soundless, only the hem of her flowing gown slithering softly across the ground.

The garment was gray, and the hair of the woman was gray and loose; she wore long lace gloves, and a black fan dangled from her left arm.

She glided rather than walked. Her eyes were facing straight ahead, wide open and yet somnambulistically blind. As she went to the edge of the plateau and looked across the bay, she seemed more an apparition than a creature of flesh and blood. Suddenly she emitted a cry, the astonished exclamation of someone who has seen the incredible. She raised her hand and used the fan to point out into the bay.

It was such a compelling gesture that Anne and Alec turned to look in the same direction. And now Anne too could not suppress a cry. "Look, Alec! A ship!"

Far out, at the southern entrance to the bay a mighty vessel sliced through the water. The black ship was clearly delineated against the gray sky: a long hull, decks, four black funnels belching out dark smoke. There were no lights anywhere; the entire ship was dark. Had it not been for the fumes above the smokestacks, one might have believed that the giant sea monster was sailing into the bay unmanned.

"It can't be," Anne murmured. "It simply isn't possible." She looked questioningly at the gray shape, and as if the Baroness had understood her words, she turned her head. She smiled, nodded, and began to speak hurriedly.

Anne could not make out a single word. "What is she saying?" she asked Alec.

"I'm not sure I've heard her correctly. She seems to believe that it's a French ship. *Le roi* . . . she's talking about the kings. . . . I don't know either."

Anne's eyes turned back to the bay. "Frenchman Bay," she said softly, as if talking to herself.

"It can't possibly be a French ship," she heard Alec saying at her side. "There is no way for that to be possible. A ship that size—it's a mystery to me how they managed to navigate past Egg Rock. Not even the ferry would venture that way at night."

A thought suddenly came to Anne, a crazy thought it seemed to her, and yet she voiced it. "And suppose it's the German ship?"

"The *Cecilie*? Never! The *Cecilie* has four yellow funnels, and these are black. I can't see a name, either, and not a flag anywhere. . . . The way she looks, she just might be the *Olympic,* but the *Olympic* landed in New York last night."

Anne looked at the ship without a name, without a flag, which was gliding ever deeper into the bay, heading for the Bar Harbor town wharf. She still could not believe her eyes. Perhaps she was simply having a daydream. She was quite unaware of the smile flitting across her face—a smile that believed anything was possible.

PART TWO

Chapter 6

The cabin smelled of soapsuds and shaving water. Weariness weighted his limbs like lead, pushing him deep into the chair. He had tried to sleep during the last few hours, after the ship had dropped anchor. But he had only lain in bed with open eyes until Pommerenke rescued him at last when it was time for his shave. Now he could hardly wait for the tiger to remove the wrap. Impatiently he tugged the cloth from his neck and went to the window of the navigation chamber.

The thick glass seemed to reveal nothing but glimmering brightness. It was one of those summer mornings when the world consisted purely of light, an all-encompassing sea of brightness, and all things within it sharply outlined and yet incorporeal as mirages. The illusion was complete. The bay with its many boats—was that not the North River? The view of the mountains—did it not resemble the Manhattan skyline? And the teeming crowd of curious bystanders on the shore—didn't the pier in Hoboken look the same whenever a ship landed? A hallucination. After three days and ten hours without sleep, it was not really surprising.

Behind Pollak's back Pommerenke cleared his throat. "If you'll allow me . . ." He buttoned on a new collar for the captain. Then he opened the wardrobe, took out a white uniform jacket, and held it out to his superior.

Pollak looked down at himself, noticing only now that he was wearing white trousers. He could not remember when he had exchanged his dark ones for these. "Why whites, Pommerenke?"

"Summer, Captain." Shadows of exhaustion lay under the tiger's eyes, but worse was the expression of perplexity that dominated his face. He had enormous skill in buttoning a jacket, even when the material had been starched stiff, but this time he did not seem able to manage it. The smooth gold buttons resisted him, and he began in the wrong buttonhole, so that he had to start all over again.

"What's the matter with you?" Pollak asked.

"You've lost weight, Captain."

"Every cloud has a silver lining." His own words made no sense to him, even less his attempt at a joke. For a moment he laid his arm across Pommerenke's shoulders. "Don't worry. At home they already know we are safe. As soon as we entered the three-mile zone, we sent a wireless message to the shipping company. Some pensioned-off captain will be going house to house in Bremerhaven to spread the news to all our families. . . ."

Pommerenke was calmed neither by the words nor by the captain's hand on his shoulder; the unusually intimate gesture explained even more clearly the situation they found themselves in. He freed himself by stepping to one side. Then, stiffly and with an effort at maintaining distance, he asked, "Any orders, Captain?"

"Sleep, Pommerenke. Sleep."

Pommerenke lowered his head. "I mean orders, sir. What is to happen now?"

Pollak understood only too well what his tiger meant. For decades their life had been conducted according to a steady rhythm. The loading of the ship, the arrival of the passengers, the sailing, the crossing, the arrival in the home port, the debarking of the passengers, the cleaning of the ship . . . and again the coal tender alongside the ship, the loading with provisions, the arrival of the passengers, the sailing . . .

During the past few days and nights Pollak had concentrated on a single goal: bringing the ship to safety. He had thought only of the next moment, nothing else. The humming of the ventilators on deck suddenly bothered him. He flipped off the switch. Pommerenke was still waiting.

"I really mean it. See that you catch a few hours' sleep. At present that is the most important order. If I recall the laws correctly, we have to be back at sea in twenty-four hours or we are stuck here for the duration of the war. . . . So I need a rested crew."

Voices were raised on the bridge. A knock on the door followed. Pommerenke opened it to the chief purser. He too had put on his white summer uniform. The material was starched stiff as a board, the trousers creased above polished black shoes.

"What is it, Kuhn?"

The purser's hand flew to his moustache, a movement that was as much a part of the man as was the moustache itself. The ends were turned upward, exactly like Kaiser Wilhelm II's, earning Kuhn his nickname among the crew—Wilhelm III. He too had not been to bed for the past three nights, and so he had been unable to apply his moustache trainer. For Kuhn that omission was no small thing; if his moustache was not in good shape, he was not in good shape either.

"You're needed on deck, sir."

"What for? When are the passengers debarking?"

"The first class is already engaged in it, since permission was received. Your cabin is empty again. The gentlemen from the bank were in a special hurry."

Pommerenke breathed an audible sigh of relief. He had not been at all pleased that Captain Pollak had given up his quarters. "If you don't need me any longer, I'll see to it that your cabin is fixed up."

Pollak seemed in less of a hurry. "I can't stop you."

"He would do better to get some sleep," he said to Kuhn after Pommerenke had left. "I want everyone who is not busy with the debarkation to catch up on his sleep. All of them are tired enough to drop in their tracks. Make do with stewards as much as possible."

Wilhelm Kuhn looked at the captain. He searched for signs of exhaustion, but he found as few now as he usually did after a drunken night. Except for the jacket, which was not quite as taut as usual, Pollak seemed refreshed and full of energy. An old rivalry between them had developed in the fifteen years they had served on the same ships. Wilhelm Kuhn was proud of being Charlie Pollak's purser, but it was not always easy to maintain his own self-esteem in the company of such a man. At heart he had been waiting for fifteen years to catch Pollak in bad shape.

"How many are going in the first batch?" Pollak asked.

"It just so happened that a ferry was in port. It can take about three hundred and fifty passengers, half of the first class. We've asked for a second boat, and if it arrives as promised, the rest of the first class should be taken care of by this evening."

"And the second and third?"

"For the moment it doesn't look good. No chance before tomorrow or the next day."

"They can't stay. They must be off the ship today."

"I don't see how. This place is pretty damned godforsaken."

"It's your business, Kuhn."

The two men had left the navigation room and stepped onto the bridge, deserted except for the helmsman. After the *Cecilie*'s anchors had been dropped, Pollak had sent every expendable man to his bunk.

"How are you getting the passengers off?" Pollak inquired. The *Cecilie* was anchored more than two hundred yards from shore. The shallow water did not allow her to come closer.

"We put them in lifeboats and lower them," said Kuhn. "It's the lesser evil, and it's quickest."

"How are the passengers taking it?"

"I thought it was going to be worse after the past three days." Kuhn was a pessimist by nature; everywhere and always he expected the worst, and he was convinced that his principal activity on board consisted of preventing the worst. "All the same, it would be good if you made an appearance. There are a couple of problems. . . ."

Pollak waved the suggestion aside. "Oh, no, this is your day, my dear Kuhn."

The chief purser did not reply. What should he have said? This was in fact his day, and in New York, Pollak would have long since gone ashore. The day before a ship's sailing and the day after her arrival—those belonged to the purser. For Pollak it was a matter of course that everything went smoothly. After all, that was what he had "his dear Kuhn" for—on such days the purser hated the form of address.

"I've had a lot of complaints because the Captain's Dinner never happened."

"If that's all . . ."

"Maybe you think it's trivial, but there's more. You'll hear a lot of complaints. I don't mean trouble, but complaints, lawsuits. That man Kreisler had to cancel his sold-out concert in London. He will be suing for restitution."

"The violinist?"

"Yes. and Mr. Mears from Chicago has threatened to bring suit for lost winnings, twenty thousand dollars, because you prevented him from sending wires."

"Kuhn, I beg of you—that's a matter for Lloyd's lawyers, not for us."

"They want to know if their fares will be refunded."

"The lawyers—"

"The lawyers, for heaven's sake. You have to let the people see you. You have to talk with them. After all, they're our passengers."

He laid special stress on the final word. *Passengers*—for the *Cecilie's* purser the word encompassed a confession of faith. To satisfy the passengers, to anticipate their every wish—that was his credo and the driving force in his life. Before every sailing he pored over the passenger lists for hours—concentrating, of course, on the first class—like a true believer studying Holy Writ. The pencil he used to make notes was sharpened to a needle point. According to an old rule of thumb, it took fifteen years to turn a first officer into a captain. For a purser the process was no quicker, but the experience that made a good purser was nowhere written; one had to amass it for oneself. This Kuhn had done. He knew most of the first-class passengers personally. The shelves in his office always held the *Almanach de Gotha* and the most recent edition of *Who's Who,* but he rarely had to consult them; his brain was a living encyclopedia of names, characteristics, preferences, dislikes, eccentricities. His knowledge also included items that were no part of his legitimate concern. He knew his passengers better than they suspected, and when new names came along, names unfamiliar to him, he made careful inquiries, discreet as a private detective, thorough as a scientist. His attention was lavished mainly upon the wealthy. Though they were not the ones who brought in big money for the shipping company—that came from steerage, from the third class—it was the wealthy to whom a ship owed her reputation. They could make her famous, give her luster, just as it was in their power to ruin her.

And so Kuhn repeated almost beseechingly, "They are our passengers. We can't afford to upset them. If they stay away next time . . ."

"Wake up, Kuhn," Pollak said, more irritated than was necessary, even in his own opinion. "The *Cecilie* won't be seeing any more passengers any day soon. Not for the present. When we sail away from here, no one will be on board but the crew."

Kuhn did not answer; he searched Pollak's expression, seemingly waiting for the captain to qualify his words. Followed by Pollak, he stepped outside and glanced over the bulwark down at the sun deck, where the passengers were milling around the lifeboats. A few of them were still wearing the life jackets they had been issued, but Kuhn noted with satisfaction that most of them had taken them off to reveal their best summer finery. The stewards who were helping them get into the boats and handing them their small luggage or pet dogs had also put on clean uniforms, snow-white and stiff as his own. It looked almost as if they were practicing a new party game.

Some of the passengers had spied Pollak. Shouts were heard. "Charlie . . . Charlie. Most of them were the voices of women, and one of them, a deeper one, now called, "Bravo, Charlie, bravo!"

"What did I tell you? They want you." The purser's expression had brightened, and he continued eagerly, despite his rooted pessimism. "It seems that our passengers are beginning to look on the whole thing as a lark. Who knows, some good may come of it. The newspapers will surely blow up the story—you might call it free advertising for the *Cecilie.*"

Pollak waved him aside. "I do not wish any reporters on board. More than that, no one at all is to be allowed on board. I have enough to do dealing with the authorities. I repeat, Kuhn, we have to get out of here in twenty-four hours, and I need a rested crew by that time."

"We don't have a single lump of coal left."

"A tender is on its way from New York. It will get here by nightfall. By that time the passengers must be off the ship."

"And the gold?"

Pollak pulled a radio message from his pocket. "A revenue cutter is on the way, the . . ."—he looked at the strip of paper—"the *Androscoggin*. It will take on the gold and silver cargo. They must have worked themselves up into a real lather, seeing how promptly they responded. . . . All right, then, everything cleared up, Kuhn?"

The purser nodded. Somehow he was still hoping that Pollak would change his mind and join the passengers on the sun deck. But finally he realized that there was nothing to be done.

"Everything cleared up, sir."

Pollak watched him until he had disappeared along the passageway. The voices were still rising from the sun deck. Kuhn was right; the passengers seemed to be taking delight in the adventure. It had not always been like this during the past three days and nights.

He had not forgotten the first moment of silent stupefaction when he had called a few selected passengers together in the smoking room, announced to them the imminent outbreak of war, and told them of the shipping company's order to turn the *Cecilie* around and make for a neutral port. "Please keep calm." Those had been his final words that night after he had explained the most essential measures. Of course there had been protests, but finally the passengers had had no choice but to resign themselves, and life on board had continued almost normally—at least for them.

Tatters of memory of the past days and nights floated through his mind: the stewards covering all windows and portholes with canvas so that no light would penetrate to the outside world; the men lowered over the railing by ropes even as the ship continued at full speed, concealing her name with black paint; others hanging from the smokestacks, painting over the yellow. Not that he believed these paltry tricks would make the *Cecilie* look like the *Olympic*. Some let themselves be misled, but by no means all. Her position had been revealed to several French and English warships, and an English cruiser, the *Essex*, had dogged her all the way. His only chance lay in the ship's speed and in the heavy fog he had encountered on the northern route. The passengers, however, had taken a different view of the situation. The fog did not give them the same sensation of safety. The breakneck speed with which they had rushed through the fog had frightened them, and at one time panic almost set in. They sent a delegation to him with a request to reduce speed. He refused, and he could not even tell them the reason for his running such a risk—that they were being pursued. . . .

And yet, when he thought back on it now, it seemed to him that all the decisions he had had to make during their flight—for that was what it was—had been simple compared to what still lay ahead. He should have been happy and proud that he had succeeded in bringing the *Cecilie* to safety. Why wasn't he? He had no words for the emotion rising in him; it almost resembled sorrow.

He stood still and looked across the bay. It was not the first time he had seen it, but that did not matter now. It must be strange for the people of Bar Harbor to see the giant sea monster in their bay. Anyone who owned a boat was on the water; there was a fleet of sailboats, motorized yachts, rowboats. The flotilla circled the *Cecilie,* and it grew ever larger. There were even canoes, dipping and rising dangerously in the wakes of the other boats.

The shore too was thickly lined with people; they stood closely ranked, waving their handkerchiefs at the ship. He could not find fault with the reception, and yet he could not rid himself of the somber feeling that gripped him—a deep, nameless mourning.

Chapter 7

*T*hat's life. By rights I should be in Venice, in my hotel with a view of Santa Maria della Salute—and where do I end up? At my own front door." Her face was shadowed by a salmon-colored hat. The broad brim curled at the slightest breeze, giving proof of the delicacy of the Panama weave.

Fred Vandermark, the second officer, was prepared to see the hat fly off her head at any moment. "Sad?" he asked. "Because of Santa Maria della Salute?"

A glance from the hat's shadow brushed him. "Why? In Venice I'd be sitting around with a bunch of Americans, which is as good as alone. The American colony in Venice—you don't know them?"

"Are there only Americans in Venice? I can't imagine that you'd ever be bored."

"Surely you don't believe I'm one of those women who have to travel to Venice to have an adventure, or to Rome or Paris or anywhere. I've always left that to chance." The hat tinged her face pink, making her younger than she was; it did not alter her eyes, which were emerald-green. She laid her hand on his arm, and her polished fingernails glowed distinctly on the white of his uniform.

"I do hope that I'll be seeing a lot of you in the days to come. . . ."

The steward, impatiently waiting a few steps away, came closer now, determined not to be put off again. "Please, Mrs. Lindsay, the boat is full. We're only waiting for you. If you'd be so good as to follow me."

"Right away, Meinert, just a moment." Her hand remained on Fred Vandermark's arm. Her other hand pointed to the shore. "Over there, in the hills. It's hard to see from here. The castlelike building with the tall chimneys. Everyone in Bar Harbor can show you the way. . . . I hope you'll come soon."

She gestured to the steward to let him know that she would really be only a moment longer. "Funny, they're all so eager to go ashore, except for me. But I'd better go now, before I say things I've never said to any man." She laughed softly, as if making fun of herself. "It must be the farewell mood. All right, then, see you soon."

"I don't know what will happen," he said, "or how long we are going to stay here. No one knows right now. But you'll be hearing from me. Good-bye."

"*Auf wiedersehen.*" Once again the breeze made a stab at carrying off her hat, once again unsuccessfully. She walked away with the steward. The wide sleeves of her salmon-colored chiffon frock fluttered in the breeze.

The stewards and cabin boys, all spick-and-span, had formed their usual semicircle at the gangplank while the passengers were going ashore. Under their caps and visors their eyes blinked in the sun; or had they fallen asleep on their feet? Kuhn stood before them; he waited until Gloria Lindsay had taken her seat in the lifeboat, and then he placed a check mark against her name on his list. An order rang out. Slowly the snow-white boat was pulled up, swung out over the side. An old lady's laughter, half flirtatious and half frightened, rang out.

Vandermark kept his eye on the pink hat, the pink dress, until both disappeared from view. He listened to the rasp of the ropes in the hoists until he finally made out the splash when the boat hit the water.

"Vandermark. Finished your morning worship?" The purser gestured at him to come closer while the stewards and cabin boys took up their positions at the next lifeboat. "I need your help," Kuhn said. "Find Mrs. Butler for me. She's holding up the procession. Surely that's in your department." He examined the *Cecilie's* second officer with a sweet-and-sour smile. Kuhn could understand why Vandermark was lucky with women; they were attracted to his rugged, virile good looks. Yes, he understood that every ship needed such officers, men who moved as self-confidently in the public rooms as on the bridge. But what he did not understand was the evident preference

Vandermark enjoyed with Pollak. "Well, how about it? Will you go find Mrs. Butler?"

"I was planning to catch up on my sleep. Captain's orders."

"I'm sure you've got a lot to catch up on—more than the rest of us, right?"

"All right, I'll fetch Mrs. Butler. Where is she?"

"You'll find the lady in the smoking room. She's collecting her bets; it seems that this time she got the better of a particularly large number of gentlemen."

Before leaving the sun deck, Vandermark looked at the lifeboat that had just been lowered into the water; it was halfway to the harbor. The many boats obstructed its way, so that it progressed slowly. Gloria Lindsay's hat and dress glowed pink across the water. Salmon-pink was her favorite color, appearing in one form or another in most of her outfits. When she came aboard, it had been her blouse, which she wore with a white suit. He would always remember the salmon color, but he was not certain whether he would ever see her again. He did not even know if he wanted to. Love affairs on board were all right, but whenever the ship landed, there was trouble. *You'll be hearing from me*—how often he had said these words to a woman at the end of a voyage and meant just the opposite.

Something else was troubling him as he looked across at Bar Harbor. How, of all places in the world, had Pollak come upon this particular spot, the least suitable of all the possibilities? He thought of the final hours of the night on the bridge; all of them had sweated blood when they sailed into the Bay of Fundy and then into Frenchman Bay—all except Pollak. More than once the *Cecilie's* keel had grazed the sandbank lying under the water, and the sound—a slight scraping—had penetrated to the bridge.

Pollak had not revealed his destination until the last moment. Of course there had been a great guessing game among the passengers. Bets grew sizable. The favorite was Portland, followed closely by the second hot tip, Newport News. But apparently only Temperance C. Butler had considered Bar Harbor.

"How ever did she think of it?" wondered Vandermark as he started on his way.

Belowdecks, in the corridors, it was very hot. In spite of the beaming sun, he had found it cool outside, but perhaps that was only because of his exhaustion. He noticed that the ventilators had been turned off. The corridors alongside the cabins were stuffed with laundry bags and rolling tables full of dishes. Workmen with ladders and tool chests were walking back and forth. In the main lounge the vacuum cleaner was humming. Two men were kneeling on the floor, scrubbing the old wax off the parquet with steel wool. The barkeep was ordering his accounts. Some of the musicians sat around at a loss in the large hall. In a way all these tableaux were an ordinary aspect of the end of a crossing. A party that had lasted until dawn was over. The guests had left, and behind the scenes the gray figures appeared to restore order to the ship. But this time there was a difference. Usually a feverish air clung to their activities; the sooner they finished, the sooner they would be able to go ashore. But today their movements were slower, more hesitant. Somehow they reminded him of life-size puppets, automated dolls whose clockwork would run down at any moment and leave them frozen in their actions. Never before had the main lounge seemed so huge to him. He could hardly believe that there were times when the dance floor was not large enough. . . .

He was prepared to find a scene of melancholy in the smoking room as well, but even at the door the noise of excited voices greeted him. The room, which always seemed a little dim in spite of its stained-glass dome, was full of men. Temperance C. Butler presided at the billiard table. Her dark eyes and her head, with its snowy white hair, were brightly lit by a low-hanging lamp.

Vandermark had difficulty making himself heard. "Ladies and gentlemen, please go on deck. You will be taken ashore. Please listen. . . ."

Temperance C. Butler, a memo pad balanced before her on the edge of the billiard table, a silver pencil in her right hand, waved him to her side. Her bracelets jangled gently, her triple strand of pearls swayed. She invariably wore dresses of a simple cut, and always they were of a uniform color, serving only as a background for her plenitude of jewelry, for chains, bangles, rings. Whenever she moved, something or other on her person gave off a soft tinkle.

"Don't scatter my debtors," she said to Vandermark. Her voice was soft and dusky, giving no hint whatever of her strong will. "Once they've gone ashore, I won't see my money again. You'd do better to help me; we can finish faster that way."

He glanced across the table; bills and coins were piled on the green felt. "Looks as if you had broken the bank at Monte Carlo."

She glanced at him. Her dark eyes sparkled. "Once I almost did, in my good years. But that's long ago."

"It can't be so long ago," said Vandermark, meaning every word of it.

"It's been a terribly long time, my boy, terribly long. But as always you're very nice to me, so help me now. De Peyster is next. Owes me forty-five dollars."

"Make him shell out his money." He had known her for years. She had changed from the *George Washington* to the *Cecilie*, where Vandermark had been serving since her maiden voyage, when Pollak made the change. Both had been preceded by a legendary reputation: Pollak, because he had once brought the *Kaiser Wilhelm der Grosse* across the Atlantic in spite of the loss of the rudder; Temperance C. Butler, because she held the record for loyalty to Lloyd—more than half a century. She had made her first crossing at the age of seven, together with her mother and father. She always reserved the *Cecilie's* imperial suite—at a premium price—and in the dining saloon her place was to the right of Pollak at the captain's table. Further privileges granted her were admission to the first-class pantry—a favor that Uhlig, the principal chef, accorded to no other passenger—and a very extensive right of codetermination in the musical program of the band. The stewards feared her because of her outrageous requests and adored her for the size of her tips, though she had the irritating habit of handing the stewards one half of a torn hundred-dollar bill at the beginning of a crossing, adding the matching half on the last day—but only if she was satisfied with the service.

"Just give me the money. I'll count it myself. Here, take the bag and stuff whatever is on the table into it. . . . Slater," she called across the green felt, "it's sixty dollars for you. I'm sorry, Harry, but Boston—you never had a chance."

Vandermark watched as she counted the bills using her thumb and forefinger, skilled as any bank teller.

"Thanks, Harry." She consulted her note pad. "Mr. Ketterling . . . Mr. Ketterling . . . thirty dollars." She was concentrating intently, although between counting she still found time to say good-bye to the gentlemen who had paid up. Her broad face with its blunt features radiated well-being, but her dark eyes remained watchful. "Almost done, my boy.

In fact the smoking room was beginning to empty until finally everyone had left. She remained in her seat for a moment longer; then she rose, put on her cartwheel of a hat trimmed with white plumes, and pinned it firmly. "Do you have the money?"

Vandermark took the plain leather bag from the billiard table. It was heavy. He had not counted along with the individual contributions, but a sizable sum must have been amassed, certainly well over a thousand dollars won on her bets.

"How did you know?" he asked.

"How did I know what?"

"Bar Harbor."

"Oh." Her voice was even softer than usual. "I knew nothing."

He had heard the men make different remarks: wasn't it obvious that she had had a tip from Pollak?

"If you had lost . . . I mean, you would have had to pay out a handsome sum."

"*If*—the word doesn't exist for me. I won. I was sure of myself. You know, I know Charlie. I've known him much longer than you have. I know what goes on in his head, and I thought. . . ." Once more she pulled the note pad from her bag, checked over her betting list, and came to a sudden stop. "That man Yarnell! He didn't pay up! A hundred dollars! Have you seen him?"

"He went ashore already—just now, in the last lifeboat."

"That's so typical of Yarnell. He stinks of money and welches on his bets. Well, I'll have it out with him next time." She closed the note pad and put it and the pencil back in her handbag. Her pearl necklace—three strands descending to her waist—jingled softly. The feathers on her hat dipped. Vandermark took the bag with the money into his left hand and held out his right arm to her. She hesitated, smiled at him, and kissed him on both cheeks. "You're a great treasure, Fred. You have an extraordinary gift. You manage to make an old lady remember that she was young once."

"I would have loved to have know you when you were young," he said.

"Really?" With a quick gesture she gathered up her long dress so that, for a moment, her feet and ankles were visible. In proportion to her build, she had unusually dainty feet and ankles. "In my time I was the merriest and craziest young girl in all of Boston," she said, "and I had the smallest feet of them all. Of course, I was never a beauty like Gloria Lindsay. All the same, it wasn't just my money the men liked about me. . . . Has Gloria gone ashore yet?"

"Yes."

She had taken his arm, and they were making their way to the deck. "Gloria asked you to visit her, I assume?"

"Yes."

"That's all right." She laughed out loud, brightly, so that the barkeep in the lounge looked up. "Two rich widows, an old one and a young one—what better luck can a young man have?"

"Three rich widows."

"True, you'd easily be able to handle even three."

He had an absurd feeling of unreality as he walked through the empty ship with her on his arm. Somewhere there was a war, the first casualties were occurring, and he was courting a sixty-three-year-old American woman. In recent days and nights he had sometimes had the same feeling while serving on the bridge; at the piano when he was playing four-hand selections with Temperance C. Butler; or in his off-duty hours, which he spent with Gloria Lindsay in her cabin, A-121. But then there had always been the unknown destination toward which the *Cecilie* was rushing, and the ocean. . . . The ocean was his familiar, safe territory, unlike land.

"You'll like Bar Harbor," he heard the woman saying at his side. "I do hope I'll see you frequently at my home. I'll have the grand piano tuned this very day." She began softly to sing the chorus of an old hit song.

> *Don't drink any more,*
> *Don't drink any more,*
> *Please, Papa, don't drink any more.*
> *Oh, listen to the prayer of poor mother and me,*
> *Dear Papa, don't drink any more.*

"We'll play it for four hands and sing along, all right? Besides, my Betty White is an excellent cook. Ask Pollak. I want both of you to come, tell him."

Vandermark struggled with his weariness. "I don't know how long we'll be here."

"What is that supposed to mean? You will wait out this stupid war here, in peace and quiet. Surely you don't believe . . . Charlie will be more sensible. Why else would he have chosen this spot?"

They had stepped out onto the sun deck. The bright light was blinding, and a shudder ran through him.

"Look around you," she said. "Does it look like war here? Bar Harbor is paradise. A little boring maybe—the sleeping beauty hasn't been awakened yet. But the ship will surely rouse her. The ship will change everything. So tell Pollak that my house is open to him, and to you too." She smiled. "You won't be able to keep the invitations at bay. Really, you should be happy to be here. Bar Harbor is paradise. Life does not give us any summer twice. . . ."

"Here is the boat."

"I never dreamed that one day I'd be leaving our good ship *Cecilie* in a lifeboat. . . . Give me the purse. I'll manage, don't worry. All right then, my boy, I hope it's a short farewell. . . . Oh, hello, Mr. Kuhn. I'm sorry to keep you waiting. You have my luggage?"

Vandermark remained behind and watched her dickering with the purser about the luggage; she seemed dissatisfied with the promise that it would be brought ashore later on, and with all his respect for Temperance C. Butler, at this instant Kuhn was unable to suppress signs of impatience. Finally they came to an agreement, and Temperance C. Butler began the process of handing the stewards the second half of the hundred-dollar notes ready in her reticule.

"What a spectacle. . . . Well, it's almost over."

Even before he heard the voice, Vandermark had known that the first officer of the *Cecilie* was nearby. Wherever he turned up, Kessler gave off a strong scent of mothballs—unless the odor was that of a particularly penetrating after-shave lotion. The question was frequently raised of whether it was really necessary for him to shave, since his round, cherubic, boyish face with the watery blue eyes seemed to get along without beard, eyebrows, and lashes. Even his hair was only a light fine fuzz.

"How about a drink?" Vandermark asked. "I've got a bottle left in my cabin, the perfect nightcap."

"If you've got time to go to bed . . ."

"I'm ready to drop."

"Go ahead, then, I can't stop you." Kessler's voice had an edge to which Vandermark had long since become accustomed. On duty or off, Vandermark invariably seemed to annoy Kessler, perhaps simply because they were so radically different. In addition, the crew tended to side with Vandermark and let Kessler know it—not surprising, given Kessler's gift for making himself unpopular, especially among the lower ranks. And one more thing: Kessler was the same age as Vandermark, thirty-two—unusually young, therefore, to be a first officer. Even Pollak had not advanced to the position until he was thirty-seven. Actually the crew should have been impressed with Kessler's career, but since he was married to the daughter of one of Lloyd's directors, he had been stamped as a favorite son of the management. This was probably unfair, for Pollak would surely have found a way to get rid of him if Kessler had not possessed the necessary qualifications for a first officer.

"What will it be, then? Will you come and have one with me? None of us has had any more sleep than the others, and we're all getting on each other's nerves."

"It's the passengers who are getting on my nerves. You'd think all this was a big joke, thought up and arranged especially for their enjoyment. God knows, I could use a drink."

Vandermark was glad that he had succeeded in lightening Kessler's mood a little. They left that part of the sun deck where passengers were continuing their departure and now passed one of the four giant funnels.

"All right, then, let's head for my cabin. It's the best champagne."

Kessler stopped short. He looked up at the funnel with its coat of black paint. "It's time to restore its true color," he stated reproachfully. He turned to Vandermark. "Do you hear me?" He sounded as if Vandermark were to blame for the smokestacks' black coating, and he continued in the same tone of voice. "If you had the proper respect for your duties, you'd take a couple of men now and see that the Lloyd colors are put back on the funnels. . . . An ignominious game of hide-and-seek—it's gone on long enough."

"My God, Kessler, the things you worry about!" He felt the heat still radiating from the funnels. "Wait for them to cool down at least." Vandermark had been in charge of the crew that painted the smokestacks in the middle of the night; by the time the work was completed, the smoke and the glowing heat of the metal had landed two of the men in the infirmary with smoke poisoning and burns, and they were still there. "I couldn't find a single volunteer if I tried. The men are worn out."

"Since when do I have to justify my orders—"

"Not to me, you don't. What are your orders?"

Kessler's pale skin blushed red. "You can save your sarcasm. Don't provoke me."

"Man, Kessler, what a stubborn mule you are. As far as I know, it hasn't even been decided whether we'll be putting to sea again."

"Not decided? How can you believe we would stay moored here?" He pointed upward at the mast where the Lloyd flag fluttered. "In wartime we are naval reserve, Vandermark. I shouldn't have to remind you—Imperial Navy. And we'll put to sea under this flag. . . ."

"I'm going to catch forty winks," Vandermark replied. "Wake me when it's time to join the naval reserve." Usually he avoided this kind of needling, but now he could not help himself—perhaps because he was exhausted, perhaps because today more than other days Kessler got on his nerves.

"Vandermark! See to it that the funnels are repainted. That's an order."

Vandermark walked on, tired and depressed, and once again he was seized by a sensation of unreality. He almost tripped over his own feet. At the head of the stairway he stepped aside while a group of men rose from the dark of the stairs and pushed its way upward.

They must be the stokers of the last shift, for their faces were smeared with soot, their eyes were red-rimmed, and their filthy vests stuck sweatily to their bodies. They seldom came on deck. The "black gang" of the *Cecilie*, a crew of over two hundred, performed its back-breaking work far belowdecks, hidden from all eyes. The way they shuffled past him, the way they stretched their heads and breathed deeply, made it clear how starved they were for light and air. Their work at the glowing furnaces which insatiably devoured coal was never easy, but it was hardest at the end of a voyage, because then the coal had to be carried from the most remote bins.

"Vandermark! What business do the stokers have on deck? Take a few of these men—"

Vandermark shed his lethargy in an instant. A few steps brought him back to Kessler, whose arm he grabbed. "For God's sake, Kessler, are you trying to get yourself killed? Pick on me if you want, but leave the men alone."

He did not need to continue. The troop of stokers marched up to the two officers. "Is something the matter?" one of them asked. "Something the matter with our taking a gander at the scenery?"

Kessler took a step forward, and for a moment Vandermark held his breath. Stokers were the toughest men on any ship, a random bunch of varying nationalities. He had seen them explode over some trivial matter and attack each other with knives and shovels. And he knew that it was not advisable to offend their pride. Tough as they were, they were equally proud of their work belowdecks; each shift tried to outdo the others, especially when, as on this voyage, speed was of the essence.

The group was still standing before them—fifteen, twenty men—dark faces, and within each the bright spot of the eyes, piercingly focused on Kessler. "Something the matter?" the ringleader repeated, and his voice with its eastern accent sounded more sleepy than threatening. "Supposed to be pretty scenery. . . ."

"Don't do anything foolish, Kessler," Vandermark whispered. Once again Kessler's light skin flushed red, but then he turned and walked away. The scent of mothballs remained, but then it too receded. Vandermark stepped to the railing and grasped it with both hands, holding on until the tremor in his knees stopped.

Sleep, he thought. All I need is some sleep. A drink and sleep. The darkened cabin and sleep, sleep. But there was another weariness in his body, one that would not be relieved by sleep.

The stokers had lined up along the railing next to him. He heard their astonished cries in every conceivable language; dirty hands with broken nails pointed across to Bar Harbor. He too gave one more glance across the bay with the countless boats, across to the boardwalk teeming with people, to the town, to the wooded mountains under a bright blue sky.

No summer comes twice—strange how the words stuck in his mind. What did it matter to him that Kessler acted crazily? What business of his was this war, though it jeopardized everything that had made up his life until now?

He discovered a salmon-pink spot in the crowd of people at the landing stage. It was the last thing he thought about when, a little while later in his cabin, he fell into a deep, dreamless sleep—and the first when he awoke.

Chapter 8

The seagulls' screeching came through the open porthole into the captain's cabin. They always arrived as soon as a ship put into harbor, and always on the side where the galleys were located, in response to the offal thrown overboard. In New York, Pollak had noticed that they escorted the ship as far out as Sandy Hook. But here it had been different. The gulls of Bar Harbor were not used to ships the size of the *Cecilie*; they had been shy at first, and it had taken a while before a few particularly bold birds had dared to come close. By now, however, a lot of them had gathered, more than in New York. Every gull of Frenchman Bay seemed to crowd around the ship, and yet their screams did not sound like an embittered battle over the offal but like a cheerful feast.

In the next room Pommerenke was busy arranging Pollak's linen and clothing.

"What do you think they'll enjoy most? The caviar sandwiches or the Westphalian ham?"

"Sir?" Pommerenke appeared in the open doorway.

"Never mind, don't let me interrupt you." All the same, Pollak's need to speak was so great that he said, "McCagg—what does the name mean to you?"

"Boston," Pommerenke answered promptly. Eighteen eighty-six. We were going from Naila, with sugar on board."

"My memory isn't getting any better either, Pommerenke."

"What makes you bring up McCagg?"

"He'll be here in a few minutes. McCagg is the commander of the revenue cutter. Look out the window; you'll see his boat. Have him brought to me at once."

Pommerenke, holding a pair of shoes, looked through the open porthole. "In the old days he wouldn't say no to a drop or two."

"What are you waiting for, then?" Pollak said. "Have a magnum chilled. The best vintage."

Pommerenke nodded silently, put the shoes away, and disappeared, giving no sign that Pollak's attitude bothered him. Pollak himself wondered what had caused his good mood. He was not convinced that it would last, but presumably it had some relation to his being back in familiar surroundings. Such things influenced him.

A very early evaluation of him had contained the notation "too emotional." It had been intended as a negative criticism, and ever since, he had leveled the same reproach against himself many times. Fewer feelings would have made his life a great deal simpler—his life with women and his life with ships. Whenever Lloyd had entrusted him with a new vessel, he had had to make a major adjustment. Even with the *Cecilie*. During the early crossings he could not overcome a feeling of unsureness; he had not felt adequate to the ship—such a thing could not be explained by reason alone—and now it had long since become a matter of his fearing nothing so much as having to leave her too one day. The situation with his cabin was similar. Only now, when he was back in it, did he realize how much he had missed the familiar surroundings: the effect of subdued lighting created by the dark mahogany paneling, the leather armchairs, the green reading lamp on the desk, the blue Chinese rug, which was his personal possession. For him, the *Cecilie* was more than merely a ship he commanded; she was his real home. . . .

The clatter of a serving cart neared his cabin outside in the corridor. Pollak opened the door to the steward; his glance went to the silver ice bucket misted over by the chill, the neck of a magnum thrusting from it.

It was a familiar sight to all the ferrymen on the North River: the captain of the *Cecilie* standing in the bow of a launch bringing him from Hoboken to Manhattan, under his arm a bottle of champagne, a magnum, as befitted a man of his stature. Champagne Charlie was the nickname they gave him, and as Pollak recalled it now, the smile of satisfaction on his face deepened.

Carefully he pulled the bottle from the crushed ice, just far enough to check the label. Then he reached for the two goblets and held them up to the light.

The steward stood by his side, napkin at the ready to polish away a smear or a water spot Pollak might discover. But the glasses were immaculate. In this too Pollak reacted like a host. There were many captains who never set foot in their ships' galleys or laundry. When Pollak found something amiss with a meal or found a carelessly ironed napkin at his place, he did not send one of his officers but went himself and complained to the people responsible, usually quite vociferously, unleashing thunder and lightning.

"Fine," Pollak said. "I'll do the serving. Should we need another bottle, I'll let you know."

There was a knock, and Pommerenke announced the captain of the revenue cutter before leaving with the steward: "Captain McCagg of the *Androscoggin.*"

Pollak remembered a face adorned with a goatee red as a fox's fur, but the man now entering sported a beard white as snow. A second memory did not betray him: McCagg had the narrowest shoulders and tiniest feet Pollak had ever seen on any man. He approached Pollak with short, quick steps. The two unequal men, the gigantic German and the fragile American, shook hands.

"Welcome on board the *Cecilie,*" Pollak said.

"I always hoped we'd meet again," McCagg replied. "I'm sorry that the occasion is so . . . . official."

Pollak himself took the man's cap and his white gloves. "We don't have to make it so official. As far as I know, there are no regulations forbidding us to start with a drink. Come, sit down."

The two captains looked at each other. Silence set in, as it always does when two people suddenly confront each other after many years and try to reconcile their memories with the present reality. Seconds passed in this way, and only then did Pollak's practiced hand uncork the champagne bottle and fill the glasses. They drank to each other without touching glasses.

"A good year," said McCagg.

"Eighteen eighty-nine—almost right. Three years before, you were captain of the *Salem.*"

"A certain McCagg was captain of the *Salem*." He spoke as if they were discussing a stranger.

"We were coming from Manila with our old four-masted barque, the *Prudentia*." Pollak refilled their glasses. "And then we saw the *Salem* in port. To run a ship like that one day—that was my dream then. That's twenty-eight years ago. . . . You were the captain of the *Salem*, weren't you?"

McCagg looked deep into his glass. "She carried eight thousand tons; now I command three hundred."

Pollak was trying to figure out McCagg's age. Sixty-three, sixty-four—ten years older than himself. "A beautiful ship and a fast ship, the *Salem*."

McCagg smiled, giving him an even more fragile look. "The *Salem* was one of the last trumps we Americans had to play on the North Atlantic, but it was too late. Our passenger ships haven't been able to keep up with the British and with you Germans for a long time now. In reality, even then we no longer had any business on the North Atlantic. In the meantime everyone has gotten used to the fact, but at that time it hurt our pride."

Pollak set his glass down on the table and leaned back, suddenly serious. "Perhaps the situation will change soon. If this war in Europe should go on for a while . . ."

"Perhaps," McCagg answered. "But they're not going to reactivate me on that account. And I don't even know whether I'd really like to get back out there on the Atlantic again. It isn't what it used to be. When I started, there was still adventure, romance, and people still had time. Now it's turned into a racetrack. More than a million passengers last year! It's nothing but business, advertising. Each shipyard tries to outdo the others with ever faster boats, more luxury on board, more exotic menus."

Pollak pulled the serving cart closer. He understood McCagg only too well; the same thoughts had gone through his mind at times, especially in recent days. But now he did not wish to acknowledge them. "Those were good times," he said. "Good times for captains."

McCagg had small birds' eyes. He peered around the cabin. "You Germans and the British have brought too many architects, too much frippery, too many cooks into seafaring. It used to be that a ship was simply a ship. Now ships are opera houses, floating palaces. The architects and the cooks run the show, not the captains."

Pollak laughed. "Sometimes it almost looks that way. Eggs are brought on board cradled in butter, and ten people are employed simply to turn them once a day. The same with fruit; if the peaches are at the wrong temperature, my chief cook thinks the world is coming to an end. And if the train bringing the oysters from Baltimore doesn't get to New York on time, he demands that I delay the sailing. Yes, sometimes I have a dream—a nightmare: we're in the middle of the Atlantic, and the engineer tells me we've run out of coal; I go below-decks and find the whole bunker filled with goose-liver pâté."

McCagg's laugh was soundless, stifled; he resisted his own mirth as if it were a cough. "Why don't you try to stoke up with pâté de foie gras?"

"Maybe that's not such a bad idea. That might be a way for good old *Cecilie* to snatch back the Blue Riband."

Unexpectedly they were involved in a conversation about ships and captains known to them both. The bottle emptied, but the two men grew no noisier, no more cheerful; rather, a mood of melancholy grew between them. Finally Pollak raised the bottle to the light. "Another?"

McCagg shook his head. He straightened his crooked black tie. "I think we should get started." In the silence of the cabin the cry of the gulls could be heard. McCagg hesitated, cleared his throat, then continued. "I'm going to have to close your bar. Maine is a dry state."

"The law is the law." Pollak seemed to make excuses for McCagg. "Close the bar. Though we're always amply provisioned, there's not much left over after this crossing. The passengers' thirst was greater than usual."

McCagg looked up. "That was a very pretty gamble." He pointed to the pile of newspapers on the round table next to Pollak's leather armchair. "They counted on everything except Bar Harbor. No one thought of it."

The newspapers had been brought to the *Cecilie* that morning by a boat crammed with all the editions of the last several days. The man must have bought up everything available in Bar Harbor, and his calculations had proved correct: the passengers, who had not seen a newspaper for a week, had fought over them and paid any amount.

"You're something of a hero."

"I haven't had time to read them yet." This was not entirely true— Pollak could have made the time—but something had prevented him from touching the papers, as if in this way he could achieve a postponement.

"What made you pick Bar Harbor?"

"I really had no choice. It was the shortest route. And then, I was afraid the English and French would try to catch me outside the other ports. All they had to do was set watches on New York, Boston, or Portland and wait for me."

"I can tell you that that's exactly what they did. Anyway, the Americans are enjoying the story. We like a man with the courage to strike out for himself."

"Except for the gold on board, probably no one would have given two hoots for us."

Again McCagg gave his soundless, strangled laugh. "Bankers are very important people among us."

"Will you take possession of the gold today?"

"Not me. That's been changed. The *Androscoggin*'s specie room isn't large enough. A naval torpedo boat is on its way from Newport News to receive your cargo. . . . Yes, today, two or three hours at the most."

"And the *Androscoggin*?"

"I've been assigned to you." He hesitated, searching for the right words.

"You mean as a watchdog?"

"Something like that. Three hundred tons against twenty thousand."

Seconds passed before Pollak spoke again. "Actually, I wasn't thinking of a long stay."

Heat filled the room. McCagg looked at the idle ventilator. "According to my reckoning, you can't have much coal left on board, or pâté de foie gras either."

"A tender is on the way. We'll stoke up tonight."

All at once McCagg seemed uncomfortable in his leather armchair. He slid to the edge, his hands on his knees. "Nevertheless, the official position is based on the premise that the *Cecilie* will be anchored here for the present. I will send the precise orders for your private perusal. Your colleagues . . . I don't know of any German ship that put to sea again."

"How many are there?"

"I don't have the exact figures, but I would guess that there might be around thirty. Didn't you at one time command the *George Washington?* Last night she lay peacefully at anchor in Boston." Again he slid around in his chair. "You won't make my job unnecessarily difficult?"

"The decision rests with New York, with the shipping company."

McCagg nodded. "Shipping companies are always practical. They're not going to risk a ship like the *Cecilie.* All right, then, I'll get it over with. The orders concerning procedure in neutral ports read: From now on you may use your wireless station on board only to receive, but you yourself may not send out any messages. Your word is enough for me. If there is any violation, I'll have to take down your antennas. There are two telegraph offices in Bar Harbor; they'll be made available to you to communicate with New York."

"So we may go ashore?" The crew as well?"

"Whatever were you thinking of? You have complete freedom of movement." He underlined his words with a gesture that seemed somewhat too large for such a slightly built man. "Looks like an involuntary holiday. In any case, you couldn't have picked a more beautiful place. If you look at it from that point of view—"

"I'll try." Pollak's eyes were directed at McCagg, and yet he seemed not to see him. "At any rate, my country is in a state of war."

This time McCagg got to his feet. He took a few steps, stopping at the edge of the blue rug. "You're not planning to play war on your own initiative?"

"So far the *Cecilie* is a passenger vessel."

"There have been stories these last few days of German passenger ships that carried armaments on board so that in case of war they could be enlisted as armed merchant cruisers."

"I know nothing about that." Of course Pollak had heard the same rumors, but the question had never been broached with him.

"I assume you are not seriously thinking of leaving Bar Harbor by hook or crook?"

"Presumably there would be no other way."

"With my three hundred tons, there's not much I could do about it. Of course I would have to try to prevent you from sailing. And don't forget one thing—out there, the other side of the three-mile zone, they're waiting for you. Even without the gold, the *Cecilie* makes a pretty booty."

"British cruisers?"

"The *Essex,* for one. We sailed past her. The fact that you evaded her clutches hasn't made the British any more friendly."

Now Pollak also got to his feet. "I shall speak with New York. You're probably right about the shipping company's attitude. They don't like losing their ships." He had gone to the porthole and was looking out. "A summer in Bar Harbor—why not? . . ."

He had spoken softly, almost to himself, but McCagg nodded in relief. When Pollak turned, he pointed to the empty magnum.

"It really is too bad that the passengers used up all the stores."

"Except for a few remnants." Pollak's features relaxed. "I mean the captain's small private reserves."

McCagg suppressed a smile. "I'll study the regulations. It would seem to me entirely possible that private reserves do not fall within the law. And even if they do, it seems impossible that they could be searched out on a ship this size. Even the best revenue inspector is powerless in such a situation. . . ."

Chapter 9

The white lifeboat lay at the dock of the Bar Harbor Yacht Club, and now, in the evening, the tide was so high that one could look over the entire shore, the lawns, the huts and landing stages of the boat-rental shop on one side of the street and the hotels on the other.

Outside one of the hotels hung the recognizable shield of the Western Union Telegraph Company, the little lamps around the lettering burning night and day. Surely an hour must have passed since Pollak made his way to the Western Union office to put in a call to New York; perhaps it had been even longer. Vandermark had lost track of time. He felt both tired and overly alert. His nap had hardly refreshed him; his limbs were weary, and his head seemed a hot-air balloon about to separate from his body. He had considered it a welcome opportunity to row across to Bar Harbor with Pollak, but then he had not gone ashore, instead remaining in the boat with the eight men who manned the oars. He could not have said why he was suddenly hesitant to go, to so much as set foot on the wooden pier, the stone banks of the wharf, as if it represented something final, something the consequences of which he could not comprehend.

The Yacht Club dock lay closer to the ship than did the steamship station where the first-class passengers had been let off, the last ones not until late afternoon. A paddle steamer had taken them away, and it had just departed when Pollak left the *Cecilie* in the lifeboat, so that the oarsmen were made to feel the wake and were kept very busy.

Now the water was smooth again. The dock lay abandoned. A few curious observers stood at the shore, using binoculars to watch the large foreign ship lying at anchor in the bay; no one dared to approach the lifeboat, as if even the people of Bar Harbor were not clear what the presence of the giant sea monster meant for the town. Perhaps it would bring them good fortune, perhaps bad—one could not be sure.

Vandermark's glance too kept turning to the *Cecilie;* she seemed huge and strangely alien, quite different from when she was berthed in Hoboken or Bremerhaven. The sinking sun was positioned directly behind her, and the ship grew in the foreground, a giant that seemed to need all of the bay and the entire sky for itself alone. It had been a long time since he had looked at the ship so deliberately, and once again he was conscious of the pride he had experienced at the time of her maiden voyage, when every port received her with pomp and ceremony.

The coal tender lay alongside, the hatches gaped open, and the dull rumble of the coal sliding down the chutes could be heard all the way to shore. The American coal, bituminous, was so soft and loose that in the unloading black clouds of dust rose. Woe if one forgot to close the portholes tightly in one's cabin; the greasy soot seeped in everywhere. Nevertheless, the coal had arrived. Did this mean that they would be leaving Bar Harbor as soon as the second- and third-class passengers had also landed?

Where was Pollak? What could keep him speaking to the New York office for more than an hour? Vandermark leaned over the edge of the boat and scooped up a handful of water. It was surprisingly cold. Was this why he had not seen a single swimmer? Though it was August, the height of summer, not a soul was in the water. He was reminded of how far north they were and how short the summers must be up here.

"The captain." One of the men nudged him. In fact Pollak appeared at the dock. In his white summer uniform he seemed less huge than in blue. The cap on his head was, as always, a little too small. He approached slowly, lost in thought. Only as he came close to the lifeboat did his steps quicken, grow more energetic. He sat down on the center bench, and his expression told the crew that it would not be advisable to bother him with questions. A black briefcase was perched on his knees; he held it tightly in his large hands, which seemed even larger in the white cotton gloves. He seemed always to select caps one size too small and gloves one size too big.

"Hurry it up a little, Hennig," he said to the boatswain's mate who was loosening the mooring rope; that was all. Erect, stiff-backed, he sat still and stared straight at the ship.

The boat took off; the men had trouble finding a good rhythm for the oars. The boat skipped and bucked, but finally the beat came regularly and they gained speed. The *Cecilie* moved closer. The superstructure and the funnels—still painted black—threw long shadows. The ship's starboard was facing the shore. The tender and the men at the hatches were shrouded in clouds of soot. Up above, at the railing, some of the crew had gathered in anticipation of the captain and the news he would bring.

Pollak's immobile figure quickened. "We'll go on deck portside," he said, adding, "Pity to soil the nice white uniform."

Vandermark wondered whether it was really the uniform or whether it might be the men waiting up there at the railing. For Pollak to avoid anything was unusual, but this was an unusual day.

They could have spared themselves the trouble of rowing to the other side, for even there groups had gathered, waiting and chattering, and they fell silent only when Pollak came in sight. The men's faces showed that they hoped for an explanation from him, but Pollak marched past them as if he did not see them, stiff-backed, his eyes directed straight ahead.

Night fell quickly now; normally the ship's lights were already turned on at this hour, but today all remained in darkness. Only the position lamps had been lit, a couple of searchlights on the superstructure and the upper deck illuminating the stairways, small lamps inserted into the paneling giving off a pale glow.

An evening breeze arose, carrying the smell of the sea, rippling the water so that it slapped the hull in little waves—and suddenly a sound hung in the air, the blare of a bugle, quiet at first, hesitant, not yet a tune, simply sounds seeming to come from afar, as if the wind were carrying them from the ocean.

Pollak had come to an abrupt stop. He listened for a while. The sounds, clearer now, came from the ship's bow. Pollak shook his head.

"Do you know what he's playing?" he asked Vandermark. "It seems to me that I recognize the tune, and yet—"

"Who is it?" Vandermark asked.

Pollak looked up, uncomprehending.

"Who's playing?" Vandermark repeated his question.

"That's right, you never heard him. It's Pommerenke. Once he was the best bugler there ever was on the high seas. You never knew that, did you? Nowadays we use a gong to call the passengers to their meals, but in the old days each ship had her bugler to announce the meals. Pommerenke was the best, a real artist. When he blew his bugle, the dining saloon was so quiet you could hear a pin drop. . . ."

Pollak gestured to one of the mates who had rowed the boat. He handed him his black briefcase. "Take this to the purser. It contains telegrams for crew members received through Western Union. I want him to hand them out at once. And Hennig . . ." He hesitated briefly. "Have Kuhn call all off-duty crew members together in the lounge . . . in an hour."

The sound of the bugle swelled. It played an odd melody, slow, almost melancholy. Pollak, head lowered, stood and listened. The mate had gone off on his errand. Pollak took off his gloves and pushed them heedlessly into the pockets of his uniform jacket.

"Come along if you like," he said to Vandermark. He sounded almost rude.

Pollak was displeased with himself. Even the conversation with McCagg that morning had depressed him. An old captain, once the commander of one of the handsomest ships, now serving on a revenue cutter! The telephone discussions with the New York offices of Lloyd and with the German embassy in Washington had done nothing to raise his spirits; just waiting for the connections had been enough to drive him crazy; there you were, in possession of your own wireless, and you weren't allowed to use it but had to stand around the office of Western Union until your legs damn near fell off. And then the conversations themselves—his throat constricted when he thought of them. He did not want to think about them, not now, or he would have had the crew assemble right now. Why the hour's delay? What would have changed in an hour? And why didn't he send Vandermark away? He had the most urgent desire to be alone, and at the same time he felt calmed to hear the second officer's steps alongside his own.

Funny chap, Vandermark. He was the type of ship's officer with whom Pollak never used to get along. Why with this one? He had often asked himself the question, and he found only one answer, which was unsatisfactory and irritating: Vandermark was the way he, Charlie Pollak, would have liked to be. Vandermark was everything he himself was not. "Why the devil did you ship out in the first place, Vandermark? Come on, tell me, what was it? The sea?"

"I don't know. I never thought about it. . . ."

"How much does it mean to you? What do you think, could you give it up?"

"Give it up? Does that mean New York decided—"

"I'm not talking about New York. I'm talking about you. Or, to be honest, about me. There was a moment—I was your age at the time—when I was faced with the question of whether to give up the sea. Afterward I often wished I could have done it—simply give it all up, from one day to the next."

"For a woman?"

"That obvious, eh? Yes, dammit, for a woman."

"It depends on the woman."

"You mean—the love of a lifetime?"

"Something like that."

"And if it's the love of a lifetime and you still can't do it? You can't get free of the other, of the first great dream of your life. You just can't do it, and then it's too late. . . ." He fell silent, and his steps quickened.

He had gone too far, had let himself get carried away. He had shown a side of himself that no one knew. He was Charlie Pollak, Papa Pollak, Champagne Charlie, the German Hun who spread good cheer wherever he went. It was a role he had long since stopped playing; he had become the part, and he would soon be it again, no later than an hour from now, when he stood before his crew. "You remind me of the moon—it shows only its bright side." Had a woman really told him that once? It had been here, in Bar Harbor, on the terrace of the Canoe Club. They had been dancing, and brightly colored lanterns had hung from the willow branches. It had been a long time ago, in another lifetime—until today . . . New York. . . . Of course that was important also, of course the most important thing of all was the ship's future. The future distressed him, but he had expected that. What he had not counted on was that the past still had the power to distress him as well, that it could catch up with him. It was here, and it was more than mere memory. It was part of his life, of this life, of the dark side of the moon that no one knew about. . . .

The high, drawn-out sound of the bugle grew gradually softer until it finally died away. Silence fell. Somewhere in the dark someone began to applaud but stopped at once when he realized that no one else was clapping. Here and there in the dusk shapes could be made out. Men stood in recesses of the wainscoting, sat in deck chairs. When they became aware of the captain, they made as if to rise, but Pollak gestured for them to remain seated.

Pommerenke stood in the ship's bow, a man of middle size in a black suit. Above him the signal line hung down from the foremast. The light of a direction lamp caught in the metal of his instrument. He lowered the bugle when he saw the two men approaching, and when he recognized them, he gave an embarrassed smile. "I'm out of practice. You can tell, can't you?" The red circle left on his lips by the mouthpiece spread into a smile, and for a moment he looked a little like a clown.

"What are you playing?" Pollak asked.

Pommerenke looked at his bugle. It was an old instrument, light-weight and shorter than the newer ones. "You didn't recognize it?"

"'Roast Beef of Old England'?" Pollak asked. "Is that what it was?"

Pommerenke lowered his head. "Not exactly appropriate, is it?"

"Why?" Pollak asked. "I always liked 'Roast Beef of Old England.' No one ever played it better than you. It's just that today it sounded different."

Pommerenke ran his sleeve across the instrument. "I'll get it again." His glance went past Pollak, over to the land. Now, at night, with its many lights, Bar Harbor seemed larger than it did by day, almost as if the town had the faculty of stretching at night.

"I've got something for you." Pollak searched his pockets and then came up with a Western Union form. "A cable for you. I pulled it out from the rest."

Pommerenke was hesitant to take it. "Did you get one too?"

Pollak laughed. It sounded like his old, cheerful laugh. "The captain is always last. What's the matter, don't you want to read it?"

Pommerenke left the cable folded and tucked it into his breast pocket. He had been married only six months ago to a young woman of twenty-three. No one on the ship knew about the marriage except Pollak, who had stood up for him at the wedding.

"'Roast Beef of Old England,'" Pollak said into the silence. "We'll introduce it again. From now on meals will be announced by bugle. And—in future I'd like to hear it sounding less sad. Do you hear? It's got to sound cheerful, as cheerful as in the old days."

A second time Pommerenke wiped his sleeve across the bugle. Then he asked formally. "Where do you wish to take your meals, sir?"

"It's going to seem funny, the captain's table without ladies," Pollak said. "All the same, I'll stay in the large dining saloon. And you can tell that to the stewards—no slovenliness, everything as always, the good china, the silver, the damask cloths. We have to keep the stewards on their toes. Stewards who are idle are a problem."

"Captain."

"Yes?"

Pommerenke seemed to be searching for words. One expected something meaningful—a request, a confession, something to match his solemn face—but then, looking straight at Pollak, he asked, "Would you do me a favor, Captain, and not stuff your gloves into your pockets that way? It stretches them way out of shape."

Pollak nodded. Then he actually reached for his white gloves, stroked the pocket smooth. "We'll both of us improve, Pommerenke, all right? I'll stop the nonsense with the gloves, and you'll see to it that 'Roast Beef of Old England' sounds merry."

Pollak and Vandermark began to make their way back. Once again they passed the silent groups. They had grown larger, and the first might already be on their way to the main lounge.

"So we're not going to be sailing?" Vandermark asked.

"Who says so?" The forced good mood Pollak had exhibited to Pommerenke seemed gone with the breeze.

"It sounded that way when you were talking to Pommerenke—the good china and silver in the dining saloon, the stewards kept on their toes. We're staying here?"

"You'll hear all about it later, in the lounge. I don't want to have to say it twice." But a moment later he continued talking anyway. "Vandermark, what do you think New York told me?"

"That you're going to get a medal."

"Yes, something like that. They're out of their minds, the gentlemen of the shipping company. I've never known those sober birds to be so euphoric. Now listen hard, Vandermark: our *Cecilie* has been booked solid! That's right. The people stormed the offices. Thousands of blind bookings for some voyage or other in some future or other. And their offices are full of flowers delivered for me. They said they felt like a branch of Wadley and Smythe—"

"But for the present we stay here?"

"That's what I asked, too. Are we staying in Bar Harbor? How long? Where are our stores to come from? Will the officers and crew continue on the payroll? I had no luck in getting any straight answers. A shower of vague praise, that's all I heard. The whole thing is simply splendid, priceless. The greatest advertising Lloyd ever had, the best press coverage ever given to Lloyd. Our competitors are seething. The *Cecilie* has become the one German ship known to every American. She's immortal, as it were—"

"Don't begrudge her her fame. The *Cecilie* truly deserves it."

"She deserves better than to make headlines for a couple of days and then be forgotten. Advertising tricks! She's never needed those."

The wind had veered, and the tide was swelling, so that one could feel the anchor chain tightening to hold the ship.

"I don't know how she'll manage to lie at anchor here," said Pollak. "I really don't know."

"You think it's going to be a long stay?"

"Afterward I spoke with Washington, with our naval attaché. . . . Yes, I'm afraid it's going to be a long stay." Pollak had stopped at the railing. He was still holding his white gloves, seemingly not knowing where to put them. He balled them up and made a fist around them.

"We have an invitation from Mrs. Butler," Vandermark said. "You and I, for dinner at her home in Bar Harbor. She said something about a good cook . . . that you knew all about it. . . . You've been here before?"

Pollak turned his head to look at Vandermark. "What else did Mrs. Butler say?"

"Nothing."

"Then let's leave it at that. There are some things I never talk about. That's always been my rule, and I'm not going to change in my old age."

The two men, standing side by side, looked across at the lights of Bar Harbor. Soon each would return to his role, captain and second officer; but in this moment, on the deck at night, the difference in rank was suspended; they were simply two men who understood each other without many words.

"I'm curious what your decision will be," said Pollak. "I mean, which will prove the stronger, the ship or the land."

At that very moment Vandermark had really been thinking of a salmon-pink dress and a salmon-pink hat, its broad brim curling in the breeze. "Are you a mind reader?"

"Sometimes." Pollak put out his hand—the fist in which he had wadded the gloves—and pointed to the shore. "The place is made to order for you."

"You make it sound as if I'd asked you to release me."

"Perhaps you will, one of these days."

"It never crossed my mind before. On the contrary. Ships have always been lucky for me."

"Ships that sail," said Pollak softly, more to himself. "And if we really are stuck here? I don't mean for a week. I mean months, years."

"Years . . ." Vandermark repeated, incredulous.

"Have you any idea what it means to lie at anchor for months, years? Twenty-four officers, doctors, pursers; sixty engineers; two hundred and thirty stokers; two hundred and thirty stewards; thirty-three cooks, bakers, butchers; thirty dishwashers; sixty signalmen, boastswain's mates, sailmakers, sailors, lamp cleaners—and how many hairdressers?"

"Nine hairdressers."

"Have you any idea what it means—a crew of more than six hundred and fifty, and all of a sudden there are no more passengers? At first it seems like a gift from heaven. They'll enjoy it for a few days, for a week, even for two—and then the empty ship will begin to frighten them. It will frighten me too."

"I suppose you'll keep the men busy."

"Of course I will. I'll keep them on their toes, but the passengers will be missed all the same."

"You've still got Mrs. Butler's great cuisine, and the hospitality of a whole lot of other ladies. Mrs. Butler believes you won't be able to rescue yourself from all the invitations."

"Don't worry about me," said Pollak. "My decision was made a long time ago. My ship and I, we belong together. If I were to lose the *Cecilie*, though . . ." He fell silent and pointed ahead to where a boat's directional lights glowed, seemingly far below them.

"See the revenue cutter? Its captain used to command the *Salem*. Now he sits on three hundred tons of rusty iron. Perhaps one day that will be my fate as well—and maybe I'll even like it. Like you, ships were always lucky for me. But do you know what? Sometimes I think it was only because I didn't have nerve enough for the other. The sea is a great thing—but the land is greater."

Abruptly the silence was broken by the renewed sound of the bugle. The melody was the same as before. Even now it had a melancholy ring.

PART THREE

Chapter 10

*I*t was as Temperance C. Butler had predicted—the German ship altered life in Bar Harbor. Not that the residents realized their good fortune at once; it came much too unexpectedly. The summer of 1914 had not begun auspiciously. Hotels and boardinghouses were half empty. And it was obvious that people feared that these Germans, who had declared war on everyone in Europe and had marched into Belgium, might drive away the remaining visitors. Already the previous year had taken a disappointing turn, and this year threatened to be even worse.

It was a puzzle. The weather could not have been better. The entertainment arranged to amuse the visitors had never been more abundant. During the first week of August the following events were scheduled: Confetti Night, with the Bangor town band; roller skating in the Casino; the Firemen's Ball with the Westcott Orchestra; a tennis tournament for ladies, with the participation of Mrs. John Jacob Astor, last year's champion; and finally—here expectations were especially high—a boxing match between Jack Twin Sullivan and Fred Mackay, the Canadian heavyweight champion, the winner to earn a bout with Gunboat Smith in New York. Nevertheless, the hoped-for invasion of summer visitors had not set in so far. The carriages and porters that congregated when the steamer arrived often drove away empty or were forced to watch as the few passengers coming ashore were called for in private automobiles.

The situation had changed literally overnight, on August 4, between midnight and sunrise, when the *Cecilie* ran into Frenchman Bay and put down her anchor at the shores of Bar Harbor. The first wave consisted of the German ship's passengers, who were put ashore here. Except for a very few, they did not stay in Bar Harbor but filled the restaurants and hotel lounges until their steamers left; in the souvenir shops the cash registers rang, for everyone wanted to go away with a remembrance of this day and this place.

And then the journalists arrived. The first landed in Bar Harbor as early as the evening of August 4, and they did not come only from Bangor and Boston. The New York papers also sent reporters, the press agencies sent correspondents; newsmen rushed in from every corner of America—only to find that they would not be allowed on board, that the German captain, Charles Pollak, would see no one. For several days they had no choice but to turn to the passengers who were taken off the ship. In spite of these handicaps, the first stories soon went out to the world. Sam Higgins of the Western Union Telegraph Company had tapped out ten thousand words by the evening of August 5—more than during any other summer altogether.

Nor did the *Cecilie's* captain grant interviews during the days that followed. The ship sported a large *No Admittance* sign, but this turn of events served only to stimulate the journalists' powers of imagination. The descriptions of the ship's flight grew progressively more sensational, the fog through which she had had to make her way increasingly dense, the pursuers ever more numerous. The story of the baby born on board, christened Cecilie by Captain Pollak after the ship—which happened to be true—stirred all America. Every newspaper ran the story of a group of first-class passengers who had offered the captain five million dollars for his ship so that he would not turn back and they would arrive in Scotland in time for the opening of the grouse season; the only truth to that one was that a couple of wealthy Americans, moved by whiskey, had talked about the idea but would never have seriously dared suggest it to the captain.

No matter whether the stories were true or invented, they were read like fairy tales come to life. Of course the ship was the principal heroine, but equally important were Frenchman Bay, the romantic inlet; Mount Desert Island, "America's Little Norway," as the journalists dubbed it; and Bar Harbor itself, a place which until then had been heard of only by a few. Bar Harbor, Eden, the undiscovered paradise—the town's name was suddenly on everyone's lips. Overnight a spate of summer visitors was loosed.

For years Bar Harbor had been dreaming of a season such as this, and now the town was hardly up to the onslaught. Within a week there was not a bed to be had. Binoculars were all sold out. The men who rented out boats had to establish waiting lists. Willard Adams, the town photographer, could hardly keep his wits about him. Everyone wished to have his picture taken with the ship in the background; because this was unnecessarily complicated and time-consuming, Adams ordered a backdrop of the *Cecilie,* placed it against the wall of his studio, and posed his customers in front of it.

The experience excited and confused the residents of Bar Harbor. Secretly they could not shake the feeling that their good fortune was undeserved or that it could disappear again as suddenly as it had come. Almost anxiously they looked for the ship each morning. Was she still there?

For the saviors of the season, the Germans, were not frequently seen by Bar Harbor at first. Of course they could be observed through binoculars as they moved about on board their ship. And every morning a lifeboat was lowered into the water and arrived at the pier of the Yacht Club to take on drinking water. Once or twice the captain had a crew row him ashore, went to the Western Union office, and after completing his errands, returned immediately to the ship.

The only contact between land and ship remained the lifeboat. The men who rowed it were not very talkative and did not thaw even when a fisherman thought to disclose to them the good fishing spots in the bay. It was therefore all the more satisfying to discover that they had followed his advice; the two lifeboats that went out to fish became the talk of the town that day. Some interpreted the incident as a major step toward friendly relations, while others, more fearful, saw in it an indication of a lack of supplies that might cause the ship to raise anchor. From that day on, the men who came in the morning to fetch the drinking water found gifts at the Yacht Club pier: fresh vegetables, chickens, eggs, bread, butter. That these things were accepted without a word was seen as a good sign.

The strain grew. One wished to have them on land. One wished at long last to see them closer up. Perhaps some young ladies harbored further thoughts. . . . Finally, after almost a week, it happened. A few stewards sauntered down the main street, mailed letters, stood around eating ice cream, bought postcards, had their pictures taken.

They did not stay long. But others followed. And when one evening—unusual in itself, for until then no lifeboat had put in at night—when one evening a dinghy really tied up at the pier and four officers in summer white came on land, everyone in Bar Harbor knew that the ice had finally been broken.

Chapter 11

*P*erhaps it was only the water-worn steps in the side of the wharf that made Fred Vandermark feel that the moment was very special. In the glow of the shore lanterns they glittered darkly; the higher he went, the lighter they appeared, and finally he stepped out on the white square cobbles of the wharf.

Firm land underfoot—once that had been a great moment. But during the years he had been at sea, fifteen of them by this time, the sensation had become blunted. Now it returned, the pulsing in his chest, his throat. The adventure of arriving in a strange place had been exhausted in the routine of Atlantic crossings, Bremerhaven to New York, New York to Bremerhaven. It had become an almost bureaucratic life, in strictly marked rhythms, according to an unalterable timetable. If it hadn't been for the women passengers . . .

Never before had he been so acutely aware of this as during recent days. He felt tired, old; and even the envelopes lined in salmon-pink which were brought to him by the drinking-water crew could not change his mood. When the invitation to her garden party had arrived this morning, and when Pollak, in spite of the cordial words with which Gloria asked him to her house—"everyone here is eager to shake your hand personally"—declined, Vandermark too would have preferred to refuse. But the others had protested, and their excitement as they came on land now told him how much they looked forward to the evening.

Fischer, the ship's doctor, spread his arms wide, and he might have been speaking for all of them as he exclaimed, "Hey, fellows, doesn't it feel good! How soft the air is!" He seemed to wish to embrace the town lying before them.

"He has to think about nature, has our doctor," one of the officers remarked.

"What I'm thinking of is the first drink. She won't keep us dry, will she?" Before coming ashore, they had emptied the last bottle of champagne from Vandermark's private stores.

"Where are we going to get transportation?" wondered Kessler, but then they saw the four-door sedan parked nearby. A chauffeur approached them. His uniform was the same color as the car, a pale beige. He raised his hand to his cap. "Mrs. Lindsay's guests? This way please, gentlemen."

He opened all four doors of the sedan; the top had been rolled back to reveal its lining of heavy silk, beige with brown stripes. The seats were covered in white leather.

"Our Lucky Fred," said Fischer. "Looks like he hit the jackpot." He turned to the chauffeur. "A six-cylinder Stevens-Duryea, am I right?"

"Right, sir." The chauffeur's hand was still touching his cap. "I'm proud to have you aboard, as it were. Arnold Googins. All Googins men have been to sea at one time or another. But there are no more ships here."

"Not a bad ship you have right now," Fischer said.

"Built to order. You'll barely hear the engine. May I ask you to take your places? Three in back, one in front."

Vandermark walked around the car and took the front seat. Fischer and Kessler were arguing about the price of the car; they were speaking in German. Kessler too seemed relaxed, expectant. Since the occurrence on the first day he had made an effort to improve his relationship with the crew as well as with Vandermark. He had gone so far as to mutter some kind of apology—weariness, strained nerves, worry about the ship. Bar Harbor and the summer seemed to have pushed Europe and the war into the background for him as well.

Googins continued to chatter as he drove. Indefatigably he called their attention to one sight after another: a hotel with dancing; a restaurant where, if they mentioned his name, his brother would serve them wine in lemonade glasses; the best tailor, who also happened to be a Googins and would give them a special rate. He drove slowly, quite as if he wished to afford an opportunity for a good look at these Germans to the pedestrians who came to a halt when the ostentatious car moved into sight.

The sedan did indeed run very quietly, and the headlamps were strong enough to light up the road. Soon they were outside the town; the narrow brick houses to the left and right came to an end, the street curved more frequently and began to slant upward. Points of light, nestled in the hills they were approaching, marked the isolated mansions.

"You will like Mrs. Lindsay's party." Googins pointed straight ahead. "Her parties are famous—at least they were as long as her husband was alive. She hasn't had a garden party for three years, since her Feast of Neptune. The grounds were decorated to make the place look like the bottom of the ocean. And the guests' costumes: mermen, dolphins, sea horses, and"—he laughed—"a lot of mermaids. But don't worry." He winked at Vandermark as the representative of the whole group. "Our ladies will go to all sorts of trouble. Every cottage will give a party for you, gentlemen. Our ladies here, each one is jealous of all the others. If Mrs. Lindsay gives a party for you, it won't be long before Mrs. Rufus King throws one. And when you've been to Mrs. King's, there'll be no holding Mrs. Biddle; and if Mrs. Biddle does something, Mrs. Gurney has to copy her at once . . . a lot of ladies. The summer won't be long enough for all of them."

On the narrow road ahead, a horse and buggy appeared, but Googins speeded up a little. The horse shied, reared, the coachman swore, and Googins swore back. Afterward he slowed and sensitively drove the car into a long, sharp curve. The wooded hills moved closer, their black outlines sharply raised against the night sky. Googins pointed to a spot of light. "that's the Villa Far Niente, Mrs. Lindsay's cottage."

The structure intermittently visible through the trees reminded Vandermark of the castles along the Loire in France: round towers, battlements, bays, turrets. Brightly lit, it floated in the darkness, silvery and unreal, and sank again as abruptly as it had arisen.

"Lucky Fred," said Fischer from the back seat and tapped Vandermark's shoulder. "Once again he holds all the aces." Fischer was a passionate poker player even though Lady Luck never smiled on him. He claimed that he had become a ship's doctor only because the profession allowed him unlimited opportunities to play poker once he had bandaged all the thumbs careless passengers had damaged in opening and closing the portholes; fortunately "porthole thumbs" were a debility incurred only in the first twenty-four hours of each voyage.

Vandermark turned to the chauffeur. "And the home of Mrs. Butler, Mrs. Temperance C. Butler—isn't it somewhere around here also?"

Googins nodded and pointed into the darkness. "We'll be passing it, but you won't be able to see anything. A little crazy, those Butlers, every one of them; and there's never been a garden party there." He laughed. "She's got something to hide."

"Money," Fischer said dryly.

"Sure, money too," Googins replied, "but money isn't anything special around here. It's just something you've got if you've got a cottage. Mrs. Butler is hiding something else, something she doesn't let anybody get near—just the opposite of the other ladies with marriageable girls in the house—a pretty granddaughter, Anne Butler. . . . Here we are." Googins was driving very slowly, almost at a walk, although there was nothing to be seen except trees.

"Could you stop for a minute?" Vandermark asked.

"Sure, but you won't see any more because of that. This is the gateway; the lanterns are never lit. The house is placed way back, quite hidden." He had stopped the car.

"Is it far to the house?" Vandermark asked.

"What do you mean?" Kessler interposed. He leaned forward. "What do you have in mind? You can't abandon us. You can't do it. You're the guest of honor, aren't you?"

"I'm just going to stop in to say hello, that's all. I'll be back in a couple of minutes. Just a brief courtesy visit, as long as I'm in the neighborhood. Mrs. Butler is going to hear that I attended Mrs. Lindsay's party, and I can't do that to her."

"Let him go." Fischer put in his oar. "You know how he is. He likes to have two strings to his bow."

Vandermark opened the door and got out. Googins was not exactly enthusiastic about losing one of the guests on the way, but all he said was, "So that you won't have to take the long way round afterward, there's a shortcut, a little gate that connects the estates. Ask Benjamin White, the butler. And make sure the old lady doesn't hear you; she doesn't like to think that the household help talk to each other." Idling, the car's motor really was barely audible. Only the steering wheel vibrated slightly under Googins' hands. He shifted into gear and drove off; the wheels made more noise than the motor.

But for the chauffeur's comment, Vandermark might not have noticed the lanterns to either side of the drive; the dense growth of ivy made them look almost like trees. He walked slowly until his eyes had become accustomed to the darkness. Under the thin soles of his patent-leather pumps he felt the sharp gravel of the drive. He was aware of Temperance C. Butler's categorical rejection of the "gasoline buggies," and in this avenue, hemmed in by tall poplars, it was impossible to imagine anything but carriages and horses.

He took his time. Even when the house came into sight after a turn in the drive, he did not quicken his steps. The broad facade had an unusual color. Was it really yellow? A large lawn surrounded the house. The grass stood high and moved in the breeze, and the wind carried an indefinable odor.

Two lanterns illuminated the main entrance. A sun-shaped disk made of bronze hung in the center of the dark wooden door. He hesitated before pulling the bell, as if the sudden shrilling might frighten the house. A glimmer of light fled across the sky, so fleeting that he became aware only of the reflection that lit up the night for a split second. A northern light—time and again he realized that he was not yet accustomed to the idea of being in Bar Harbor. The scent had intensified, heavy and sweet. Was it the reason for his coming to a stop and hesitating? A summer long in the past . . . the same scent . . . what could it have been? Only when he looked up and discovered the espaliers along the house, the leaves, and among them the peaches, did he remember.

His last summer at home. It had been fifteen years ago. At the time he was barely seventeen years old. His valise stood on the gravel path in front of the house. It was the first valise of his own. He wore his blue suit, the shirt with the stiff collar. His wallet held a railway ticket to Hamburg; a ship ticket, third class, one way to New York; a check for five hundred American dollars.

His last summer in Güstrow. His last day in his parents' home, the farmhouse. His mother, her eyes red-rimmed with weeping. His father, stony-faced, pacing back and forth in his workroom. The announcement from the high school that he had been expelled still lay on his father's desk. Blue ink shading into purple—intolerable, dishonorable—something to do with a woman. The wife of his professor of German, of all people . . . Güstrow, a small town, but honorable. An honorable father and a dishonorable son. In 1899 there was only one solution to such a problem: America. That was where one pushed off the undutiful sons, the hopeless cases. He had been a hopeless case.

The valise outside the house. The carriage that was meant to take him to the railroad station. His father, unable to make himself say a word of farewell; his mother, white handkerchief clutched in her hand, rumpled and damp with tears. And he himself, aware only of the scent of the ripe peaches coming from the espalier next to the porch. Freedom!

He did not make it to New York that time. He spent the five hundred dollars in Hamburg, pawned the ship's ticket for half its value. He shipped out and never returned home as long as his father was alive.

Later, years later, his mother sold the farm and moved to Bremerhaven to be close to him, her beloved son. She never forgave her husband; she forgave her son always.

He had never doubted his mother's love, as he had always been sure of his luck with women—both undeserved, to his mind. Anyway, did the men who really deserved it ever have any luck with women?

Now his mother was proud of him, second officer on the *Cecilie*. She cut out every newspaper announcement under the heading "Maritime News" that carried his name. She filled scrapbooks with pictures. And she always met him at the Kaiser Wilhelm Quay: that was her, with the large white handkerchief—still damp, but now with tears of joy.

Chapter 12

He breathed in the scent of the peaches, and just as he had been many years ago, he was overcome by a feeling of promise—that the whole world lay open to him, that everything was still ahead of him. . . .

Inside the house someone began to play the piano; it was not one of the old hit songs Temperance C. Butler loved, but something with scales and trills. Someone was practicing, stopping, repeating passages. Vandermark thought he recognized the piece, a Czerny étude from the *School of Velocity*. He followed the music, walking around the side of the house. Stone steps led to the terrace. Tall French doors emitted light; some stood open, and the wind played among white curtains. In one of the rooms he saw a black grand piano. A girl sat before it; she had conspicuously pale hair. Beside her, on the floor, was a pair of sandals.

He walked on slowly, step by step; his attention was wholly concentrated on the girl at the piano, so that he did not notice the woman sitting in a leafy corner of the terrace until he almost bumped into the table beside her. The woman's mouth fell open, though no sound passed her lips. But the book she had been reading slipped out of her hands and fell to the ground.

Is that you? Had she actually whispered the words? Vandermark was not certain. She sat motionless, staring at him as if he were a ghost. Her response was more than mere startlement.

"I'm so sorry. . . ." He sketched a bow. "Vandermark, second officer on the *Cecilie*." He picked up the book and placed it on the table. "I heard the piano. . . ."

"Don't mention it." Her voice was toneless. She moved the hurricane lamp in such a way that he was more clearly illuminated. Gradually she seemed to regain her composure. "It's the books," she said. "I always read such exciting novels. Not the proper literature for sensitive nerves. I shouldn't . . ." She had taken up her book, but now she put it back on the table. "So you are the second officer of the *Cecilie*. Mrs. Butler has told us a great deal about you. We have been expecting you all day long, you and your captain. . . . Are you alone?"

"Yes. Captain Pollak—"

"Anne!" She interrupted him by rising and calling the name. "You want to see Mrs. Butler, don't you? I'm Edith Connors."

"The golfer?"

"Oh, Mrs. Butler has been telling tales out of school. I hope not too many."

It sounded like small talk, but Vandermark was not deceived. The secluded spot on the terrace, the simple dress—as if it were her ambition to make herself invisible. He liked this type of woman, inward-turning, silent, promising so little in love and capable of so much.

"It seems that was all there was to tell," he said.

She smiled for the first time. "I like that."

"I believe you."

"Anne—are you coming?"

"Wait." He would have liked to be alone with her a little longer. But the piano had stopped, and the girl stood in the doorway. She wore a sleeveless dress and held her sandals by the straps.

"Yes? Did you want me?"

"A visitor for your grandmother. An officer from the *Cecilie*. Vandermark—you know, the one she's been raving about."

Anne came forward, at ease, curious. When Edith Connors had called her name, he had remembered Googins' remark about the granddaughter Mrs. Butler was *hiding*, and somehow he had expected a well-bred but not overly pretty girl—simply, a rich heiress. Consequently he was all the more surprised to see the girl he had met the evening the *Cecilie* sailed from New York.

"Anne Butler," she said.

"Fred Vandermark."

Did she fail to recognize him? The glance she directed at him left the question open.

"Come with me; I'll take you to Grandmother. You are alone? Without Captain . . ." She groped for the name and then continued. "Grandmother has been expecting you. All of us have been expecting you, isn't that true, Edith? There's no living with Grandmother since she came home. She takes it out on us that her European trip was canceled."

She led the way across the terrace into the house. In the music room Vandermark pointed to the piano. "Was that you?"

"Yes . . . Czerny. Every year when I'm on vacation I make a start. It's horrible to have a grandmother who is perfect at everything." She put her sandals on the floor and slipped her feet into them. Then she looked at him with her easy, curious expression, but her eyes held something more. "I'm glad you didn't say anything in front of Edith about New York."

He nodded in silence. So he had not been mistaken—she was the girl from the ship. And yet, she was a different person now. That night she had been fearful, close to panic. Now she was relaxed, sure of herself. Perhaps the difference was due to the surroundings, the house, the lofty rooms with their dimmed lights, the shiny wood floors. Even inside the house the scent of peaches lingered on the air. . . .

"It's just because of Edith," she said. "Edith is—how shall I put it—"

"My feelings would have been hurt if you had not remembered me."

"Oh! You're one of those."

"One of those what?"

"One of those men whose feelings are hurt the moment one doesn't recognize them."

"Yes, that's right, I am one of those."

She laughed. "That can't be true. That kind of man never admits it. The two don't go together."

"It seems that you are just as knowledgeable about men as your grandmother."

"I try to learn from her."

"I'm sure she's an excellent teacher."

"Her? A rotten one. Much too impatient—especially when she's in a foul mood. And she came back in an awful mood. She mistreats us all. You know, usually she keeps busy unpacking all the things she's bought up in Europe and finding space for them in the house. This time she misses that, so for the past week the house has been turned upside down. Today she found a huge box of lace she bought years ago on the Riviera—it must have been the whole store—and she is convinced that she's the only one who can wash and stretch the lace properly. . . . But come, you'll see for yourself. Don't be surprised if you get your share of her temper."

She led him through a hall into the service section of the house—the kitchen, the pantries, the servants' quarters. At the end of the corridor light streamed out through a pane of opaque glass.

"She's in the pressing room," Anne said over her shoulder to Vandermark before opening the door.

On the *Cecilie*, Temperance C. Butler was a Byzantine empress, but the woman he saw now, in a faded housedress, bending over a stretching frame, looked more like an Indian squaw.

"A visitor for you," Anne announced.

"I don't have time for visitors. Don't bother me now. This is ticklish work, but if I don't do it myself, the lace will be completely ruined."

"Grandmother."

At last Temperance C. Butler looked up from the frame. "Fred Vandermark!" She pushed away the footstool, stood up, placed the round lace stretcher on the pressing table, and walked up to him with outstretched arms. "Welcome." She pointed at herself, not in embarrassment, but flirtatiously. "I'm the born housewife. Sewing, ironing, cooking . . . in my days the girls were thoroughly trained in all of those. . . . You've met? Anne, my granddaughter. By the way, your tinkling—not exactly earthshaking. You should ask him"—her index finger tapped Vandermark's chest—"to give you a couple of lessons. He's got the patience for it. He is the only man patient enough to play duets with me. But run along now and let White know that we have a guest."

"I can't stay long," Vandermark quickly said.

"Is that right? I saw it coming. So many obligations that there's no time for us."

"This is the first occasion I've had to come ashore at all."

"And Charlie? Charlie didn't come with you? And when Vandermark did not reply at once, she added, "What's the matter with Charlie?"

"I don't know. . . ." The answer was truly not easy. Should he tell her that on his ship Pollak was busy with the same work she was about here, spring cleaning? That he had been pushing the crew for a week to bring everything up to spit and polish and that he continually discovered something else that could be made more perfect? Or should he tell her that for hours he locked himself in his cabin with McCagg and kept two stewards busy chilling and serving the champagne they consumed? "We don't see much of him," he said at last. "And he only goes ashore when he has to get in touch with New York. Tonight he was invited, as I was, to Gloria Lindsay's garden party, but he declined."

"Gloria Lindsay's party! So she did manage to steal a march on me. You're going alone?"

"There are four of us. The others went ahead."

"Did she send a car for you?"

"Yes."

"Which one?"

"A six-cylinder sedan, tan." He looked at Anne. She was standing at the pressing table, apparently studying the pattern of a lace cloth.

"The Stevens-Duryea," Temperance C. Butler said. "Anyway, that shows how highly she prizes you. But tell Charlie I'll send my best carriage to the dock. I will expect him for dinner day after tomorrow, and no excuses. The carriage and Jenkins will be ready at the Yacht Club pier at six o'clock. All right, now I'll let you go. I hope you enjoy the garden party. Not to my taste, Gloria Lindsay's garden parties, but what can you expect? After all, ten years ago she was still—no, I don't want to be catty tonight. This is one of my gentle days. I'm sure you'll have a good time. And you'll meet all the people one has to know in Bar Harbor. . . . Anne will see you out."

She stood on tiptoe and kissed him on both cheeks, in the traditional way, except that there were four kisses—left, right, and once more left, right. "Two, that's normal, as it were," she remarked. "But four, that's a genuine sign of love—because you came to see me first. . . . Anne!"

Once more she led the way, silent and, it seemed to him, thoughtful. Earlier she had worn a green-and-white headband that held down her pale hair, but at some point she must have removed it. When they stepped out on the terrace, he noted that she no longer wore her sandals but was barefoot.

"I'm told there is a shortcut," Vandermark said.

"Did Googins tell you? Are you in that much of a hurry?"

"Well, not all that much."

"But I can show you the shortcut too. Grandmother and Mrs. Lindsay are slightly on the outs, but the staffs of the two houses get along all the better for that." She smiled. "We are always kept up on the latest news of what's happening over there."

The table in the corner of the terrace was abandoned. Edith Connors had disappeared, and with her the hurricane lamp and the book.

"Who is she, by the way?" he asked.

"Edith Connors?"

"Yes."

"Is it love at first sight? It wouldn't surprise me; it happens to most of them. Are you married?"

"No, why?"

"Then you haven't got a chance. She only falls in love with married men. She likes things to be complicated. But tell me . . ." she came to a stop and turned around. "However do you do it? I still can't believe it. You walk in, and Grandmother is a different person. All day long she was insufferable—and suddenly she's beaming. How do you do it? I wish I could do it."

"I don't know if it works the same way between two women as it does between a man and a woman. Besides, that's part of our profession, getting along with the ladies."

"So that's how it is. That's why she loves to travel so much."

"That's the reason for half of the traveling ladies, didn't you know? Ocean voyages are an age-old cure for broken hearts; according to the theory, seasickness cures lovesickness. You never traveled with your grandmother? Why not?"

She laughed merrily. "Maybe because I've never had a broken heart."

"Really? What a pity."

"Is it essential?"

"It makes our job easier."

"I can understand that."

He could not make her out. She responded so differently from what one might have expected of a girl her age. And of course there was another thing: he had always given young girls a wide berth. In dealing with the women he encountered, there were certain rules of the game that were always observed, so that sometimes he seemed to himself like an actor who plays the same part year after year—always the same cues, the same scenes, the same settings. The only difference was the women themselves.

They had crossed the broad lawn and found themselves on a narrow gravel walk. Didn't her feet mind? In any case, she walked as if used to it. They passed several outbuildings; here and there a lantern glowed. In the shadow of low fruit trees a paddock appeared, and the animals came to the fence, trotting alongside Anne to the edge of the lawn. Vandermark watched as Anne laid her hand on one of the horse's necks. "Tomorrow it'll be time," he heard her say. "Tomorrow we can go for a ride."

The ground began to slope toward a yew hedge so high, so dense, and so evenly cut that at first glance Vandermark took it for a wall. Nor was he aware, until Anne came to a stop, of the gap, quite overgrown, where the little garden gate was concealed.

"Here we are," she said, gliding into the darkness of the hedge. The click of a latch, then she disappeared. "Come on. . . ." He could hear her voice. She held the gate for him and pointed into the garden lying ahead.

Vandermark had not exactly expected to find himself in the kind of backyard that went with a modest one-family house, but he was hardly prepared for such spacious grounds. Light bathed the various sections—walks, a pond, a pavilion—but there was no sign of its source, which must be concealed in the trees and bushes. In these islands of light people moved about, the guests clustered in groups, servants scurrying among them. The image was a little like a stage set for a musical comedy, especially against the brightly lit, castlelike building, which seemed like a bizarre backdrop.

He had heard the stories of rich Americans who bought up entire European palaces, disassembled them stone by stone and numbered them, had them brought across the Atlantic, and rebuilt them. "Where is it from?" he asked. "From Europe?"

"Mr. Lindsay always claimed as much, but in reality it was designed and built by an architect from Chicago. Do you know what Grandmother says? It's not Louis Quatorze but Chicago Quatorze."

Above his head a bird took flight. Vandermark was aware only of the rush of wings and saw no more than a dark shadow, but Anne said, "an *Otus asio*. This is its hour."

"A what?"

"A tufted screech owl. They're wood creatures, fairly large. They grow to as much as twenty-five inches."

"Is that one of your specialities?"

"Animals? Yes a little. At the moment I'm trying to track down two eagles."

"Would you take me along sometime?"

"You?"

"Yes, me."

"Tell me, is it true that Gloria Lindsay has set her sights on you?"

"Now you're talking like your grandmother."

"Has she?"

"Perhaps it's just the other way around. Perhaps I'm the one who's chasing her."

"But she's older than you, way beyond thirty. . . ."

In New York, on the ship, at their first brief meeting, it was she who had been unsure; here it was he who felt on foreign soil. "What happens now? Will you let me come with you?"

"You really want to come along?"

Gloria Lindsay—she came from a world he was familiar with; but Anne. . . . Nevertheless, or perhaps precisely because of that, he said, "Yes."

"It's complicated. We have to hike through the woods. I don't know what the white uniform you're wearing will look like afterward."

"Will you let me come? Yes or no?"

"You're easy to seduce, aren't you?" She laughed, and as she laughed she ran away, disappearing into the dark so that only her light hair remained visible for a moment.

He entered the garden. The lawn under his feet was cropped close and soft as a carpet. The sounds of music met his ear along with the sound of human voices. Once he stopped and looked back; perhaps it was wishful thinking, but he imagined that somewhere in the dark, concealed by the hedge, Anne was standing, following him with her eyes.

Chapter 13

"It's going to the dogs, your Europe," the man said, his tone implying that he was bearing glad tidings. "It's at an end—a corpse, or nearly. This war is the last nail in the coffin. This is where you've got to be, here in the good old U.S.A. You guys are really lucky. Your captain, how come he didn't come with you? I'd have liked to shake his hand; he's some guy. Here in America we've got a soft spot for tough guys like you. . . . Please, call me Cyrus, just Cyrus. None of your European formality."

Vandermark had never met any of the men who surrounded him shaking his hand, patting his shoulder, and congratulating him before he passed on to the next group. He did not know how many people he had introduced himself to or how he could store their first names in his memory. He had not yet caught sight of Gloria Lindsay, the hostess—only men.

"You're Fred? I'm Gus. Well done! When anybody asks me, I always say, refuse the European loans. Have you heard the latest Kaiser joke? Well, the Kaiser took his dog for a walk. . . ."

It was a different group, a different man, but for Vandermark the voices were always the same, the faces were all the same. Almost all the men were dressed in black, and they seemed to be members of the same race—even the same family. All of them drank a great deal, which required only that they extend their arms for a servant instantly to refill their glasses.

Catching sight of Kessler's slightly sour expression—presumably his response to the joke about the Kaiser—he pulled him along to another group.

"... saving me a lot of money, this war in Europe. Saving all of us a lot of money, right? If I think how many dollars my wife left behind in Europe all these years. ..."

"As long as it's only money. My wife had her heart set on a duke for our daughter, a Russian duke—and we all know about the Russian dukes you find in Paris. At home they owned a couple of sheep, and right away in Paris they play at being aristocrats. ... Oh, hello, you're from the *Cecilie?* Fabulous, the way you threw a monkey wrench in the English machinery. Can't stand them, the English, damned snobs. You're Fred, aren't you? And how do you like it here? If you're ever looking for a job, Leonard Kellog, New York—that's all you need to know. All doors are open here to a man such as yourself."

Another man interrupted, laughing. He pointed to a woman who was coming toward them wearing a pink silk kimono. "I bet Fred knows exactly which doors are open to him, am I right?"

"Excuse me." He went to meet her, relinquishing the group to Kessler. He hoped they would not tell too many Kaiser jokes. But Kessler seemed past the point where he responded with anger, for Vandermark heard him laughing. Fischer, the ship's doctor, and the other second officer were also surrounded by men and presumably were made to endure the same comments and advice.

He was glad to see Gloria. She moved slowly in the narrowly cut kimono, its pink silk embroidered with golden dragons. They came to a stop facing each other, and he pulled her to him, very close, so that he felt the heat of her body through the silk. Her lips were the same color as the gown. "Well, did you meet everyone?" she asked.

"Pretty much everyone. But I won't be able to remember any of them."

"Weren't they nice to you?"

"Three offered me a job, the last of them one Leonard Kellog."

"If Leonard says it, he means it."

"Good. And what does he do?"

"Leonard? I don't know what *he* does, but his company supplies shipping firms with milk and butter. Just about half of all the ships that sail from New York—Lloyd too, I think. He owns close to forty thousand cows—Jerseys, Holsteins, and Shelburns—and he was a friend of my husband's."

"That means I'd almost be staying in the same line of work."

"You know what line of work my husband was in?"

"He owned shipyards, didn't he? In Baltimore?"

"The yards still exist, and they're mine now. I mean, I own the stock. Sometimes it scares me to own something about which I understand little or nothing."

He wondered if she expected him to pursue the subject. He was tempted, but he said, "What about it, are there no ladies at your garden parties?"

She pointed to the right, past an artificial pond to a Japanese teahouse. "I always separate them at the beginning. The men should be by themselves, and so should the women. Most of them are married and don't have anything to say to each other anymore."

"Do you take such a pessimistic view?"

"About parties, always."

"Then why do you give them?"

"My husband loved parties; maybe that's the reason. I don't know . . . yes, I do. I arranged this particular evening actually with you in mind, to get you here. Come, let's keep moving." She led him, both hands around his arm, and abruptly they found themselves in a section of the grounds that seemed like another world. It was a Japanese pleasure garden with artificial water courses, arched bamboo bridges, exotic plants, and in between, half concealed by the greenery, strange stone figures: animals, fat-bellied Buddhas. Water lilies blossomed on a pond. Once again he felt as if he had stumbled into the stage set for a musical.

"I invited her," Gloria said. She led him to a small pagoda and sat down on a bench under the overhang.

"Whom did you invite?" he asked, although he knew at once whom she meant.

"Temperance C. Butler. And her granddaughter, Anne. Did you see Anne?"

"Yes."

"What do you think of her?"

"She's very young."

"Earlier, when the others came with Googins and you weren't

with them . . . it's absurd, but I'm jealous. Before I met you, I didn't know the meaning of the word. Now I'm jealous of every woman you knew before me and all the ones you know besides me."

He took her hand. "But I can't get rid of them just because of that."

"Thanks," she said. "Thanks for seeing my problem in the proper perspective. It helps. This past week went on forever. I missed you terribly. I shouldn't be telling you, I know—but why not? If you're not in love, it's easy enough to be smart."

"Won't your guests be wondering where you are?"

"You don't like me to say such things?"

"Of course I do. You tell me very nice things, but maybe I'm conceited enough already. . . ." He was in a strange mood; it had to do with the memories the scent of peaches had aroused in him. He was not someone who looked backward, but tonight the past was stronger than the present.

"Of course, my guests will be wondering where I am." He heard Gloria's voice at his side. "But the guessing game is part of my parties. Who will it be this time? A silly game, and boring, but what can I do? Look at this house, the gardens. Everything is outsize and senseless. These ornamental bushes, these water lilies cultivated in the hothouse—and it takes just one foggy night to destroy the whole thing. It devours enormous amounts of money. And though I've got it, I simply can't forget that my life used to be different. You know my life story?"

"The way I heard it—a Ziegfeld girl who became the wife of one of the richest men in Baltimore, John Lindsay."

She turned to face him. "That's more or less how it was, but not quite such a fairy tale. At the end I was in New York working for Flo Ziegfeld, but the places I performed in the years before . . . dear God, they weren't famous. I was one of the countless show girls dancing in the back row, dreaming of a fabulous career and doing anything— literally anything—to get it. I got what I wanted. I was poor, and I wanted to be rich. I made it at the last minute. I was twenty-six when I married John Lindsay ten years ago. Twenty-six, Fred. That's the age when a show girl starts to panic. John wasn't the first rich man who wanted to marry me—but see, money wasn't the only thing I was interested in. I was looking for Mr. Right, too. That's the other side of my life story. John had a couple of terrible traits. This castle here was one of them, but we were happy together. His death was a great shock for me. You understand. . . ." She was silent for a time. From afar they heard voices, noisy and animated. "What's the matter with you today?" she asked at last.

"I think it has to do with the ship—this state of suspended animation, not knowing what is going to happen." It was only part of the truth; he could not find the right words to express the rest.

"Has anything been decided?"

"Yes and no. For the time being the *Cecilie* will remain in Bar Harbor, but no one seems able to tell us what 'for the time being' means. Not even Pollak. I think he's expecting this war in Europe to drag on for some time."

"Could you quit your job?"

"And then what? Take a position with Leonard Kellog?"

"There are other possibilities."

He did not dare to ask what they might be—or rather, he was unwilling to ask because he was afraid of the answer. But why exactly? Would another chance like this one ever come along again? Even two weeks ago he would have shrugged off the whole thing. He had always lived for the day, without worrying about the future. Today had always meant more to him than tomorrow. But now he was thinking, *Time is running out.* It was an alien and unfamiliar thought, and yet it had taken root, pursued him. . . . What had Gloria just been saying? *I made it at the last minute.*

Suddenly he remembered the morning before the last departure from New York. The hotel room he had maintained for years, paying for it not with his salary as a second officer but out of the sums his mother slipped him on the side. The woman with whom he had spent the night had left the bed and disappeared into the bathroom. Soft noises as she dressed while he pretended to be asleep until the door had closed behind her. The view from the window onto the avenue below, the taxi that carried her away. And later, the gold cigarette case she had left for him on the table. The inscription. That was the moment he recalled most clearly: himself on the edge of the rumpled bed, lost in the melancholy calculation of the extent of his collection of cigarette cases by the end of his life. *For Fred from. . . .* That would be all that remained—a display case crammed with cigarette cases and cuff links.

Was the affair with Gloria Lindsay any different? Would it have a different outcome? He had been standing at the gangway when she had come on board in New York. A beautiful, rich woman traveling alone. All his affairs during recent years had begun this way. The trip over, the trip back, the hotel room with the blue wallpaper . . .

"Do you know what I'm discovering?" he said. "I'm finding out that I'm growing old."

"When you're with me?"

"When I'm alone."

"I find out the same thing every morning in front of the mirror. When you're alone, you're always finding out terrible things. . . ." She was silent before asking out of the blue, "Is that a rule of the shipping company?"

"What do you mean? What rule?"

"That ship's officers must be single."

"On the contrary. They much prefer us to be married. Besides, in Bremerhaven every mother of a marriageable daughter is out to catch those officers who are still available. For them, the most important part of the newspaper is the page listing the crews of the departing ships. That's their oracle; they check it off, they make their inquiries, and then they spread their nets. Any invitation in Bremerhaven is a kind of manhunt."

"But they never caught you."

"My mother sees to that. She watches over me very jealously—at home."

"You're the only son, aren't you? And she always spoiled you rotten."

"Can you tell?"

"That's not all. It's clear that you're accustomed to being loved. We women are peculiar in that. When we are girls, we want our braids to be just as long as those of our girl friends—and later, we want the man another woman loves. But we are most irresistibly drawn to the man who gets around, as they say. Actually we ought to be frightened of him, but we always imagine that the only reason he has so many women is that he still hasn't met the right one—and that we are exactly what he has been looking for all along. My father was a little bit like you, and my mother was determined to get him. He never changed, but she turned a blind eye."

"What did your father do?"

She rose. On the large terrace behind the house servants were setting up the cold buffet. Drawn by the sight, the men appeared from all over the grounds, and the women were also moving toward the house.

"If you want to put it that way, he was also in shipping. Nick Frohman—does the name mean anything to you?"

"No."

"Charlie Pollak ought to remember, or your chief purser. Nick Frohman was a well-known figure on the passenger ships plying the North Atlantic. When the pursers found his name on their passenger lists, they immediately put up a sign in the smoking room: *Professional Gambler on Board*. . . . Yes, that's what he was, a professional cardshark. His favorite workplaces were always ships; he found his best marks there. He saw nothing of the world although he traveled all his life, nothing but his cabin and his cards. He never stopped sailing back and forth between America and Europe. The captains, all of them, were on to him, but no passenger ever lodged a complaint. He didn't cheat, and often the passage—he always traveled first class—cost more than he earned. He was a gambler. He never had any money for us. One day my mother packed her bags and left him. She could not understand my staying with him."

"What became of him?"

"He died when I was twenty-two. His last years were pretty depressing. He had gout, and his hands might as well have been paralyzed. He refused to admit it; he believed that he would get better. I can still see him in my mind's eye, sitting there in my room in New York with a pack of cards in his hands. The apartment house was on a side street off Tenth Avenue, near the Hudson, and all day long you could watch the huge luxury liners across the river in Hoboken. He was still hoping that one day he would again be able to go on board and play cards. When he finally took it in that his hands would never get better, he died. . . ."

"You were very much attached to him."

"Yes. He was a person who—well, when you were near him you were quite simply happy. I don't know why. . . . Come on, let's join the others. I have to introduce you to my ladies. They're all dying of curiosity."

"Do we have to—now?"

"Another hour, and the whole thing will fall apart. They'll have drunk enough, heard enough, seen enough. The only thing they want to know anyway is, Will *he* stay behind when we leave? You will stay, won't you? I've had a room prepared for you. You can come and go as you like."

"Isn't that a terrible imposition?"

"The staff is delighted to have something to do. There's only this large, empty house and nothing more. Since my husband's death I . . . let's see . . . the first year I did not come at all. The second I spent ten days. Last year I was here for three weeks. And all the rest of the time—nothing and no one. It's time to wake up the sleeping beauty of this house."

Why did he hesitate? Was it his old urge for freedom, or was he simply eager to prove to himself that he could not be so easily seduced?

"There are times when I'd like to know what you're thinking," she said.

"Right now I'm thinking about us."

"And what are you trying to figure out?"

"I'd like to be able to see into the future."

"Let yourself be taken by surprise. Right now, we have one whole summer."

Chapter 14

The last notes of the march tune were drowned by the thunderous applause of the audience, a burst of enthusiasm never before heard in Bar Harbor at the regular Sunday band concerts. There were even some shouts of "bravo" and a demand for encores. The listeners attending the performance from their cars supported the shouts with a loud honking of their horns.

Anne Butler had trouble reining in her shying horse to bring the light two-wheeled victoria to a stop. "Hush," she said, "hush," and held the reins taut until the nervously prancing horse calmed down. Never before had she seen such a crowd on the Village Green, the old meeting place of Bar Harbor. The square, hemmed in by locust trees, was, in spite of its name, green only in the spring, when the newly sown grass sprouted; now, at the end of August, the grassy expanse was brown from the long drought, and in many spots the pale, sandy soil seeped through. The weekly market, the performances of traveling circuses, boxing matches—all these took place on the Village Green, as did the band concerts every Sunday morning during the season. The bands of the police and the fire department took turns, depending on which was able to scrape together a sufficient number of musicians. Last Sunday had been the first time that the stewards' band from the *Cecilie,* a thirty-man wind ensemble, had preempted the program. Its success had been overwhelming.

"Encore! Encore!" The shouts of the crowd, reinforced by the rhythmic clapping and the tooting of car horns, seemed at last to have won out. From her seat Anne Butler saw the chimes raised over the heads of the crowd, the many little bells sparkling in the sun, filling the air with a bright tinkle. The crowd fell silent; the circle contracted around the bandstand as the thirty men in blue-and-white uniforms picked up their instruments. When the thirty instruments sounded simultaneously, there was at first a breathless silence. But then the audience recognized the tune—"America"—and right in the middle of the selection they broke out once more into applause. Some began to sing along: "America, America, God shed. . . ."

"Terrific guys." The man who addressed these words to Anne had grasped the bridle of her horse, which was threatening to shy again.

"Thanks, Higgins." She recognized him as a Higgins, but there were many Higginses in Bar Harbor, and they all looked so alike that Anne could never tell them apart.

"Hard to believe, eh? When we play, they stand around like dead fish, our worthy fellow citizens. It's a big deal if they give us a little polite applause. And now it's a completely different story."

"Are you Sam Higgins?"

"No! Sam works for Western Union. . . . They really are something, those guys. And what a repertoire they have! They're going to steal the first prize away from us at the Eden Fair. But I'll say this for them, they're damned good." He noticed the pile of books tied with twine lying next to Anne on the buggy seat. "You're on your way to Dolly's?"

"Yes, if I can get through here."

"You better go by way of School Road. They're not going to finish here for a long time. I wonder what you'll think of Dolly. She's fallen head over heels. Can you imagine Dolly in love?"

Was he Dolly's brother? Anne thought it better not to ask. She steered the victoria away from the green. There were simply too many Higginses in Bar Harbor. Too many Higginses and too many Googinses. They were everywhere—in the post office, with the steamship line, in the fire, police, and sanitation departments, on the parish council. The female Higginses and Googinses were no less active than the men. One Mrs. Higgins was the town registrar, another was a midwife, one gave piano lessons, another ran a sewing school, and Dolly Higgins was the local librarian.

The band could still be heard at a distance. It was a warm day, hot for Bar Harbor. On the houses the awnings were lowered. The portals of the Baptist church stood wide open; the service had ended an hour before. A Sunday calm also blanketed the schoolhouse and its large yard; farther back, in a side street, lay the lending library, a white, narrow wooden house with green shutters.

Anne tied up her horse and buggy in the shade of a large maple and walked on, carrying her bundle of books. The clatter of a hedge clipper was the only sound in the quiet street. There were many similar clapboard houses in Bar Harbor, many of the same narrow front yards with box hedges; but Dolly Higgins was the only one who kept her hedge trimmed in the shapes of animals. This effort required constant care, and even now a man was busy snipping away at the bushes—a Higgins, of course.

It was cool and quiet in the hallway. The umbrella stand, which normally was not large enough to accommodate all the ladies' parasols, was empty today, Sunday. The sole gear hanging on the hat stand was a visored cap with the golden Lloyd insignia. Anne was taken aback, and she remembered the earlier remark that Dolly Higgins was in love. She had not taken it seriously, for if there was such a thing as the model of an old maid, the perpetual wallflower, then it was Dolly, in spite of her cheerful name.

Anne entered the reading room; usually Dolly Higgins sat at the large circulation desk, but now the chair was empty. Between her tenth and twelfth years Anne had loved nothing more than this reading room with its green-painted walls and the pulley lamps of green glass; she loved it especially on foggy days, when the lamps were lit even at high noon. The sight had aroused in her the desire to become a librarian herself when she grew up; but Dolly Higgins, pale, nearsighted, and always wearing the same black dress with cuff guards of muslin, had sobered her.

"Dolly!" She put down her pile of books. From the next room, where most of the library's holdings were kept on tall shelves, she heard Dolly Higgins's voice, high, a little breathless as always—but the laughter? When had she heard Dolly laugh like that, a wholly abandoned laugh? A man's laughter joined hers. A man who laughed with Dolly Higgins—that was truly something to turn the world upside down.

"We'll fill the gaps, don't worry. The first shipment will be arriving at any moment." The man spoke English fluently, like all the *Cecilie*'s officers, even if his accent was more marked than Vandermark's.

"If you had any idea what a small budget I have for new acquisitions." The voice was Dolly's. "Downright ridiculous, and every year they reject my plea for an increase."

"We'll fill the gaps," the man reassured her again, "and we'll do it with brand-new books. If you'll permit me, I'll help you catalogue them."

"Really?"

Anne Butler felt it was high time to make another attempt at making her presence known. A tiny bell stood on Dolly's desk, and now Anne pressed her finger on the button, wresting from the bell a loud and piercing ring. There was a moment of silence before Dolly Higgins appeared in the doorway; behind her loomed the figure of a man in a white uniform.

"Anne Butler! On Sunday? Has Miss Connors run out again already?" Even today Dolly Higgins wore a black, high-necked dress, but her bearing was different, as if she had discovered that she had a body under the dress. "By the way, allow me to introduce—this is Mr. Kuhn, purser on the *Cecilie*."

The chief purser seemed momentarily embarrassed; his index finger brushed the ends of his moustache upward. "The granddaughter of Temperance Butler?" he inquired. "Delighted to meet you. You never honored us with your presence, but your grandmother. . . ." He looked at Dolly Higgins as if to ask whether he was behaving properly.

Dolly Higgins briefly laid her hand on his arm. "Imagine, Anne, he's donating books to us, mint-new books from the *Cecilie*'s library. They've still got the label from Brentano's in New York, where they always buy them for the passengers before a sailing. We met by chance, quite by chance, in Hamor's Shell Shop. Mr. Kuhn is also a shell collector. Shells are his hobby. We got to talking about the fact that all of a sudden everyone here is looking for books about Germany, and the only thing I have is a description of a journey up the Rhine and a slim volume about Bayreuth."

"And *Grimm's Fairy Tales*," Anne added.

"Oh, yes, of course, *Grimm's Fairy Tales*—the book almost fell apart in your hands. But Mr. Kuhn will change all that—"

"Perhaps I'm in the way here," the purser said.

"Oh, no! You must stay until the books arrive. I'll make some coffee right away. I just want to give Anne her next load of books."

Usually Dolly Higgins seized any opportunity to check over every single book that was returned to her, to look for underlined passages, but today she refrained. "Here, these books are for Miss Connors." She leaned across the table and whispered, "He's a godsend, this Mr. Kuhn. He even knows something about cataloguing. I always thought what they said about Germans' sense of order was exaggerated, but he really is like that. He understood my method at once, and he's even made some suggestions to improve it. . . . Remember me to Miss Connors, and please"—she laughed—"in future, if you'd pay attention to the Sunday closing hours. . . ."

This time the man outside on the ladder lowered his hedge clippers; he took his pipe out of his mouth and looked at Anne. "Well, Miss Butler, did you see for yourself? Hard to believe, isn't it, if you didn't see it with your own eyes. It got to her after all, our Dolly, in her old age. A ship with a crew of six hundred—oh, well. But I still wouldn't have thought that one of them would be for her."

"You're Daniel Higgins, aren't you?"

"No. Daniel, he works at the livery stable on Roberts Street. I'm Ezra Higgins, the cemetery grounds keeper."

He bestrode his ladder, turned his head, and stared at the street, where an open motorcar was approaching. A man in civilian clothes was behind the wheel, and two sailors from the *Cecilie* occupied the back seat. The car stopped in front of the library, and the two sailors began to carry stacks of books into the house. Ezra Higgins winked at Anne and said, "It's spreading, the German fever, among the Bar Harbor ladies."

Ezra Higgins attacked the next box tree with his clippers, and Anne got into her carriage.

Ezra Higgins's remark was correct. Any topic for conversation other than the Germans—they had been here nearly three weeks now—no longer existed in Bar Harbor. Every morning when Jenkins returned from town with the papers, he had news. Leota Hebard, "Top boutique for Feminine Fashions," had hired one of the stewards as a salesman. The Dyer Bakery was selling German pretzels, for the widow who ran the business had assigned suzerainty over her ovens to one of the bakers from the *Cecilie*—and, certain insiders claimed to know, the bakeshop wasn't the only place he had been admitted.

Dollivers on Main Street had enlarged its men's salon and advertised in the paper, *Beards trimmed in the German fashion.* And according to White's information, many families considered it good form to have a "house German" who was invited to dinner and on excursions. Mrs. Fabri had bought out the entire Star Movie Palace twice a week for the crew of the *Cecilie,* and on Mrs. Palmer's orders each man was offered a choice of cigar or chocolates at the box office—an act of generosity that was, of course, duly enshrined in the Bar Harbor *Record.*

The band concert on the green had ended. Anne Butler became aware of that fact because the streets were filling up and she and her victoria made only slow progress. Many members of the audience accompanied the band back to the Yacht Club pier. The men had stopped playing, but one of the drummers was beating a march tempo. Anne followed the parade to the Rockaway Hotel, across from the dock. From her seat she could see over the crowd as the men climbed into the lifeboat and handed each other their instruments: the trumpets, the horns, and the trombones disappeared; only the large tuba remained visible, glittering in the sun, a golden chimney above the white boat.

The small square above the dock had never had a name, but that had changed when it became the principal gathering place of the Germans. "Lovers' Lane," the natives now called it with meaningful overtones, and it deserved the romantic appellation. Whenever one of the *Cecilie's* lifeboats put in, young women quickly appeared at the dock, tripping up and down under their parasols, waiting for "their" Germans. And at night, when the sailors had to go back to the ship, this was where sweet partings took place.

The lifeboat with the stewards' band had cast off; once more the crowd on shore broke into an ovation, and many hands waved the boat on its way. Out in the bay the *Rockland* hove up; she had to give the *Cecilie* a wide berth to get to her landing place. For a while she disappeared behind the sea monster, her siren ringing loudly through the bay as she steered for the shore. She lay deep in the water, and the passengers crowded her decks.

"Hello there."

Anne had long since spied the four officers on the terrace of the Rockaway Hotel, and she also recognized the voice, but she pretended to be deaf and blind. He had risen to his feet, come over to the wooden balustrade, and looked at her.

"Hello. Are you always in such a hurry? Too busy for some ice cream?"

Her feelings told her to drive on. There were no reasonable grounds for her behavior and even less justification for the jealousy she felt, and the anger. The worst part was that she was afraid he could read her feelings in her face—and that was something she wished to avoid more than anything in the world. So she stopped the carriage and made a huge effort to make her surprise seem as convincing as possible.

"Oh, Mr. Vandermark."

He came down the broad stairs. His tanned face, his blue eyes, his dark-blond hair that had grown longer and wavier in recent weeks— when she was alone, she always tried to tell herself that it was only the white uniform and the charm of the new that accounted for his effect on her, but when she came face to face with him, as she did now, her defenses broke down, and the feeling that seized her was so new and unfamiliar that it frightened her.

"So formal?" He had stepped to the side of her carriage and was looking up at her. "Your grandmother keeps telling me that I'm one of the family."

"I'm sure that's true for Grandmother."

"Not for you?"

"You've given me little chance to feel that way—" She regretted her words at once. If only she had driven on! For weeks she had been waiting for him to pay more attention to her, for weeks she had been pretending indifference, always arranging matters so that she was not at home when he came to the Yellow House in the afternoons to play piano duets with her grandmother—and now she was giving herself away.

"Are you going to read all those?"

"What? Oh, the books . . . no, they're for Edith Connors."

"How about a dish of ice cream? Come along." He stretched out his hand, and although she really did not want to, she got out of the carriage.

"Why ice cream, of all things?" she asked, to keep up a remnant of resistance.

"I don't know. I didn't really think about it. It's just that you look as if you like ice cream."

If she was seen sitting on the terrace of the Rockaway Hotel with Vandermark, it would not be long before the whole town would be talking; even now she could feel the curious glances. The story would make the rounds this very day; that's how things were here. Why not? Perhaps it would even reach Gloria Lindsay. Maybe Gloria did not care—and then again, maybe she did. Anne's tactic of staying in the background, waiting, which she had employed up to now, suddenly seemed a mistake. She had gained nothing by it. At the Club, whenever she had wanted to snatch an admirer from another girl, she had gone about it differently. The trick was very simple. Who knew, perhaps it would work as well now.

"I ought to be jealous," she said, looking straight at him.

"Of whom?"

She smiled knowingly. "When two houses are so close to each other, you can't help but know exactly. . . ." She had succeeded in speaking casually, even jokingly, but as she tied up the reins, a tremor ran through her hands. It was true that she knew exactly how often he visited Gloria Lindsay. She knew about the evenings he spent at her house, about the nights. Whenever the staff whispered or her grandmother let fall a remark, she pretended indifference. She had no need of secondhand news. Her room faced the Lindsay grounds, and night after night she could see with her own eyes the two figures taking a walk—white and pink among green bushes, appearing and disappearing. . . . Every night as she sat at her observation post on the window seat in the darkened room, Anne swore to herself that this would be the last time, and yet she sat there again the following night, waiting and hoping that Googins would drive up in the car to take Vandermark back to Bar Harbor. But the motorcar never came as long as she was awake.

They had taken seats on the terrace. Vandermark had introduced her to the other officers, but they had not stayed. One at a time, claiming one or another pretext, they had taken their leave.

"Is it always like that?" she asked.

"Of course. We have a secret language, a sign that means 'Clear the field for me.' It is the most important maritime signal."

"Oh, so that's how it is. Then your chief purser surely also signaled 'Leave me alone with Dolly Higgins.'"

"Who is Dolly Higgins?"

"She takes care of the Bar Harbor library. I've just come from there." She told him what she had seen and heard in the library, asking at last. "Is he married?"

Vandermark nodded. The waiter arrived, placing before Anne the lemon ice she had ordered.

"Poor Dolly," she said. "I just hope he doesn't tell her, or not until the end of summer."

Vandermark smiled. "Does it hurt less at the end of summer?"

"You're making fun of me. You treat me like a little sister."

"I don't know. I never had a little sister."

"And you've never been interested in young girls, either."

"Not especially."

"What's so awful about young girls?"

The smile vanished from his face, only a memory of it lingering in his eyes.

Anne pointed to the ice-cream dish. "Is it that young girls eat too much lemon ice?"

"In any case, only a young girl can devour a dish that size with such gale speed."

"What should I have ordered to make you think of me as grown up?"

"I never said that you are not grown up."

She felt his glance. With other men, she loathed this sort of silent examination. Strangely, it was different now. Nevertheless, she said snappishly, "Do I pass muster?"

He did not answer. In Anne's experience it was a good sign when a man did not know what to say, but Vandermark's silence annoyed her. Until this summer she had thought that she knew enough about men to always keep the upper hand. According to her grandmother's theory, there were no problems as long as you kept the upper hand.

"Did you find the eagles?" he asked.

She looked up. "So you do remember that you stood me up that day."

"Now, that sounds very grown up," he said, "and very feminine, turning the facts upside down. I could not impose myself on you anymore. You didn't invite me to come along."

"Do you want to come along today?"

"Today?"

He did not sound enthusiastic. She could tell that he was thinking of his appointments, with her grandmother, with Gloria Lindsay.

"Yes," she said. "Today."

"Right now?"

"No, let's say five o'clock." She picked the time because it was sure to disrupt his plans. She saw his hesitation, and suddenly her heart was beating so loudly that she was sure he could hear it.

"Fine," he said. "Five. I'll call for you."

Had he really said yes? And did he think he could also keep his other appointments—or wasn't he thinking about them? That other time, weeks ago, she had waited for him all morning. That would not happen to her again, at least not in the Yellow House, in front of witnesses.

"No," she said. "How about meeting me at the Baroness'? You've heard of the Baroness?"

"The Frenchwoman?"

"Yes. She has a log cabin at the foot of Green Mountain. Anybody can tell you the way. We'll meet there at five?"

"It's a deal. And now how about some more ice cream?"

She shook her head. "You really don't know anything about young girls." Her heart was still pounding, no longer anxiously but in anticipation. She was pleased with herself, and she began to enjoy sitting with him on the terrace of the Rockaway Hotel, allowing herself to be stared at by the passersby. The *Rockland* had docked. One motorcar after another drove away from the steamship station loaded down with new summer visitors and piles of baggage. Between the vehicles a man now appeared, wearing a dark suit, carrying his own traveling bag, and directing his rapid steps to the Rockaway Hotel. Alec Butler! A dark suit was a rarity in Bar Harbor during the summer. All the men, even older ones, wore light-colored clothing, at least light-colored trousers, and all wore light-colored straw hats. Alec was clad, not only in a dark serge suit, but also in a dark felt hat, and his valise was black. Anne had recognized him immediately, but he would probably have walked right past her if she had not called out to him. He came up short and then cautiously approached.

"You didn't come on the *Rockland*, did you?"

He nodded silently and then sketched a greeting in Vandermark's direction. "Good morning." He had met Vandermark in the Yellow

House at the first dinner party Temperance C. Butler had given for Pollak and Vandermark.

"Please come and join us," Vandermark suggested.

"I—" He looked at his bag. "First I want to check whether everything is in order with my room."

"Your room?" Anne asked. "Are you trying to tell us you've reserved a room at the hotel? What's going on, anyway? Why did you come back? Didn't you tell me you had so much to do in Boston? And why do you want to live at the hotel?"

"Because I'm only staying a day, two at the most—something that came up suddenly. Has to do with a lawsuit." His last words were directed, not at Anne, but at Vandermark.

"You're looking at me as if you were bringing suit against me." Vandermark rose. "It's time for me to go along anyway." He gestured toward the dock. "I have to catch the next boat."

He waved the waiter over and paid. Anne sat still, missing none of the looks meant for Vandermark. Odd—there were other good-looking men on the terrace, but none attracted so much attention. What was it about him?

He put out his hand. "It was nice to see you. See you again soon."

She held on to his hand for a moment longer than necessary, smiling at him. Now that he had made a secret of their appointment, she was very certain that he would keep it. Somehow she felt an urge to carry the game even further in front of Alec. "I do hope that we really will meet soon," she said. "You'll have to tell me more about maritime sign language."

"I'll give you a course in sign language," he replied.

"For beginners?"

"I believe you're ready for the advanced course."

She watched as he crossed the street and went to the dock, where one of the *Cecilie*'s lifeboats was just putting in. There were other white uniforms on the boardwalk, but she saw only one.

"So now and then he still goes back to his ship," she heard Alec observe.

Anne laughed. "You really did look at him as if he were the accused and you were the prosecuting attorney."

"You mean to say he still hasn't taken up permanent quarters at your house?"

"At our house? I'm sure Grandmother would have offered, but he already has a permanent bedroom elsewhere." She felt extremely aware of having the upper hand with Alec, and especially with the Anne Butler who had spent every evening for weeks at the window of her room watching two figures in the neighboring garden. That Anne Butler was gone for good. . . .

"What was all that nonsense about maritime sign language?"

"Surely you're not jealous?"

"May I order something for you?"

"Thanks, no. I had a large dish of lemon ice. Besides, I have to be leaving too."

"You're letting him pay for your ice cream?"

"Does a second officer earn so little? I really do believe you're jealous."

"I simply asked you a question. It's up to you how you interpret it."

"Why can't lawyers ever give a straight answer?" Instinctively she compared the two men—Alec, the attorney, sitting somberly and stiffly by her side, and Vandermark, the ship's officer, to whom everything seemed to come easy, who took life easy.

"Is it love at first sight?" Alec's glance went past her to the dock, where the *Cecilie's* lifeboat was moored.

"At least that's a very direct question."

"And the answer?"

"Maybe." She had always discussed her admirers with Alec, her serious and not so serious flirtations, and it had never bothered her when Alec's sharp tongue passed judgment on the young men. But this time it was different.

"If you'll take my advice," Alec said after a silence, "stay away from him."

"But why?"

"He is . . . I think too many women like him."

"So? Oh, I get you. A man who is that good-looking cannot have a good character."

"I didn't say that."

"But it's what you meant. The old Puritan ethic, according to which it's a sin for a girl even to have a pretty face. A decent honorable person can only live in an unattractive shell—like Dolly Higgins. 'An honest face,' people say, and what they mean is 'an unloved old maid.' But even Dolly has fallen in love, and you should see how becoming it is to her."

Alec sat still, his head somewhat ducked, his features expression-less, and stared out across the bay at the ship. "One of those too?"

"Of course."

"It's becoming an epidemic."

Anne laughed. "Ezra Higgins calls it the German fever, though the sickness they're spreading is anything but unpleasant. Are you really going to take a room at the Rockaway?"

"It makes sense for the short time."

"Will we see you? How about dinner tonight? Grandmother would be offended if you were in town and didn't visit."

"At nine, as usual?"

"Yes. Nine o'clock on the dot." She rose.

Vandermark had reached the end of the dock and stepped into the lifeboat. He did not turn around, did not look back, and suddenly Anne doubted that he would come.

Chapter 15

I can't take you any farther." The driver pointed across the clearing. "You'll have to walk up there if you want to get to the Baroness. Just follow the markings and you can't miss it." He looked at the bill Vandermark was holding out and shook his head. "Much too much. This summer—it's the seven fat years all rolled into one. Our business never had a summer like this one. But I hear your salaries have been cut."

"Is that right. Is that what you hear? It hasn't happened yet. So take it."

"Half, that's plenty." The man made change. "Enjoy yourself. A crazy lady, the Baroness, but it's the best view of the bay." His fingertips touched the visor of his cap. "Was an honor to drive you. Anything else I can do for you?" The driver's hands were already curled around the steering wheel.

"What time is it now?" Vandermark asked.

"Just past four o'clock."

"Thanks."

The driver hesitated before starting the motor. Did he suspect that Vandermark was sorely tempted to get in again and be driven back to Bar Harbor? Then he turned the car around, and Vandermark followed the markings on the trees.

He was never late for any rendezvous—but an hour early? Insane.

What was the point of it anyway? A nineteen-year-old girl. He had had time to think about Anne Butler, plenty of time. Usually he had no need of much reflection to take the measure of a woman. But Anne? What was she? She was very young, very inexperienced. She did not know about love yet. Was this what attracted him—being the first? Until now it had been precisely this thought that made him avoid young girls—the responsibility connected with them. And now he was here, an hour early, because suddenly he could no longer endure the ship. Wouldn't it be better to turn around? As yet nothing had happened; he could still turn back without hurting her. The thought had never occurred to him in connection with any other woman, but this girl aroused many feelings that were new to him.

He had been walking quickly and was out of breath by the time he reached the plateau at the foot of Green Mountain. After walking through the forest, he was blinded by the bright light. Far out in the bay the ship lay at anchor, unreal, a mirage, not to be trusted. Perhaps he was dreaming the whole thing: that he was here to meet a nineteen-year-old girl, that he found himself in a foreign country, that his ship was anchored in an alien bay many thousands of miles away from home. . . .

"*Monsieur l'officier!*"

He turned to face a female figure who seemed just as much a dream figment. She wore a dress such as he had never seen on a living creature, with a corseleted bodice and a wide hoopskirt; it was made of peacock-blue silk shimmering into all colors, so that it was not immediately noticeable how threadbare the material was. She held a yellow parasol over her head; its long silk fringe quivered in the wind. She drowned him in a wave of words in a unique kind of French, and he understood only that she took him for a Frenchman and the *Cecilie* for a French ship. He had heard enough about the Baroness to figure out the situation, but her appearance was quite different from anything the descriptions had led him to expect. Her gray hair was powdered white, and her face was pink with rouge, but here and there she had missed, so that she almost resembled an old masterpiece with peeling paint.

"I have been waiting for you a long time," she continued. "The King has kept me waiting for a long time."

Children's voices rang from the log cabin. There was a whole brood of them. They stood before the window where the souvenirs were displayed.

"What does the King command?" The woman's voice dropped to a whisper. "Will you assume protection over me? Support my demands?" Her gray eyes clung to him, would not let go. Suddenly her face lit up. "Of course! You want to see the documents, the proofs. Come with me, *monsieur*. I have prepared everything."

"I——" he began and fell silent under her gaze.

"Follow me." She shifted her parasol to her other hand and walked ahead. Her hoopskirt brushed the ground.

When the children caught sight of her, they came running, forming a circle around her. The plateau echoed with their voices. The Baroness leaned down, spoke to them softly, and pointed to the tiny pond near the sparse bushes. The children ran off jubilantly, and the woman walked on. At the door of the log cabin she came to a momentary halt, waiting for Vandermark. "Come in, *monsieur l'officier*, come in."

He followed her inside, into a dusky room. She pointed to a writing desk on which lay bundles of papers, rolls of parchment. On the wall next to the secretary hung an old flag of blue silk, the fleur-de-lis stitched on it in silver.

Vandermark felt a gentle but firm pressure pushing him into a chair. The Baroness stood at his side, laying out the papers for him. "See for yourself."

The paper rustled—or was it her hoopskirt? The documents were old, on stiff parchment, their borders darkened. Others, bearing more recent dates, seemed to be court writs; then again, she showed him invoices, lists of attorneys' fees, taxes. He could not concentrate enough to actually read them, but some words caught his attention, dates. The penetrating whisper continued at his side, incomprehensible for the most part except for isolated words, shreds of phrases: "The King . . . his wish . . . this island . . . enemies . . . I will endure. . . ." And still more papers were spread before his eyes.

He did not know how long he sat there. He had lost all sense of time. He was caught fast in a dream, powerless to free himself.

A hand touched his shoulder. A voice spoke softly at his side. "Take these to the King. Then he will know that I am alive, that I am waiting for him. . . ." She took his right hand, pushed a golden ring on his little finger. Her face held a mysterious smile. "Be careful. Show the ring only to the King, no one else."

She released his hand, turned away, and went to the door. Light scattered the room's dusk. The Baroness walked out, a dark silhouette in the sun.

Vandermark felt dizzy when he finally stepped outside. Sky and bay formed a limitless blue horizon. Somewhere the children's voices rang out, and then someone called his name. The shade of a tree held a girl in a white dress, she too a dream creature. He looked at his hand, almost astonished that the ring really did grace his finger. It was a plain gold circlet, thin from much wearing, its original inscription barely visible. It might be lilies or lettering. He concealed his hand behind his back as he went to meet the girl. . . .

He was growing tired, but the girl ahead of him walked with light, quick steps at an even pace. Now and again she stopped and pointed upward, and the piece of sky visible through the treetops held the large, circling bird.

How long had they been walking? One hour? Three? He had not managed to regain his sense of time. At the beginning the trees still sported markings and they met other hikers, but that had been long ago.

The path grew increasingly narrow and difficult. They had to negotiate rocks and fallen tree trunks, and sometimes the path disappeared entirely under moss and ferns and berry bushes.

Anne stopped and turned to look at him. "Shall we rest a little?" Her face was slightly flushed, but her color seemed due less to exertion than to her joy that they had discovered the eagle's roost.

He nodded and looked around for a suitable spot. The terrain was rocky, but there was an earthen mound thickly covered with moss; tiny pink blossoms glowed in the sunlight streaming through the tree trunks. They sat down. Beside them in the underbrush there was the rustling of some wild animal they had startled. Then all was silence.

"This really is a wilderness," he said. "I'd be hopelessly lost here."

"It's not really so bad, not on a day like today. All you have to do is take your bearings from the bay." She moved closer to a tree trunk, leaned her head against it. "Of course it's another matter when it's foggy. Then you really can get lost." She toyed with a blade of grass. "It's a good excuse for courting couples. It's almost a proverb in Bar Harbor. If a girl stays out too late, they only say, 'She was overtaken by the fog.'"

"Haven't we stayed out too late?"

She smiled at him, and once again he wondered if she was as innocent as she seemed. Basically the situation was, after all, quite unusual: a young girl alone in the woods with a man who was a stranger to her. Was she quite unaware of it, or did she enjoy playing with fire? But if so, why hadn't she taken advantage of any of those moments on their way through the woods? Had she merely been lacking in courage? Was she waiting for him to take the initiative?

"Your grandmother allows you a great deal of freedom," he said.

"She knows she can trust me. Edith Connors thinks differently about these matters, but Grandmother . . . she didn't let herself be tied down either when she was a girl. The thirst for freedom runs in the family."

"Does she know about our . . . excursion?"

"I didn't tell her in so many words, but she always knows everything. If she hadn't wanted me to go, she would have told me straight out. For her it's very simple. One always knows where one stands. It's very practical too, whenever I bring a young man to the house. I can tell from looking at her face whether she approves of him or not."

"And you submit to your grandmother's judgment?"

"She's always right. And besides . . . really, all she has to do is frown, and the young man understands that he hasn't got a chance. That makes a lot of things easy for me. I'm rid of him without a lot of talk and scenes." She laid back her head and closed her eyes. She sat quite motionless. Her chest rose and fell as she breathed.

Vandermark observed her and once again asked himself which of the two was the real Anne—the young girl whose hair curled at her temples and who thought of nothing but eagles and horses, or the woman who went off into the woods with a stranger and who sat next to him daydreaming with closed eyes and half-parted lips? What thoughts were going through her mind? What desires moved her? It seemed to him impossible that they were the thoughts and desires of a child.

Her hand lay close to his. She had rolled the sleeves of her white dress up to her elbows. Her skin was smooth, warmly golden in the dim light. Was she waiting for him to take her hand? Or would the gesture frighten her? Such questions—for a man like himself. He knew the proper moment; it was one of the secrets of his success with women, the proper moment. And now. . . .

She opened her eyes, turned her head, looked at him with a smile he did not know how to read. "A penny for your thoughts," she said.

"A fortune for yours."

"Mine?" She paused briefly. "I was thinking about you—that you're a lucky man. I mean, one who has luck in his own life and brings luck to others. I've been looking for the eagles for weeks, and today, when you came with me, I found the roost. That's what I was thinking . . . that you've brought me luck."

He was as sobered as he had been earlier, when she had spoken about subjecting her admirers to her grandmother's inspection. Women's sense of reality was something he had stumbled over time and again, and for a moment it was on the tip of his tongue to say that it was time to return to Bar Harbor. Judging from the low position of the sun, it must be well past six o'clock. At eight-thirty Googins would be waiting at the dock with the car, but he would have to go back to the ship before then, to change clothes. If he did not wish to be late, it was high time to start back.

"It's still a penny for your thoughts," she said.

"They're not so simple."

"I thought everything was simple for you. Aren't you called Lucky Fred on board? And luck means that everything is simple. I mean . . ."

"You mean, getting anything you want?"

"Something like that. Surely you've always gotten anything you wanted."

"I don't know. Maybe it's just the other way around."

"I don't understand."

"Maybe I didn't want anything. I take life as it comes." He folded his hands, and as he did, his eyes fell on the Baroness' ring. He had never worn a ring. Once he had tried, when his mother had given him a signet ring for his thirtieth birthday, but he could not get used to it. But this plain, worn gold circlet did not bother him. On the contrary, he felt as though he had been wearing it for years, a talisman that would bring him luck.

A jay fluttered up from a tree and emitted its warning cry; an animal moved in the underbrush. The shrill tone of an alarm whistle rent the silence. A second one replied, then a third; the signals came closer, encircling them.

Anne had jumped to her feet. Her bearing, her expression, everything about her spoke of fear and resistance. It was so unusual to see her frightened that with one step Vandermark moved to her side and laid his arm protectively about her.

Boys in scout uniforms began to appear among the trees. A man seemed to be their leader. He too wore a scout uniform, and he had a hunting rifle slung over his shoulder. He was looking straight at Anne, threateningly, almost punitively. Now he came to a stop. Vandermark held Anne firmly within his arm, but instead of a flesh-and-blood body he was holding a figure of stone—frozen, completely lifeless. Once again an alarm whistle shrilled. The boys gathered around the man with the rifle, turned on their heels, and disappeared into the woods as suddenly and eerily as they had come. One final, already softer signal, and then the silence returned.

Anne's tension lessened, at first imperceptibly; slowly life returned to the petrified body, warmth, breath. Vandermark's senses were all attuned to the transformation; a young girl, a creature who was still a mystery to herself. Softly he said to her, "Don't be afraid."

She looked up at him. For seconds her eyes held him fast. "I'm not afraid." She spoke in a tone different from her usual one. "The man is completely harmless." She released herself from his embrace, and her movements were also different. "Every time I go into the woods, he puts on the same performance." She had turned away so that he could not see her face.

"Who is he?"

"He runs a summer camp for boys and takes them for hikes through the woods. He has a bee in his bonnet—he's convinced himself that he has to save the forest from hikers. He hates it if they picnic and make fires. He's afraid that the woods will burn down to the ground one day." She had spoken rapidly, almost precipitately. The gesture by which she now pulled the rolled-up sleeves of her white dress down to her wrists and buttoned them was equally hasty.

"The day the *Cecilie* put down her anchor in Bar Harbor, Storm finally went round the bend," she continued. "Now he feels compelled to hunt down German spies as well." She turned back to Vandermark, smiling. "He thinks the only reason the *Cecilie* landed here was to put spies ashore. Every time he meets me in the woods, he warns me. He says the woods are full of German spies. He says that they are making sketches, maps of the paths, of the water reservoir." She laughed. "This forest here seems to attract crazy people. The Baroness in her log cabin, Storm in his camp . . . but the craziest one of all is my Uncle Sol on his cliff. Shall I introduce you to the craziest member of the Butler family?"

"He lives here?"

"Yes. He's my grandmother's brother, but he hasn't been down to Bar Harbor for years, or to the Yellow House. He's barricaded himself in his rock castle. You must meet him so that you will be properly warned how crazy we Butlers can be."

"Your grandmother is a good example."

"People are always telling me how much I resemble her as far as my character is concerned. But Uncle Sol—compared to him, we're terribly ordinary. Come with me, then you'll see for yourself."

"How far is it from here?"

"Please." She stood before him with glowing cheeks. She really was a child still. She did not yet know herself. Only her reason was grown up; her heart and her senses were still asleep. She longed to be awakened at the same time that she feared it.

"Please," she repeated.

Vandermark thought of Gloria Lindsay. If he did not return to Bar Harbor at once, she would spend the evening waiting for him in vain.

He nodded. "All right. Show me your Uncle Sol."

As before, she assumed the leadership. The silence of the woods, the dusk that grew increasingly thick, her white dress glowing at its heart. She walked with light, quick steps. Now and again she stopped, took her bearings, smiled at him, and walked on.

A crazy day, he thought. A baroness made him a gift of an old ring, and he wore it like a talisman imbued with magic properties. A man and a dozen boys were on the hunt for German spies. A young girl persuaded him to risk his luck. . . . Then he stopped thinking. He only followed a white dress. . . .

Chapter 16

It was the hour when all through the grounds the sprinklers were turned on. Through the open window of her bedroom Gloria Lindsay heard the gardener's steps and soon thereafter the soft drumming of the drops on the leaves of the rhododendron bushes growing against the wall just under her window.

She lay on her bed wrapped in a large Turkish towel. The fifteen-minute rest after her nightly bath was part of her beauty program, as were the five minutes of exercise every morning and much else that went into the battle against aging. Perhaps *battle* was not the right word. What she did to remain young resembled rather the strict discipline she had used in earlier days, as a dancer, in her daily training.

The gardener's steps distanced themselves, the soft rustle of the sprinklers remained. During her first summer in Bar Harbor, hearing the sound outside her window in the mornings, she had always believed that it was raining. When she realized that it was only "Lindsay rain," she was seized by a sensation of security such as she had never known before. The grounds were extensive, August was dry and hot, and water was expensive in Bar Harbor. Her husband's fortune, his shipyards in Baltimore, his real-estate holdings—they stood for a dimension she was still unable to comprehend in those days. But "Lindsay rain" outside her window—that was a language she understood. You're not poor anymore! You'll never be poor again! She rose and went to the window. During the afternoon a few clouds had moved in, but they had drifted away again; tomorrow was going to be another hot, cloudless day. It was the hottest, driest August she had ever spent in Bar Harbor. Not even at night did it cool off. Somehow the weather was wearing down her nerves, especially the warm nights that granted her little sleep. She heard a car. Probably Googins driving into Bar Harbor to pick up Vandermark. Or was it Mel Shubert? He should have been here long ago, according to his telegram. Perhaps he had already arrived and no one had told her he was in the house.

She closed the window and went into the bathroom. She took off the towel and stepped naked to the large mirror. During her years as a show girl she had learned to take her own measure as severely as did the dance directors, the costume designers, and especially Flo Ziegfeld himself. Nothing escaped his eye. He saw every additional ounce, each broken fingernail. He sat in on rehearsals, an elegant dandy who seemed bored by everything, but all the girls on stage trembled when his melancholy eyes sharpened, his narrow mouth contracted still more, and he raised his manicured hand to point at one of them: "I'm sorry, but I think Nora should be taken out of the show."

How would he judge her today? Though she weighed not a single ounce more than she had in those days, her body had altered. She was thirty-six years old; there was no changing that fact. She barely belonged on the young side of life. At forty a woman started on the other half of the road, no matter how beautiful she was. Right now the four-year difference in age between her and Vandermark did not matter—but ten years from now?

There are no guarantees, she thought, not in this area. The idea did not alarm her. It only admonished her to be cautious. That was why she had asked Mel Shubert to come. He was part of her earlier life; he knew her as few others did.

She listened to the noises in the house. A window being opened, a chimney flue being rattled—or was it a table being moved? She always felt a stranger here. She did not even know the precise number of rooms in the house. It was like a hotel, the same anonymous bustle in the halls, on the floors above and below her. She had had this sensation from the first day. A hotel with only two guests—John and Gloria Lindsay.

She pulled on a robe and went to the dressing room. Here too there were the sounds: someone preparing the room where Vandermark slept. There was no direct connection between his bedroom and hers. Brice, her butler, had burst out a week ago with the idea of changing the visitor's quarters to those of her late husband. It made her smile to remember his expression when she rejected the suggestion—unbelieving, confused, embarrassed. Surely it was unnatural and unnecessary to play hide-and-seek in one's own house. But she knew what she was doing. You did not win a man by making it too easy for him or tying him to yourself too closely, especially not a man like Vandermark.

She had opened the closet. Most of the time she made her selection quickly, but today it took a long time before she decided on the dress of red chiffon with white polka dots.

In the hall it was already turning dark; actually the corridors were never bright. The dark paneling, the dark pictures, and the dark carpeting swallowed the light. The stained-glass windows in the staircase shone in the glow of the sinking sun. Everywhere servants were busy. She knew only a few of them by name. In the hall a manservant was just turning on the candelabra, in the dining room the table was being laid for dinner; the gardener was carrying a flower arrangement for the dining table through the hall, and Brice appeared through the swinging doors at the back.

Samuel Brice could have been the manager of a luxury hotel in his black-and-gray striped trousers and his cutaway. He bowed. "There will be three for dinner, is that correct?"

She nodded.

"Will Mr. Shubert be staying for a while?"

"I couldn't say now."

"I've given him the tower room."

"He's here already? Why wasn't I—" She did not finish the sentence. There was no point to it, she knew. In this house nothing would ever happen unless the butler saw fit.

"Mr. Shubert simply wished to change his clothes and wash up. Drinks will be served in the library."

Once again a protest was on the tip of her tongue. The library was one of the rooms in the house where she had never come to feel at ease—huge, somber, intimidating. But John Lindsay had taken his drinks in the library, and the custom was maintained.

She felt delivered when she heard steps coming from the grand staircase. Mel Shubert wore one of his velvet suits, which he owned in every shade of brown. A monocle dangled from a silk cord, and his left hand held the inevitable cigarette in its holder. His appearance always reminded Gloria that he was the son of a Russian magician and had been on the stage since childhood. Perhaps she only had this response because she knew his story and had seen old photographs. The monocle, the cigarette holder—to her they were remnants of the time when his father had made him disappear in public.

"Mel!"

"Goldie!"

Such had been her stage name—Goldie Frohman—and it always made her feel very young and a little sentimental when he called her by it. They hugged.

"How nice of you to take the time."

"When Goldie calls, Mel comes running." His voice exactly matched his brown eyes and his velvet suits, and although he had lived in the United States all his life, he carefully continued to cultivate the Slavic accent of his father. He was not very tall, extremely slender, and no one would guess that he was sixty years old.

"Did you have a pleasant journey?"

"I didn't see much. I'm hatching the illustrations for an edition of the *Nibelungen*. Then there are a couple of plays I have to costume, and Flo is already pressing me for sketches for the Follies of 1915. I've taken on too much again, and my whole life is a sketchbook in front of my nose. I simply can't say no; that's my trouble." He had taken her arm. "But who can say no when the money you've been waiting for for thirty years suddenly starts falling from the skies?"

"How long can you stay?"

"I have to be in Boston day after tomorrow. They're planning a production of Charpentier's *Louise*. The conference has been scheduled for an eternity and postponed time and again. Thanks, by the way, for sending the yacht for me." He gave her a searching look. "Where is he?"

"He'll turn up for dinner. In around half an hour or so."

"Your call aroused my curiosity. I always figured it would happen one day. Actually, I thought it would happen sooner."

"I thought it would take longer."

The library was a long, high-ceilinged room. The ceiling was painted with frescoes, and the shelves were stuffed with luxury editions of the French classics, as new and untouched as on the day they were bought. Only a few books looked used—the section of pamphlets and monographs about cattle breeding. Cattle had been John Lindsay's hobby. He probably owned everything that had ever been written on the subject. Unordered shipments of books were still arriving, and art dealers all over the world continued to offer her paintings of the kind her husband had collected: calves, cows, bulls. The walls of the house were hung with them. Just as other families commissioned portraits of their children, so John Lindsay had had his stud bull rendered in oil. Above the mantel of the library hung a large painting of the Shelburn bull. The name was engraved on a gold plaque at the bottom edge of the frame: Caligula. Gloria could not look at the picture without remembering how often she had listened while her husband explained the bull's family tree to his guests. And there stood the telephone where every evening he had spoken to the farm's dairyman—conversations that sometimes went on for hours.

They had sat down in front of the fireplace. The logs were lit and burning. At their back the servants came and went. A serving cart was pushed toward them, the glasses filled.

"How is the show going?" She had attended the opening night of the Follies of 1914 on July 1 in New York. She went to all Ziegfeld openings. It was still part of her life.

"We're sold out at every performance."

She smiled because he had said *we*, but she felt the same way. As always, Mel's presence calmed her. His whole manner, his movements, his silence had a beneficial effect. And then there were his hands. When she watched him as he held the cigarette holder or played with his monocle, she was always reminded of her father. Nick Frohman had needed the cards for his hands' restlessness. *We*—yes, they had a great deal in common. Both of them had risen from the bottom, and both had had the will to rise.

When she met Mel Shubert—eighteen years ago—he was a painter whose pictures no one bought and who at best was allowed to concoct decorations for department stores. He was discovered practically overnight, and today theaters fought over his stage designs. Their friendship had begun when he destroyed her great illusion of becoming a ballet dancer. "You just haven't got it, Goldie. And besides, you're three inches too tall." It had always remained the same between them—he had told her the truth, no matter what the situation. And she did not marry John Lindsay until Mel Shubert had declared, "Yes, he's the right one." He himself was a bachelor. Since he had become famous, there were rumors making the rounds that he preferred men to women, but his case was both more simple and more complicated—he needed neither women nor men.

Finally the servants left them alone. Gloria Lindsay, relieved, leaned back in her chair. "Sometimes I'd like to chase every one of them out of the house, these servants, the maids, the chauffeurs. Every year there are new faces. I don't even know the names of most of them. All I do is pay them. Twenty people, a fortune in wages every month."

"You can afford it, can't you?"

"That's not the point. It's just that needless expense goes against the grain with me. I'm here three weeks out of the year, at most. What I'd really like to do is sell the house."

He inserted a new cigarette into the holder, but he did not light it. "Did you want to talk to me about the house?"

"In a way the house has something to do with him. Until he turned up, everything seemed all right—the house here, the house in Baltimore, my footloose life from hotel to hotel, my trips, the parties, all the commotion. I was sick and tired of it, but what else was there? But now . . . how shall I put it? Now what I want is a very ordinary house for two people to live in. The last few years were very comfortable. It was like a party that never ended. But I'd forgotten how it is to be with someone you love."

"As bad as all that?"

"Hopeless."

He raised his hands defensively. "You're giving me quite a responsibility."

"You're the only one—"

"He's got no money, I take it."

"I don't know how much a ship's officer makes. . . . No, he has no money. And I can't talk with him about it."

"I'm not a lawyer, but if you'll go see Lyman, he'll draw up a marriage contract for you that safeguards you 100 percent."

"That's exactly what I don't want. Maybe my money is important to him, but I don't care, don't you see? John Lindsay's money was important to me, but he risked it. And besides, money alone wouldn't interest him. Money alone—I'm sure he could have had that before, more than once."

"How old is he?"

"Thirty-two."

"Thirty-two," Mel Shubert repeated, and on his lips it turned into an entirely new, shimmering word. "Then it ought not to be the money, not primarily anyway." He leaned forward. "But I'll have to see him. Does he know that I'm supposed to size him up?"

"He's used to my having visitors, but he might be able to see through it. I'm sure I would have seen through it, and he's very like me. . . . Were you able to find out anything about naturalization?"

"I had a talk with Lyman about it, without naming names, as we agreed. It shouldn't be a problem. The fact is that several such applications are already in the works, and more are expected in view of the many German ships trapped in America now. In New York three stewards have been sent to Ellis Island until the formalities are completed, and it is expected that the petitions will be granted. The attitude in Washington is unequivocally pro-German." Perhaps he was remembering that he himself was of Russian origin, for he added, "As yet."

"So you think he wouldn't have a problem?"

"Not once your name was brought in, your wealth taken into consideration, the sureties you can furnish; everything would go smoothly. Probably he would even be spared the stay on Ellis Island. But is that what he wants?"

"Sometimes I think he does, other times I'm not so sure. The same with his ship. Sometimes I believe it means nothing to him, that he'd give up the sea and his career as a ship's officer without blinking an eye. And then there are times when I think the ship means more to him than anything else in the world and that he'd never give it up for a woman."

"What's your hurry? The war won't be over so soon, and they won't let the ship leave."

She sighed, as if to make fun of herself. "I've told myself all that. When he's here by my side, everything is all right. But if he spends so much as one night on board the ship, by morning I'm afraid to open the window for fear that it might no longer be lying in the bay. . . . Yes, Brice, what is it?"

The butler had stepped into the library. He approached cautiously. "Dinner was to be served at nine o'clock."

"Is it nine already?"

"On the dot."

"Has Googins returned?"

"Not yet."

"Well then, I think we'll wait a little."

"Now you know the situation," she said when they were alone again. "I'm holding the worst cards of my life, and I want to win the game just the same."

"Your father won a lot of games with a bad hand."

"But he's seen my hand! He knows how bad it is. I haven't concealed anything from him. He knows exactly how I feel, he knows that all he has to do is say one word. Three weeks—counting the time on the ship, four—we've known each other . . . and it's really all up to him, but he always evades me on this question. He does not show his hand." She laughed. "Yes, Mel, there you have me—clever, cool, sensible Gloria Lindsay."

He stared into the fire, a thoughtful, melancholy smile on his face. "At the right time you are always sensible, and you are unreasonable at the right moment too. But you've really aroused my curiosity now. By the way, all New York is busy wondering. And you do realize, don't you—this is going to come as a hard blow to several gentlemen. But most important, how would the chairman of your board of directors take it? Would you risk losing someone like Marcus Keisor? Would you be that foolish?"

"Perhaps not all that foolish, no. I asked him to come here. I didn't let the cat out of the bag right away. He came for the day and stayed three. And why? Because the two of them got along splendidly, and usually Marcus dislikes any man who's interested in me on principle. Fred is a man who—I don't know how to explain it. . . . Brice, for example. Brice was won over completely. The reason is ridiculous—dinner napkins. Not one of our guests ever bothered to put the napkin back in the ring after dinner. And there's no sense to it, they go into the laundry anyway. Fred always puts his napkin back in the ring, and Brice *loves* him for it; that's how a true gentleman behaves, that's all."

"That would hardly impress Marcus Keisor."

"True. I was prepared for it to go wrong. Marcus—with his direct, hard way, his head full of nothing but steel and figures—and Fred. I had invited some other houseguests, and everything was very relaxed, you understand, but after the very first evening the two were like old acquaintances. And after three days Marcus was convinced that Fred could 'run the show,' as he put it. And he means it. Every time he telephones me, his closing sentence is 'When can I expect your friend in Baltimore?' It seems Marcus is afraid of only one thing: that I'll marry a man who has no connection with shipping."

"So the financial problem would seem to be solved as well."

"That's what I thought too. And if Marcus takes up for a man! But Fred didn't take the bait. . . ."

A motorcar stopped outside. Then voices sounded in the hall—Brice's, the butler's, and another one. Mel Shubert looked at Gloria questioningly, but she shook her head. There was a knock on the door, and Brice entered. "It was Googins," he said, "alone, without Mr. Vandermark. What shall we do now? Would you like us to serve dinner?"

"He did not come?"

Brice avoided her eyes. "No."

"He did not call?"

"No, Mrs. Lindsay. Mr. Vandermark . . . he does not seem to be aboard the ship. Barnes Higgins drove him to the Baroness at four o'clock, and Mr. Vandermark has not yet returned. If I may take the liberty, I'd like to suggest that you begin dinner. Foster is already in despair."

"Foster? Who is Foster?"

"The new chef, Mrs. Lindsay. The cheese soufflé is falling."

Silence reigned for a moment. Then Gloria Lindsay set down her glass and rose. Her earrings, long drops of coral and pearl, seesawed as she turned to Shubert. "That's how it is, Mel. We are subject to the chef's orders, or he will walk out on us. Good chefs are hard to find in Bar Harbor—isn't that right, Brice? Mrs. Biddle has already tried to woo him away from me. And cheese soufflés are his pride and joy. It isn't advisable to offend him in this matter."

She took Mel Shubert's arm; as she left the library with him and walked to the dining room, she wondered if Brice knew more than he was telling. Might Vandermark be across the way, in the Yellow House? If so, Brice would know almost immediately if he did not know already. Why did he have to stand her up today of all days? What was keeping him? Who was keeping him? None of her thoughts were evident on the outside. This had always been her strength, even on the stage. There were girls who had better figures than hers, who were better dancers, better singers, but it was she who never cracked, who saved the day, who could always be relied on. Self-control—it was a word always writ large in her life.

In accordance with the style of the house, the dining room was also overly large and built for many diners; nevertheless, the parade of servants, the constant coming and going, the elaborate ritual of serving, the changes of plates, silver, wine-glasses, were almost enough to make one forget that only two of them were at table. Gloria ate and drank and made conversation with Mel Shubert. "I hear Flo Ziegfeld looks ten years younger since he married Billie Burke. Is that true?"

Soon they were immersed in the latest New York gossip. Her glass had to be refilled more rapidly than usual, she laughed more frequently, but it required the most minute attention to notice the glances she now and again cast at the place that remained empty.

Chapter 17

It was one of Temperance C. Butler's unalterable principles never to wait dinner for anyone, and so the first course was served promptly at nine o'clock in the Yellow House. That Anne was missing from dinner was unusual. Nevertheless, Temperance C. Butler wasted no words on the event, and a glance from her cut off all remarks Edith Connors and Alec tried to make about the empty place.

Meals were important occasions in Temperance C. Butler's life, and she could afford to let them be. Her digestion stood up under any excesses, and she was lucky enough never to gain weight. Of course she was no sylph—rather, she was "well grown," in her own phrase—but no matter what sins she committed, her weight remained constant.

Like most gourmets, she adored talking about food at the table, and nothing inspired her more in this field than the day of fasting Edith Connors kept once a week. Today was one of these, and while Edith Connors nibbled at her apple and took an occasional sip of milk, Temperance C. Butler indulged in detailed commentary on the dishes brought to the table. She began with her tricks for the preparation of lobster bisque—the mortar and pestle for grinding the shells must be heated—and thereupon dwelt long and lovingly on the art of correctly stuffing a partridge—a skill mastered by only a very few chefs. One of them was the *chef de cuisine* in the Palace Hotel in Montreux, and she had personally invaded his domain to seize the recipe.

With a luxuriant sigh she put down a cleanly gnawed leg and dipped her fingertips in the bowl of warm water. Shaking her head, she looked in Edith Connors' direction. "To lose out on the first partridges of the year is a mortal sin. When will you ever learn, Edith? A woman of forty or more should stick to the pleasures fit for her age, and eating is as much one of them as bridge, golf, or religion." She dried her hands with the napkin and turned to look at Alec. "And why are you poking at your food? You'll never get anything like it in all of Boston. It took years for me to get Betty White to the point of making the stuffing properly." She turned a look full of love and compassion on the remaining partridges. "You should take pity on them. I'd like to go on"—she placed her hand on her stomach—"but where would I put desert? . . . Peach Orientale." She turned to the maid who was coming in with the tray as if on cue.

The dessert was served. Pitted peaches poached in sugar syrup and wine—"a few pats of butter add the glaze"—and served on a bed of whipped cream and ground almonds. Temperance C. Butler had already achieved such a degree of satiety that her thoughts no longer centered exclusively on food. "Alec, remind me that I want to talk to you about a legal problem. You won't charge me a fee, will you?"

"You could afford it."

"That's what everybody thinks. It's Harvey again, and with him it's always a matter of money. My sons always want money from me. I feel like that performer—I can't think of his name—the one who hangs suspended over the stage and claims that three magnets are holding him up. My sons are holding me up."

"What about Harvey?"

"It's his opinion that I'm spending too much. I should hold on to my money rather than squander it. He's afraid there won't be enough left for him. They're all afraid, the two boys as well. Somehow they must have gotten wind of the fact that on her eighteenth birthday I settled part of my estate on Anne. Now the fat is in the fire. Harvey is threatening to contest my action. Can he do that?"

"It depends how much you settled on Anne. After all, she isn't your only grandchild, and her father wasn't your only son."

"We'll talk about it later. What's the matter, don't you like the peaches? I remember there was a time when you couldn't get enough."

Alec sat with lowered eyes; the dessert dish in front of him was almost untouched. Without his aunt's remark he might have gone on eating out of politeness, but now he put down his spoon. He wadded up his napkin and pushed his chair back from the table. It was evident that it cost him an enormous effort to remain seated. When the grandfather clock sounded ten thirty, he pulled out his watch, wound it, and then, casting a glance at Anne's empty place, said, "I don't understand you. Since when do you put up with this sort of thing?"

Temperance C. Butler feigned astonishment. "I beg your pardon? I don't understand." She gestured White to her side. Their two heads huddled together, they spoke softly, then White returned to his station near the door. Temperance C. Butler folded her napkin and pushed it into the silver ring. She rose and said, smiling, "You'll permit me . . . my coffee in the music salon. . . . Surely it won't bother you if I play a little?" She took a step and then pointed at Alec's place. "What's the matter? Don't you roll up your napkin?" She looked at Edith Connors. "We have guests who do, don't we, Edith? Good manners never hurt anybody."

Alec blushed, and although Edith tried to restrain him with a warning gesture, he said, "I can imagine which guest. He's here often enough."

Temperance seemed to enjoy his outburst. "What's the matter with him, Edith?" she asked. "Do you know what's gotten into him? Does he begrudge me my little pleasures? That I've finally found someone who will play the piano with me? How often have I pleaded with you, Alec? I plead with you even now. How about it? Something easy, a nice little song, 'I'll cling to you, Just like the ivy'—even fitting, don't you think?"

"So Anne is with him?"

"There is a strong probability."

"And you allow it?"

"Me? As far as I'm concerned, the two of them have been far too slow."

"I beg your pardon!"

She laughed. "I like him, Alec. Surely it's all right for me to admit it? I like to have Fred Vandermark around. I'd be very sorry if one day he stayed away because a certain neighbor. . . . Unfortunately I am no longer of an age when I can do something about it myself, prevent it from happening. You'll excuse me now."

Alec made as if to follow, but Edith Connors held his arm. "My God," she said when Temperance had disappeared into the music room, "you've known her long enough. One word critical of Anne, and she begins to attack. And Vandermark has won her heart. I must tell you, all of us reap the rewards—she hasn't been this amiable and even-tempered in a long time."

As if in confirmation, the first sounds of a melody rang across from the music room, accompanying Temperance C. Butler's voice:

I'll cling to you,
Just like the ivy. . . .

"If she thinks her sons are the only ones after her money—!"

"But Alec! It's not that simple." She fell silent; one of the maids had entered to clear the table. Edith opened the French doors and went out on the terrace. The evening was mild, still warm, and the scent of peaches filled the garden. A few books lay on the table. She sat down, pulled the hurricane lamp closer, and was about to open her book.

"Please, Edith," Alec Butler pleaded, "the truth. How serious is it between the two of them?"

"For him? I can't say. He's here frequently, but he comes only to play piano duets with your aunt. And Anne . . . one might believe she's avoiding him."

"That doesn't mean anything. On the contrary. . . . But she confides in you."

"Once upon a time." Edith Connors hesitated before speaking again. "You know, one day Anne discovered that I'm an old maid. And since then . . . well, she simply thinks that I do not understand anything about these matters or that I have always made mistakes. Perhaps she's right. In any case, she has not taken me into her confidence. And somehow I prefer it that way."

"And what do you think of this man Vandermark? Your personal view."

"That really doesn't matter. This house belongs to Temperance C. Butler."

"I just don't understand. No one has ever been good enough for her, and now, suddenly. . . . Everything else aside, he's a complete nobody."

"You forget, her second husband was also a nobody. She likes a man to be dependent on her. She holds the gold hoop high, and the man has to jump through it. She loves the animal-trainer act."

"And you think Vandermark will jump?"

"Not absolutely. Besides, it all depends on Anne."

Alec lowered his head and fell silent. He was glad that he could speak with Edith, but he did not feel relieved. Anne—where was she at this very moment? She had left the Yellow House in the afternoon. Now it was almost eleven o'clock at night. She had taken the victoria. Tormenting images rose in his mind. Vandermark was not a man to gaze at the moon with a woman.

"You are asking me riddles," he heard Edith Connors' voice. "I had no idea that you had such feelings for Anne. Does she know? Have you ever told her?"

"Why have I been working like one possessed? Why have I built up my practice? Why have I just bought a house, on top of all that?"

A smile flitted across Edith's face. "Forgive me. But if you think she'd understand all that. . . . These are arguments for future parents-in-law, but not for a young girl like Anne. She's in no hurry about marrying. I don't know what plans she has for her life; she probably doesn't know herself. Her plans to go on to the university—I don't take them very seriously myself. I think it's more to balk her grand-mother's lust for dominance. Anne does not let her grandmother lead her around by the nose, and Temperance is clever enough to give her lots of rope. The two of them are very alike in this. Temperance al-ways lived as she pleased. She did not give up her own life in favor of husbands or children. She always put herself first. Anne is the same way, and that's what reassures me. She isn't the type to easily give in to an emotion and forget everything else. Just think about her flirta-tions at the Club. She thinks it's wonderful to make a young man fall in love with her, but she herself remains quite untouched."

"Her flirtations at the Club! My God, you can't compare them with Vandermark. Of course Anne was superior to those boys. But Vandermark—that's something else again."

Did Edith Connors nod silently? Alec would have preferred that she contradict him. He pulled his chair closer to her, searching her face. Until now he had never asked himself what her calm features concealed. Edith was one of the family; she was something like the spirit in his aunt's house. But her own life, where had it run its course? Her earlier remark went through his mind—that Anne saw her as an old maid who knew nothing of "these matters." His instinct told him exactly the opposite.

"You must help me," he said. "You know what is at stake. What happens now can decide her whole future. You are always comparing her with her grandmother, but she doesn't have the same tough core. She is a dreamer, she can be hurt. If the wrong man . . . I don't want to stand by and watch this man Vandermark make her unhappy."

"I understand you; but you know, no woman is spared that."

Alec stared out into the garden. All was calm. In the lodge, where Jenkins lived, a light shone. The shadows of two horses could be seen in the paddock. The third was missing. Alec listened because he thought he heard a carriage, but he was mistaken. The sound of the piano was still coming from the music room, but the song was different now.

"What shall I do?" he asked Edith. "Give me some advice. I can't stand by and watch."

"There is nothing you can do. No one can do anything. It will come to an end suddenly. Perhaps sooner than you think. You won't lose her. This one summer—it won't be more. And what is one summer compared to a lifetime?"

"I don't understand you." Her words had hurt him.

"Some things repeat themselves."

Her voice was so low that he could barely make out the words. Her head lowered over her book, she sat still, and all at once a memory rose in him. It had been many years ago. He was fourteen at the time, quarantined in this house with diphtheria. Edith Connors had taken care of him. Night and day she had stayed with him during the crisis. Every time he emerged from the fever he had seen her: her figure in the light of a shaded lamp, her soft, calming voice, her hand laid against his forehead. During his convalescence he had frequently faked attacks of fever simply to have her go on caring for him.

"Did you ever know," he asked, "that you were the first woman I was ever in love with?"

She turned her head and looked at him for a long time. Then she said, "It comes a little late, your confession." She shrugged her shoulders. "That seems to be the story of my life—belated confessions." Her book had closed, and now she leafed through it to find the page where she had stopped reading.

Alec rose. "It seems pointless for me to wait any longer for Anne. I'll write her a note. Or better still, you tell her that I'm leaving Bar Harbor on the three o'clock steamer tomorrow. If she wants to see me, she can reach me at the Rockaway Hotel or in Marshal Harmon's office."

Edith Connors placed a bookmark between the pages before looking up. "What's your business with the marshal?"

"I have an appointment with him in my capacity as an attorney. We will go to the *Cecilie* together." When she did not respond, he continued. "It's going to be quite a shock for them—a million-dollar lawsuit."

"What are you talking about?"

"Read the Boston papers tomorrow."

"What do you mean?" She put the book down on the table. "Either stop hinting or tell me what it's all about."

"Didn't I tell you?" It seemed to help him to be able to work off his inner tension. "The banks whose gold the *Cecilie* was supposed to transport have brought suit against the shipping company. They want one million forty thousand four hundred and sixty-seven dollars from Lloyd."

"But on what grounds?"

"Default of contract concerning freight transport."

"But they got their gold back."

"They wanted to give it out in loans. That's how banks make their money. In this case they lost a cool million in interest. The court shares their opinion. On July thirty first Germany was not officially at war, and when the ship turned around in peacetime, she broke the contract that had been concluded between the banks and the shipping line concerning the transport of the gold."

"They're splitting hairs."

"Lawyers live on hairsplitting. In any case, the court has ordered that as marshal of Maine, Harmon seize the ship as a precautionary measure until the case has been adjudicated."

"You seem to be enjoying the case."

"I won't argue with you there."

"You're representing the banks?"

"Me? Oh no, I'm not that important yet; they have New York lawyers. I've joined them with a minor suit for a cool three hundred thousand dollars. I represent a Belgian, a passenger on the *Cecilie*; his suit also complains of nontransportation. If he had been able to return home in time, he could have safeguarded his property before the Germans marched into Belgium. The suit has been admitted."

Edith Connors looked at her folded hands. "How can they do that to Charlie Pollak? He made every effort to—"

"It does not concern him. The suits are addressed to Lloyd."

"Of course it concerns him." She reached for the stole hanging across the back of the wicker chair and placed it around her shoulders. "And what will happen now?"

"You mean legally?"

"Yes."

"The shipping line has the right to contest the action. The deadline for them to do so is the first of September. Then the hearings will begin. But such a suit is never settled with a hearing. It can go as far as the Supreme Court and drag on for years. Until the final verdict, the ship remains secured—that is, she may not leave United States waters, war or no war. Tomorrow Harmon will hand the captain the necessary document, and a vessel of the United States Coast Guard will be ordered here, but otherwise the case has no effect on either Pollak or the crew."

"War or no war, did you say?"

"Yes."

She looked at him. "You realize that if the ship stays here, so does he? . . . All the same, it will all come out right, Alec. You know you can count on me as an ally."

He was standing by the table. In the glow of the hurricane lamp his face appeared pale, his features drawn. When the music started up again in the house, he pressed his lips tightly together.

"Why don't you go in and keep her company for a little?" Edith Connors laid her hand on his arm. "Be nice to her. One can never have too many allies, and she is the one who tips the scales. Don't forget, she has a high opinion of marriages within the family. Her first husband was a distant cousin. And she never misses an opportunity to express her delight at the fact that her children bear the Butler name. She went so far as to keep her name when she married a second time. That's your trump card, Alec—that you are a Butler."

"She'll see through me."

"Of course. All the same, she'll be flattered. I know of a young man on Beacon Hill to whom a single lady left her entire fortune—only because three times a week he spent an hour playing the piano with her. . . ."

Chapter 18

The last lifeboat in the shuttle service between Bar Harbor and the *Cecilie*—called the "trash collector" by the crew—took off from the Yacht Club pier just before midnight.

It was one of Pollak's regulations that at midnight everyone had to be back on the *Cecilie*. The officers were urged to punish infractions with curtailment of wages and confinement on board. Now and then there were latecomers who used rented boats, and occasionally a man would stay out all night, but these were exceptions. Most of the men were spontaneously drawn back aboard long before taps, and sometimes the last lifeboat was almost empty. This night only two figures stood at the pier.

By midnight all Bar Harbor was fast asleep; the streets lay deserted, the shops' illuminated signs had been turned off, and the sailboats at the docks and buoys bobbed sleepily in the swell. The only louder noise came from the storage sheds, where the day's catch of fish was being packed into the kegs with ice so that the morning steamer could take them away.

The ship out in the water dominated Frenchman Bay even more than by day. But this nighttime ship was not a sea monster with its long black hull, its many decks and superstructures; it was a creature of light, floating in the dark.

"I never used to look at it this way," Vandermark said, "not with such eyes."

Anne did not take her eyes from the ship as she said, "It's almost too beautiful. I keep waiting for it to melt into thin air."

They were sitting side by side on the stone steps leading down to the dock to wait for the last boat. Horse and buggy stood at the wharf.

"I'd like to take you on a tour of the ship," he said. "Of course, she isn't the same *Cecilie* that she was in New York. Without passengers she is missing something. All the same, I'd like to show you around."

"It's very late."

He looked at her. "What have you got against ships?"

"I'm afraid of them. My mother and father died on a ship."

"I'm sorry. I didn't know."

"How could you have known? Grandmother never speaks of it, and neither do I. My father was her favorite son. I was only five at the time. . . ."

"Please don't force yourself to talk about it."

"Why not, as long as I've started? . . . It was supposed to be my first sea voyage. My mother and father were going to take me to Europe."

A couple of sailors came walking along the boardwalk, girls on their arms. They saluted Vandermark, walked on; their steps died away, their shapes turned to shadows.

Vandermark waited for Anne to resume speaking.

"The ship was called *Kaiser Wilhelm der Grosse*," she said at last. "It was the year nineteen hundred, in June. I was in New York for the first time, and the heat was awful. Different ships were moored at the Lloyd docks in Hoboken, being loaded. I remember the names *Saale* and *Main*—can that be right?"

"Yes, there were such ships."

"Bales of cotton caught fire on the dock. Within minutes everything was in flames. The fire spread to the ships—"

"I know. I know the story." It had been one of the worst disasters by fire of all time, claiming more than two hundred lives. The *Kaiser Wilhelm der Grosse* had gotten off lightly. The ship already had her steam up and was able to get away from the docks out into the Hudson, to quell the fire there. For the other three ships there was no escape. They burned to the waterline, until at last their hawsers burst in the blaze and they were washed away on the tide.

"Now I understand why you never came with your grandmother."

"I shouldn't have started. But now at least you know why I behaved so oddly that time in New York, on the ship. . . ." She looked up at him and then, quite surprisingly, kissed him. It was only a fleeting touch; her lips barely grazed him, and then she laid her head on his shoulder. It was the gesture of a child seeking protection from an adult, but Vandermark thought he detected the restrained fervor of a woman seeking the man underneath.

Before he could respond, she moved away. "Thank you so much for a lovely day."

She sounded conventional, distant; Vandermark thought that all of a sudden her voice resembled that of her grandmother. In any case the tone was the same one Temperance C. Butler used to thank him for playing the piano with her—condescending, the attitude of the grande dame. In Temperance C. Butler he found it amusing, but in Anne it troubled him; more than that, he felt offended. It was a surprising discovery that she had the power to hurt him.

"Shall I see you tomorrow?" She had gotten into the victoria and taken up the reins.

"What's on the program?" he asked evasively. "The eagles again?"

"We could collect shells or rocks. There are places where one can find wonderful bits—rock crystal, rose tourmaline—the area is famous for it. But it's a long way to the good spots."

"I'll think about it."

"I understand. You have to reconcile the two of us, Gloria and me. Let me know the next time she lets you have the day off."

She cracked her whip, and the horse started. Vandermark watched her drive away and did not know whether to be angry at her or at himself.

Gloria!

He had left her in the lurch. And the reason was a spoiled little girl who teased him with her whims. During the last few hours he had always quickly pushed aside the thought of Gloria, but now she came to the foreground. He felt very close to her, closer than ever. . . .

In the silence the cough of the lifeboat's outboard motor, which had been installed in Bar Harbor, sounded excessively loud. A mate stood at the dock, staring at Vandermark. For a moment Vandermark was undecided. The Western Union sign shone in the darkness. Shouldn't he at least telephone Gloria, give her some kind of explanation?

"Are you coming, sir?"

His freedom—the ship had always been that. Nothing and no one could hold him back when the ship was ready to sail. He made a sign to the mate to indicate that he was coming. The wooden planks up the dock, sagging under his footsteps filled him with relief.

He was the last. The boat took off as soon as he had gotten in. It was only sparsely occupied, and the men sat silently on the benches. Sometimes a match flared up behind a cupped hand as a cigarette was lit. Vandermark was reminded of the ferry across the Hudson when the crew returned at night from Manhattan to the ship, loud, boisterous, some of them tipsy and boasting of their latest adventures.

The ship came closer, grew and grew; the black hull hove into sight, the decks, the funnels, the masts. The ship lost the magic with which she was imbued when seen from land, but Vandermark preferred her this way: the power emanating from the ship, especially the feeling of security she lent him.

On top of the rock where Sol Butler made his home Vandermark had thought, The *Cecilie,* she is my rock. Would he ever have harbored such thoughts had it not been for the involuntary stay in Bar Harbor? Anne, Gloria, women in general—they meant the land. *Cecilie,* that was the name of the sea. *Land*—it sounded dark. *Sea*—it sounded bright and open. Anne, Gloria—names and women were interchangeable. *Cecilie*—she was unique.

The lifeboat had entered the ship's circle of light. McCagg's revenue cutter lay fifty yards before the bow. Behind it a second boat had been made fast, noticeable now, at night, only by her directional lanterns. The outboard motor stopped; a few men reached for the oars and maneuvered the boat underneath the gangway.

"After you, sir."

Vandermark climbed up the swaying ladder. Two cabin boys saluted as he stepped on deck. It was only three yards above the waterline, and at this hour it was deserted. The air was hot and sticky. Silence reigned in the crew's quarters. The men preferred to spend their time on the open decks; some of them even spent the night on the lounge chairs of the promenade deck, which used to be reserved for first-class passengers.

A ship without passengers—even after all this time the situation was still unfamiliar, and the fact that the crew gradually tended to take on the role of the passengers only served to stress the unnaturalness of it for Vandermark. As every night, the promenade deck was peopled by hundreds of men. To pass the time, many had recourse to earlier occupations and skills. There was already a theater group, and a pair of brothers—engaged as machinists on the *Cecilie*—had been busy for ten days reconstructing their old act as tightrope walkers. During the day, Vandermark had watched them rehearsing a couple of times, but when he now saw the men on the wire on the brightly lit foredeck, he was surprised all the same.

The wire had not been put up very high, barely skimming the heads of the audience. The man did not have a rod but kept his balance with an opened umbrella. His feet felt their way forward on the wire inch by inch, uncertain, almost fearful. Over and over he was forced to stop until his swaying body regained its equilibrium, but he remained aloft; and when he had reached the end of the wire, the audience broke into loud applause. The man stopped on a small wooden platform. He bowed. Pearls of perspiration glistened on his forehead, and wherever his flesh-colored jersey was not embroidered with black sequins, it showed dark sweat stains.

"Encore! Encore! Do it again!" The calls, isolated at first, increased, grew louder, more demanding, and when the man did not respond, almost angry. It was clear that he was not eager to make his way back across the wire, but the watchers would not relent. They stamped their feet and shouted; the loudest among them were those who had newly joined the throng, attracted by the noise.

Vandermark would have liked to intervene to end the performance, but just then a drum flourish began. The man on the platform spread out his arms, and slowly seeking support, he forced his right foot onto the wire. Silence fell among the audience; only the drumbeat rolled on as the man felt his way forward along the wire, tilted to one side, caught himself, gained one yard after another. Vandermark turned away; he could not watch any longer. The drumming increased in speed and was abruptly drowned in shouts of jubilation.

The night was wind-still and very warm. No one on board seemed to be thinking of sleep. From the tennis court on the game deck the thud of balls could be heard. Gramophone music came from the Viennese Café, from a worn roll whose melody was barely recognizable—could it be "International Rag"? A few cabin boys had made themselves comfortable in the palm garden and were playing chess. The ivory and ebony men they were using were part of the first-class equipment.

Never before had Vandermark realized so clearly how the crew had taken over the ship. The process had been extremely slow. During the first few days the crew had behaved as always. Each man had his place, and it did not occur to him to use the decks and especially the social rooms set up for the passengers. Only gradually and with a certain amount of stealth, as if on some forbidden errand, had they made themselves masters of the ship. Pollak had not ordered them to refrain; on the contrary, he had encouraged them, especially the crews from the nether regions of the ship, the stokers and machinists. And to everyone's astonishment, it was precisely they who had adjusted most quickly to the new situation and visibly enjoyed escaping the dark, the dirt, and the heavy labor and playing at being lords of the ship.

Of course Pollak saw to it that the six hundred and fifty crewmen were not without occupation. Every other day he had the ship polished and burnished, but for the rest they were free to do as they wished. Since the day they had cast anchor in Bar Harbor, he had treated his men with kid gloves and shown as much understanding for their moods as he had previously had only for the eccentricities of first-class passengers.

Pollak himself kept almost entirely out of sight. Vandermark was puzzled—Pollak, who loved gregariousness above all things, locked himself in his cabin. He spent time with McCagg, but that was his only entertainment. He did not move off the ship. Except for the one evening with Temperance C. Butler, he had refused all invitations. He left the ship only to negotiate with the New York office. But even these trips had grown less frequent, and sometimes lately he had deputized his chief purser. What was the meaning of his behavior? Did he wish to set an example to the men? Did he think that only his presence could hold them together? Was he worried that otherwise they might run off?

Vandermark knew that the young unmarried men discussed the possibility of quitting. To this day the crew was complete—and yet the *Cecilie* was no longer the ship she had been. The crew had changed, a transformation had taken place. Vandermark could not have said exactly what it was; he simply felt that nothing was as it had been and that it never would be again.

He remained standing at the railing and looked across at Bar Harbor. The night was dark but clear, and the few lights still burning in the town were very distinct. Suddenly he recalled his dream of the previous night. He had jumped overboard to swim ashore. The land seemed close by, easy to reach. People on shore were waving at him, encouraging him. He swam and swam, but the shore receded farther and farther. Finally he turned around to go back on board, but the *Cecilie* was no longer there, only high waves rolling in from far out in the ocean. . . .

Though he was tried, he knew that sleep would elude him once he was alone in his cabin. Would it not be better to return to shore? He went down to A deck. The corridors were deserted, the wall sconces dimmed as night-lights. The only bright ray of light streamed from the chief purser's office, where the door stood open.

One could be almost certain of finding Wilhelm Kuhn in his office at this time. He sat at his desk, his uniform jacket slung over the back of the chair. He was in his shirt sleeves and had rolled up the cuffs and unbuttoned his collar—comforts Kuhn seldom allowed himself. Behind him, in a corner of the room, a ventilator was humming, but the air was sticky nevertheless.

"How can you stand it in here?" Vandermark asked.

Kuhn reached into the shelf behind him and handed Vandermark a letter. The envelope was covered with many stamps and cancellations, so that his mother's delicate writing was almost hidden.

"Mail?" he said. "When did it arrive?"

"Today. Two sacks at once. They seem to have found a route now, by way of Genoa, with Italian ships."

Vandermark pocketed the letter. "Where is Captain Pollak?"

"In the smoking room. The usual card game. I have some problems, but he is unapproachable when he's playing with McCagg. I'm worried about Pollak. Our whole situation worries me. I can't see an end to it. . . ." On the desk before him lay the large ledger, its columns filled with entries in his precise, vertical hand, but underneath it Vandermark spied the passenger list from the last voyage. Had Kuhn been perusing it? Had he quickly placed the ledger on top of it when he heard Vandermark approaching?

"What do you expect Pollak to do? Turn off the war? Conjure up passengers and supplies? Give orders to set sail?"

Kuhn nodded. His expression was serious. "Something like that, yes. I believe the whole crew is secretly waiting for something of the sort—"

"And here I thought you of all people had adapted to the new situation."

"Why?" Wilhelm Kuhn brushed up his moustache.

"Does the name Dolly Higgins mean anything to you?"

"That's unfair, extremely unfair." Kuhn seemed both embarrassed and flattered. "You have something going with one woman after another, and no one says a word. I am really performing good works; these Americans have an antediluvian picture of Germany, and it can't do any harm if a few sensible books. . . . But how do you know about it anyway? I've only been there a couple of times. Anne Butler? Of course—Anne Butler."

"Whoever, you did not make a bad impression on Dolly Higgins."

"It's quite harmless. It's only—"

"That's all right."

"She's smart as a whip, and she knows many of our previous passengers personally. . . . And you think I made a lasting impression on her?"

Vandermark nodded smiling. Wilhelm Kuhn, who in New York went ashore only to go to a particular shop to buy a particular kind of fruitcake that his wife particularly loved for its decorated tin box— Wilhelm Kuhn had fallen prey to the seductions of Bar Harbor. The fact suddenly cheered Vandermark up. "I'll look in the smoking room," he said. He stopped again when he was in the doorway. "One question. What about our salaries? Today I heard something about their being cut."

Kuhn looked at his ledger. Vandermark almost had the impression that he would have preferred talking more about Dolly Higgins.

"The salaries for August are in the safe," Kuhn said. "They will be paid out in the normal way. But what will happen in September. . . ."

"So there is something to the rumor?"

"What do you care? Did you ever live on your salary? I can't be more specific, but of course Lloyd has no income." He opened his desk drawer, pulled out a bundle of papers, and held it up. "Bills, Vandermark, nothing but unpaid bills. Fresh meat, fresh vegetables, water. Are you aware that for drinking water alone we spend ten dollars a day?"

Vandermark listened to the chief purser with the absurd feeling of being on the wrong ship. How could this be the *Cecilie*, how could this be Wilhelm Kuhn, who worried about paying bills for drinking water?

"I tried to talk it over with Pollak," Kuhn continued. "I think I have a couple of ideas. For example, we could open the ship every Sunday for guided tours. I'm certain we'd get five hundred visitors a day, and if we charge a dollar a head. . . . We could print postcards of the ship and sell them; that would bring in some more. What do we have a print shop on board for? But forget it. Lately you can't count on Pollak. I, for one, don't know how long Lloyd can last."

Vandermark remembered the second boat alongside the revenue cutter. "By the way, has McCagg got company?" he asked. "There's another ship lying to, if my eyes don't deceive me."

Kuhn's expression grew more somber. He tightened the knot of his tie. "When I came back on board, there was no second boat. But ask McCagg. He's in the smoking room. He's the one who should know. They're playing poker. That's something Pollak always has time for."

"Why don't you come along?"

"To play poker? I've never held a card in my whole life. I don't need any more trouble than I had when there were gamblers on board."

Vandermark hesitated before asking, "Did you happen to know a Nick Frohman?"

"Nick Frohman, did you say?" Kuhn pondered. "Nick Frohman . . . a professional gambler?"

"Yes."

"It's been a long time, twenty years or more. Yes, I remember Nick Frohman. He generally traveled on English ships. His name was on the blacklist the shipping companies shared among themselves." Kuhn's memory was like an archive. Names, dates, facts—it held all of them fast. Nick Frohman too was in his file.

"I ran into him once or twice," Kuhn continued, proud of being able to show off his knowledge. "He traveled first class, like most of the professional gamblers, and like most of them he had his gimmick. They always concentrate on a particular passenger during any one voyage. Their problem is only how to make contact with their pigeon quickly and unobtrusively. Nick Frohman traveled with a little girl, eleven, twelve years old, his daughter. A cute little thing with reddish-blond hair and green eyes. She made friends with other children, her father got talking to the parents, and lo and behold, a game was arranged." Kuhn leaned back in his chair. "I always had something against gamblers. But if I had to make the choice now—the *Cecilie* here in Bar Harbor or back on the high seas with a handful of gamblers on board—I wouldn't hesitate. If only we were back on our route." He stared into space, and in his eyes was the expression of a man looking at something indescribably beautiful. "On our route, Vandermark. . ." he said softly. "My God, will it ever happen again?"

The chief purser's words stayed with Vandermark as he made his way to the smoking room. And something else occupied his mind: an eleven-year-old girl with reddish-blond hair and green eyes, traveling with her father on luxury liners and helping him line up victims for the gaming tables. The funny thing was that he envied the child. He pretended that his own father had been a professional gambler and had taken his son along on his travels to act as a decoy. What a life! Always on beautiful ships, in elegant first-class cabins. Surely, given such a life, he would have loved his father. . . .

In the smoking room only one table was illuminated. The four men sat in a cloud of cigar smoke. It was the usual group: Pollak, McCagg, Dr. Fischer, and the chief engineer. The glasses and ashtrays stood within easy reach on small round serving carts next to each place. Bills and coins were piling up in front of McCagg. The men made their bids in subdued voices. "Three cards . . . one . . . enough . . . I'm staying."

"I'm folding." Fischer threw his cards on the table. The others did not respond at once. Silently their eyes traveled over the hand that lay spread out before them on the green felt covering the table. Fischer pushed back his chair. As he got up, he noticed Vandermark. "You're just in time. We're all losing our shirts to McCagg here. Take my place. This isn't my lucky day."

Vandermark went to the table. The chief engineer had also left the game. Only Pollak and McCagg were still holding their cards and scrutinizing each other. Without turning his head, Pollak spoke. "Back on board, Vandermark?"

Vandermark thought of a little girl on a big ship. Why wasn't he with her? Why hadn't he at least telephoned her? Suddenly nothing in the world seemed more important than to hear her voice. A lifeboat was always ready at the gangway, and surely he would find a mate as wide awake as himself who would row him there and back. He had to hear her voice.

"How about it, which of you is in?" McCagg shuffled the cards and dealt.

Vandermark picked up the five cards at Fischer's place. "Not your lucky day, did you say?" He held the cards out to Fischer, and the doctor's eyes popped.

"Hand it over." Fischer sat down again. He stared around the table challengingly. "Who's going to open?"

Vandermark left.

The bay seemed even more serene and deserted than before. The only sound was the dull thudding of a motor as a white yacht moved toward the Egg Rock lighthouse. Bar Harbor was dark. Vandermark stood forward at the bow of the boat. He was too restless, too impatient to sit down; somehow this night journey had a quality of precipitate flight.

"Shall I wait for you, sir?" asked the mate as they docked.

Vandermark was already standing on the pier. "Wait a quarter of an hour. If I'm not here by then, go back alone."

The Rockaway Hotel had already put out its lights, but the Western Union office was still open. The man at the counter, who had fallen asleep with his head cradled in his arms, jumped up. The Villa Far Niente had had one of the first telephones in the town; its number was 27.

Vandermark was prepared for a wait; it was past one o'clock. But Brice answered immediately after the first ring.

"Hello? Mr. Vandermark?"

His voice sounded as if he were speaking from the entrance hall.

"I know it's late, Brice. Would you put me through all the same, please?"

The extensions were distributed all through the house, and one of them was in Gloria's bedroom.

"I'm afraid I can't do that."

Vandermark thought he could picture Brice at the telephone, shaking his head regretfully.

"Did Mrs. Lindsay retire so early?"

"She waited a long time. . . . You were expected for dinner, isn't that right? We were having your favorite appetizer, and for desert the apple pie you're so fond of. . . . I'm sorry, Mr. Vandermark. Mrs. Lindsay . . . has left."

"Left?"

"Yes, Mr. Vandermark."

"But at this hour there is no—"

"Just a moment. Where are you now, if I may ask?"

"I'm calling from the Western Union office. Why?"

"Perhaps you can still catch up with Mrs. Lindsay at the landing stage east of the steamship station. It's not far from where you are. You can't miss it. The *Nirvana*. It stands out from the other yachts."

"White?" Vandermark asked. "Three-masted?"

"Yes."

"She's put to sea, Brice. But why? I mean, what happened?"

"I had no way of reaching you. It was a surprise for us too. There was a visitor, an old friend of Mrs. Lindsay's. He arrived tonight with the yacht."

"An old friend?"

"Mr. Shubert, yes. He intended to stay until tomorrow. Well, first we waited dinner, but when Googins came back without you. . . . It was shortly before midnight when Mrs. Lindsay called me in and told me that Mr. Shubert's things should be packed and that Googins should get ready to drive them to the yacht. It all happened from one minute to the next. Mrs. Lindsay had changed her clothes and was ready to go in ten minutes. . . . She left a letter for you."

"Did Mrs. Lindsay say where she was headed?"

"She had me reserve a room for her in New York, at the Plaza. For an indefinite period. . . . You will come?"

The telephone hung from the wall in a corner. The Western Union official sat behind his wicket; he stared sleepily into space, but his posture gave away the fact that he was listening. Vandermark looked at the clock and saw that the quarter-hour was almost up. Brice's voice came from the earpiece, almost guilty, pleading, as if he were responsible for the situation.

"I'll send Googins to Bar Harbor tomorrow night. He'll be available to you every night, Mr. Vandermark. You'll come to dinner, won't you? The chef will make a special effort, I'm sure. Mrs. Lindsay's sudden departure, you know—we are not used to it. And she gave me specific orders that the house was open to you as before. . . . I'll keep the letter for you here."

"Thanks, Brice. You'll hear from me. and I apologize for calling so late."

The mate was still waiting in the lifeboat. The yacht had passed out of sight. The light of Egg Rock streaked across the bay. An eleven-year-old girl who enticed gamblers on luxury liners—he could still see the image; it occupied him more than the telephone call.

When they reached the *Cecilie,* a lifeboat was just taking off. McCagg was returning to his revenue cutter. It was unusually early for him. Perhaps Fischer's hand had promised more than it held.

Chapter 19

The wind had risen suddenly, a stiff southwester leaping across the water in gusts. The sky was clear, of a transparent blue, and the sun resembled a burning glass globe, but it gave off little warmth.

The lifeboat rocked on the waves. Only a few fishing skiffs were on the water, and a couple of intrepid sailboats—nothing else. The few people on the boardwalk did not walk upright but bent forward against the wind, hands clamping down their hats.

The captain of the *Cecilie* sat in the bow of the boat wearing his dark uniform, Pommerenke by his side. Their luggage was stowed under the bench, Pollak's black, dented valise and his tiger's seabag. Pollak raised his head, shaded his eyes with his hand, and looked to the southwest. He had predicted the change in the weather. That morning, even before sunrise, before there was the least sign, he had given the order to haul up the starboard anchor to allow the *Cecilie* to turn a few degrees in the wind. And as he turned to the officers who were accompanying him now, he said, "You'll get even more wind, southwest, and then fog—a real pea-souper." He examined them— Kessler, the first officer; Vandermark; and Kuhn—as earlier he had scrutinized the sky and the water. "Look after the crew while I'm gone. Keep the men busy. Think of something that will occupy their minds. Twenty-four hours of fog, and the men get jumpy."

The beaming ball of the sun and the cloudless sky seemed to contradict his words; nevertheless no one doubted his prediction. Kessler pulled his cap deeper onto his forehead. His skin did not tan but only peeled when he got too much sun, and after the four hot weeks in Bar Harbor it was rough and flaky, as if he had a rash.

"We should have the crew go through a real maritime drill again," he said, "an emergency simulation. They've become land rats."

Vandermark and Kuhn exchanged a look, but Pollak remained relaxed. "Don't go too far, Kessler. It's enough if you have all the brass polished. That's an ideal foggy-day occupation."

The lifeboat neared the shore. It headed, not for the Yacht Club dock, but for the steamboat landing; there the ferry to Rockland, which made the connection to Boston, lay ready to depart. The decks were almost empty, for the strong wind had driven most of the passengers inside. Only here and there an isolated shape stood at the railing. The smoke from the funnels was swallowed by the wind, and the steamboat whistle that blasted now seemed also to be carried off by a gust, so short and thin did it sound.

They were running late because of a few orders from New York that Simoni, the sparks, had produced at the last minute. Pollak had looked them over quickly and put them in his pocket. The men had become uneasy when they learned about the suit against Lloyd and the seizure of the *Cecilie* pending the final verdict, but Pollak seemed little influenced by the news. At first he had even refused to appear in Boston as a witness in the hearings—"Let the lawyers settle it among themselves"—but suddenly he changed his mind, and beginning last night he became more expansive and cheerful than he had been in a long time. The customary poker game lasted until three in the morning, but Pollak gave no sign whatever of being tired; rather, he was as bright and chipper as on his best days.

The lifeboat had arrived at the landing stage. Before anyone could help him, Pollak grabbed his valise. Pommerenke, the walking barometer of his master's moods, also in full dress uniform, slung his seabag over his shoulder.

William Pauker, captain and co-owner of the *Rockland*, was waiting for his famous colleague at the gangway. Vandermark's attention was riveted on a single female figure on the ferry's upper deck. A silk scarf was wound around her hat, partially concealing her face. She wore a severely tailored traveling costume of tobacco-brown material etched with a pale plaid. A gold chain glinted in the lapel buttonhole.

Now she raised her hand as if to grasp the fluttering end of the scarf, but it might as easily have been a sign to someone still on land. Involuntarily Vandermark looked at Pollak—and he was not mistaken, the captain too was looking at the figure on the upper deck. Was he also raising his hand to return the woman's signal? And what was the meaning of his smile as he turned to Vandermark?

"All right, fellows, I'll be back in three days at the latest. I'll telegraph to let you know what boat I'm coming back on."

"I hope all goes well," Wilhelm Kuhn said. "Give it to them good."

Pollak placed his hand on the chief purser's shoulder. "I'll give it to them—you can count on it. All right, then keep your head above the fog. And you, Kessler"—Pollak glanced across the bay at the *Cecilie*—"you are responsible for the lady. Take good care of her."

The *Rockland*'s siren drowned out his final words. Pommerenke had already gone on board, and immediately after Pollak followed him, two men pulled up the ladder. Under the boat's stern the water began to churn and foam. Clumsily the *Rockland* turned from the dock.

Vandermark looked for the woman on the upper deck, but the place was empty.

"He's pretty relaxed about the trial," Kuhn said.

"We never should have turned around." Kessler stared at the retreating ferry. "That's what started it all. Now we're trapped. And if we don't help ourselves, we'll never get out of the trap."

They were alone on the landing stage by now. The men who had hauled in the gangway of the *Rockland* and untied the hawsers had disappeared into the little station house. Without the windbreak of the ship, the gusts hit them with full force. The tide was at its fullest, and the waves smacked over the wharf wall. The lifeboat that had brought them lay high in the water. The first gulls that had followed the *Rockland* were already returning, coming to rest on the damp edge of the shore.

"We're trapped," Kessler repeated grimly.

"And I'd had such a pleasant idea of how it was going to be." Kuhn too looked at the ferry, which was sailing around the *Cecilie*. "I would have served out my last few years, four, maybe five, and at sixty I would have retired and opened my own agency. With the stock of regular passengers I know personally, it would have been a success."

"Let's not get melancholy before the fog even sets in. How about a game of billiards in the Rockaway Hotel?" Vandermark had only meant to dispel the depression left behind by Pollak's departure, but Kessler slewed around, his spotty face reddened by the wind, a feverish glow in his eyes.

"Playing billiards, sitting around hotel terraces, running after women . . ."

Vandermark laughed. "Which one of us can he mean, Kuhn?"

But Kessler had no intention of changing his tack. "In the captain's absence—"

"It's okay, Kessler," Vandermark interrupted. "I get it. No billiards. You are in command."

"It's almost eight thirty," Kuhn said. "Time for me to make my call to New York." Calm and level-headed, he sized up Kessler. "Winter clothing," he said at length. "I'll ask the New York office for winter gear. Pollak thought the time had come. . . . When I think that it was July when we left New York. Midsummer. And now we're asking for woolen underwear." He walked away, coat collar turned up, shoulders hunched, one hand on his cap to keep the wind from tearing it off his head.

Kessler gave a forced smile. "Go ahead, have your game of billiards."

"I don't care about it, I really don't."

"I want you to take over day duty, from noon to eight o'clock."

"All right."

"I mean to help you out. Nine o'clock, that's your time, isn't it?"

It was my time, Vandermark thought. The water glinted in the sunlight, but the foamy crests of the waves had suddenly turned from white to gray. In spite of the sun, in spite of the cloudless sky, there was a livid quality in the air. Far away on the horizon a thin gray line had appeared. A closed carriage drove down Main Street, came to a stop. Jenkins alit from the box and came up to Vandermark.

"One more thing," Kessler said. "No shore leaves granted after eighteen hours."

Vandermark looked at Kessler. "Not even the stewards?"

"The whole crew. No shore leave for twelve hours. At eighteen hours thirty I want to see the crew on deck, wearing life jackets. You will carry out a life-jacket drill and an inspection of all the lifeboats. You have to admit we've fallen into a pretty muddled routine. We understand each other?"

"All right."

"Beginning at twenty hours, you can go off skirt chasing."

"Your authority extends to that as well?"

For a moment it seemed that Kessler would lose control again, but he caught himself in time. "You'll have to admit the whole situation can get on a person's nerves. I'm not the type who can enjoy this sort of thing—" He gestured widely. "I've made every effort, you know that. I've really tried everything, but somewhere I have to draw the line. I mean, after all, we are. . . ." He did not complete the sentence. "Someone wants you, Vandermark."

Kessler returned to the lifeboat. The wind pressed his white trousers tightly to his legs. Jenkins, who had come closer, said, "If the wind doesn't stop, the bay will be closed by afternoon. . . . Mrs. Butler sent me to inquire if you would have tea with her."

Vandermark looked at the coach. A hand reached through one of the windows, its bracelets and rings sparkling, and waved at him.

"Does the fog last a long time?" he asked Jenkins.

"Sometimes it's no more than twenty-four hours, but it's happened that we couldn't see the hand in front of our face for a week at a time. You never can tell beforehand; not even the fishermen know."

He walked ahead and helped Temperance C. Butler to alight from the carriage. She wore a woolen stole and a kerchief around her head.

"I have to take your arm," she said to Vandermark. "My legs are not too steady today." And with that she gathered up her long flowered skirt with a quick gesture until her knee came into sight, revealing a large adhesive plaster. "That's what happens when you climb a ladder to pick peaches at my age."

Jenkins, embarrassed, looked away and made a desperate effort to screen the scene with his body. Temperance C. Butler was not troubled. She simply could not forego this opportunity to show her slim legs, and in fact she had the slender, well-shaped legs of a young woman. Her cheeks had a rosy glow, and her eyes flashed.

Letting her skirt drop, she took Vandermark's arm and steered him toward a small café across the street. A few marble-topped tables and some chairs were still standing on the sidewalk, but the umbrellas had already been removed. She pointed to one of the tables. "You don't mind sitting out here, do you? People are so squeamish—as if a little breeze could blow them away." When the waiter came, she ordered two teas without consulting Vandermark. They were the only customers.

Vandermark had followed Jenkins with a certain amount of reluctance. It was the first time in five days that he was back on land, and he was not surprised that she referred to the fact immediately.

"You've made yourself scarce, my dear man."

The waiter brought the tea. Vandermark thought of Gloria's letter, which Brice was still keeping for him. Five days on the ship—it was a long time, but he had still not figured out what he should do.

She leaned across the table. "Problems?"

"The lawsuit in Boston," he said, not quite truthfully. "Of course we worry about what is going to happen."

"It's an effrontery. But that's how bankers are. I hope Charlie Pollak isn't taking it too badly."

"It's a matter of his ship."

"Nonsense. The people are on his side, the public. At worst it will go on and on. Charlie will give it to them."

Vandermark had to smile, because she had used Kuhn's very words. And then he remembered the woman on the deck. He looked at Temperance C. Butler. "Was Miss Connors taking the *Rockland?*"

She evinced no surprise. "I had to send her to Boston for a few days."

"Exactly today?"

"Just a coincidence."

Vandermark thought of the day the ship had been emptied, of the bets Temperance C. Butler had collected in the smoking room. He remembered his conversation with Pollak that very same evening.

"Pollak and Miss Connors knew each other before, didn't they? In Bar Harbor?"

"It's a strange place," she said, not giving a direct answer. "Here people fall in love with each other whom no one would ever have expected to. I met both my husbands here—that tells the whole story."

"Were they serious?"

"Marriage is always serious, at least for me. I always took marriage seriously, the men themselves less so."

"I meant Charlie Pollak and Edith Connors."

"I told you, Bar Harbor is a strange place; here the impossible is possible. No one is proof against it, not even Charlie Pollak, or Edith Connors either. Gloria Lindsay is another good example. She met John Lindsay here. Everyone thought John was crazy, but it was a good marriage. And look at me. I entered into a marriage here that I was sure would be a success, and it went radically wrong. And in my second marriage, where I myself counted on a catastrophe, everything worked out wonderfully. A strange place, that's all."

"How serious was it between Charlie Pollak and Edith Connors? Was he thinking of leaving the sea?"

"You'll have to ask him about that. I only know that it was enormously complicated, too complicated for my simple nature. I never understood why they called it off at the time. It seemed to me a pointless sacrifice on both sides. . . . Edith had a dozen chances to marry afterward, good matches, but she turned them all down. If that isn't complicated!"

"Perhaps she loved him"

"That's precisely what I mean, Fred, precisely. To love someone so much that you can't ever feel anything else, no. . . ." She shook her head. "It's sad enough that we have only one life, but only one love— that's asking too much." She looked at him. "We agree on that, don't we? That's one of the reasons I like you. . . . Well then, think about it."

Though he thought he understood her meaning, he asked, "What is it I'm supposed to think about?"

"Well, you're going to have to make a decision one way or the other. Charlie Pollak—that was a different matter. A ship was waiting for him in New York, ready to set sail. But when will the *Cecilie* set out to sea again? First I thought it was a matter of days or weeks. Now . . ."

He gazed out into the bay, where the ship lay at anchor. The wind had fallen somewhat, but the gray stripe on the horizon had broadened—a fogbank coming closer, just above the surface of the water. Soon it would be touching the outermost of the Porcupine Islands. The sky above it was still clear and bright.

"I wish you well." Temperance C. Butler laid her hand on his arm. "Of course I'm also thinking of myself. I like having you near me. I'd like it to stay that way. Keep that in mind when you're deciding. It's a fact that when a man chooses a wife, it is always an advantage if he is on good terms with her father. In this instance, I'm representing Anne's father. To put it bluntly, Anne has a considerable fortune, and she will be even richer after I die."

"That really is putting it very bluntly."

"The usual situation is for a girl to marry a rich man, but the reverse has been known to happen—a man takes a rich wife."

"That was always my hope."

"I knew we'd understand each other."

"But in this case, aren't you planning too far ahead? Anne and I—"

She stopped him with a gesture. "That's your business. I only wanted to let you know that you can always count on me. By the way, before I forget. . . ." She opened her handbag, pulled out a check, and held it out to Vandermark. "I canvassed my friends in Bar Harbor, and this is what I collected."

He examined the check. It was made out to Wilhelm Kuhn the *Cecilie*'s chief purser, and it amounted to two thousand dollars.

"Two thousand dollars? What for?"

"A contribution from the residents of Bar Harbor for the maintenance costs of the ship."

"And you wheedled the money out of your friends?"

"If I couldn't do that, my dear Fred! All winter long in Boston I do nothing but get people to open their pocketbooks for 'good causes'—people who are determined not to give me a cent. I'm feared. But here in Bar Harbor it was different. The *Cecilie* is close to everyone's heart." She smiled. "I'm sure the amount would have been considerably higher if I could have collected from my neighbor as well."

He was still holding the check. "How much of it is yours?"

"I must like you an awful lot, Fred. Usually I can't stand for someone to see through me." She rose and gestured to Jenkins, who was waiting across the street with the carriage.

"Will you pay for the tea?" She held out her hand. "Will I see you soon?" Vandermark hesitated before answering, and she continued, "There are people who are made nervous by the fog, but I love foggy days. No one bothers you. Wouldn't you like to play the piano with me again? I have received a new shipment of sheet music. How about today?"

"I've been assigned to duty. As long as Pollak is in Boston—"

"Come whenever you want."

He watched as Jenkins helped her across the street. A remarkable woman, a mixture of cordiality and coldness, of sentiment and calculation. With her one never knew what the next moment would bring. She was a storm passing overhead, a tornado of words, smiles, batted eyelashes, gestures, rattling jewelry. One ducked, one longed for it to be over, but once one had escaped her, one felt revived, in spite of some exhaustion.

He paid for the tea and went to the Western Union office. Why didn't he telephone Gloria at her New York hotel? Had Googins really driven into town that night to wait for him? He saw Kuhn's figure through the office window. He seemed to have just finished his call. Vandermark waited for him, and they walked to the dock together.

"They don't have any winter clothing for us in New York," Kuhn announced. "Too early in the year. And I presume that they have nothing at all on hand, that all the supplies are in Bremerhaven."

Vandermark gave him the check from Temperance C. Butler, explaining its origin and purpose. The chief purser held the paper in outstretched fingers. "I'll have to ask Pollak whether we are allowed to accept it."

One of the lifeboats pressed into shuttle service was moored at the Yacht Club dock. "Are you coming?" Vandermark asked. "No tryst?"

"Not until tonight. Dolly Higgins wants to go to the concert— that is, I'm not sure whether I really ought to go."

"Why ever not?"

"I don't know, at my age . . . somehow it's quite ridiculous, isn't it" Perhaps it's only because she looks so much like my wife. Yes, there's an extraordinary resemblance; that's what it must be."

"And her name is Dolly. And she's from Bar Harbor. The strangest things happen here."

They had come to the end of the dock. The layer of fog across the water had moved closer. It looked as if the *Cecilie* were resting on a gray silk pillow. The sky was still clear, and the sun hung above the bay, a perfect circle rimmed in red.

Chapter 20

Goggins drove the Stevens-Duryea at a crawl because the fog was so thick in the hills. Judging from the noise of the wheels, they must have been going uphill, but when the car stopped, Vandermark was not even certain whether they had already arrived at the Villa Far Niente. The fog had wrapped the large building in mist; its outlines melted, the light of the candelabra on either side of the entrance oozed away without providing illumination, and the windows seemed to be made of bright paper.

Hour by hour the fog had enclosed the bay more and more, but during the day colors had served to provide some points of reference. Vandermark had tried to hold himself in check, but the increasingly dense fog made him nervous. For the first time he felt that they were prisoners, that they would never leave the bay again. The hours had dragged on endlessly. The ship lay motionless, as if already rooted in the ocean floor, and the crew, depressed, slouched across the decks. There was one good thing about the fog, however—no one had been particularly upset at Kessler's canceling all shore leaves for twelve hours, and the inspection of the life jackets and lifeboats had even been welcomed as a distraction. Kessler had scarcely shown himself; together with the engineers, he had gone below to inspect the engines.

Vandermark had finished his tour of duty at twenty hours and had gone to his cabin to change his clothes. This had always been his favorite moment of the day, when he had his bath, laid out clean clothing, dressed, filled his cigarette case. Once, in Mexico, he had attended a bullfight and before it had watched in the dressing room as the torero was being readied—and he often recalled that ceremony while he changed. The tension that prevailed in the bullfighter's dressing room, the secret significance that seemed to cling to every gesture—it was no different for him; he too was preparing to enter the arena. . . . But this particular evening his elation had not set in, and he had even hesitated before leaving the ship at all.

"Will you be needing the car again, sir?" It was Googins. As on previous days, tonight too he had been waiting at the dock. His raincoat was shiny with mist.

"I'm sure I won't, Googins. And if I do, Brice will order a car for me."

"He won't get one, not with this fog. Have Brice call me if you need me."

"Good evening, Mr. Vandermark." Brice stood in the doorway, wearing his dark cutaway with gray-and-black striped trousers. "I'm glad to see you. I hope Googins drove carefully. He tends to be a little reckless."

"We did not encounter any other cars, Brice."

"Your coat, sir?" The hall was brightly lit, and the vases were filled with flowers. Through the open door of the dining room he spied two servants. From the floor above he heard steps and subdued voices.

"Are there other guests?" Vandermark asked.

"Oh, no, sir, you're the only one. Will you have something to drink?" He did not wait for the answer but walked ahead into the library. A fire was burning in the grate.

On the table a flat silver dish held a red-bordered white envelope.

"Your drink will be brought in a moment. Dinner at ten?"

"Only for me, Brice?"

"Foster insists that he'd rather cook for one person who enjoys food than for a dozen guests who don't care about eating."

Vandermark looked around the room. "There's always work in such a house, I imagine."

Brice crossed his arms behind his back. "Just to have all the brass polished once a month . . . you know how that is from your ship, don't you? But it's something, if I may be so bold, that Mrs. Lindsay does not understand. She cannot imagine how much there is to do. If you'll permit me, I'll put through a call to New York now."

"New York?" Vandermark had the absurd impression that he was listening to a conversation between two strangers. "Have you heard from Mrs. Lindsay?"

"She usually telephones at nine o'clock, sir. Sometimes the connection is bad. I'll initiate the call, in any case. And you'll let me know when you want to have dinner."

Vandermark nodded and mumbled his thanks. He would have liked to follow Brice, to convince himself with his own eyes that the table had actually been set for him in the dining room. Was there a single place setting on the large table? He sipped his white wine and sat down by the fireplace. He picked up the letter but did not open it. She had written it five days ago. Who knew whether her words were still valid? Why was he here anyway, alone in this strange house? Why wasn't he across the way, sitting next to Temperance C. Butler on the piano bench? The offer she had made him that very morning—he was still astounded. Eschewing diplomatic embellishments, she had aimed straight at her target, had not beaten around the bush or glossed the matter over with fine sentiments; rather, she had spoken very baldly about money. Did she really believe he was for sale? He was not offended; on the contrary, he was tempted to find out how high a price he could command from her, how many conditions he might set, should things come to a head.

He could no longer endure sitting by the fire alone in the huge, silent library. He left the room and went down the hall to the west wing, where "his" room was located. He was not surprised that here too there were fresh flowers and the lights were lit. He opened the armoire and looked at the gear that had accumulated during recent weeks: black trousers, a white dinner jacket, shirts, underwear, patent-leather pumps, bow ties of taffeta, and pajamas with embroidered monograms. After cigarette cases, this was generally the next level of gifts: pajamas and a dressing gown with embroidered monograms. If he had still owned them all, they would have constituted a genuine dowry, but more than once in his life he had abandoned wardrobes of this sort with all their contents. You could get a new dinner jacket and patent-leather pumps anywhere.

Why was he thinking such thoughts? Hadn't Gloria advised Brice to continue to treat him as if he were the lord of the manor? Or was it only his vanity that suggested this to him? Gloria. Gloria Frohman. Gloria Lindsay. The telephone directory of Bar Harbor still listed "Villa Far Niente—Mr. and Mrs. John S. Lindsay, Baltimore."

Shipyards, freight lines, real estate, cash. He had always lived for the day and felt good about it. The telephone on the night table next to the bed rang. He picked up the receiver, prepared to hear the butler's voice, but an unknown woman said, "I am completing the connection." He sat down on the edge of the bed. All he could hear was a rustle and crackle in the line and many voices superimposed on one another. "The Plaza Hotel here. I will connect you with Mrs. Lindsay."

The line fell silent. Then, without introduction, her voice: "Is that you, Fred? Hello? Where are you? At the Villa Far Niente?"

"Gloria!"

"I'm glad I finally got through, and glad you're there."

"Is this your call?"

"I tried to put it through an hour ago. I was told you were lost in the fog. . . . I got away just in time, it seems."

He could barely make out her voice. It had grown increasingly soft, and other voices joined in the background. "It's a very bad connection. Please talk a little louder. What are those voices?"

"Oh, that. Friends of mine . . ." Again he could not hear her. "Gloria?"

The Plaza switchboard cut in. "With whom are you speaking?"

"Mrs. John Lindsay," he said stressing *John*. The connection seemed dead. No sound but that of his own breathing. Then, suddenly, Gloria was back, this time distinct, very near, and without the background voices, as if she had gone to a different room. "We were interrupted. What were you saying?"

"I didn't have a chance to say anything yet."

"I can barely hear you. Shall I get the switchboard back again?"

It seemed impossible to carry on a sensible conversation, and so he asked only the most important question: "When are you coming back?"

"Why don't you come here?"

"Why did you leave so suddenly?"

"Did Brice give you my letter?"

"Why, Gloria?"

"Wasn't it a good idea? I thought, maybe it's a good idea—a little distance . . . a. . . ." Her voice came in waves, now loud, now soft. He could make out only a word here and there.

"I can't get away right now," he said.

"The lawsuit in Boston?"

"You've heard about it?"

"It's been in all the papers. I'll start collecting."

"Collecting?"

"Among my friends—for Charlie Pollak, for the *Cecilie,* for the court fees. . . . Can you hear me?"

"Yes."

"Where are you? In the library?"

"No."

"I can only hear a rustling. . . . Is that because of the fog? I'll call again. Tomorrow night at nine. Hello? Nine, is that a good time for you? I'll stop now before we're cut off again."

"Gloria! I have to talk to you." He fell silent, for the line was already dead.

He had an image in his mind's eye: a luxury suite in the Plaza; Gloria in full evening dress; many friends, a swarm of men. Jealousy filled him. But wasn't that the real purpose of her departure? In her place he would presumably have done the same.

Brice was waiting for him in the hall. "Was it the call you initiated?" Vandermark asked.

"No, sir. The call came from New York. What about dinner?"

"Couldn't I simply have a couple—" But when he saw the disappointment on the butler's face, he said, "All right, then, let's be surprised by whatever Foster has to offer. I'll have my dinner in the dining room."

"It can be served at once, sir."

And so he actually sat at the table, which even without the extra leaves was roomy enough for ten persons. The appetizer, the soup, the entree, the entremets, the main course. White wine with the fish, red wine with the roast. His eyes told him that everything must be extremely tasty, but his palate distinguished only cold or hot, salty or sweet, nothing more.

Brice entered, approached softly. "Everything is excellent," Vandermark said automatically, "really excellent. Please tell Foster. . . ."

Brice cleared his throat. "Excuse me, there is someone who wishes to speak with you."

Vandermark placed his napkin on the table. "On the telephone?"

"No, sir, here . . . Miss Butler."

"Anne Butler?"

"Yes, sir."

"What does she want?"

"She wouldn't tell me."

Only to see Brice's reaction, he said. "Have Miss Butler come in."

"Sir, of course I asked Miss Butler to come in, but she refused."

Vandermark did not rise until he had folded the napkin and pushed it through the ring. Brice accompanied him into the hall and opened the front door.

He had forgotten how thick the fog was. She stood only a few paces away, wrapped in a voluminous cape similar to the one her grandmother had worn that morning. He could not have said what its color was in the impenetrable gray of the fog. She had her back to him and was staring into the grounds.

"Anne."

She turned. The cape was too long for her and too full. Perhaps it really did belong to her grandmother, and she had simply tossed it on in a hurry.

Anne's face wore a strange expression—a mixture of stubbornness and curiosity, if he was interpreting it correctly. He had no doubts about his own feeling: it was relief. He inhaled the damp but invigorating air, and he was excited by the thought of walking through the fog with Anne.

"I'll just get my coat," he said. "Then I'll come with you."

"Wait." She put out her hand to hold him back. "You have to return to Bar Harbor at once. They've been trying to reach you everywhere. It must be urgent."

"Who is looking for me?"

"The chief purser, Kuhn, is waiting for you outside the Rockaway Hotel. You're to go there as quickly as possible."

"Did he telephone?"

"Dolly Higgins . . . Kuhn was already on his way. Dolly Higgins called us for him. she thought you were at our house . . . not here."

"What is it all about?"

"Dolly didn't say anything more. Only that it's very urgent and that you should leave at once. They were just leaving the concert when Kuhn got the message."

"Wait here," he said, but again she held him back.

"It's better if you have Googins drive you . . . it's quicker."

"Wait all the same, all right?" But when he returned with his coat, she had disappeared. He looked around searchingly, even when he was in the car, and once he thought he could see her, but in the dense fog his eyes could just as easily have deceived him.

Googins drove fast. Nevertheless, the way seemed twice as long, and when they finally arrived at the Rockaway, it looked as if Vandermark might be too late. Here at the water's edge the fog was a real soup, the hand in front of one's face barely visible. The houses formed a thick wall of shadow, and the street outside the hotel was deserted; there was no sign of any human being.

Googins turned off the motor and got out also, and it was he who first noticed the sound of engines. It was very soft, as if packed in cotton wool, and it came from the water. Vandermark rushed to the shore, following the noise.

The tide was low, and the boat lay below the dock. It was not one of the *Cecilie's* white lifeboats. In the glow of a lantern abruptly turned on him he distinguished a gray rowboat with an outboard motor.

"Over here," a voice said. "Careful. The planks are slippery." A hand was stretched out to him. He grasped it, sought for a foothold, and bumped into someone. Wilhelm Kuhn's face emerged in the glow of the lantern, pale and tense.

They must already have loosened the lines, for at the same moment the boat pushed off. A hand pressed Vandermark down on a bench. There were other men in the boat, but besides Kuhn he knew none of them. Their uniforms were unfamiliar to him. And then at the stern he spied the fluttering cloth, red and white, with the blue, star-studded corner.

"What is this?" he asked Kuhn. "What happened?"

"McCagg sent the men," Kuhn answered. "McCagg was afraid. . . . Do you think Kessler may be cracking up?"

"Kessler? What about Kessler?"

"I don't think that McCagg is the kind to sound the alarm without good cause."

"You mean the order for us to return on board came from McCagg?"

"Yes. He claims that strange things are happening on the *Cecilie*. He claims to have intercepted a wireless message. . . . The ship is said to be blacked out. . . . And he says that she's been under steam for the last hour. He's afraid that Kessler might try to put out to sea."

"Put to sea?" Vandermark stared into the bay. The fog was not quite so dense on the water, but there was no sign of the *Cecilie*.

"McCagg telegraphed to our ship," Kuhn continued. "He did not receive an answer."

"I simply can't imagine. . . ." Vandermark shook his head. He tried to ward off the thoughts that were beginning to crowd his mind: Kessler's behavior that morning at Pollak's departure; the cancellation of shore leaves, which he had instituted for a period of twelve hours; the life-jacket inspection; the inspection of the engines. And one thing more: day after day Kessler had had himself rowed into the bay, far out beyond Egg Rock, and always he had taken along lines and maritime maps to chart and record the depths. The pastime of a pompous ass, the butt of the crew's jokes. Now, however, the matter took on a different cast.

A wave slapped against the boat, and water sprayed upward. The outlines of the *Cecilie* began to emerge vaguely in the fog. Suddenly the air had a different smell, carrying the odor of coal and sulfur. He was not mistaken; during the first hour after the engines were started, the four funnels always spit out these mordant fumes.

The idea came to him so suddenly that he put it into words at once. "No, it's impossible," he said to Kuhn. "How does he intend to put to sea at low tide?"

"It's already rising. It will be high by three o'clock in the morning— only two hours from now."

The boat had slowed; the *Cecilie*'s hull was clearly visible. Vandermark was interested only in the four funnels. Was it the fog that cloaked them? Was it clouds of smoke?

The boat lay to too late. It bumped hard against the hull, and the motor died. As the men took to the oars, the boat scraped the ship's side. Kuhn had stood up. They must be coming to the gangway.

The man in charge of the boat raised his lamp, but the gangway had been drawn up.

"Give me the lamp," Kuhn called to him. "Someone is sure to see us."

The men dipped their oars sideways in order to hold the boat in place. The only sound was the soft slap of waves between boat and ship's side. And then, another noise, coming from inside the ship. When Vandermark laid his ear on the metal of the hull, he recognized it: coal being poured out onto the grills of the furnaces.

Chapter 21

The fog pushed the smoke and soot downward from the funnels. They had gone on board at the stern, across a rope ladder which had finally, after many unanswered flashes of the lantern, fallen over the side. The decks were in darkness; no light burned anywhere, not even the fog lamps.

They made their way forward, feeling along the railing. Vandermark had expected the decks to be thronged with crew members, but they encountered only a few men, and these gave them contradictory information. No one knew exactly what was happening. Only one thing was evident: the *Cecilie* had her steam up, and the first officer was on the bridge, where he had barricaded himself hours ago. He had set up a watch who admitted no one.

The lifeboats that had been used for the shuttle service with Bar Harbor had all been hauled on board and hung in their davits. When they came to the foredeck, they saw that McCagg's revenue cutter and the Coast Guard vessel had placed themselves horizontally before the *Cecilie*. Their searchlights were turned on, but their rays were not strong enough to penetrate the fog.

Vandermark, Kuhn, and the ship's mate who had thrown them the rope ladder stopped at the foot of the stairs leading to the bridge. The wide glass front of the bridge had been carefully blacked out; only here and there, where the curtains did not close tightly, did a thin line of light seep through. A guard was patrolling inside the bulwark.

Vandermark listened to the noises coming from the ship's interior. The engines were running. The sound was hollow, as when the engine telegraph was switched to neutral. When the ship was under way, the sound grew softer and lower. He felt the chief purser's eyes upon him. "What now?" the look was asking, and at that moment he realized clearly that the responsibility rested with him. Though Wilhelm Kuhn was the senior officer on board, according to maritime rules only one person could call the first officer to account in such a situation, and in the absence of the captain, that was the second officer.

"Let's go up," Vandermark suggested. At the same moment a door opened above. Light streamed out, a figure became visible. Hesitantly Dr. Fischer came down the steps.

"What's happening up there?" Vandermark barred his way.

Fischer shook his head. "He's crazy—or else he's the only sane one among us. I don't know. He won't let anyone talk to him. I tried, but it's hopeless."

"Does he really mean to put out to sea?"

"He's taken it into his head. He's been hatching the plan for a long time, just waiting for an opportunity."

"You think some of the crew was in on it?"

"No, I don't. Kessler's too cautious for that."

"But he can't move the ship all by himself. He needs people to go along with him. Who is up there with him?"

"A couple who are on his side, a couple who are undecided, and a couple who are trying to make him listen to reason. He has managed to win over the chief engineer."

"Is he there?"

"No, in the engine room"

Vandermark turned to the ship's mate. "Gather a couple of reliable people. Don't do anything for the moment, but hold yourself in readiness near the engine room."

The mate shuffled his feet. "I can't go against the first officer's orders."

"What orders have you received?"

"None so far, sir."

"All right, then. Get your men together. And wait for Kessler's orders."

Vandermark nodded to Kuhn, and the two of them climbed the stairs. The revenue cutter's searchlight seemed to have found a penetrable spot in the fog. It slid across the dark glass front of the bridge. It was followed by the signals of a Morse lamp, but the wall of fog closed around the ship again at once, opaque and protective. The guard silently raised his hand to his cap when he recognized Vandermark and Kuhn and allowed them to pass. A jumble of voices came from the bridge. As Vandermark and Kuhn entered, the men fell silent.

Vandermark had expected brightness, but the room was in semidarkness. Only a single wall lamp and the engine telegraph with the illuminated dials and discs gave off light, so that Vandermark could not immediately recognize all the men. Kessler stood at the window on the spot usually occupied by Captain Pollak. And like Pollak, he too had placed his feet half on the red runner and half on the dark wood floor. It was this ridiculous, trivial detail that gave Vandermark the necessary composure. The men stepped away from each other, making room for him. Of the third officers, two were present, as were some of the engineers, some helmsmen, one mate—and then he saw Simoni, the wireless operator.

Vandermark stopped in front of him. "I've heard that you sent out a message. You're aware of Captain Pollak's orders?"

"Just a moment," Kessler intervened. "I decide what is allowed and what is forbidden. I give the orders here—do you understand, Vandermark?" He had not spoken loudly, but his voice held the sharpness of a wire strung too taut. "And now I must ask you to leave the bridge. I don't need you here."

Vandermark sensed the growing tension among the men. "No wireless traffic," he said. "That is Captain Pollak's order. I demand an explanation from you, Simoni."

The sparks looked at Kessler and back at Vandermark.

"I gave the order," Kessler said. "I take full responsibility." Vandermark did not expect what he said next. "Tell the second officer what he wants to know, Simoni. Go ahead."

Simoni pressed his arms close to his sides. "I had intercepted a wireless message," he began haltingly, "from a German ship a hundred miles out to sea." Simoni glanced at Kessler, but the first officer did not help him out. "I reported it to the first officer. . . . He ordered me to make contact." Simoni took a deep breath. "I called the first officer's attention to the ban—"

"That was not the question," Kessler cut in. "Stick to the facts, the content of the message."

"The message indicated that we would be protected from the English if we . . . if we were to try to get out of here."

"When was this?" Vandermark asked.

"Two hours ago."

"And you telegraphed a reply?"

"A coded message: 'Put out to sea at high tide, three o'clock.'" Again Simoni breathed deeply. "I again called the first officer's attention to the consequences—"

"Shut up," Kessler shouted, suddenly losing self-control. "Cowards! You're nothing but a bunch of cowards!" He took a step toward Simoni and shouted, "And now the other thing! Tell the second officer the other thing, Simoni."

The wireless operator looked at the message he held in his right hand, which Vandermark now noticed for the first time.

"Tell our second officer that not everyone is a coward!" Kessler barked. When Simoni remained silent, he tore the paper from his hand and held it triumphantly aloft. "Do you want to have to hide in shame from the *Kaiser Wilhelm der Grosse?* Why can't we do what they have done? We are at war. All this talk of passenger vessels! The *Kaiser Wilhelm der Grosse* was a passenger vessel as well, but when war broke out she became an auxiliary cruiser of the Imperial Navy. She has sunk three enemy ships while we here—"

"What about the *Kaiser Wilhelm?*" Vandermark interrupted.

Again Kessler waved the wireless message. "She lay outside Rio de Oro taking on coal. A British cruiser took her by surprise and ordered her to surrender. The commandant refused, and the battle lasted ninety minutes, until the *Kaiser Wilhelm* ran out of ammunition. But she did not surrender! She scuttled herself. She set us an example. She showed us where our place is. Not here, in cowardly concealment. We too have the duty—"

"The *Kaiser Wilhelm* scuttled herself?" It was Kuhn. His voice sounded hollow, aghast. "When did it happen?"

"A week ago," Simoni answered, "on August twenty-sixth. The news only came through today."

The men stood still, heads lowered. Gradually Vandermark was beginning to imagine what must have happened on board during the last few hours. With the help of this news, Kessler had tried to incite the crew, to soften them up for his plans. The *Kaiser Wilhelm* was more than a ship; she was a piece of German history—the first speed steamer with two screws. And the first ship that had won the Blue Riband for Germany and North German Lloyd—under Pollak's command. And now she had scuttled herself!

Until this moment the war had been an event occurring far away, on the other side of the Atlantic. The fact that they and the *Cecilie* were stuck here, in this secluded bay, really had nothing to do with it. A magic spell had brought them here, a spell held them fast. The war and Bar Harbor—they were two mutually exclusive things. But this piece of news suddenly made the war real and present.

Kessler returned to his spot by the window. He drew himself up, tried to make himself taller than he was. His feet once again straddled the red rug and the teak. "I don't believe there is anything more to discuss," he said in the voice of a man who was sure of himself. "We have already wasted too much time."

Vandermark let his eyes run over the men, and he knew that he could expect no help from them. "There is no order from Pollak," he said directing his words not only to Kessler but to the whole group. "And there is no order from the shipping company." He waited for a response, any sign of agreement. Where was Kuhn? Why didn't he say something? Why didn't he offer support?

"The shipping company is no longer in a position to give orders," Kessler responded. All vehemence had disappeared from his voice. He spoke softly and insistently. "We are at war, and that means that we are subject to the Imperial Navy. We will put out to sea at high tide. We will at least try. We must try. It is our duty, our only duty."

No one responded. No contradiction, no agreement. The men stood with lowered heads, as if paralyzed. The air in the room was spent.

"All in favor of our putting to sea raise their hands." Kessler had spoken without intonation, as if voicing a mere formality.

Again no one responded. Silence reigned on the bridge. Only one sound could be heard: the engines in the ship's interior. Suddenly a voice came from the background.

"Coffee, anyone?"

All heads turned, staring at the steward. Beside the bridge there was a small pantry. Had he calmly been making coffee there while the discussion went on in here? He was holding a large metal coffeepot, and there was the scent of real coffee. Only Pommerenke had served coffee on the bridge, never a steward.

"Coffee?" he repeated, not quite as unself-consciously as before.

A ripple ran through the group as Kuhn stepped forward and went toward the steward slowly, with weary movements. Nor did his face express anything but exhaustion. His eyes were barely visible behind the heavy lids. "Who gave the order to serve coffee here on the bridge?" His words were slow, formal.

"I thought—"

"Who? Who gave the order?" Kuhn's expression grew even more somber as he waited for an answer, even more melancholy. "Coffee! Don't you know, man, how scarce our coffee supply is? Didn't Captain Pollak issue orders that coffee is to be served only once a day, in the mess at breakfast?"

The men could not believe their ears. To think of the coffee supply at this moment was absurd. But the chief purser continued hesitantly, like a man who had to make an effort for each word. "I wrack my brains trying to figure out how to feed you all, how to put together a decent meal for six hundred and fifty men. I juggle and cheat in the books. . . . Coffee . . . the man makes coffee! Against the captain's express orders!" His lids lifted, and without transition, from one second to the next, the weariness seemed to fall from him. He took a step forward. "Who . . . who on this ship dares to act against the orders of Captain Pollak—who?" His voice trembled with anger, his whole body shook with rage. "Is it the general belief that his orders can be contravened because he is not on board? Do you think he would have tolerated all this nonsense for even a moment? Do you really believe that? This damned, harebrained nonsense, Kessler—do you think he would have listened to you for even a second? Put to sea . . . with his ship . . . with the *Cecilie!*" He turned back to the group. "I want the bridge cleared at once. Only the assigned watches will remain. . . . No, wait! Bosun Wolters! Go to the chart room. Take down the names of everyone present. Have each of them make a statement and sign it!"

"Take down names, statements, and sign," the mate repeated.

Kessler shot around to face Kuhn. It looked as if he wanted to attack him, but then he stopped in front of him. The men moved back, so that the space around the two became larger.

"What gives you the right. . . ." Kessler's protest sounded weak. "Captain Pollak transferred his authority to me during his absence. I bear the responsibility for the ship." He fell silent. Red patches mottled his face.

Kuhn stared at him, lids lowered again. "I would advise you to leave the bridge and return to your cabin. If you have a spark of honor, you won't show your face again on deck until Captain Pollak returns. You can draw up your own statement and hand it to Pollak. And one more thing—settle the matter with the chief engineer. Have them stop heating up the boilers and turn off the engines. . . . And you, steward! Pass the damned coffee around, as long as it's been made."

Suddenly the air on the bridge was filled with voices. The men surrounded the steward, perhaps because only in this way could they turn their backs on Kessler and distance themselves from him.

Whatever the reason, the first officer saw himself isolated. The die had been cast against him, and he knew it. He made an impotent gesture that took in the whole room—expressing in equal parts threat, resignation, contempt, and admission of defeat—and then he left the bridge. Vandermark followed, waiting until his figure disappeared down the stairs.

The four funnels of the *Cecilie* were still spewing out smoke, dark clouds of fumes visible only for moments when the searchlight of the revenue cutter swept past them. When Vandermark turned, the blackout curtains had already been removed from the bridge; the glass front glowed with bright light.

On the steps he met the chief purser. "Surely you'll take care of the rest," Kuhn said. His face was expressionless, his eyes sleepy. "The *Kaiser Wilhelm der Grosse* . . ." he mumbled, "scuttled. I wonder if Pollak has heard?" Before Vandermark could reply, Kuhn marched on, his hand seeking support from the railing.

Vandermark looked up at the bridge. The men had retired with Wolters to the chart room to make their statements. The large, bright area was deserted. Pollak's place at the glass front was empty, Kessler had disappeared. The responsibility for the ship rested with him now. Automatically he placed one foot in front of the other, automatically he told a mate, "Bring me a Morse lamp. No—" he corrected himself. "Get me the megaphone."

He waited, leaning against the bulwark. He felt the fog on his face, in his lungs dampness mixed with acrid smoke. On land the fog had a different taste. Had he really been on land as recently as an hour ago? Had he really sat at a table letting himself be waited on? Perhaps he was there still, perhaps he lay in bed dreaming. . . .

"The megaphone, sir."

Vandermark took hold of the metal funnel and raised it to his lips. He did not know how to begin, but the old skilled mechanism took over on its own. "Second officer of the *Cecilie* to the captain of the *Androscoggin*." He felt as if his words were drowned by the fog. He repeated the call and waited.

The searchlight of the revenue cutter began to move, wavering back and forth, cutting across the ship, and then the answer rang out of the fog.

"Captain of the *Androscoggin*. What's going on? Are you in trouble?"

"No trouble."

"What about your engines?" The voice came through the fog.

"We were checking the engines and the boilers. Purely routine."

"You're sure there's no more trouble?"

"Quite sure. The engine inspection is finished. We chose tonight so as not to molest anyone with our smoke."

"Did you inspect your telegraph installation?"

"Yes, but that was an error. The captain had left no orders to do so. . . . Can you settle it with him when he returns?"

"I'll settle it with him."

"End second officer of the *Cecilie* to the Captain of the *Androscoggin*."

"End."

The searchlight that had been beamed on him cut away. He returned to the bridge, took over the watch, and when Wolters had finished taking the statements, retired to the table in the chart room. A large sea chart of the North Atlantic showing the summer and winter routes of all passenger liners hung on the wall. Would the *Cecilie* ever return to the route, and they with her?

He could not put his thoughts in order. There was the night of July 31, when Pollak had called them to the bridge and informed them of his decision to turn back; there were the days that followed, the race with their pursuers, and then the morning when they put down their anchor in Frenchman Bay; there was a wardrobe where his clothes were kept, the voice of a woman on the telephone. . . .

The images and the times mingled, overlaid each other. There were faces—Kuhn, Pollak, Kessler—and then suddenly his father's face. Why was he remembering his father just now? A forgotten face, a forgotten voice that suddenly came to life: *Every real Vandermark left a piece of himself on a European battlefield.* Yes, that was his father, the last in a long line, endless generations of career officers. As a child he had had to listen to his father's tales from the family chronicle. Everywhere Vandermarks had taken part. They had not been absent from any campaign of the last three hundred years. The names of great rulers and generals were mentioned, the names of places where the Vandermarks had earned their medals and their wounds. The wounds were the most important part to his father. He had elaborated, all the while pacing back and forth in the library, his stiff artificial arm fastened to the pocket of his coat; it had been at Sedan that he lost his arm, and his tales always ended with a description of that day. And then the closing sentence: *I hope you too will one day have a chance to fight for the Fatherland.*

He thought about Kessler. He would have been a son to his father's liking. But himself? His glance fell on his hand, on the ring the Baroness had placed on it. Again a stream of images, of memories flooded him. It was like wandering through a foggy landscape. Reality intruded only occasionally; the steps of the ship's mate on the bridge, the flickering of the lamp when the current tripped, the silence that took over as the engines stopped.

Chapter 22

Vandermark was in his cabin when he heard the *Rockland's* whistle. The ferry was expected, but he had not counted on its being so punctual. It was easily docked, and he hurried with his packing. He was in his old cabin; he had never had any other in all his years on the *Cecilie*. It was not large, and he shared the bath with the ship's doctor. Pollak had given the officers permission to move into the empty luxury cabins of the first class, but Vandermark had not availed himself of the offer.

There was not much to pack. The seabag would not be full. After all, what could one need for the six days at sea the crossing would take?

The *Rockland* was the first ferry to arrive in Frenchman Bay for two and a half days. The fog had blanketed the inlet for sixty-two hours. For almost three days there had been no sky, no water, no land—nothing but impenetrable gray. Sometimes the only sign of life was the shadow of a fishing cutter or, once a day, the boat that brought mail and newspapers. The *Cecilie's* fog lamps had burned without letup. The shuttle service with Bar Harbor was curtailed.

As if by secret agreement, the crew forbore discussing the events of that night. A short announcement had appeared in the Bar Harbor *Record:*

A few fishermen, returning late last night, had the shock of a lifetime: the *Cecilie* emitting smoke from her four funnels. Jonas Googins of the *Mallebar* said he had believed that the German ship was about to steal away in the fog and darkness as silently as she had appeared on August 4. It turned out, however, according to the information supplied by Captain McCagg of the *Androscoggin,* that it was simply a matter of routine inspection of the *Cecilie*'s engines. Bar Harbor residents can breathe a sigh of relief, since the departure of the German vessel would doubtless have meant a painful loss.

The crew seemed to have adopted this version as their own; they spoke about the fog, about the drinking water which was gradually becoming exhausted, but not about Kessler.

On the evening of the third day after Pollak's departure the fog thinned. Today it had been rainy since morning, a steady drizzle trickling down in thin sheets outside the cabin's portholes. When he heard the two short signals of the *Rockland,* Vandermark interrupted his packing to open the porthole. The ferry was already engaged in docking. The boardwalk and the square in front of the steamboat station were solidly crowded with people. They stood closely ranked beneath their umbrellas. From a distance they appeared to form a black roof relieved by an occasional bright dot.

When the *Rockland* had made fast, the roof began to move; umbrellas shook, kerchiefs flickered, hands waved. Was the reception meant for Pollak, returning from Boston with the ferry? Vandermark went for his telescope, returned to the porthole, and rested his elbows on the broad ledge. The scene moved closer, the objects grew larger, more precise, and the people clearly recognizable—their expressions, their movements. And then he discovered the banner stretched between two wooden posts of the steamboat station, white writing on a green background:

WE WANT CHARLIE TO STAY

The lettering was already beginning to run in the rain. Could it be that the crowd down on the wharf was chorusing an echo of the words written on the banner? Yes, all the mouths moved as one: *We want Charlie to stay.*

Through his spyglass he could see the captain of the *Cecilie.* Charlie Pollak towered over the crowd by a head. Someone tried to hold an umbrella over him, but he waved the well-wisher away. Kuhn and McCagg were walking beside him; Pommerenke followed, his seabag slung over his shoulder, Pollak's little black valise in his hand.

Their progress was slow, hemmed in as they were by the crowd accompanying them along the way to the Yacht Club. Time and again they were stopped by someone who wished to have a word with Pollak, to shake his hand. The crowd pressed onto the pier, and the people went on standing there after the lifeboat had cast off.

Vandermark took the telescope from his eye and laid it aside. It was so unmistakably a demonstration for Pollak that it could only have been occasioned by the events of the last few days—the trial in Boston and the item in the Bar Harbor *Record.* Vandermark was reminded of Temperance C. Butler's check, but the welcome prepared for Pollak was without a doubt a much more emphatic proof of how much the residents of Bar Harbor wanted to hang on to "their" *Cecilie.*

He packed up the remainder of his belongings, gave a last look through closet and drawers, and pulled the string tight on the seabag. Softly the ship's noises reached his ears, indicating that the *Cecilie's* crew was intent on outdoing the people of Bar Harbor—everywhere running footsteps and slamming doors. He could visualize the men flocking together at the starboard railing to offer their captain a welcome. For a moment it was as if he could feel the ship listing slightly to starboard. He had to smile at himself. Not even six hundred men would make the *Cecilie* lose her balance. But perhaps, he went on fantasizing, it was the ship herself, the *Cecilie,* welcoming her captain in this way, with a gentle bow. . . .

He sat down on his bed, let his thoughts wander. In the last two days he had frequently fallen into this state. He could spend hours daydreaming, forgetting the world around him. He was startled when the door opened to admit Fischer, the ship's doctor.

"If that isn't typical of Pollak," Fischer said. "The *Rockland* is the first ferry to make it back here, and right on the minute of the timetable."

Vandermark rose and closed the porthole. The crowd on the Bar Harbor wharf had dispersed.

"Pollak is expecting the crew in the mess." The doctor gave a glance at the packed seabag. He showed no astonishment, and he asked no questions. Perhaps he had expected something of the sort. "Pollak has seen Kessler. As soon as he came on board, he headed for the first officer's cabin." Fischer smiled. "Nothing remains a secret from the stewards."

"Do you know what they talked about?" All this time Kessler had not show himself. He had received the chief engineer and two or three others; he had had his meals brought to him in the cabin, but he never left it.

"We'll find out from Pollak, I assume," Fischer said. "How about it? Aren't you coming? It's time."

"I have to speak to Pollak alone."

Fischer stopped once more in the doorway. "I'll see you?"

"Of course."

The mess was on the same deck as his cabin. Even if Vandermark was not attending the meeting, he was there in spirit. He saw it in his mind's eye—the crew crowding together, the lively discussion as the men waited, the silence that would set in when Pollak entered. Why wasn't he there? What was he afraid of? That someone would make him change his mind?

He left his cabin. Loud voices came from the mess. Had Pollak already finished with what he had to say? He did not like such assemblies and generally left them to his first officer or the chief purser; when he addressed them himself, he kept them short.

Vandermark was undecided. The men crowded out into the corridor. Their uniforms were wet through from the rain, and the woolen cloth gave off a strong odor. Over their heads Vandermark saw that the mess was smoke-filled. Meetings called by Kessler carried an absolute prohibition on smoking, but Pollak had always permitted it.

The first of the men were now leaving the mess. Someone bumped into him—Simoni. He mumbled an apology and stopped, unsure, bothered. Of all those who had been on the bridge that night, Simoni had perhaps looked forward to Pollak's return with the greatest anxiety. Each time he met Vandermark, he began to speak of the event, accused himself on account of the message that had been sent, and for making public the news about the *Kaiser Wilhelm der Grosse.* Vandermark had tried to reassure him but without success.

"He didn't say a word about it," the wireless operator now said. "Do you think he will report me? What is he going to do with me?"

"What happened, anyway?" From the bits of conversation among the other men Vandermark had gathered that they shared the wireless operator's amazement—Pollak had not mentioned the events of that night, had not said a word about the first officer.

"What did happen?" Vandermark repeated his question.

"I beg your pardon?" Simoni seemed totally preoccupied with his own problems.

"What did Pollak have to say?"

"He seemed in a good mood. A couple of jokes about the weather, a couple of unpleasant facts he would have to share. Lloyd is running out of steam. No income. As of immediately, wages will have to be cut. Twenty-five cents per head a day for the crew, a third of the previous salaries for the officers, including captains. Possible retroactive pay after the war. The amount of provisions for the ship will be cut. Fish three times a week—we're to catch it ourselves—and on Sundays visitors will be allowed on board for an entrance fee of one dollar."

"At least Kuhn will be pleased."

"I beg your pardon?"

Never mind. . . . And that's all? Nothing about the trial?"

"Yes, of course. Not a lot, a couple of snide remarks about lawyers and bankers—" Simoni stopped short. "A passenger brought suit? Did I understand correctly?"

"Yes."

"Well, the suit was rejected—it's finished, I mean. And about the seizure of the *Cecilie,* Lloyd's demurrer was granted. The suit goes on to the next court. All in all, everything stays as it was; the *Cecilie* remains at anchor outside Bar Harbor. . . . He's sure to put me on report, what do you think? Just between the two of us? Is he going to let me go? I've been with her from the start. From the start I've been the sparks on the *Cecilie.* Surely you can understand. You've been here from the start yourself, haven't you?"

"I think you're worrying about nothing, Simoni," Vandermark said. "You'll see. Pollak will settle the matter with McCagg in his own way. The two of them will take care of it over a bottle. You've known Pollak long enough. . . ."

They were pushed aside by men streaming out of the mess.

"Hey, fellows, what are you doing? Make way for us. I had enough shoving down at the dock. Move over, fellows, or all my gorgeous uniform buttons are gonna pop off, and Pommerenke hates sewing on buttons. Right, Tiger?" It was Pollak's good-natured voice, and it was himself, towering over the others by a head, with his walrus moustache and a new, shorter haircut.

The men retreated to the walls, leaving the way free for him. Simoni threw a fearful look at Vandermark. "He's going to—"

"Hello, Simoni." Pollak headed straight for the wireless operator, stopping in front of him. "Everything clear?" The sparks swallowed, searched for words, mumbled something indistinguishable. Pollak laid his hand on the man's shoulder. "Deuced right about the fog four days ago. Damned exact forecast that came in over the wireless. But don't tell a soul, Simoni, or my reputation as a weather prophet is down the drain."

"Yes, sir, Captain."

"And see to it that you conjure up some better weather for us." He turned to the men around him. "Is there anybody here who objects to better weather? You, Vandermark?"

"No, sir."

"Would have surprised me, in your case. Always a fair-weather guy, you were. Come along, Vandermark, I need you. . . . Move over, fellows, move over."

Vandermark followed Pollak and Pommerenke. On the one hand he was glad that Pollak had taken the initiative; on the other, Pollak was taking the wind out of his sails from the outset. He was capable of it; hadn't he just finished demonstrating his skill on Simoni?

No—he, Vandermark, would not let himself be deflected from the warpath he had assigned himself. He would simply inform Pollak of his decision, and that would be the end of it. No long explanations, no discussion. If you allowed yourself to get into an argument with Pollak, you always ended up the loser.

Shaking a few hands here, waving to a group of men there, Charlie Pollak walked through his ship. Arrived at his quarters, he handed Pommerenke his cap and his white gloves. There was no need for him to tell his tiger that he wished to be alone with Vandermark; Pommerenke decided all on his own that he had an urgent matter to discuss with the quartermaster.

"Sit down, Vandermark," Pollak said. "How about a drink? No? Too bad. You don't mind if I have a little something?" He fetched a bottle of coffee liqueur from the closet, along with a glass. He drank standing up, turning his back on Vandermark, and what his expression and demeanor did not reveal, his back showed: he was exhausted, tense, drained.

He must have sensed Vandermark's look. "Something wrong with me?" he asked as he turned around. "My hair? Is that it? I tell you, never go to a strange barber in a strange town. I thought I was doing God knows what to make myself look better, but I shall penitently return to Pommerenke's ministrations. He's found the trick of camouflaging my big ears a little." He sat down in the leather armchair and leaned forward, his hands on his thighs. "Now let's talk about you, Vandermark."

The cabin was dusky, the curtains half drawn, the atmosphere stale, as if no one had remembered to air it out during Pollak's absence. "You want to quit, am I right?"

Vandermark nodded. He was relieved that the truth was out and that Pollak had spoken the words.

"I thought something of the kind as soon as I realized you weren't at the steamboat landing. I thought to myself, That's not like my second officer; he cares too much about the formalities. You always had a soft spot for formalities. A good thing, formalities. . . . But I do understand. I mean, I can understand your wanting to quit. No further on the old tub, salaries reduced, and old Charlie ain't what he used to be either."

No discussion, Vandermark reminded himself sternly, no explanations. Now he knows, he says he understands, so let's not have a single superfluous word.

"Yes, sir," Vandermark said. "I wish to quit, entirely without formalities."

"Without formalities?" Pollak rose and stopped in front of Vandermark. "A heavy blow for a captain, losing his first officer and a second officer within an hour of each other. I'll have to digest that one." He went to the closet, poured out a second glass of coffee liqueur, and drank it down, shuddering as if it were bitter medicine.

He's trying to get at you through your emotions, Vandermark thought; he's trying to soften you up. Only then did he become conscious of what Pollak had said. "Kessler is quitting?" he asked.

"What? Oh, Kessler, yes." Pollak patted the breast pocket of his dark jacket. "I've got his request for separation from Lloyd's service right here." He smiled, and the smile suddenly made him look tired. "A stickler for the formalities, my first officer."

"You will recommend that it be accepted?"

"His resignation? No."

"But you said—"

"We came to a different agreement. The resignation would not have solved his problem. Quitting isn't the solution to everything, and especially not in his case. Kessler will leave the *Cecilie* tonight, and along with him the chief engineer and two crew members. They will try to make their way back to Germany. . . . No, it's not as quixotic as it sounds. They hope to find a neutral ship in New York, an Italian one that will take them to Genoa. I'll give them a week's head start, we agreed on that, and only then report the disappearance of the four men. I hope it solves his problem. Now, about you."

"I don't have a problem. I want to quit, that's all."

"Pollak went to the window. "It's sticky in here, isn't it? Not aired. The stewards get negligent if you don't keep after them." He pulled the curtains aside and pushed open the porthole, which was disguised to look like a window. The rain had stopped and the sky was clearing. The mahogany paneling of the cabin, which had looked black only a moment ago, took on its dull reddish glow again.

"Then about *my* problem," Pollak said, turning away from the window. "I need a new first officer." He spoke casually, as if he were merely thinking aloud. "Can you tell me where, given this situation, I am to find a new first officer?"

Vandermark looked at his hands. That was the trap. But he would not fall into it. "Are you offering the job to me?" he asked.

"I would recommend it, yes."

"And Lloyd generally follows your recommendations."

"Generally, yes."

Vandermark also stood up. "You don't need a first officer. Can you tell me why the ship needs a first officer? Or a second, or a ship's mate, the stokers, all the stewards? What for? That's my problem, if you want to know—that I feel highly superfluous on a ship that is stuck here forever. I've got to get out of here, Captain. I can't stand it any longer. I'm beginning to feel stifled. I can't sit around waiting for a miracle that never happens. Or do you think there will be a miracle?"

"In New York the mood is good. German victories in Belgium and France. The people at Lloyd seriously believe that it will all be over by late autumn and that then we'll go back on our route."

"And the lawsuit?"

"It could be settled. If necessary, they'll pay a million in damages; let's face it, it's the kind of situation any shipping firm is insured against."

"But do you believe it? I mean, that we'll get away from here before the year is out and be back on our regular course."

Pollak took his time before answering. Vandermark would have given a great deal to know Pollak's thoughts at this moment, his true thoughts, his true worries and fears. The calm he showed, the sense of humor—they were only the surface, only the tip of the iceberg.

"It's no longer a question of belief with me," Pollak said at last. "I simply have no other choice. Funny, I always knew that the *Cecilie* would be my last ship. Perhaps that's why I'm so attached to her and expect everyone else to feel the same way."

Vandermark was reminded of Edith Connors, and of the fact that three days earlier she had gone to Boston on the same ferry as Pollak. "You'd have every possible opportunity in this country." he said.

"My God, Vandermark, you're so young! Only a very young man could say something like that. I have only one opportunity, and that is the *Cecilie*. But as I said, I can't expect you to feel the same."

"Does that mean you'll let me go? You won't raise any objections?" Vandermark was honestly surprised, almost disappointed.

"No, no objections. I told you I understand."

Pollak had gone back to the window. The sky had cleared. The cloud layer was so thin that the sun was visible behind it. Vandermark had stepped to Pollak's side, and they looked out together. On the shore some passersby were strolling without umbrellas. The banner was gone.

"I have only one request," Pollak said.

"Yes, sir?"

"I'd like to preserve the formalities. I need your written request."

"Sir?"

The two men were speaking without looking at each other, their eyes directed on Bar Harbor.

"Bring me a written request. I'll forward it to New York, and then we'll have to wait and see what the decision is."

"And until then?"

"Yes, until then. . . . Until then you can deputize for the first officer. At your previous salary."

"Sir, I intend leaving the ship today."

"I see no way of giving my approval to such an action, much as I
would like to. Write your request, and then we'll see. It's a pure formality, I know, but the naval service is an awful stickler for forms. . . .
Are we agreed?"

The sun had finally managed to break through the clouds, a few
pale rays flitting over the water and making it glitter.

One of the *Cecilie*'s white lifeboats was on its way to Bar Harbor. Had Kuhn given the order? Pollak? And then Vandermark saw
that on the Village Green—after the three days of fog and the rain,
the grass had regained its color—a few workmen were erecting the
stand for the band concert. Tomorrow was Sunday, and Bar Harbor
seemed convinced that the steward's band of the *Cecilie* would be
performing again.

PART FOUR

Chapter 23

In previous years the horse show had been the culmination and conclusion of the season. Temperance C. Butler particularly liked to remember the last one, when she had taken three first prizes: best single span, best coachman, most handsome bridle. It had been a big day for her, and in addition she had bet on the winner in the mile-and-a-half race for three-year-olds.

Yes, in those days there had still been horse racing in Bar Harbor. The long oval track in Robin Hood Park at the foot of Newport Mountain was lying waste now, overgrown with weeds, and the grandstand was beginning to decay. The horse show had, at least for the present, been done away with. The Eden Fair remained to cap the season.

There too there were prizes to be won, and Temperance C. Butler was not only a member of the fair committee but was also among the regular prize winners. For the last five years she had collected first prize for the best homemade apple pie. There were prizes for everything and everyone at the Eden Fair—for the best bread baked in a woodstove, for the best honey, the best fruit of every sort, the most beautiful strains of flowers; and besides these, of course, there were prizes for many athletic contests—tug-of-war, sack races, egg-and-spoon races. . . . A genuine flood of prizes descended on the just and the unjust on the last Sunday of the fair, giving rise to tears and to joy, as well as starting enmities that occasionally lasted until the following year.

But the Eden Fair was threatened with the same fate that had befallen the horse show. The attraction diminished, the visitors stayed away. The celebrations on the Village Green had shown a melancholy decline for the last two years, the number of visitors so low that the take did not even cover expenses.

What a difference this year! The fair committee had received so many applications from exhibitors and stall holders that its members decided to move the fair out of town into Robin Hood Park. The old grandstand was transformed into a kind of music pavilion, with a platform for the bands and a large dance floor. The meadow at the center of the old racetrack was used to build an amusement park such as Bar Harbor had never seen. There was a large festival tent, merry-go-rounds, a hippodrome, shooting galleries, grab bags; and nestled among them were many smaller booths selling refreshments, balloons, and the typical souvenirs of Bar Harbor. Even the Baroness had made her way down from her mountain to hawk Indian jewelry under the shade of a blue awning.

Though it was only eleven o'clock on this Sunday morning, the fairgrounds were already doing capacity business, and the crowd along the booths was so thick that Temperance C. Butler reached for Pollak's arm to give her support. She leaned on him, smiling with the attractive helplessness that only those women possess who need no help at all.

"Well, did I promise you too much, Charlie? We owe all of it to you. Why are you making a face? Are you afraid that people will spend all their money here and not have enough left over to visit the *Cecilie?*"

"You seem to think of nothing but money."

"But look around you!" She gestured widely. "The stall holders are taking it in by the shovelful."

"You are the greediest person I know."

She laughed out loud. "Thank you. I take it as a compliment, coming from you. I *am* greedy. Greed is one of the strongest and purest emotions I know—and so good for one. Where do you think I get my excellent constitution? My sound heart? Greed, my friend. I am greedy for life, and that keeps me young. Whenever and wherever, I'd always get the first prize for greed."

She pulled him along, still laughing. Her carriage had called for him at the Rockaway Hotel and dragged him here, more or less against his will. As always, he had been ready with an excuse—he had an appointment at noon with McCagg—but she got around him by arguing that he could not possibly desert those of his crew members who were entered in the contests at the fair.

"And besides, Charlie, after the Eden Fair summer is over. You'll see. It's unique—not even once has our fair been rained out, but one or two days later it comes pouring down in sheets, and fall is here."

It was hard to imagine rain on a day like today. All of September had been beautiful as a dream. Even this first Sunday in October was like a summer day. Dust whirled up by the many vehicles hung over the winding, sandy road that led to Robin Hood Park. The woods on Newport Mountain boasted the colorful dress of Indian summer, but Temperance C. Butler knew that it would take only a single night of frost to destroy the entire array. Yes, it was almost time to leave Bar Harbor and return to Boston. But until that moment there were still a number of matters to be settled. . . .

They had come to a stop at one of the refreshment establishments, which practically consisted of nothing more than coarse wooden benches and tables in the open air. Here too it was crowded. The waiters could hardly keep up with serving and pouring, and Temperance Butler could not refrain from calling Pollak's attention to the purses they wore on their belts, filled to bursting.

"It's not that I'm really greedy," she said.

"I didn't mean it that way."

"It's crazy, I know, but I'm always jealous when I see people *taking in* money. I have plenty of money, I always have plenty of money, so it can't be that. But all of it is invested—I don't see it, I don't get to touch it. Nothing but those stupid, dull checks. But never cash. I dream of having a little store where on an evening, I can take the money from the register. I love cash registers! The little bell. The noise when they fly open. All the lovely compartments, blinking with coins. The paper money under the clamps. My love of traveling has something to do with it also. It's the best moment when, before leaving, I go to the bank and get the foreign notes, all new bills. At my bank in Boston they know that I won't accept anything but new money. . . . How many visitors did you have on the *Cecilie* yesterday?"

"I'd have to ask Kuhn."

"What's your estimate?"

"Two hundred. I really don't know."

"A dollar a head? You should raise the price."

"Kuhn did raise it, to the best of my knowledge, for the length of the Eden Fair."

"Kuhn is a good man. I hope he puts the gate aside without telling Lloyd all about it."

"It's all recorded in the books, if I know Kuhn."

"You're too honest. Charlie. It's your only fault. . . . Shall we dance?"

"Dance?"

"Please, Charlie. I'm dying to dance with you."

The dance floor was beneath the grandstand. Three bands had been hired to take turns for the duration of the fair, and at the moment *Cecilie's* stewards' band was doing its stint. The musicians had taken their places and were putting their music on the stands.

"What shall it be?" Pollak asked. "A waltz?"

"Of course a waltz." She made a sign to the steward who acted as bandleader. "You know what I like, don't you, Flocke?"

The fact that she remembered all the names and never confused them was one of the reasons Temperance C. Butler was so popular on board the *Cecilie*. The man sketched a bow. "Of course, Mrs. Butler. I know."

They returned to the middle of the floor. "He would never dare to open with anything but a waltz," she said. She waited for the music to begin. "Do you know this one?"

Pollak was not really in the mood for dancing, but he quickly forgot his feelings. The pleated skirt of her lavender dress swirled as she turned, her bracelets jingled, and she was light as a feather in his arms.

"Well, have you guessed? No? I'll tell you, because you'll never figure it out for yourself. It's the 'Cecilie Waltz.'"

"The 'Cecilie Waltz'? Who wrote it?"

"I'll give you three guesses. Well?"

"Strauss? Waldteufel? Leo Fall?"

"Three wrong guesses. But anyway, you've paid your tiger a big compliment. . . . Yes, you heard me right, the composer of the 'Cecilie Waltz' is Gottlieb Pommerenke."

"Gottlieb? His first name is Gottlieb? Can you imagine my forgetting that? To me he's simply Pommerenke. And he composed the waltz?"

"I gave him the commission, against an appropriate fee, of course. . . . It really is a joy to dance with you, Charlie! How about it, shall we show these young whippersnappers a thing or two? A waltz to the left?"

Her good mood had infected him, and while all the couples circled to the right, they danced in a counterclockwise direction. Nevertheless, Pollak was glad when the waltz ended and she said, "That's enough for a start. Come along, we've earned some refreshment."

The tables at the foot of the grandstand were all occupied, but for Mrs. Temperance C. Butler the headwaiter naturally had a table left, in the shade, under a green awning. The next moment two tall glasses filled with a green liquid were set down on the table.

Pollak's face expressed suspicion. "What is that?"

"Woodruff punch—nonalcoholic, of course. Not quite the thing for you, is it?"

"You know me too well."

She smiled at him. "Summer of ninety-seven. That was the first time I sailed with you. It was on the *Friedrich der Grosse,* and you were still first officer. Ever since, I've been loyal to you—seventeen years." She drank her punch through a straw. The rings on her fingers sparkled. "Those were wonderful years."

Pollak took off his cap and used his large white handkerchief to wipe his forehead and nape. His expression had grown serious, pensive.

"Problems?" she asked.

"Can you tell just by looking at me?" He shook his head. "They're always same problems as long as the *Cecilie* lies in Bar Harbor."

"It's been two months . . . yes, to the day. And what a summer it's been! You'll have to admit as much."

He nodded. "You'll be leaving Bar Harbor soon?"

"It's time for me. Boston is waiting. As I said, after the Eden Fair the season is over. That's how it's always been—the visitors leave, the hotels close. Beautiful as it is here in the summer, in the winter Bar Harbor is a very lonely place."

"I know—"

"Oh, yes, I almost forgot. Was it October?"

"'October, All Over.' You know it?"

"No."

"An old seamen's verse warning about the dangers of the North Atlantic. I don't remember where I heard it first. Mostly people think only about the icebergs that drift down on our course in the winter and spring, and they forget the storms that come up from the Caribbean in the summer."

"And how does the verse go?"

"'July, stand by, August, you must. September, remember, October, all over.' Everything is all over in October."

Temperance C. Butler was twisting the drinking straw between her fingers. "Some things seem to repeat themselves." Her glance went past Pollak out into the bay, only a blue strip of which could be seen.

"You mean Anne and Vandermark?" Pollak asked. "I had the impression that everything is all right there. In any case, it isn't the ship that's holding him."

"I'm worried, Charlie."

"You? Because of those two? Vandermark is very nice."

"You misunderstand me, Charlie. Of course Vandermark is very nice. I've got nothing against him. Quite the opposite. But it will all be over when we leave here . . . for him, I mean. October, all over."

"But he spends a lot of time with her, doesn't he?"

"Anne is in love with him. It may be that he thinks he loves her too. But I know better. I sounded him out—I tried to talk to him about money. He didn't rise to the bait. Or, if you like, he rose, all right—he became evasive. Well, if that isn't a sign. . . ."

Pollak looked at her. "The world is full of women who don't get the man they love. It's always been that way, and it will probably always be."

"Sadly, yes. But I don't want Anne to be one of them. She wants him, and I want her to have him. She is my granddaughter. She is a Butler, and the Butler women get what they want. Hasn't Vandermark ever talked to you about it?"

"No. We avoid each other since that time; I mean, he does. He avoids any conversation, and he never mentioned the matter again. He does his work punctiliously, but that's all."

"You offered him the post as first officer?"

"Yes. He's leaving it up in the air. And I am too; it's still better than a final no."

"You'd hate to lose him, wouldn't you?"

Pollak's expression became closed. "The ship needs a first officer, and he'd make a good one."

"I'd like to see him take the job before he resigns. I have something in mind, you know. You're aware that I know a lot of influential people in Boston, especially in shipping circles. And it makes a difference whether I present them with a second officer or a first officer of the *Cecilie.*"

This time Pollak could not help but smile. "You've planned it all very carefully, haven't you? In the future he is to be your first officer; that's what you have in mind. If it's any comfort to you, I won't stand in your way. After all . . ."

"After all?"

"A lot has changed in these two months, and especially in the last couple of weeks."

"You mean—the war?"

"Yes."

'We won't be traveling together next summer?"

"It doesn't look like it. Who knows if we'll ever be traveling again."

"I've never seen that side of you."

"I've never seen it myself."

"Homesick, Charlie?"

He shrugged his shoulders. He picked up his cap, twisted it in his hands, and put it on his head. His glass stood untouched.

"Woodruff punch without alcohol—that can't help but make you blue," she said. "Before I leave for Boston, I'll have them raid my cellar for you. I'm sure some good vintage champagnes are left."

"Don't let McCagg find out."

"Don't try to tell me that McCagg despises a good champagne. . . . By the way, what about the Captain's Dinner?"

"Captain's Dinner?"

"You owe me one from the last crossing. I don't care about the other passengers, but I want *my* Captain's Dinner before I leave Bar Harbor. You believe in the formalities, after all."

"You shall have your Captain's Dinner." After some initial reluctance, he began to like the idea. "Yes, you're right. We will put on a magnificent Captain's Dinner."

"Perhaps we can sail around the bay a little?"

"Not exactly, but it will be a dinner with all the trimmings, I promise you—printed invitations, everything *comme il faut.*"

"Promise?"

"Promise."

"Tell me, Charlie, can you still officiate at weddings on board?"

He was always prepared for her crazy ideas, but this time he was not certain whether her words might not hide a larger intention. "Well . . . I really don't know," he replied. "On the high seas, of course—but here? Why?"

"I was just wondering And because it's always impressed me—a captain who marries a couple, baptizes a child, consigns a body to the sea. Simply the fact that a captain is absolute master on his ship. If I'd been born a man, I don't think there would have been any other career for me." She rose. "I have obligations. I must attend my fair committee. At two o'clock we start giving out the prizes in the main tent, if you want to come."

"I don't know if I can stand it here that long."

"I'll be expecting you. If not, don't forget tonight, dinner at my house. An hour earlier than usual, at eight, so that we can be finished before the fireworks start."

He watched her walk away. Her manner of walking in itself distinguished her from all the other women. It was as if her feet always moved to a dance tune. She was a remarkable woman, no doubt about it. But to live with her . . . Why did women always have to go to extremes? Either they were not emotional enough or they were too much so; either they were entirely selfless or as egotistical as Temperance C. Butler. Strange that she, of all people, had seen through him. Seemingly casually she had asked, "Homesick, Charlie?"

Some boys on stilts walked by, presumably to enter one of the athletic contests. The image unlocked a memory: his son on his first stilts, homemade and so high that someone had to hold them for him while he climbed on. The boy had insisted on having them so high, to make him taller than his father. That was the most important part of it for him. For a while, whenever he waited for Pollak at the wharf in Bremerhaven when his father returned from a crossing, the boy was on his stilts.

Temperance C. Butler had hit the nail on the head—it was homesickness.

Chapter 24

"Heave-ho! Heave-ho! A win for the *Cecilie*! A win for the Germans! Heave-ho!" The audience's shouts of encouragement were directed, not at the team from the revenue cutter, but at the twelve men in the blue and white athletic suits with the Lloyd insignia sewn on the chest.

"Heave-ho! Heave-ho!" the first ship's mate of the *Cecilie* urged the crew. "Only one yard more!" The cable to which the twelve men clung was pulled tight to fraying. The red cloth tied at the center trembled, but it had stopped moving. The twelve men in red-and-white suits who clung to the other end of the cable, their heels dug into the dirt, their faces flushed, were gaining ground. For seconds the crowd fell silent, and the only sound was the labored breathing of twenty-four pairs of lungs.

"*Cecilie! Cecilie! Cecilie!*" The audience, concerned for the victory, resumed its shouts of encouragement. "Heave-ho! Heave-ho!" the ship's mate's voice exhorted.

The red-and-white team was hanging almost horizontally from the cable; the men had to change their grip, thus bringing about the final decision. The *Cecilie*'s team pulled, gained ground—inches to start with, then a foot, step by step—until there was no stopping them. What had cost them so much effort earlier now appeared effortless. The referee's shrill whistle ended the contest in the tug-of-war, and the announcement of the winners was drowned in the jubilation of the crowd: "The Germans won! The Germans won!"

"Your boys seem to be winning everything," said a voice behind Pollak, who was standing in the audience. It was the familiar voice of Captain McCagg, and Pollak came close to embracing him.

"Damned ambitious, your boys."

"You must excuse me," Pollak said. "I fully intended to be at the dock."

"But you preferred devoting yourself to the successes of your crew, is that it? I said to myself, I've got to get there right away to give my people at least some moral support. An unpatriotic crowd around here, don't you think? What's next?"

"I think the sack race."

They moved with the crowd to the next battle station. A section of the racetrack had been staked out with colored flags and ropes. A pile of sacks lay at the starting line, and three men from each team were getting ready.

"Have a good trip?" Pollak asked.

"I sure never would have dreamed that I'd ever go to Washington just because I'm thought to be a good friend of Captain Pollak of the *Cecilie.* . . . Damn! What did I tell you? Your boys have taken the lead again. Is that part of your maritime training? Sack races? Hey, you guys"—he turned to his own men, who were just about to slip into their sacks—"what's the matter with you? No morale? You represent the United States of America! Show those Germans!"

"What's up in Washington?" Pollak asked. "What did they want with you?"

"Hey, they really are ahead. Up and at 'em, guys! Show those Germans! . . . I felt terribly important—Captain McCagg of the *Androscoggin* in Washington. . . . Don't give up, guys. You're throwing the victory away. . . . Look at that, Charlie. Nothing but a lousy third place. What were you saying?"

"Washington," Pollak repeated. He sensed that he would have to keep pushing if he was to get McCagg to talk.

"Damned bureaucrats," McCagg grumbled. "Three days they kept me sitting around in outer offices. And rain all that time. Was the weather here like it is today while I was gone?"

"Invariably beautiful."

McCagg looked at the track. "They're losing the third heat too."

He turned to face Pollak, suddenly serious. "Why didn't you tell me about Kessler and the others?"

"Did I get you in trouble?"

"A little. Not enough to really matter to me. It's just that I didn't know what they were talking about when they brought it up."

"I should have told you. The first week I had to give the men a head start—that was our agreement—but after that I should have informed you. It was only that I heard nothing further from the four men, and I did not know how they made out. So they know about it in Washington?"

"You reported it to Lloyd?"

"After a week."

"Lloyd passed the information on to Washington. With the lawsuit pending, they didn't want any more trouble, and so. . . ."

"Did they know what became of the four of them?"

"It seems they really did manage to get an Italian ship. There are some similar cases."

"From other ships?"

"Yes, but they weren't so lucky. Three men were arrested on a train from Baltimore to New York; a couple in New York itself, at the harbor; and two, who went off in the opposite direction, in Milwaukee. Washington is expecting the number of cases to increase. Do you know how many crewmen from German ships are on Ellis Island today, waiting for action on their naturalization applications? Eighty."

"Out of thousands," Pollak replied dryly.

"The worm has turned, Charlie. Since the battle of the Marne there have been no more German advances. I believe less than ever in a short war."

Pollak forced himself to smile. "And you're surprised that my boys here intend to win everything?"

Nearby another contest had begun. The crowd surged in that direction, and the two men remained behind alone. From the fairground came the sound of voices, of the merry-go-round, the music, the barkers. A different band was playing on the bandstand.

"I could do with a drink." McCagg led the way to the refreshment stands. Colorful liquids sparkled in large pitchers.

"I can't recommend any of them," Pollak warned. "No liquor."

"We're a dry state. Didn't I tell you?"

"It's the one thing I didn't take into account when I picked Bar Harbor."

McCagg gestured to Pollak to follow him. The short, slender man used his elbows vigorously to clear a path through the crowd. They crossed the oval of the racetrack, and McCagg headed for the large parking lot at the edge of the woods. There were hundreds of cars and carriages, not only from Bar Harbor but also from the rest of Mount Desert Island, all of them covered with a thick layer of dust. The parking lot was fully exposed to the sun, and there was a smell of oil, of gasoline. The car for which McCagg headed stood in the last row near the edge of the woods, in the shade of a huge chestnut tree. The driver was asleep in the front seat, but McCagg woke him. "I won't be needing you for a while. Our team could do with some reinforcement. And it wouldn't hurt you to lose a couple of pounds."

Opening the back door after the man had gone off, he gestured invitingly. The roof of the large limousine was so high that even Pollak could sit upright. McCagg reached under the seat and brought out first a bottle and then two silver cups. "Best Jamaica rum, Charlie."

"And the long arm of the law?"

"Very short, on occasion."

The two men each emptied a cup. Only then did they take off their caps and lean back in the leather upholstery. They remained silent, downing a second and a third drink. McCagg sighed comfortably. "Filthy weather in Washington," he said. "If it weren't for this stuff here, I'd have come back with the granddaddy of all colds. It's gonna change here soon, too. Autumn and winter in Bar Harbor are a damned dreary time."

"I've been told that once today already."

"It's true. Once the autumn storms start, you get the same kind of waves here that you get on the Atlantic."

"Doesn't sound all bad to me."

"You can ask Roscoe Higgins, the harbor master. His people will be busy starting in October chasing the marker buoys torn loose by the storms."

"October, all over. . . ."

"What?"

"Just a seamen's verse." Pollak held out his silver cup. "I hope we don't have to be stingy with it."

"One bottle won't carry you far enough—an old sailor's saying. But seriously, ask Roscoe Higgins."

"On the other hand, the lobsters are better starting in October."

"Sixteen knots north wind, and the water temperature barely above freezing."

"Just right for lobster."

"If you don't have to empty the traps yourself. Damned unpleasant in icy water." McCagg cleared his throat. "The *Cecilie* isn't exactly built for ice. If Frenchman Bay freezes over—"

Pollak sipped thoughtfully. "What are you trying to tell me, McCagg? Are you seriously trying to make me believe that Frenchman Bay freezes over in the winter? Roscoe Higgins will be chasing buoys, but on skates."

"There's been known to be drift ice."

"So what? It won't hurt the *Cecilie*. Cheers."

"Cheers."

"What else happened in Washington? Tell me."

"They came to the conclusion—"

"They?"

"Our Navy Department. How shall I put it? . . . They want . . ."

Pollak did not rush him. He could easily put himself in McCagg's place. Besides, the rum was helping. Sitting with McCagg was helping. The homesickness was there, but this way it was easier to bear.

"They . . . the gentlemen of the navy . . . feel that the *Cecilie* would be safer someplace else."

"So?"

"Damn, how did I get stuck with this?"

"Perhaps because you can do it best."

"Well, then, there are a lot of reasons for all of it. For one thing, political reasons—the collapse of the German troops in Belgium, the growing political influence of the English. But other things are involved as well, especially you yourself."

A group of sailors from the *Cecilie* came wandering away from the fairgrounds. They were singing and swinging a prize cup, passing it from hand to hand. They headed for one of the cabs for hire, got in, and drove off, still singing.

"So I am the reason?" Pollak resumed the conversation.

"They don't trust you. The fact that you escaped the English once—somehow they're afraid that you'll pull off a similar miracle one day, only in the opposite direction. Fortunately they don't suspect what happened while you were in Boston. None of that leaked out. They just think, now that the long foggy days are approaching. . . . You're a fog artist. Admit it."

"I certainly wouldn't ever have tried at a time when they were expecting me to."

"Strictly between ourselves—are you going to try?"

"Not the slightest cause for worry. Don't forget the two English destroyers outside the three-mile zone."

"You checked it out for yourself while I was gone? I heard. Last week, a fishing party. All I thought was, He sure went dammed far out for a couple of fish." McCagg rubbed his bushy white hair. "To be honest, Charlie, I think it's possible that you'll try. When you come to think of it, it's only natural."

"Yes, it's natural. I've played around with the idea. Maybe more. That's why it was a major blow to me that Kessler tried at the wrong time. He spoiled everything. Now it's too late. You can reassure Washington completely on that point. And what other reasons are there?"

"Money. Always money. There are the bankers who'll worry about their money as long as the lawsuit isn't settled. And then—the *Cecilie* is a costly business for all concerned. It's costing us Americans money: one revenue cutter and one torpedo boat on constant guard. They figured it out for me down to the last penny. And Lloyd in New York doesn't think all that differently. The stay this far north increases maintenance costs considerably."

"The Navy Department and Lloyd are in touch with each other?"

"They got together in this matter, yes. Both of them would like to see the *Cecilie* lying in a harbor where the cost of maintaining the ship wouldn't be so high."

"And where would that be?"

"Cheers. A good, clear rum, isn't it? That would be Boston, Charlie."

"And where in Boston?"

"I'm glad you're not making it too hard for me. You know Shirley Point and Deer Island? There's one more beautiful place there in the outer harbor. The *Köln* and the *Ockenfels* can move apart a little, and you can have a snug berth between them. There are other German ships there. Your boys would have company. Boston has a lot of advantages. No icy winters. The girls are as nice there as they are here. . . ."

Pollak was thinking of something else while McCagg went on talking. When he had gone to Boston to testify, he went out to Deer Island. The day was sunny, the ships glittered like his own. And yet everything differed from Bar Harbor. The *Cecilie* in Frenchman Bay— that was a sight to make one think about her putting out to sea within the hour; one looked at the mast as if prepared to see the blue peter there—the blue flag with the white square at its center, the common signal for departure. In Boston, seeing the German liners, he had been forced to think of ships that, tied to the dock, were waiting for the wreckers, ships that would never put out to sea again. . . .

"Of course, it isn't Bar Harbor." He heard McCagg's voice at his side. "There are controls, barricades, and you would have to spend a few days in quarantine."

"I was there. I saw. I saw the ships, too. I spoke with the captains."

"Weren't they happy?"

"They didn't complain. You know, McCagg, sometimes at night, on the *Cecilie,* I wake up suddenly with the craziest feeling that the sparks is standing in the doorway with a telegram from New York: *Transferred, sail at once and take passengers on board.*" A thought brushed him, vague, still forming. "How can I get to Boston in my ship? The *Cecilie* isn't a canoe. With twenty thousand tons, I can't hug the shore. Sooner or later I have to go beyond the three-mile zone. And there goes your grand design."

"You will be given a guarantee from the Navy Department."

Pollak smiled. "They don't trust me, but I'm supposed to trust the English."

"The English will pull out for the period in question."

"Why?"

"They are not interested in turning you into martyrs to boot. The fact that a German captain and his ship are enjoying so much sympathy here is a thorn in the English side anyhow. Besides, two American destroyers will be keeping you company on your journey from Bar Harbor to Boston. The Department assumed the guarantee toward Lloyd."

"If both want it, why bother asking me?"

"You have a reputation for being self-willed. I was supposed to sound you out."

"Who knows about the plan?"

"Two or three men in the department in Washington, the naval attaché of the German embassy, and only the principal agent of Lloyd."

"Then let's leave it at that for the moment. I don't want any unrest among the crew. I'll think about it. I've got a few days, haven't I?"

"No deadline was set. I hope we can still share many a bottle."

"Reinforcements are on the way. A charitable contribution from the Yellow House. Good vintages."

"I hope they arrive soon, Charlie—there's one more thing. However you decide, I am the commander of the *Androscoggin* for only two weeks longer. . . ." He began to stutter. Perhaps he had drunk more than Pollak had. "Well . . . Christ, Charlie, I feel like a damned traitor. . . . They . . . they're giving me a ship again!"

"Yes," was all Pollak replied.

"Nothing grand. But it seems that we Americans are suddenly back in the freight business, as a neutral country. They're taking the oldest barges and the oldest captains out of mothballs."

"Congratulations. Who is she?"

"Not a she. Three thousand tired tons, rickety but not slow. Used to transport bananas. Was already written off. But a shipyard in Savannah put her back in service. Could be that come the first gust of wind, the tub will fall apart into its component parts, but I just couldn't resist going out on the Atlantic one more time. . . . I'm a bastard, telling you about it just now, the very moment when you . . . dammit, Charlie."

Another group of sailors passed close by. They could not see them, only heard them singing an old sailor's chanty: "Yo-ho-ho, and a bottle of rum."

Pollak reached for the bottle. "These cups are much too small." He put the bottle to his lips and waited for the sensation of warmth that normally ran through his body. But what he felt was only something hard in his chest. "Tell me, McCagg, how many hours will she run before she reaches Boston?"

"Fire her up enough, and she'll manage it between sunrise and sunset."

A different feeling engulfed Pollak, pushing aside the pain until only one thought remained: I will be standing on the bridge again, I will be standing on the bridge again!

Chapter 25

*H*e lay on his back and watched the eagles through half-closed eyes. There were four of them. The mother and father circled high in the sky, their wings spread wide, almost without flapping; somewhat closer to earth, not so serene, not so assured, as if the air might be full of holes, were the smaller birds with the lighter plumage. Ten days ago the fledglings had left the aerie for the first time; their excursions grew longer from day to day, and even now they vanished from his sight when the parents extended their circles and allowed the wind to carry them off.

"Anne?" He looked over his shoulder, but she was not there. The sun stood high in the sky, and the forest floor radiated warmth. He lay back down and closed his eyes, sleepy with the noonday heat, the scent of the woods, the soft, lulling sounds around him, their gentle monotony, impervious even to the signal whistle that sometimes shrilled in the distance. He could not feel his limbs, only a sweet, sluggish weightlessness to which he wholly gave himself over. Flying, circling—that was how he felt.

He must have fallen asleep, for when he opened his eyes, Anne was with him, leaning over him. The sun touched her hair, turning it even lighter, almost transparent. A pine twig was caught in the strands. She held out a small basket filled with blueberries. She said something, smiling with lips stained blue with berry juice.

Blueberry mouth—that was his only thought. He stretched out his arms and pulled her down to him. *Blueberry mouth.* He kissed her very softly, his lips closed. Her head came to rest on his shoulder. Seconds, minutes. Then she straightened up again. She sat near him on the ground, her yellow linen skirt spread over her crossed legs.

He raised his hand, laid a finger on her lips. "Blueberry mouth," he said. "That's what I'll call you from now on."

"Only when we're alone, I hope."

"It's nice when we're alone." He liked it when she looked at him from so close; she was a little nearsighted, and at those times her eyes took on an expression of hesitancy, of uncertainty.

"All the same, we have to hurry now," she said. "The awarding of the prizes. That's the most important part of the fair for Grandmother."

He reached out for her, but she shook her head. "One day," he said, "if we are alone for long enough, and if you don't remind me of your grandmother for long enough, I might forget myself and tell you that I love you."

Suddenly her back stiffened as she continued sitting on the ground. "Grandmother is deeply offended if we don't all participate. We'll be late as it is."

"Blueberry mouth . . . you're making a mistake." But he stood up. He gave her his hand and pulled her to her feet. She picked up the basket of berries, and they walked to the parked carriage.

"Where did you find the berries?" he asked.

"The woods are full of them; a sign that the summer is over."

They got into the carriage, and Anne picked up the reins. Once Vandermark had tried to drive, but the horse, used to Anne, had been difficult.

"Has it been decided yet when you go back to Boston?" he asked.

"Very soon."

"And school? Did you give up the idea altogether?"

She nodded. "I'm afraid I bit off too much. I always thought I was different from my friends, but it will happen that I'll do what they do—marry. Does that surprise you very much?"

"You said it yourself, they all do. It's normal."

"It's high time for someone in the Butler family to behave normally. One of the teachers at school always said, 'Act normally, that's crazy enough.'"

He did not reply, precisely because he sensed that she was waiting for a response. There had been many hints of the same nature. They had increased in the last few days, and he often imagined the conversations that took place in the Yellow House between Anne and her grandmother.

The road went downhill, and the horse ran swiftly. In the distance they heard the noise and the carousel music of the fair, and then the roof of the bandstand appeared through the trees. Anne drove the horse even harder, but by the time they reached the main tent, the prize giving was almost over.

The large tent was filled to the rafters, and everywhere along the wooden tables victories were being celebrated. Vandermark and Anne had difficulty making their way forward. The jury sat on a dais, Temperance C. Butler at the center with a little bell in front of her.

"Quiet! We must ask for quiet!" The speaker was one of the judges at her side. "Now we come to the prize for the best pastry. Quiet! May I ask the pastry chef of the S.S. *Kronprinzessin Cecilie* to come forward. . . . Quiet! Herr Karl Holzapfel. Please come forward."

The prize-winning creation was carried from behind the stage to the judges' table. In the meantime Vandermark and Anne had made their way to the dais and were able to see the work of art close up: a ship made out of icing, the hull covered in chocolate, the portholes marked by something silvery which was certainly as edible as the spun sugar rising from the four funnels. An unimaginable din broke out as a short man with thinning hair climbed up to the stage: clapping, stamping, whistling, cheering, all of which grew even louder when Karl Holzapfel raised his work up high and presented it to the audience. Temperance C. Butler waved her bell in vain, the band blared a fanfare in vain; the noise did not abate until, holding his certificate, the *Cecilie*'s pastry chef left the stage. A few of his coworkers were waiting at the foot of the steps and led Holzapfel away in a triumphal procession.

"He deserves it," Vandermark said. "He drove the whole galley crazy."

The bell rang once more. A new winner was called up and showered with ovations. Anne tucked her hand under Vandermark's arm. "There is nothing they won't give a prize for. I can't wait to find out what we won."

She was not kept in suspense long. The final prizes were handed out, someone made a closing speech, and then the jury rose. Temperance C. Butler was the first to leave the dais. Anne and Vandermark went to meet her, putting her between them.

"Let's get out of here," she said. "It's all too much for me. Let someone else do it next year. The heat. I need a sip of water. . . . You're certainly late enough."

The tent orderlies made room for them, screened them until they were outside. Temperance C. Butler hurried to the nearest refreshment stand and, like someone parched, whispered, "Water." She drank one glass and a second before her vitality returned. She mustered Anne and Vandermark with a mixture of benevolence and sternness. "Really, you were terribly late."

"What did we win?" Anne wanted to know.

"We? You mean, what did *I* win. . . . Jenkins? Where is Jenkins with the certificates? I hope he's keeping them safe. . . . All right, I'll tell you the first prizes I got. The new strain of sunflowers, the peaches, and the two white doves. Three first prizes, more wouldn't look good . . . I mean, if you're a member of the jury yourself."

"And Betty White's apple pie?"

"*My* apple pie, Anne. According to the bylaws, prizes are awarded only to property owners or taxpayers of Bar Harbor—with the exception we made this year for the crew members of the *Cecilie*."

"What about the apple pie?"

"The prize for the best apple pie of 1914 went to Mr. Foster."

"Who is Mr. Foster?"

"The chef at the Villa Far Niente."

"So the prize went to . . . Gloria Lindsay, according to the bylaws."

A silence ensued, and Vandermark felt the two women's eyes turned on him. He no longer spent his evenings at the Villa Far Niente, as they doubtless were aware. Did they also know that his telephone calls to the Plaza Hotel in New York had become less frequent as well? He wouldn't put it past Temperance C. Butler to be able to procure such information; it would not even be difficult for her, since the Western Union operator was a Higgins.

"Why are you looking at me that way?" he said. "I didn't bake the pie." Temperance C. Butler joined in his laughter.

Only Anne remained silent, and her expression said that she did not know what there was to laugh about. "You don't understand what this prize means to Grandmother. She's won it five times. Isn't that right? . . ." She turned to her grandmother. "You didn't by any chance cast your vote for Foster too?"

"But I did, my dear. Mrs. Lindsay deserves the prize. She assumed most of the cost for tonight's fireworks. A pretty little check arrived from her, for a pretty little sum. The fair committee agreed that she would have to be rewarded. Politics, my dear, diplomacy—it has nothing to do with emotions. And of course the prize had to be something important. The apple pie just happens to be very important." She paused. "You can win it back next year. It would be a fabulous entrance for Fred if his wife . . . oh, excuse me. I anticipate, and I meddle in things that are none of my business."

Anne and Vandermark said nothing, but Temperance C. Butler did not seem to be troubled by the embarrassment she had caused. She took Vandermark's arm. "You know about tonight? Dinner an hour earlier. I'll send Jenkins to the Rockaway at six thirty."

She had fallen into the habit of disposing of his time since he had begun to visit the Yellow House almost daily. "In my house there are firm rules, Fred, and I'm too old to change my ways." Thus, she decided when Jenkins was to call for him, how long his excursions with Anne were to last. He had his regular place at the dinner table, his armchair near the fireplace. And all was done with a gentle tyranny of which he generally became aware only after the fact.

"There's time enough if Jenkins comes at seven-thirty," Vandermark observed.

"Of course there would be time," she replied. "But I would enjoy talking to you alone for half an hour before the other guests arrive. I think there are some things we have to talk about, Fred, just the two of us."

Vandermark had something like a vision. The festively set table in the dining room of the Yellow House. He saw every detail—the candles, the glasses, the flowered china on silver plates, the place cards—and Temperance C. Butler at the head of the table, bedecked in jewelry. Now she raised her hand, rapped her ring against a glass, and her dark eyes looked at him across the table. "Ladies and gentlemen, it is my honor and my pleasure to announce to you. . . ."

"You'll have to excuse me now." He heard Temperance Butler's voice. "I still have some obligations. Are you coming with me, Anne?"

Anne did not look at her grandmother as she spoke. "I think there

are times when you are too straightforward. . . . We won't keep you
from your duties."

Temperance C. Butler opened her parasol and, displaying an
amused smile, walked away.

"I'm sorry," Anne said when her grandmother was out of earshot.
"She probably doesn't even notice how she pushes everyone around."

"I doubt that she does anything thoughtlessly."

"Sometimes she gets terribly on your nerves, doesn't she?"

"Lately she does."

"We're used to it; we live with it all the time. You have no idea
how much we look forward to her going away every summer. You have
to take her as she is."

"Do I have to?"

"Oh, come on. Let's not let her spoil our day. We haven't even
made the rounds of the fair. We haven't gone on any of the rides. You
haven't even won one flower for me at the shooting gallery. Please. I
want an armful of paper flowers from you. . . ."

She pulled him along to the lanes of booths. To the left and right
the calliopes of the merry-go-rounds blared. The children were in the
minority. Three-quarters of the horses, swans, and motorcycles were
occupied by sailors from the *Cecilie,* and most of them had their girl-
friends along. A different expression, of course, had taken root in the
sailors' vocabulary—*my fiancée from Bar Harbor.* However seriously
the girls might take it in every case, for the men it had another, less
weighty meaning; and at the thought Vandermark's mood brightened.

"Look who's here." Anne had discovered Dolly Higgins and the
Cecilie's chief purser. "They're having their picture taken. Look."

Willard Adams, Bar Harbor's photographer, had brought his
backdrop to the fair. To increase the semblance of authenticity, Adams
had had a piece of wharf wall put up in front of it. And on it sat the
couple, behind them the painted panorama of the bay with the ship.

"Smile! A little more cheerful!" The photographer's exhortation
from behind the monstrous camera could not have been meant for
Dolly Higgins, for she was beaming broadly. It was Kuhn who was
looking somewhat self-conscious and unhappy but finally bowed to
the demand.

After Adams had completed the procedure, Kuhn came up to
Vandermark. "Do you think it would be all right for me to ask the

photographer for the plate?" he asked, nervously rubbing his mustache. "Let her have her picture, but I don't want any mischief to be done with it. Now it's your turn, my man! No dodging it! To the wall with you."

Willard Adams, who knew precisely how to treat the men to whom he owed the small fortune he had made in a single summer, joined them. "It is an honor. And of course there's a special price for you. All the gentlemen from the *Cecilie* get my special rate. Please, over this way."

"Do I have to, Anne?"

"Please, Fred."

"Willard Adams is an artist in his field."

"No chickening out."

All three of them—Anne, Dolly Higgins, and Kuhn—were urging him, pushing him toward the backdrop. Curious bystanders crowded around, commenting.

"It won't take a minute," Adams assured them, but then he took ten minutes running back and forth between his subjects and the camera, and he still found more to be set right. "A little closer together. Your arm around the lady. Head slightly to the left." Finally he disappeared behind the box on top of the tripod and pulled the black cloth over his head. "And now, attention. Hold still. Smile. Yes, that's it, splendid . . . done."

The odor of magnesium hung in the air. Adams filled in a green order form, tore it off the pad. "You can have the picture tinted if you like. Large size, matted, the whole thing fifty cents."

He held the green slip out to Vandermark, but Anne was quicker and grabbed it. "I'll take care of it."

It was very difficult for him to keep his composure. Humiliated by a paltry fifty cents. Rarely a day passed now that he was not reminded how meager his check was. Jenkins was sent to the dock so that Vandermark would not have to pay for a hired cab; he was handed cigarettes; and whenever he brought Temperance C. Butler a few flowers or a box of candy, the word *spendthrift* was immediately used.

Actually he should have been pleased, for with his salary cut by a third, it was true that he could not make any large gestures. But this sort of care went against his grain. He had always lived for the day. As long as he had anything, fine; when there was nothing left, that was fine too. Now others were wondering whether he had fifty cents to pay a photographer.

The four of them had walked on. Anne and Dolly Higgins, arm in arm, went ahead to one of the shooting galleries; Vandermark and Kuhn followed.

"Have you seen Pollak?" Vandermark asked.

"What the two of you are up to, it's childish," Kuhn said, "to tell you straight out for once. Avoiding each other—childish. I can't understand Pollak, but you even less—turning down a third gold stripe."

"I must speak to Pollak."

"It's high time the two of you straightened things out. Childishness between two grown men! Perhaps I can give you a retroactive increase for the third stripe."

"Where can I find Pollak?"

"I think somebody said that he was with McCagg, and McCagg's car is in the parking lot. They're celebrating the fair in their own way. . . . God knows I could do with a drop. . . . What do you think, how many copies can be made from one plate? I don't want to end up hanging in Willard Adams's shopwindow on Main Street."

"What harm could it do," Vandermark asked, "since the two women look so much alike?"

"You're right about that."

They had arrived at the shooting gallery.

"Ten shots, ten cents, the barker called out, and when he noticed the officers, he held the guns out to them. "Half-price for the gentlemen from the *Cecilie.*"

Chapter 26

*Y*o-ho-ho, and a bottle of rum, a bottle of rum." It was the chanty that finally drew Vandermark's attention to the two men. McCagg's light voice carried the melody—Yo-ho-ho—while Pollak's bass droned along—A bottle of rum, a bottle of rum, rum, rum.

The two captains sat in the shade of the chestnut tree. They had spread out a car blanket and leaned comfortably against the tree's thick trunk. Their caps lay in the grass. The movement with which McCagg tried to hand the bottle to the captain of the *Cecilie* turned out to be somewhat too lavish. The hand circled like a rudderless ship while McCagg issued commands to it—starboard, half-speed ahead—and when he heard Vandermark's footsteps, he concealed the bottle behind his back.

"Halt!" His flashing eyes scrutinized Vandermark. "Remain . . . beyond the three-mile zone." His voice obeyed him better when he sang than when he spoke. "No one . . . enters the harbor . . . without my permission."

"You may give him permission to approach." Pollak's voice was steady, but when McCagg brought the bottle out again for Pollak, the latter's hand also missed its mark on his first attempt to grasp the object.

"Come, Vandermark, step closer. . . . What's going on? Are we still winning prizes?"

"It seems so, sir." Vandermark hesitated. The moment did not seem propitious for putting his request to Pollak. On the other hand, he suddenly felt something like envy for the two men sitting companionably together, drinking themselves into a stupor.

"You Huns," McCagg said. "You insist on winning it all, don't you? Don't leave anything for my boys. . . ." Blinking, he stared at Vandermark, seemingly recognizing him only now. "You're Pollak's new first officer, right?"

"Second officer, sir," Vandermark replied.

Pollak placed his arm around McCagg's shoulders. "Drop the subject. You've touched on a sore point. We don't wanna touch any sore points, not this wonderful day. Give him permission to put into port."

McCagg smiled. "You mean, let him transgress the laws? Is he a good law transgressor?"

"I think so."

"And can he sing? I need somebody who can sing."

"You could test him."

"All right, let's test him. Give him a drink to wet his whistle. I'll start . . . and you join in. Ready? His light voice took up the tune.

> *Three sailors set out to sea,*
> *They felt so good, they felt so free.*

Either he did not notice or he did not care that they did not join in his chanty. Vandermark sat down on the ground next to Pollak. Pollak held the bottle out to him. "A good, honest drop."

McCagg, eyes closed, leaned against the tree trunk and sang to himself.

> *The waves were high, the winds were strong.*
> *Three sailors sang their sailor's song.*

"When did McCagg get back?" Vandermark asked.

"Is that why you came?" Pollak pointed to the car. "Somewhere in there are some silver cups, on the back seat, if you don't want to drink from the bottle. Go on, take what you can get. I don't know how much more of it he has. How about it?"

Vandermark took the bottle. He drank, returned the bottle to Pollak. It made its way back to McCagg. Vandermark felt better. It was not just the liquor but also the presence of the two men, McCagg's song, Pollak's reddened face. The bottle returned to him; he took another swig. "I'm way behind you," he said.

"Try. Maybe you'll catch up, though it wouldn't be easy. . . . It's not so easy to catch up with two captains suffering from homesickness. . . ."

It was an astonishing confession from a man such as Pollak, plunging Vandermark into an embarrassed silence. He felt like an intruder. Now Pollak was humming along with the song "Three Sailors Set Out to Sea."

"Well, my boy?" he asked at last.

Vandermark hesitated before replying. "Can you assign me to duty tonight?"

Pollak lowered the bottle. "What was that? We have orders to set our course for the Yellow House. Highest-priority orders. Defiance to be punished with the galleys—at least." He passed on the bottle.

"Galleys seem appropriate to me, sir."

"Leave out the 'sir.' What was it, then? Ship duty? Not a hope, my boy. Our course reads: Yellow House."

"It's easy for you to laugh, sir."

"What's your reason, sailor?"

Vandermark took another swig. "There's a smell of engagement in the air, sir."

Abruptly Charlie Pollak was sitting bolt upright. It was the same posture he assumed when the evening at his captain's table had gone on too long. The more he drank, the more erect he sat, and when he eventually rose, he could walk away as straight as if he were toeing a line drawn on the ground. He turned his head and looked at Vandermark through slitted lids.

"Did I get it wrong? Wasn't that what you were after all the time? How else are you going to get the money? Did I take the wrong view of it? I thought, Look at that, three stripes aren't good enough for him; he wants the big money. Am I being too frank?"

"Not at all."

"And Anne? How far did it go? Did you make any promises? An officer of the *Cecilie* who makes false promises. . . ."

"Not so much as a word."

"Words aren't the only way." No matter how much Pollak might have drunk, his head was working clearly. "All right then, what's the matter? If I'm to cover for you, I have to know where I stand."

"There are no grounds . . . not for an engagement."

"What makes you think something of the sort is in the wind?"

McCagg broke off his song. "Hey, how about you guys? Why are you talking? We're singers now, not talkers." His hand energetically demanded the bottle. He held it up to the light and saw that it was empty. He laughed. "You're powerful law transgressors, you Huns." He supported himself on his elbows, got to his feet. For a moment he staggered, trying to get his balance. Finally he pulled his uniform jacket straight, and his torso came to rest. "I will retire for consultation."

He disappeared among the trees. They could hear him mumbling to himself as he passed water. When he returned, he planted himself before them. "The court has found that not enough laws have yet been transgressed." He went to the car slowly, step by step, his arms stretched out at his sides as if he were tightrope walking. They heard him poke around, then silence, then the sound of a cork being pulled out of a bottle.

"McCagg has every reason to celebrate," Pollak commented. "He's being given a ship, I mean command over a real ship."

"He's leaving us?"

"Yes, the poker game is breaking up. Too bad. But a ship is a ship, isn't that so, Vandermark? They'd suit you well, three stripes. . . . No, no, I don't want to blackmail you; the last thing I'd do is exploit such a situation. It's your decision alone. . . . Is the old lady behind it? Temperance Butler? An unusual woman. Not easy living with her, but I bet she has great plans for you. Just so you don't regret it later, Vandermark. Truly an unusual woman. You know what she asked me, just today? Actually asked me if I could still legally perform marriages on board."

"Will you assign me to duty?"

McCagg had returned. His coat was open, his collar had disappeared, and his tie dangled loosely across the white shirtfront. He showed them the full bottle, put it to his mouth, drank, and passed it on to Pollak.

"I'm curious who's gonna win this race. I tell you, I'm not all that easy to beat. I shall defend the honor of the American revenue service just as long as I can." He resumed his seat by the tree trunk.

Vandermark looked at Pollak. "Is it really a contest, sir?"

"You mean, by tonight my steering mechanism won't be in work-ing order? Don't worry, my boy. I shall arrive at the Yellow House by a straight course, and I'll stick my neck out for you. You do realize that Temperance Butler will see through the business about duty on board?" He placed his hand on Vandermark's arm. "You are herewith assigned the duty, Second Officer. Not exactly gentlemanly, what you're doing; but to be honest, I like it better than if you were only after the money. I'll stick my neck out. . . . You are assigned to duty. But don't you dare leave the ship this evening."

"Of course not, sir."

"And you'll have to provide me with a substitute. You may just be able to get away with blowing the engagement sky-high, but to play havoc with Temperance C. Butler's seating plan, that's going too far."

"Thank you, sir. Perhaps one of the other officers can take my place. How about Mankiewitz?"

Pollak raised his hand and pointed at the parking lot. "How about that one? Hey, Kuhn! Over here! We're over here."

The *Cecilie*'s chief purser stopped, searching for the source of the voice. Then he discovered the group of three and came trotting on the double. When he saw the shape the two captains were in, he heaved a sigh of relief, took off his cap, and mopped the perspiration from his face with a handkerchief. "One hell of a hot day," he said. "One hell of a crowd. Nice little place you've got here."

"You're a godsend." Pollak grinned. "You'll have to step into the breach, Kuhn."

"I'll have to what?" Kuhn's glance went from one to the other, coming to rest on the bottle that happened to be in McCagg's hand.

"Give the sailor a swig," Pollak said.

"Another Hun," McCagg replied. "A damned invasion of Huns. Does he know how to sing? Hey, sailor, can you sing?" He passed the bottle to Kuhn.

Kuhn sat down next to Vandermark. He drank slowly and with pleasure. It seemed that he would have liked to keep the bottle for himself; in any case he was slow to respond when Pollak put out his hand.

"There I stood like a fool with the two girls." He addressed Vandermark. "You promised to come right back." He laughed. "I suspected something of the sort. A man needs to be with other men now and then, right? I took to my heels as well." He put out his hand for the bottle, but he had to wait before it returned to him. "What did Pollak want with me? What breach am I supposed to step into?"

"Later," Pollak said. "I'll explain it to you later. And now, McCagg, let's have your song!"

McCagg ran his fingers through his white hair and began "Three sailors—" He stopped abruptly, looked at the others, and began to count, pointing at each one. "One, two, three, four. There are four of us." He started a second time.

> *Four sailors set out to sea.*
> *They felt so good, they felt so free.*

He made a sign to the others to join in, and four throats sang freely.

> *The waves were high, the winds were strong,*
> *Four sailors sang their sailor's song.*

Chapter 27

*A*t this hour Bar Harbor was like a ghost town. The fair had drawn everyone to Robin Hood Park, and even the visitors who had arrived by the noon ferry were driven to the fairgrounds at once. It was the perfect hour for a man who loved his voluntary solitude. And that was why Harry Gumm had set out for the harbor.

Everyone in Bar Harbor knew Harry Gumm, but people rarely saw him. A real-estate broker, he bought and sold houses; but he left his own habitation only when it was absolutely unavoidable. You went to see Harry Gumm where he lived if you wanted to buy or sell. It had to be a most unusual deal to make him abandon this principle.

In spite of the time of day and the hot weather, he was dressed in navy blue. Only the top button of the gray silk vest was visible; the gray pearl in his tie was hidden by a fold of cloth. Harry Gumm cared about soberness in a profession that had a reputation for being flighty. Once, on one of the rare occasions when he had attended a public event, he was mistaken for the Spanish ambassador. If his father had lived to see the day—Fernando Gomez, who had swept the wharves in the harbor of Cadiz. . . .

Harry Gumm walked at a leisurely pace but made straight for his goal: the harbor on West Street, where the private yachts had their slips. A friend from Great Head had called him when the yacht appeared there, and so it had been simple for Harry to calculate when it would arrive in Bar Harbor. As he watched, the *Nirvana*, its motors throttled, was just putting into harbor.

Harry Gumm watched the yacht with approval though also with the necessary seriousness, which seemed to him all the more appropriate as he missed the familiar surroundings of his office in the Hotel Saint Sauveur—three rooms where nothing alluded to his profession, for they were at the same time his living quarters. Yes, Harry Gumm lived in a hotel—the proper setting, he felt, for a confirmed bachelor. The ladies of Bar Harbor had tried their utmost to break down his resistance; and although he had now reached sixty, they were still trying.

The yacht's motors fell silent. Sailors busied themselves with her hawsers. Harry Gumm's glance traveled across the yacht until he discovered the woman, or at least the broad-brimmed hat, behind a cabin window. It had been worthwhile to take the walk. He was pleasantly excited.

Harry Gumm preferred doing business with women to dealing with men. In a way it was more complicated, more boring, to work with women, especially widows. But he had also made his best deals with women, and he never forgot that it had been a female client who assured his monopolistic position in Bar Harbor. It had been thirty years ago, when he had sold an entire peninsula for a hundred thousand dollars—one hundred thousand!—and a part of it had been his own property.

To be sure, such a deal came along only once in a lifetime. Those days were gone for good. There was barely any land left that had not been cultivated, and everything was solidly owned. Now the real business was in houses. They too were solidly held, but the owners changed, died, moved away, and new ones came looking for a place to live. He knew almost all the properties, or at least all those worthy of a Harry Gumm, and therefore he hardly needed to get out of his office. Some of the houses had gone through his hands more than once.

The time for musing was over. Gloria Lindsay had appeared on deck. A salmon-pink ribbon fluttered from her straw hat. Harry Gumm did not care much for yachts—after all, they were not what he sold— nor did he have an eye for women, but that the one on deck was one of the most beautiful women he had ever seen—he was well aware of that. He went to meet her as the gangway was put down. He walked slowly, with dignity, his expression serious. Nothing escaped him. Was

Gloria Lindsay traveling without luggage? The man who followed her carried only a small bag. Was that all? She had sent him a cable signifying that she wished the sale of the Villa Far Niente to go forward as expeditiously as possible; she could not stay in Bar Harbor for more than two, at most three, days. The lack of luggage confirmed the statement. Or was more to follow? Something was concealed under a large tarpaulin on the yacht's foredeck. Had Gloria Lindsay brought along an automobile?

"Did you have a pleasant journey?" He bowed to her.

"It's always a very long trip. How nice of you to have taken the trouble. What's the situation?"

"Good, good." He looked at her searchingly, suddenly somewhat worried. It was precisely the ones who were in such a hurry, who put such straight questions, who seemed so impatient, who sometimes had a sudden change of heart. And Harry Gumm had to admit to himself that this transaction meant more to him than any other deal in recent years. When Gloria Lindsay's cable had come to his desk, he had been quite unable to believe it at first. The Villa Far Niente for sale! A house that had never gone through his hands. Not even when the property was acquired had he functioned as the agent. At the time, John Lindsay had bought it directly from Temperance C. Butler—a fact that had been a thorn in his side all these years.

"Do you have a buyer?"

"Oh, yes. I think I have the right one. Besides myself, no one knows?"

"Of course not. The only thing I care about is that the matter be settled quickly and smoothly."

"You can depend on Harry Gumm."

"And you know I want to sell it as is. Fully furnished."

"Your cable was extremely clear. You did not give me much time, but I haven't been idle. There are two seriously interested parties. . . ." He realized that her attention was being distracted. A car came along the shore road, filled to bursting with sailors from the *Cecilie*. They were brandishing something, and their voices were raised in song.

"Many people at the fair?" Gloria Lindsay asked.

"I wouldn't go out there if you paid me. An anthill. There must be thousands."

"I believe we have discussed everything?"

Harry Gumm was disappointed. He had counted on her asking

him to come to the Villa Far Niente with her. "If you really want a quick sale, it would be good to straighten out a few other points."

"Can't I leave it all to you?"

Harry Gumm's expression grew even more grave. It was one thing that he never had to advertise in the newspapers, that his memory was enough, his connections—or at least his client file, locked in his safe; but he still attached great importance to having his work recognized.

"A house such as the Villa Far Niente does not come on the market every day, and it doesn't suit just anyone. There is, for example, the question of the staff."

"The staff? Brice will go with me, as will Foster, the cook; perhaps even Googins if I can succeed in prying him loose from Bar Harbor. But otherwise I would have thought that the new owner could take on the staff."

"You see, that already lets out one of my interested parties, Mr. Amory from Chicago. I tracked him down by telephone through half the country until I found that he'd gone fishing in Canada. I caught up with him there. But Mr. Amory insists on bringing in his own staff."

"But the people know the ins and outs of the house. The gardener, for example—"

"Mr. Amory would not have left much of the garden standing. He needs three holes for golfing at his doorstep; to practice, that's all."

"But you had another party."

"Someone from Bangor."

"From Bangor?"

"Don't worry. There's a lot of new money in Bangor, no worse than old money. Virginia Bradley. She owned a house in Bar Harbor once before, Alpine Cottage. I sold it for her at the time. She thought she would like Newport better. Now she is returning, a penitent."

"She is seriously interested?"

"She knows the Far Niente. She would have been happy to close the sale right then and there, over the telephone. I had invited Mr. Amory to come here tomorrow, and Virginia Bradley the following day, but I can change the arrangements. And as to Virginia Bradley's solvency"—he loved such words—"I have a letter of credit from her bank. We can have all the legal details settled in three days."

Harry Gumm was displeased with himself; he had laid down all his trumps at once instead of skillfully prolonging the conversation.

But how could he when Gloria Lindsay was so inattentive? She listened with just half an ear; her glance kept wandering to the sailors from the *Cecilie,* who had gotten into a white lifeboat and were putting out.

Of course Harry Gumm had wondered why the Villa Far Niente came on the market so suddenly. He knew that since the death of her husband Gloria Lindsay rarely came to Bar Harbor. For eleven months out of the year the house stood practically empty, but other people allowed themselves the same lavishness. Why, then? Could there be a kernel of truth in the rumor of an unhappy love affair with an officer from the *Cecilie?* It would only confirm his theory—and the theory of his old friend Sol Butler—that love affairs can end only in a mess.

Gloria Lindsay was still staring after the boat, although it was no more than a white dot on the blue surface of the water.

"I hope you won't change your mind." Harry Gumm had an unerring instinct for the moment when the tone between himself and a client could afford to become more personal, but now he was uncertain whether he might not be rushing things.

"Does that happen sometimes?"

"Now and then."

"Especially with women?"

"I didn't mean that. It's fifty-fifty."

She stood before him, cool and reserved; and now, when he had stopped expecting it, she smiled. "In business matters I'm extremely reliable, quite without emotions."

"Oh, anything to do with a house always involves the emotions." He laid his hand on his heart. "For me, in any case. Do you intend buying something in another ocean resort? Closer to Baltimore? I might be able to be of help to you."

"Watch out." She took his arm and pulled him a few steps to the side. "Take care."

Above them in the air, held by four ropes, dangled an automobile, a brand-new sedan, its body a brilliant blue, the roof silver. The crane from which it was suspended veered to the right. Two men ran to the wharf and took possession of the car, which was gently lowered.

Harry Gumm knew that the garage of the Far Niente already held two cars. And now Gloria Lindsay was bringing still a third, though she intended staying no more than three days. His suspicion was aroused again, but his broker's sense told him, She really wants to sell. Not at any price, but sell all the same.

The car was now on firm ground. The ropes were loosened, Gloria Lindsay's traveling bag was stowed in the trunk, and one of the men cranked up the engine. The motor caught at once. Gloria Lindsay shook hands with Harry Gumm. "Until tomorrow, then. Around what time? You'll be along, won't you?"

"I can bring Virginia Bradley to your house at ten o'clock."

"How about eleven?"

"Fine, eleven o'clock." Harry Gumm hesitated. "One more thing. I don't know if you ever looked at the title. Your husband bought the property from Temperance C. Butler, and in case of a subsequent sale, she assured herself of the first option."

"Gloria Lindsay touched her hat, as if to make sure that the wind would not carry it off. "She cannot be seriously interested."

"I don't believe she is. Nevertheless, she should be informed. I'll be happy to see to the matter." Yes, he thought, only too happy. "It's a pure formality." He knew that it was time to end the conversation.

"Very good," Gloria Lindsay said. "Do whatever you think proper. Until tomorrow, then. And thank you again for coming."

She walked off; at every step her legs moved visibly under her narrow skirt. As she got into the car, the red silk lining glowed bright in the side slit of her skirt. The devout Catholic in Harry Gumm was outraged at her shamelessness, but the man himself found the sight very stimulating.

The car drove off, and Harry Gumm left the dock. He had grown warm in the sun; to this was added the inner heat caused by this major deal and all that went with it. He imagined Virginia Bradley's reaction when she learned that she could look over the Villa Far Niente as early as tomorrow; of course he would not tell her straight out that his other potential buyer had quit the field—quite the contrary. Then he started rehearsing the telephone conversation with Temperance C. Butler. . . .

He started on the way back, slowly, with dignity. The boardwalk was more crowded now. In front of the Rockaway Hotel the first visitors were gathering for the trip to the *Cecilie,* which was scheduled for three o'clock. Harry Gumm was drawn back to his office, and yet he stopped and looked out into the bay to the German ship.

He was not one to have a sentimental affinity with the ocean and with ships. He was dedicated to the land, to houses solidly rooted in the soil. Ships were an uncertain, incalculable matter, like women. Nevertheless, as he looked at the sea monster, something like gratitude gripped him. His business had been very quiet in recent years—and "quiet" was putting it mildly. Prices of houses had gone down, and even at the lower prices no one wanted them. Since the German ship had cast anchor in Frenchman Bay, the tide had turned. Suddenly Bar Harbor had become fashionable again, and during the last six weeks he had done more business than in the whole previous year.

Harry Gumm was a forward-looking man, and he wondered what would happen should the *Cecilie* disappear some day. Would Bar Harbor become a sleeping beauty once more?

As he stood at the shore, his imagination began to work. He transformed the ship into a house. He turned her into a floating hotel. A crazy idea? All it took was to find the right people for such a project. . . . How much might such a ship cost? He sighed. He could no longer imagine the bay without the *Cecilie*.

Chapter 28

S he held the reins loosely, leaving it to the horse to set his own pace. She was in no hurry to arrive at the Yellow House. She would be unable to conceal her mood from either her grandmother or Edith Connors. Beside her, on the black leather seat of the buggy, lay the bunch of paper flowers he had won for her at the shooting gallery; but what should have been the memory of a happy day filled her with sadness. And the basket of blueberries at her feet made matters worse, not better.

She had expected so much from this day! But hadn't yesterday been the same, and the day before? Always she had waited—for what? For a miracle? Now, in any case, she was driving home alone with a bunch of brightly colored paper flowers that only reminded her how eager he had suddenly been to get away. He had to talk to Pollak! On a day like today he left her. And then, on the pretext of looking for Vandermark, Kuhn had also gone off and not returned, and she had been left standing with a Dolly Higgins who had tears in her eyes. . . .

Blueberry mouth—wasn't it her own fault? Why had she insisted that they go to the prize giving? In the woods, in the clearing, alone with him, it had been very different. *Blueberry mouth* . . . he had embraced her, kissed her. Her head had rested on his shoulder. . . . She had wanted to stay. . . . Why in the world had she had to play at being the dutiful granddaughter? She did not understand herself. She had acted like someone who doesn't know what she wants. She had done everything wrong. And the blame rested with her grandmother. Her everlasting good advice, her tutelage—they hemmed her in, made her unsure of herself. . . .

She was so deeply lost in thought that she did not hear the car coming up behind her. Only when the reins flew out of her hands and the horse galloped on its own did she become aware of the tooting horn. She had difficulty regaining control over her horse. Finally she brought the buggy to a standstill at the side of the road. Once again the horn behind her tooted, and then the car speeded up to overtake her. The silver roof glittered in the sunlight. Through the narrow rear window she saw a broad-brimmed woman's hat with a salmon-pink ribbon.

Seconds passed before she understood. Only one woman wore such a hat—Gloria Lindsay.

It came too unexpectedly. During the first few days following Gloria's departure, Anne never lost her fear that she would suddenly return. After a week Anne began to feel more secure. When she opened her window at night and looked across at the garden of the Villa Far Niente, where no red dress emerged, and no white uniform; when she saw the closed shutters in its west wing; then she was filled with triumph, the triumph of a woman who has driven another from the ring. Only one shadow remained—his telephone calls from the Western Union office to New York; according to information given to her grandmother, they grew increasingly rare. In exchange, Gloria Lindsay's name turned up with increasing frequency in the society columns of the New York newspapers; a fashion show, which she attended in the company of X; Y, with whom she had danced the night away on the Amsterdam Roof. . . . Vandermark had to put up with many a sarcastic remark, not only from Temperance C. Butler, but also from Anne, who began to enjoy the game.

Now Gloria was back, and Anne thought she understood. He had known. That was why he had been so strange, so different today. He had only been looking for an excuse. She tore the whip from its mounting and was about to beat the horse—something she had never yet done—when she saw that the sedan with the silver roof and the bright blue body had stopped near the fork in the road. The rear door opened, and Gloria Lindsay got out.

Anne had no choice but to stop as well. But she made no move to get down from her seat, keeping the reins between her fingers. For a moment it was not clear whether Gloria Lindsay would take the first step, speak the first word, and as long as the moment lasted, Anne clung to a thought that she had relied on in recent weeks to put down any doubts: she, Anne, was nineteen, and Gloria Lindsay was thirty-six, an aging woman who was attractive only because of her skillfully created appearance, her makeup, her striking hats and dresses. But as Gloria Lindsay came up to the buggy, the image collapsed. The woman standing before Anne was a beauty, a genuine beauty. Next to her Anne felt ugly, her hair badly dressed, her clothes out of fashion. Involuntarily she pushed her feet under the seat, and if she could have, she would have hidden her hands as well, so coarse did they seem to her.

"I didn't recognize you at first," Gloria Lindsay said, "nor did my driver. I'm sorry that we frightened your horse. Are you all right?"

"Yes."

"You were at the fair?" Gloria's eyes went to the paper flowers lying on the seat next to Anne.

Anne nodded. "And you? You just arrived?"

"Yes, I'm coming directly from the yacht. Very crowded at the fair, I've heard."

"They just had the prize giving. You won too."

"Me, a prize?"

"Your cook, for his apple pie." Anne was extremely proud of being able to carry on a normal conversation in a voice that, in her opinion, also sounded quite normal. "Officially, of course, the prize went to you," she continued. "The bylaws of the fair committee . . ." She smiled knowingly. "Your check for the fireworks found its mark. Did you return because of the fireworks?"

"Of course. As long as I've paid, I want to see how they go about burning my money. Nice to see you. Give your grandmother my best. She is still here, isn't she?"

"It was a long summer this year."

Once again Gloria's eyes strayed to the paper flowers. "You fortunate child. I always dreamed that someday someone would win a bunch of paper flowers for me at a shooting gallery. . . ." She raised her hand. "Good-bye."

Anne waited until Gloria Lindsay had returned to the car and the sedan had driven off. She looked at her hands; they lay in her lap, very still, and yet she felt that they were trembling. Automatically she took up the reins, automatically she steered the buggy. Her head was empty, her whole self was empty, a hollow space that gradually filled with pain.

She had chosen the back entrance, through the kitchen; she could always say that she had intended giving Betty White the blueberries. When she came into the hall, she heard her grandmother's voice. She was standing at the telephone, a wall instrument; it was the only one in the house—Temperance C. Butler considered extensions unnecessary. Anne, holding the paper flowers, made for the stairs, but her grandmother signaled to her to stay. She quickly concluded the conversation. "Anyway, thanks a lot, Harry. . . . Yes. . . . Perhaps I'll talk to her myself. . . . No, not the apple pie. Five times in a row is enough."

She gestured Anne to her side. Her raised eyebrows indicated the paper flowers. "Anyone who manufactures that sort of thing deserves to be drawn and quartered. Imitating nature in a criminal manner. Surely you don't intend keeping these hideous things for your old age."

"At least they won't wilt."

"I beg your pardon?"

Suddenly Anne could no longer control herself. "She came back. Can you believe it? *She* came back."

"First give me those." She took the flowers from Anne and rang for White, who appeared at once. "See that these are taken to Miss Anne's room. And then please bring some tea."

"Now?"

"Yes, we'll have tea earlier today. Everything is topsy-turvy as it is. How did Betty take the business about the apple pie?"

"Quite composed, outwardly," White said. "But I know it's eating away at her. She's looking to take the blame, and she thinks maybe she used the wrong variety of apples."

"God forbid. You know what it was. Explain it to her. I only hope tonight's dinner won't be made to suffer. You can always tell from the food when Betty is upset, I think. Now tea, please. . . ."

She led the way into the library. She took her seat and motioned Anne to sit down. "How do you know she's back?"

"I met her just now."

Temperance C. Butler gave Anne a long and searching look. "I do hope you said or did nothing rash."

"I wish I had. God knows, I wish I'd attacked her and scratched her eyes out."

"There are better ways, Anne, not quite so crude."

"I would have enjoyed the crude way."

"Let's not argue about it. I assume, then, that you comported yourself in a manner proper to an Anne Butler."

"Just as you taught me."

"Did she say anything about the house?"

"Which house?"

White entered with the tea tray. When they were alone again, Temperance C. Butler said, "She is selling the Villa Far Niente! To Virginia Bradley! I am spared absolutely nothing! Her pug dogs will be yelping all day long in the grounds. How can a person stand so much ugliness day in, day out? Herbert Bradley was no Adonis, by God, but compared to the pugs he was a raving beauty."

"She's selling Far Niente?" Anne was so confused that she could not tell whether this was good or bad news.

"Harry Gumm, that old thief, offered the property to me."

"You don't seriously intend—"

"No, of course not. He simply wanted to use me as competition to Virginia Bradley, to drive up the price."

"Why is she selling?"

The two women's eyes met, two allies who had no secrets from each other. "I'm not really sure," Temperance C. Butler said. "She said nothing to you? No? It can mean any one of a number of things. I'll find out soon enough." A gleam entered her dark eyes. "We will invite Gloria Lindsay to dinner tonight. Yes, that seems a good idea. . . . Of course, that will make thirteen at table; enough to give White a few more gray hairs."

"You want to invite Gloria Lindsay? Here?"

"*She* is the thirteenth, my child."

"I don't want to see her! Together with him! What can you be thinking of? Invite her, by all means, but I won't be sitting at the table. I don't understand you at all."

"I didn't expect you to. But perhaps you'll listen to me. You're dreaming. You're dreaming that life is wonderful, summer without end. The more you cling to the dream, the sooner you'll have to wake up. It's sad, but that's the way life is."

"I don't like what you're saying. I don't believe that it's like that."

"You may not like it, but it's the truth. Try to understand. Life with a man one loves is harder than with a man one doesn't love. It sounds paradoxical, but that's how it is. I know what I'm talking about. I've gone through it myself."

"What does that have to do with Gloria Lindsay, and particularly with . . . him?"

"Very simple. There will be many more occasions in your life when you will have to be pleasant to women whom you can't stand. Why not begin tonight?"

"Do you really believe that she would accept your invitation and come?"

"I most certainly think so—if she knows that he will be here. Let's not underestimate her. She is a person who goes into the lion's den."

"I'm not so sure . . . but if you think . . ."

"Look, Anne . . ." Her grandmother's voice was gentle and sweet. "It's better for you to realize that Fred—that you will have a husband whom other women like. There will always be some swarming around him."

Anne looked up. "He's older than I am. In ten years . . ."

Temperance C. Butler smiled. "Now you're talking like a Butler. But in this instance your arithmetic is wrong. Even in ten years, even when he's white-haired, it will be no different for him. Men like him never lose it. It's better that you be prepared. There is a method to fight it—you have to be on good terms with your rivals. . . . Yes, love is a complicated business."

Anne sat still, her hands folded in her lap, her eyes lowered. She was the picture of attention; she was in fact trying to listen, but her grandmother was using a language she could not understand, did not wish to understand. If that was love, then she did not want ever to love another human being.

Temperance C. Butler reached for Anne's hand. "I know how you feel, believe me. I was young once too. . . . More tea?"

Anne rose. As a child, she had always curtsied to her grandmother when she came and left. It was a custom that meant a great deal to Temperance C. Butler, and sometimes, when Anne felt that her grandmother was treating her like a child, she still curtsied—a good way of telling her grandmother that she was going too far in her tutelage. But the curtsy she sketched now had a different meaning. It was like a visor she was dropping.

"May I go now?" she asked like a well-brought-up child.

Her grandmother nodded. "Of course, my dear. And you'll see—you will get him."

Anne walked to the door with the short steps of a child. She stopped once more.

"Please place her so that I don't have to be looking at her all the time." She was still walking slowly as she crossed the hall, but once on the stairs, she began to run.

The first object to meet her eyes as she entered her room was the bunch of paper flowers lying on top of her bed. She threw herself across them and cried. A long summer—and oh, how short.

Chapter 29

"Our roses never stayed in bloom this long before." Brice pointed to the espalier next to the front door. "Incredible, this summer. . . . Are you sure you wouldn't like me to bring you a parasol?"

"Thank you, Brice, my hat will do." Gloria Lindsay tied the bow of her straw hat tight under her chin. "Something else?"

"Dinner?" the butler asked. "If you're expecting company . . . the staff would like to see the fireworks tonight. If dinner could be served an hour earlier. . . ."

"When do the fireworks begin?"

"They're scheduled for nine o'clock."

"I'm not expecting anyone."

"I thought . . ." The butler began to speak, then mumbled an excuse.

Gloria Lindsay was still busying herself with tying the bow. "Nothing fancy. You can give the staff the evening off." She was not even certain that she would spend the night in the house. She could go back to the yacht at any time. Perhaps that would be better than spending her last nights here alone.

"Something will be prepared for you, of course," Brice said.

"Thank you. I'd like to spend some time in the garden. Afterward we can go over the monthly accounts."

She was relieved to be alone at last. Since her arrival Brice had not quit her side. He had always found something else to report, and she had even been made to admire the fruits Foster had preserved—several hundred jars, separated into varieties and supplied with labels, filling the shelves of the cellar. She had patiently played at being mistress of the Villa Far Niente and postponed telling Brice that she was about to sell the house. Later, when they were going over the accounts together, she would certainly tell him.

In the garden, too, the roses were still in flower. Everywhere there was the glow of red. But here and there piles of fir branches had been readied to cover the beds for the winter. The little pond and the artificial brook were drained, and some of the stone and bronze figures in the Japanese garden had already been covered with wooden slats.

I should have spared myself the sight, she thought. She had been determined never to return to Bar Harbor. Harry Gumm could have sold the house even without her presence; all it required was her power of attorney. But the question of the staff was not so easily solved. And she had to decide which personal effects should be moved from the house to Baltimore.

She had intended to begin at once, and she had made a start in her bedroom. But when she opened the closet in his room and saw the dinner jacket and his other belongings hanging there, she abandoned the project.

That was why she had left the house and gone to the garden. But here too everything reminded her of him. She had walked with him along every one of these paths. There, on a bench by the teahouse, they had sat the first night. No—it was a good thing that she was selling Far Niente. She must get free of memories that could only hurt.

She turned around, retraced her steps. It would only take an hour to make a list of everything she wanted to take with her to Baltimore. The sooner she put all of it behind her, the better. In four days she could be back in New York, or in Baltimore, or perhaps in Palm Springs. . . . Anyplace was better than Bar Harbor.

The new car was parked on the graveled turnaround in front of the garage. Googins had raised the hood and was lost in contemplation of the motor. He was enthusiastic about the model, and he looked up at her and nodded approvingly. The telephone was ringing in the house. One of the windows of the hall was open, and the sound rang out across the yard. Gloria stopped, listened to the ringing, almost frightened. She had secretly been waiting for it, and she had been afraid. In New York, her telephone conversations with him had been torture. Afterward she had only felt more unhappy.

The instrument was still ringing. Then the ringing stopped. She was not certain whether the caller had given up or whether someone had picked up the receiver. She opened the front door and stepped into the hall.

Brice was standing by the telephone in the alcove with the stained-glass windows. When he caught sight of her, he put down the earpiece and went toward her. "For you. . . . Your neighbor. I'll transfer the call to the library."

"It's all right, I'll take it here." His disappointed face had betrayed to her at once that it could not be Vandermark. She picked up the earpiece and the receiver and announced herself. "Gloria Lindsay speaking."

"My dear! This is Temperance Butler. I hope I'm not disturbing you. It's only—to make it brief, Harry Gumm called me. What a surprise!"

Gloria looked around, but Brice had already retired. "It had to happen sometime."

"I understand. Such a huge house. And you've spent so little time here recently. . . . You're sure I'm not disturbing you?"

Gloria Lindsay made no great effort to pretend cordiality but asked quite dryly, "You're not interested in the Villa Far Niente?"

A laugh interrupted her. "Good old Harry. He's taking his revenge. No, I'm not interested. At my age one stops buying houses. Your deal will go off smoothly. That's not why I'm calling. I wanted to invite you to dinner."

"I—"

"Don't say no right away. Only a few good friends. Charlie Pollak of course, and—"

"I only just arrived. And I'm not staying long."

"All the more reason for coming to dinner. It will be our last chance, as it were, to see each other. We are leaving in a few days as well."

Something or other had been distracting Gloria all this time. First it was the noises penetrating into the hall from outside through the open window; now the front door opened and closed, and steps came across the stone floor of the hall. A mirror hung before her eyes, and when she looked in it again, she encountered another pair of eyes. . . .

"Hello, are you still there?" The voice came from the earpiece, which she had lowered. She put it back to her ear and tried to avoid the mirror.

"How about it, can I count on you?"

He was standing behind her now. She sensed his presence without seeing him. He leaned down toward her, and then his lips touched the nape of her neck.

"Or are you expecting guests yourself?"

She held the earpiece so that he too could hear the voice. In the mirror she saw that he shook his head and laid his index finger across his lips.

"No," she said. "As I told you, I only just got here myself. And tomorrow morning Harry Gumm is bringing the first client by. You'll forgive me. . . ."

His hands were on the ribbons that held her straw hat. Carefully he loosened them, lifting the hat from her head. She shook her hair loose, and he smiled at her in the mirror.

"Perhaps you'll change your mind. . . ." Temperance C. Butler clung to her objective tenaciously. "We will be eating at eight, because of the fireworks."

"I don't believe I'll be able to manage it."

"Too bad, really. I'm so very sorry. . . . But I'm sure one of my guests will be even sorrier."

"You mean Charlie Pollak?"

"You know exactly who I mean. It will be a big disappointment to him when I have to tell him that you couldn't come. Well? Do you really want to do that to him?"

"Not willingly," Gloria Lindsay said. "I'll think about it."

"You see. . . . I'll have them set a place for you, just in case. And do forgive this informal invasion by telephone."

Gloria Lindsay lowered the telephone. He took it from her hand and replaced it. She turned around, hesitant, suddenly worried that she was imagining the whole episode. "Hold me," she said. "Hold me very tight." He took her in his arms, and she said, "She actually got me to the point where I half promised her. She saved her trump card to the last, because she knew that if you were there, I would come. . . . Hold me. Tighter. Only this moment."

He held her close in his arms and said, "She made you a false promise. I will not be at the Yellow House for dinner tonight."

"But she said—"

"Kuhn will be taking my place. It was decided before I knew that you had returned, before I saw the yacht." Abruptly he whirled her through the hall until, breathless, she stopped him.

"Tell me . . . have you been drinking?"

"Enough to be terribly intoxicated. I've had a cold shower, and I drank a whole pot of coffee. I thought I'd sobered up when I came here, but now . . . I don't know, perhaps now it's something else."

The swinging door that led to the housekeeping wing sprang open, and Brice came storming in. "Mr. Vandermark!" He came to a stop. "Excuse me. . . ." He bowed, embarrassed and beaming at the same time. "Excuse me." He retreated again.

"You disappointed him terribly," she said. "Him and Foster."

"I know." A motion of his head indicated the large hall. "I couldn't. I could not sit in this house alone. It seemed too large even with you. And . . ." He paused. "I couldn't come to New York, either. I could not follow you. I could say that it had to do with the *Cecilie,* with Pollak, with some of the things that happened . . . every excuse I used on the telephone. But I couldn't because it would have looked like—"

"Capitulation?"

"The word isn't quite right, but basically, yes, like capitulation."

"And you believe it's easier for a woman?"

"I asked myself, did you have to go to New York?"

"Yes, I had to."

"Because of me?"

"No. Because of myself, because of my—terrible word—self-esteem. And especially so that I could come back to capitulate."

They stood facing each other. All casualness had disappeared. Gloria noticed an expression of seriousness in his face that she had never seen before. And yet she thought, It has been too easy. She did not believe in gains that came easily; nothing had ever been handed her on a silver platter, though it might have looked that way from the outside.

"If it's because of me that you're not going to the Yellow House—"

"I told you, the matter was already settled."

"If she finds out that you were here—and she will find out—then I don't know what she'll do. In any case, she won't like it."

"No, but she'll have to accept it."

She was reluctant, but she had to speak. "And Anne? You would think that New York is far enough away. But there are so many good friends who telephone."

"Forget it. It's not important."

"Then you'll stay here tonight?"

"I can't. I—"

"I understand." So it had been too easy after all. She had suspected as much.

"I must return to the *Cecilie* for duty. I promised Pollak. I'm not allowed to leave the ship."

"Oh. Can I . . . did I tell you that I'm selling the house?"

"The Villa Far Niente?"

"The whole kit and caboodle, just as it stands. I already feel that it no longer belongs to me." A smile was gradually spreading across her features, still thoughtful but at the same time tender. "Couldn't you take me with you? Couldn't you smuggle me on board?"

"It wouldn't be the first time," he said.

"I'll pack a few things."

"Let's leave right away." He reached for her hat on the table by the telephone. "You don't need anything else. If I'm to smuggle you on board, you'll have to do as I say."

"I'm sure you have a great deal of experience."

"All sailors have that kind of experience."

He had had his hired cab wait outside, but she pointed to the blue-and-silver sedan. Googins had still not finished his inspection.

"A beauty," Googins said. "The car's a real beauty, all right." Hopefully he added, "You're going driving? May I drive you?"

"Sorry, Googins, we're going alone. Tomorrow you can try it out."

"Not until tomorrow?"

"Mr. Vandermark will do the driving today."

"I'll explain it all to you, sir." Googins opened the door. "You'd best get behind the wheel right away; then you have all the buttons and knobs right in front of you. . . ."

There was no stopping Googins; he would always think of something more.

When they were finally under way, Vandermark asked, "A new car? Why a new car?"

"I meant it for you."

"For me?"

"Let me explain. It's the silliest idea I ever had, and I hope you'll forgive me. I wanted to give it to you—for revenge, for jealousy, call it what you will. It was to be my wedding present to you and Anne Butler, and the note that was to go with it has been ready in my head for a long time. 'Dear Fred Vandermark, in memory of some lovely hours, this little gift for you, so that you may be spared having to ask your young wife immediately after the wedding for money to acquire a suitable vehicle' . . . and I thought up something so mean."

"And you think I'll accept the car?"

"It would be a fitting punishment for me. It was sinfully expensive."

"I'll think it over," he said. "Perhaps I'll come up with a better punishment yet."

Chapter 30

The first rockets burst over the bay, and for seconds the cabin was bright as noon.

She released herself from his embrace. "The fireworks."

He reached for her, pulled her back. He was in a strange mood of elation; the long, hot day, the liquor, all the coffee, their reunion—his body and his head were setting off their own fireworks.

"Don't you want to look?" she asked.

"I want to look at you."

"You'll have plenty of time to look at me." The loud bursts and crackles of the exploding fireworks came through the open porthole. Sometimes the noise seemed far away, and then again as close as if the rockets were being released from the *Cecilie.* Darkness and light alternated in the cabin; the reflection tinted the walls—red, yellow, green, blue.

He held her close, but she turned her head toward the open porthole. "They're *my* fireworks. They're blowing up my money—and I don't get anything out of it."

"But I'm getting something out of it. Don't be so self-centered."

"What do you get out of it?"

He looked at her, at her face, her naked body, her skin changing with the changing colors. "I never slept with so many women at one time before . . . with silvery ones, red ones, green ones, purple ones."

Her head sank back; for a moment she lay motionless. Then it was she who pressed herself against him, seeking him, inciting him, urging him on, letting him spend himself. . . .

"Which one," she said softly, close to his ear, when it was over, "which of them was it this time?"

"I think the purple one."

She sat up, leaning over him. Her loosened hair changed color. She began to kiss him. Her hands roamed his body. "You don't know all of them yet. . . ."

He pulled her hands toward him. "I think now I'd like to look at the fireworks."

She slid from the bed and ran through the cabin to the porthole. He watched her for a while, then he rose, picked up his dressing gown, and draped it over her shoulders. Across the bay the rockets soared, sizzling balls of fire suddenly transformed against the sky into bright fountains of light, into wheels of sunshine, into trees of stars.

"I'll have to leave you briefly," he explained. "Not for long."

"Why now?"

"I'm on duty." He began to dress. "It will take me half an hour, no longer, my inspection tour."

"Tonight?"

"I had to work on Pollak for a long time before he would assign me to duty. Now I can't just—"

"All right, no need for you to apologize. There should never have to be apologies between us. I'll wait for you."

As he left, she was still standing at the porthole looking out. The festival fireworks were over, but more rockets were rising into the sky; some came from private yachts, and many more from the hills behind Bar Harbor. By the time Vandermark stepped out on the upper deck, these stragglers too had disappeared. The air smelled of magnesium and sulfur. A few charred fireworks had fallen onto the *Cecilie*'s deck. He checked the men of the fire watch he had assigned. He climbed up to the bridge, received the report of the watch officer. In the mess the victors of the Eden Fair were being given a celebration.

Wilhelm Kuhn and Captain Pollak had left the ship at seven thirty in order to arrive at the Yellow House in time for dinner. It was strange to walk through the ship, to have the responsibility, and to know that she was waiting for him. He was very sure of his feelings, for the first time in his life. At the same time he imagined being the *Cecilie*'s first officer. The third gold strip . . . it was not ambition. His ties with the ship were of a different sort. Loyalty, gratitude. The years on the *Cecilie* had been happy ones. And finally Gloria—this was where he had met her. . . .

His rounds had taken longer than half an hour. He announced his return by knocking before he entered the cabin. The little lamp next to the bed was lit, and a large serving cart draped in white linen, with candles and glasses, offered a complete dinner such as was served to first-class passengers.

"May I invite you to dinner?" She was wearing one of his pajamas, with the cuffs of the overlong sleeves turned up. He went to the table, took the bottle from the ice bucket, looked at the label. "I'm famished," she said. "I haven't eaten since noon."

He sat down at the foot of the bed. "How did you manage it?"

She spread the napkin on her lap and helped herself to venison in pastry; she poured a little Cumberland sauce over it and broke off a chunk of white bread. "I rang for the steward."

"Impossible." He pointed to the wine label. "On the whole ship there isn't another bottle of Chateau Leoville. Not even for Captain Pollak."

"Perhaps he just doesn't like it. Aren't you hungry?"

He rose, fetched a chair, and sat down across from her. She held out her empty wineglass. He poured. "You rang, and the steward came, and. . . ."

She laughed. "If I haven't learned by now how to get along with stewards!" She waited until his glass was filled as well. They clinked glasses. Her loose hair, the pajamas that were too large for her—she looked very, very young.

"Goldie," he said. "Little Goldie Frohman."

She smiled. "That was when I learned how to get along with stewards. When we traveled first class, meals were included. But by the end sometimes we had enough only for second or third class, and they don't include meals." She took a sip. "You know, in first class, on the promenade deck, the stewards go back and forth all day with their serving tables. Sandwiches, soup, tea, coffee, cake, fruit, ice cream, all at no extra cost. The only thing is, you have to have a deck chair; that's the problem. There are never enough, not even for all the passengers in first class—

"But Goldie Frohman got a deck chair."

"The stewards had a soft spot for little Goldie."

"That's when you learned."

"I learned a lot more. *Jumping rope,* for example. Do you know what that means? No? You know the thick red ropes that serve to separate the ship's classes? They're carefully watched. It's not easy to get from third to second class or from second to first."

"We don't like to see it, no."

"But my father needed first-class cardplayers. That's why he invented jumping rope, as he called it. I had to distract the stewards so that he could slip from one class to another. There's always a way—that's what I learned."

Vandermark raised his glass. "To Nick Frohman and his daughter Goldie." He tried to imagine Gloria as a twelve-year-old girl. "How did you wear your hair in those days?"

"Loose."

"And a sailor suit?"

"Yes, white or blue, depending on the time of year."

"And a ribbon in your hair?"

"Of course. And I had a sailor hat with long streamers. Tell me, when is your next tour of inspection?"

"In two hours."

"Your uniform . . . isn't it uncomfortable and hot?"

He felt her foot nudging him under the serving table. She leaned forward and began to blow out the candles. The room sank into semi-darkness; only the bed remained in the glow of the little lamp, and so did the woman lying there, ready to give herself to him. She stretched out her arms. "You can choose," she whispered. "The red one or the purple one."

Later her head rested on his chest. She breathed softly.

"Are you asleep?" he asked.

"No." She slipped her arm under his head. "I'm thinking."

He did not ask what she was thinking about. He had no questions for her, not now.

"Shall I tell you what I'm thinking?"

"Well?"

"I'm thinking that you might be making a mistake. Anne Butler—"

"Surely that's settled between us. Isn't it?"

"Not quite. I want to say one more thing about it. If I don't say it now, I never will. . . . You and I, we made it very easy for ourselves. Even tonight—it's so easy to love each other. What I'm trying to say . . . even if you were to marry Anne, that wouldn't change anything for me. I mean, I'd be prepared to go on with it. We could see each other whenever we could arrange it, wherever it's convenient, for a night, for a few days. . . . Nobody would have to know about it—I think we'd be clever and careful enough. My conscience wouldn't bother me."

"And my conscience?" he asked.

"You're no better than I am."

"What a strange declaration of love."

"You know I really mean what I say." Her voice held no bitterness, no cynical undertone. She really did mean what she said. A woman who hoped for no more than could be hoped for. She was not making a chess move, was setting no trap for him.

"Aren't you expecting me to argue with you?" he asked.

"Perhaps. But what people want and what they get, those are two different things. You know how I feel. Of course I'd like to have you for myself alone. If that can't be, I'm prepared for any compromise just so long as I don't—lose you altogether."

"That really is a strange declaration of love."

"You see, I know I'll never really have you all to myself. Only one woman ever had a man all to herself, and what did it lead to? They were driven out of Paradise."

"She wasn't like you. If she had been more like you, it never would have happened."

"You sound as if you mean it."

"I do mean it. If I ever forget, remind me."

"We're talking away all our lovely time. . . . When do I have to leave the ship?"

"Early in the morning is best. Do you want to go back to the house?"

"I think I'll live on the yacht for the time I'm here."

"It's closer and simpler. A ship's mate will take you there."

Two hours later he made his rounds. He was in the engine room when a ship's mate announced that Pollak and Kuhn had returned. Vandermark went to the gangway and welcomed them. He did not ask how the evening in the Yellow House had gone, and Pollak did not refer to it; he seemed in a good mood, while Kuhn was taciturn and barely able to keep his eyes open. Their arrival revived the ship once more; a restlessness went through the decks, ebbed away, and by the time Vandermark had finished his rounds, quiet had finally set in.

Gloria was asleep. Before he lay down next to her, he opened the curtains so as to wake up in time. But he could not sleep anyway. Perhaps he was overtired, perhaps too wide awake. He spent the rest of the night lying beside her, his eyes open.

Chapter 31

*T*he French doors to the garden were ajar, and the yellow curtains were drawn halfway in order to keep the sun from fading the tapestry she had brought back from Europe the previous year. On the dot of nine o'clock Temperance C. Butler came into the breakfast room, her skirt whipping, her steps springy.

"Good morning," Edith Connors and White said in chorus.

"A lovely good morning," she answered, unmistakably good-humored. She sat down in the chair White held for her and placed on the table her small reticule embroidered with colorful glass beads.

"May I pour your tea?" White took the cozy from the teapot.

"I hope it's not as dark as yesterday's."

"We are using a different mixture."

"Why a different mixture?"

"It's a remnant. You told us not to order any more tea because it would not be worthwhile."

"Quite right, White." A smile flickered across her face. "Sometimes I forget what I myself asked for. . . . To cut the white Bourbon roses—was that also an order from me? I was in the garden, and guess what I saw—someone must have cut about twenty of the Bourbon roses."

White cast a covert glance at Edith Connors. *Take care,* the look said, and she answered it with *Yes, take care.* Over the years they had learned to catch moods, prepare for approaching mischief.

"You gave the order to Jenkins," White said. "Yesterday, for the centerpiece."

"Correct. The table really did look wonderful. My compliments to Jenkins. And to your wife as well, by the way. The wine sauce for the turbot was excellent, and the venison. . . . I'll go to her myself and tell her." Her glance traveled the length of the table. "White."

"Yes, madam?"

"Where are the morning papers?"

It was no use that Edith Connors lowered her head to indicate that she had found White's remark concerning the centerpiece extremely ill-advised. It had happened, and the consequences were already setting in. He would have to answer, and his reply would make matters even worse. Once Anne's name had been pronounced, even Temperance C. Butler could no longer pretend that the empty place had gone unnoticed.

"Miss Anne wanted to go for the papers today," White mumbled.

"And where are they? You know perfectly well that *after* breakfast the papers no longer interest me."

"Perhaps the boat was delayed."

"Today? In this weather? It's all right, White, but in future please see to it that Jenkins goes for the papers. I do not want new customs to become entrenched here, not even in the final days of our stay."

It was typical of her that she made no further comment on Anne's absence as long as the butler was in the room. She simply took no cognizance of anything she did not wish to be aware of. Last night Edith Connors had had another chance to study at length this talent in Temperance C. Butler, and even if reluctantly, she had admired it. Without blinking an eye she had accepted Pollak's explanation of Vandermark's inability to join them. "That's right, give him a hard time for a change" had been her only comment, and then the subject had not been mentioned again. Whether it was difficult for her or not, she had preserved the amenities, had been cheerful, had dominated the table talk, later had sat down at the piano—and at no time had Anne fallen short of her grandmother's example. . . .

The small hand with the heavy rings pointed to the china bowl that held the quince jelly, and Edith Connors handed it across the table. One had to appear punctually for breakfast; Temperance C. Butler insisted on it, but she was not talkative in the mornings. The others could talk if they liked; she buried herself silently in the Boston papers. And should she let fall some remark or other, it was invariably a "Look at that! William Bragdon!" She always sounded cheerful and encouraging, although she was referring to an obituary. Today she missed the papers, and after a brief period she laid her napkin aside, stretched, and turned her look on Edith Connors, not unfriendly but still with that firmness used to remind children of their lack of obedience. "I assume you knew all about it?"

It was clear that she was speaking of Anne, even though she did not mention the name."

"Yes. I saw her drive off."

"And you let her go. Don't you find that highly improper? Who in the world would hang around a steamboat landing so early in the morning? Only chauffeurs, hotel servants, and dock workers. I'm only too aware of all the gossip Jenkins picks up down there and offers up in the kitchen later. Servants' gossip, not meant for the ears of a young girl."

Though arguing with Temperance C. Butler was generally a lost cause, Edith Connors could not prevent herself now. "I can understand that it was important to keep up appearances last night. But do we have to continue the charade this morning as well? What happened last night was terrible for Anne. I can imagine what she must have gone through. I can also imagine why she drove into Bar Harbor so early today."

"She went for the papers, I thought."

"Please . . ."

"Do you think Anne is running after him? Do you really believe that?"

"It's enough for her to be unhappy."

Temperance C. Butler looked at her hands; she pulled off one of the rings, a sapphire, tried it on a different finger, put it back in its original place. The soft, filtered light in the room tinged her skin the color of dark honey. Her white hair was freshly washed and held back with two decorative combs.

"Unbelievable." She spoke the word as if it were the name of a priceless jewel. "If I know you, Edith you intend to stand by Anne. Am I right?"

"I'll speak with her when she gets back."

Temperance C. Butler's expression grew dour. "You will not speak with her. You will stay out of it. Think about yourself. You couldn't manage your own life."

The strident noise when Edith Connors' cup turned over filled the quiet room. The tea ran across the cloth. For a moment it seemed that Edith Connors would jump to her feet, but she remained seated, as if rooted to her chair. Temperance C. Butler rang the little handbell and pointed out Edith's mishap to the maid who entered. The girl put a napkin under the tablecloth and placed a clean cup in front of Edith Connors.

"Pour some tea for Miss Connors, as long as you're here," said Temperance C. Butler. "For me too, please."

When the maid had left, Temperance stretched her hand across the table. Using her most conciliatory tone, she said, "Forgive me. Last night took it out of me too."

Edith Connors remained silent. Years ago, when such moments happened, she had promised herself she would leave, find a new situation, begin a new life, catch up on all that she had missed. But after living with Temperance C. Butler for thirteen years, only her nerves rebelled for an instant; she herself had become reconciled to her fate.

"What happened, after all?" she heard Temperance C. Butler say. "A man shies at the last minute—my God, that happens every day."

"If it were not for Gloria Lindsay, maybe."

"You read too many novels. Novels are full of women who let a man make them unhappy. I don't know why. It seems it's what women like to read."

"Or because it happens in real life."

"I've never been able to do anything but despise such women. I don't mean it personally, Edith. Anne is a Butler. Anne takes after me. Don't you worry about Anne."

She took a sip of tea, shook her head, set down the cup, placed her hand on her reticule. "If all else fails, she just won't marry Vandermark and will marry Alec. . . ."

Edith Connors raised her eyes. "Alec?"

"Why not? He's a good lawyer. He stands to inherit a considerable fortune—and perhaps sooner than we think. In contrast to Sol, who thinks that life on his cliff is especially healthful, I'm of the opinion that his way of life will lead to the grave all the sooner. In any case, I've set my mind on having this year end with a wedding. And you'll see, I'll get my wedding, one way or the other. . . ."

"A wedding is not always the cure-all, especially not for Anne."

"Anything can be turned into a tragedy. Anne will not do that. I know her better. Anyway, it still is not certain that she won't be Mrs. Vandermark. Obstacles are made to be overcome. Of course I was annoyed last night. But at least he showed good manners. No, no, as far as I'm concerned, it's not a lost cause yet. I won't give up just yet—if only because of Gloria Lindsay. Allows herself to be invited and doesn't show up. She'll be sorry. She'll find out with whom she's dealing."

"I'm thinking only of Anne."

"I am too, and that is why I will leave no stone unturned."

"Perhaps it would be better . . . I mean, some men don't like having their decisions made for them."

"Really, Edith, you don't know the first thing about men. Don't tell me now that you don't like Vandermark."

"No, it's not that." She had never felt certain that Anne and Vandermark were really suited to one another. Sometimes she had been tempted to warn Anne. But might envy be behind her concern? On a day that was now far in the past she had banished love from her life. The decision had brought her peace. Though because of it her life had lost fullness, was now only half a life, she found she could handle it much better than before. And that was why she was in this house, would remain in this house, like White, like Betty, like Jenkins, a shadowy existence under the mighty tree named Temperance C. Butler.

"You do like Vandermark, be honest." Temperance Butler would not let go. "And shall I tell you the reason?"

"Could we change the subject, please?"

"All right, let's talk of something else. But simply to give up, just like that? No. There is still the money. He likes a good life, he loves luxury. I know that he thinks about it, perhaps not first and foremost, but it is a factor in his deliberations. I know that Gloria Lindsay isn't exactly poor either. Perhaps it's simply a matter of who offers him more; perhaps the whole problem is that simple. . . . I must say, he would even rise in my estimation if it were so. I love people with a clear view of reality. But let's wait and see. And now we really won't talk about it anymore." She listened. A carriage was driving up outside. "I've thought about it. Tomorrow we will go to Bangor. Anne needs an evening dress for the Captain's Dinner. The rags she has here are good enough for the Canoe Club. . . ."

Once more contradiction rose in Edith Connors. "Perhaps Anne won't want to attend the Captain's Dinner? Didn't Pollak say that he planned to invite Gloria Lindsay as well?"

"So what? You are invited too, Edith, my dear. We'll buy a dress for you too."

"Anne won't go." Edith Connors clung to the thought.

"She will, and I won't even have to persuade her. You'll see."

Steps came across the terrace, and then one of the doors opened. Anne entered the room, the newspapers under her arm, wearing a light-blue dress, her face shaded by a straw hat decorated with a few artificial flowers. Sun streamed into the room through the open door, along with the scent of roses, sweet and heavy.

"Was the boat delayed?" Temperance C. Butler asked without looking at Anne. She reached for the bell. "I'll order some more tea."

"Don't trouble yourself."

"I'll have some more myself. I asked you whether the boat was late."

"I spent too much time." The hat threw shadows across Anne's face. "It was such a beautiful morning." She placed the papers on a small side table next to her grandmother's place.

"Isn't that one of my hats?" Temperance C. Butler raked her grand-daughter with a sharp look.

"Yes."

"My God, I haven't worn it in an eternity. Where did you find it?"

"In the attic."

"What were you doing in the attic?"

"I cleaned up some things from my room. Otherwise everything piles up on the last day."

The maid entered.

"A pot of fresh tea," Temperance C. Butler ordered. "And ask Betty if there's a piece of blueberry cake left."

For a moment silence reigned except for the maid's footsteps and the closing of the door. Anne was still standing next to her grand-mother's place. Edith Connors had a keen awareness of the current run-ning between the two women, the tension between them. Anything seemed possible—an outburst of tears, of anger. She was least prepared for what actually happened. Temperance C. Butler put out her beringed hand and said, "I haven't yet heard a 'good morning' from you."

Anne took off her hat, hung it over her arm, leaned down to her grandmother, and kissed the old lady's cheek. "Good morning, Grandmother."

She put her hat aside, sat down in her regular place, and addressed Edith Connors. "You were up early too."

"Yes."

"You should have come with me. It was so lovely down at the harbor, hardly any wind, cloudless—you could see out to Egg Rock. And everywhere people were busy picking up the burned-out fireworks. One fell on the terrace of the Rockaway and singed an awning."

"I was glad that Edith was here to keep me company." Temperance C. Butler picked up the topmost newspaper. "By the way, we decided to go to Bangor to do some shopping."

"With the carriage to Bangor?"

"We used to go in the four-in-hand, remember? But if you prefer, we can rent a car."

Edith Connors observed Anne covertly. She had seemed pale under the straw hat, but her color was as fresh as ever. Was it possible? Edith Connors wondered. Was it possible that Anne caught her grandmother's thoughts? Was it possible that she would accept her grandmother's decision without opposition?

"I was just about to make the same suggestion," Anne said now. "I've been racking my brains what to wear to Pollak's Captain's Dinner."

"And what were you thinking of?" Her grandmother's voice was very gentle.

"I think I'd like a white evening gown."

"White was always an exceptionally good color for you. And for that night I could lend you my garnet choker. . . . Ah, there's our tea."

The maid went around the table and poured. She placed a piece of blueberry cake in front of Anne. Then she retired. The breeze from the garden brought the scent of roses. Someone was raking the gravel. The only sound at the table was the rustle of the newspaper. Temperance had pushed her chair back a little, and it was evident that she would no longer take part in any conversation. Everything was as it had always been, and soon Temperance C. Butler was talking to herself. "Look at that, Randolph Calhoun. At sixty-one." And, as if delighted to have an outlet for dammed-up feelings, she added. "He did his Judy a favor after all, dying before her."

Chapter 32

The narrow, windowless room with the walls of riveted iron plates was filled with the drone of the printing press. The two men in blue fatigues could barely fit into the *Cecilie*'s print shop, and therefore Pommerenke remained standing in the doorway. "The menus." He placed his hands around his mouth. "Are the menus ready?"

The man behind the press shouted something incomprehensible. The light of the ceiling lamp, directly above him reflected off the lenses of his wire-rim glasses in such a way that his eyes were invisible.

He made a gesture which Pommerenke took to mean that he was to shut the door. The man flipped a switch, and the deafening noise stopped. A shelf along the wall held the preprinted envelopes for the menus and concert programs that were freshly printed each day during a crossing. More than half had been left over after the last trip.

The printer wiped his hands on a cloth, opened a desk, and with his fingertips pulled out the menu that had been printed up for the Captain's Dinner. Carefully he laid the card on the little folding table. "My best handmade paper. And my most handsome font. I hope Captain Pollak is pleased."

Pommerenke took one of the cards. The front sported Pollak's photograph, surrounded by a wide border. The type underneath read:

DINNER
on board
S.S. *Kronprinzessin Cecilie*
October 1914
in
Commemoration of
THE SUMMER IN BAR HARBOR
by Captain Charles Pollak

The printer looked over Pommerenke's shoulder. "Nine of them. And the place cards, with the names. No change there?" He put the cards in a manila envelope. "I dunno. Smells of good-bye to me."

Pommerenke did not seem to have heard the remark. "If you've already finished the menus, why are you still printing?"

The two printers exchanged a look. The one with the glasses, who had handed him the menus, retired behind the press. He placed his hand on the machine. "Some noise. I sure have missed it all this time. You wouldn't believe how you can miss something like that." He smiled. "Word got out that we're printing something today. Everybody came running and wanted a copy as a souvenir. We thought . . . but we're doing them on ordinary paper. I'll be glad to put one aside for you."

"No need. I'll get it from the captain. He never saves his."

"Really does look like we're leaving," the printer said again. "The menus, and the dinner altogether." He took off his glasses, wiped the lenses. "There's something going on, something in the wind. . . . "

Pommerenke was used to such questioning. The crew looked to him as a man who knew everything about and from the captain, who knew his innermost thoughts, as it were. But first of all, this was not true, and second, Pommerenke was a man who knew how to keep his own counsel.

"We all have our own thoughts." The printer put his glasses back on. "Gonna have to happen sooner or later. Or do you think we're going to stay here forever?"

Pommerenke took the envelope. "Thanks a lot." He had closed the door behind him when the press started up again.

The noise came dully into the narrow corridor, like the beat of an iron heart in an iron body. Pommerenke began to walk faster. Down here he always felt uneasy. The gray metal walls, the gray floor, the murky light of the naked bulbs, the multitude of pipes, the air shafts—this region of the ship was a little like a mine. Something Pollak had once said came to his mind: "The gold glitters above deck, but it's mined down there." The sentiment was deeply felt by the men who worked down below. It was they on whom everyone depended for the reliability, the punctuality of a ship, they whose existence the passengers knew only as the thud of the engines, as the smoke rising from the four funnels. When would it be like that again? When would the *Cecilie* be carrying passengers again? When would she return to her Atlantic course, when would she be running east, heading for home?

The corridor grew wider, the lighting brighter, and then he felt the soft carpet under his feet again and was on the deck where the large dining room was located. It used to be only natural to find these surroundings brightly lit of an evening. Here was the shining center of the ship, where everyone congregated. Since they had been at anchor in Bar Harbor, this area had fallen silent. No passengers, no music, only quiet and darkness. Tonight old times were finally back—or nearly. There was more bustle than there had been in a long time. Stewards rushed back and forth, serving carts rattled, dumbwaiters rumbled, swinging doors flew this way and that.

Before he went to fetch the menu cards in the printing shop, Pommerenke had briefly looked in on the kitchen to pass on Pollak's last-minute instructions, and there too he had found humming activity. All of the cooks had gathered, making it seem as if dinner were being prepared for a hundred guests rather than nine.

For weeks he had not seen a steward in uniform but only in civvies; now four of them were standing in full dress at the entrance to the first-class dining saloon, dashingly opening the doors for him. The large room, at the exact center of the ship, was twenty-one yards wide and rose through three decks. White columns supported the galleries, and at the center a cupola of stained-glass mosaic arched over the space. The white and gold of the walls, together with the blue of the rug and the drapes, created an atmosphere of cool splendor in the daytime, but now, at night, in the light of the many small table lamps and the great chandeliers, it had something magical about it, seeming like a fairy cave at the bottom of the ocean.

The chief steward had suggested serving dinner in one of the smaller saloons, but Pollak had refused to entertain the idea. A Captain's Dinner took place in the dining saloon, nowhere else. And all the tables must be set—this too he had insisted on. And finally he had ordered that the captain's table, usually placed to one side, be moved to the center of the room, exactly under the glass dome.

The cloth of white damask, the cut-glass goblets, the vermeil utensils—Pommerenke took in each detail. Everything was as it had always been for the Captain's Dinner except the china. The dishes used for this night were white with a cornflower-blue border, the decoration consisting of an eagle and a crown. Pommerenke took up one of the smaller plates, turned it, and examined the hallmark of the royal factory in Berlin.

"Everything all right?" The chief steward had rushed over when he saw Pommerenke pause at the table. "Captain Pollak didn't expressly order it, but it seemed a good opportunity to use it one more time."

Pommerenke nodded. The china had been made on special consignment. The shipping company had ordered it to commemorate the ship's godmother, and it had been used only twice before, in 1908 and in 1913, when Crown Princess Cecilie herself had been a guest on board.

"May I have the menus?" the chief steward asked.

Pommerenke handed over the envelope without a word. Suddenly he was engulfed by a deep sadness.

"He put the Chateau Leoville on the menu," he heard the steward say. "I hope there's enough of it left; well, he'll know what reserves he has. And Roederer. I thought we were out of it."

"The last four bottles . . ."

"That will never be enough."

"Then we'll have to add the Burgeff. There are a few more bottles of that."

"First Roederer and then Burgeff? Please clear it with the captain. I don't want him yelling at me afterward. And the place cards? What is the seating plan to be?"

Pommerenke told the chief steward the seating plan. Pollak at the head, his back to the musicians, and then in clockwise order Gloria Lindsay, Kuhn, Anne Butler, Vandermark, McCagg, Edith Connors, Dr. Fischer, and at Pollak's right hand Temperance C. Butler.

Someone came up with a serving cart; it was covered with bags of confetti, streamers, colorful snappers, inflatable snakes, and paper hats.

"Over there," the chief steward instructed. "We won't need it until dessert." His gesture turned out too wide, his voice rang too loud. Pommerenke's heart contracted.

A few more hours, and all the tables would be cleared, the confetti and streamers swept up, the lights turned off. The ship would sink back into darkness.

Simoni, the wireless operator, was just closing the door when Pommerenke arrived at the captain's quarters. Simoni was about to pass him silently with only a gesture of greeting, but Pommerenke stopped him. "Something special?"

"I only took the latest weather reports to the captain." Simoni was pale, stubble indicating that he had not shaved for several days. "The usual," he added quickly. "I have to hurry back."

Pommerenke looked after the departing figure. Of all the crew, Simoni was the one whose daily activity had changed the least, who continued to perform his duties rigorously, delivering his reports to Pollak three times a day. And more, even at night his wireless station was lit up, and he sat before his instruments as if expecting a message of the utmost importance. The order to take off? To return home? It could not be anything else. . . .

Pollak was sitting at his desk in his parlor. In front of him lay the message from Simoni, maps, tide charts, notices. He did not look up as Pommerenke crossed the room and went into the adjoining bedroom. The three-quarter-length dress coat was already brushed and hanging in the closet. Now Pommerenke took the medal ribbon from the leather box, pinned it to the coat, and a hand's breadth below it, next to the third and fourth buttons, the Order of Cecilie, a blue-and-gold star. The manual movements soothed him, distracting him from his thoughts. He went into the bathroom and turned on the wall sconces over the marble dressing table. He gave a turn to the roll of crepe paper over the neckpiece of the barber's chair. He heated water. Finally he began to strop the straight razor against the leather. He had left the doors open; usually Pollak came on his own when he heard the sounds of razor against leather, but today Pommerenke had to go back to the parlor. "Time for your shave, Captain."

Charles Pollak looked up. "So late already?" He pulled open the desk drawer and with one movement of his hand swept the charts and notes into it. Then he rose and followed his tiger. In the bedroom he stopped to look at the dress coat. "Are the medals and ribbons necessary?"

"You always used to wear them to the Captain's Dinner."

"They get in the way when I'm dancing. I always manage to tear the ladies' tulle dresses." His hand caressed the dark fabric. "A good piece of cloth. I've been wearing this one since I made captain."

"Unfortunately. You need a new one."

"Why are you so stern with me today?"

"After every crossing you said you would go to the tailor."

"After the next crossing I will go to the tailor. That's a promise. Satisfied?"

Pommerenke did not reply. He had been with Pollak for thirty years, and there were still moments—like the present one—when he could not figure him out. His cheerfulness, his even temper—were they genuine or pretended? Would he explode any moment over some triviality? Anyway, what did it mean, the dinner, the charts on his desk? Or was it all simply a way to pass the time, a man playing at being a captain? . . .

Pommerenke pointed to the barber chair.

Pollak sat down, unbuttoned his shirt, leaned his head back. "Close, now. When Temperance C. Butler has had a little wine, she likes to dance cheek to cheek."

"There are still four bottles of the Roederer." Pommerenke whipped the white cloth around Pollak's neck and tied it at the nape.

"Careful. You want to throttle me? Four bottles of Roederer, did you say? And the Pommery Mrs. Butler sent?"

"You drank it up. The chief steward suggests that we add on the Burgeff, but there's not much of that left either." He beat the soap sudsy and stood before Pollak with the brush.

"Add on? Has he gone crazy? Then we simply serve only the Burgeff and start a little later with it. It won't last long tonight anyway. No champagne left on board. . . ." He sighed. "And on my ship. Pommerenke, we're going to the dogs."

"May I begin? It's high time." For a while the men did not speak while Pommerenke went about his work. Once he encountered Pollak's eyes in the mirror, surprised, almost punishing, and Pommerenke had to agree with him; usually his hand was steadier. The fact that the *Cecilie* was lying at anchor in calm waters should have made shaving easier, but the opposite was the case. At sea, on the cruising ship, he had never nicked Pollak while shaving him, not even when there were heavy waves. But lately, here, it had happened several times. . . . He had finished the second shave, picked up the alum stick, and touched the small, bloody cut on the ear. The peal of the ship's bell could be heard from the distance.

"Really high time." Pollak leaned over the basin and splashed some camphor water into his hands. When he was about to get up, Pommerenke pushed him back into the chair, trimmed his moustache, and went over it with a small brush.

"Enough," Pollak said. "There's no way to make me any handsomer." He let himself be helped on with his coat, then reached for his cap and his white gloves, which had been laid ready. "And you?" he said. "What about you? Are you prepared to let yourself be deprived of it, ladies on board, dressed to the nines?"

"Just let me straighten up a little here."

"There's plenty of time for that. Get your trumpet. I want to hear a grand welcoming flourish."

"You must go now. I'll follow shortly."

"A forceful 'All aboard,' that's what I want to hear. And then, on the dot of nine, my good man, when the first course is being served, you'll blare out your 'Roast Beef of Old England,' or if you prefer, the watchman's call from *Fidelio*. You can choose."

"Aye, aye, sir."

"All right, then."

The door closed behind him. Though it was padded on both sides, Pommerenke could still hear Pollak's firm tread. A few minutes later, after he had straightened up the bathroom and turned out the lights, he went to get his trumpet.

A light rain had fallen all day, but when Pommerenke came out on deck, he found that it had stopped. Instead, the temperature had dropped. The clouds had parted, and the lights of Bar Harbor sparkled brightly.

The boat bringing the guests was already under way. At first he only heard the motor, but soon the skiff emerged into the *Cecilie*'s circle of light; its speed slackened, the boat hove to, and two searchlights caught hold of it.

Pommerenke had to lean far over the railing to be able to see. The gangway was decorated with white chains of light.

Pollak stood on the platform awaiting the ladies. Temperance C.

Butler was the first one out of the boat. Two cabin boys helped her, leading her up the narrow steps. It was a lovely picture—the woman in the long fur, on her head a sparkling tiara. Now she put out her hand to Pollak. The fur opened, necklaces twinkled brightly. Already the second lady came along, wearing an evening coat of gold lamé over a red dress.

Pommerenke straightened up. He took the trumpet from its case and took his place in the shadow of one of the deck superstructures, where he could not be seen from below. He raised the trumpet to his lips, closed his eyes, and breathed deeply.

The first sound of the signal suddenly hung bright and clear in the air: *All aboard, come all aboard.*

Chapter 33

$\mathcal{H}$er laughter rang out above the sounds of the small orchestra that was still playing decorous dinner music. The tiara in her white hair was crooked, and behind it she wore a green paper hat with a white tassel.

The steward standing next to her was pouring confetti into her cupped hand. The gentlemen quickly covered their glasses with the palms of their hands before the rain of confetti descended on the table.

The confetti was followed by streamers. The triple-stranded pearl necklace swung as Temperance C. Butler released the rolls into the air. From the time she had come aboard she had looked forward to this moment; important as a good meal was to her, she had been waiting impatiently for the dessert to be cleared. She stretched both hands out to the steward to let him fill them again until the table was covered with the multicolored confetti and streamers.

The Wiltinger wine that had been served with the filet of turbot had barely stretched to cover the demand; the Chateau Leoville with the venison had died out before its time, and now the last two bottles of Burgeff had been opened. The mood at the table became increasingly uninhibited—except for McCagg, who had been made a little tired by the all too lavish meal, and Anne Butler, who sat stiffly at Vandermark's side. Time and again she threw a reproachful glance at her grandmother, quivering each time someone laughed, as if she, the youngest, were responsible for the behavior of the older members of the party.

"She's acting much too foolish." Anne Butler fished confetti from her glass.

"She's having a good time. What's foolish about that?" He made a sign to the steward to bring Anne a clean glass, but she shook her head.

"I won't have any more to drink." Her voice held the same vehement undertone as before, when she had refused to put on the paper hat her grandmother had assigned to her. There had almost been a scene, but Anne abruptly gave in to her grandmother's decision and put the "ridiculous thing" on her head. She had been given one of the most attractive ones, of black shiny paper, which suited her light hair very well. She wore it perched far back on her head, and her hand kept creeping up to the thin rubber band under her chin as if she were tempted to take it off.

Somehow the steward had managed to give Anne a clean glass without her noticing, and Vandermark thanked him with a nod. Like planets circling the sun, the stewards moved around the table unostentatiously, quite soundless and in the background, but at hand at the slightest nod.

Vandermark picked up his glass. To his left McCagg seemed impervious to conversation; in honor of the evening he had bought a new pair of patent-leather pumps, and they were pinching. Dr. Fischer, across from him, was engrossed in a conversation with Edith Connors, and judging by the snippets Vandermark heard, they seemed to be discussing remedies against seasickness. Kuhn had laid sole siege to Gloria Lindsay; he was flirting actively, at the moment kissing her hand one more time.

"We seem to be the only ones here who have nothing to say to each other," Vandermark observed.

She turned to him with the same reproachful look she had given her grandmother. "Isn't it the gentleman's job to keep his dinner partner entertained?" She picked up her glass, clinked with his. She raised it to her lips, but when she set it down, it was as full as before.

From the head of the table the stifled laugh of Temperance C. Butler rang out. Pollak was whispering in her ear, and she pulled his head even closer. Under the transparent chiffon her full arm was outlined. Now she let him go. Both had streamers draped around their necks; on Pollak's dark coat they looked like additional badges of honor; on her, like exotic jewelry. Temperance C. Butler looked across the table and then back at Pollak. "Charlie! Where's your speech? Everybody, don't we want a speech?"

Shouts of agreement came from all sides. The men sat up straighter, checked their neckties; the ladies pulled their dresses straight. The stewards came running to make sure that all glasses were full for the toasts. "Yes, a speech, Charlie!" Temperance C. Butler's request traveled around the table. Captain Pollak sat tall and straight in his chair.

"Of course there will be a speech." He smiled at Temperance C. Butler. "I never could refuse you anything."

Temperance threatened him with a raised forefinger. "Don't try to get out of it, Charlie."

Pollak looked over to McCagg. "McCagg! You promised that tonight you would be the speaker."

McCagg started up. He had gotten hold of the largest of the paper hats, a top hat with a band of stars and stripes. He squirmed in his chair and finally decided to get to his feet. He used both hands to raise himself, slowly, awkwardly. He kept one hand on the table for support while he sought for a spoon with the other and tapped it against his glass. "Damned good drink, that Burgeff. . . ." He fell silent.

"Is that part of the speech?" Everyone laughed, and Temperance C. Butler interjected. "Silence! Silence for Captain McCagg."

McCagg reached for his hat, straightened it on his head. "Ladies!" As he bowed, he tottered. "Gentlemen." He looked at Pollak. "My dear Charlie. I'm a lousy speaker. I'm known as the captain who makes the worst speeches . . . on the whole ocean. . . . My dear Charlie . . . the ocean . . . our ocean . . ."

Perhaps it was the liquor, perhaps only emotion; in any case he seemed to have totally lost the thread of his speech, if he had ever had one. He looked around despairingly and reached for his glass. "Here's to Charlie Pollak. Here's to his ship. To Bar Harbor and to this summer. . . ." His voice gave out. He was standing very steady, with an almost military bearing. Again his glance, searching for help, circled the table. "Good-bye, Charlie, regretfully. . . ." Holding his glass, he made his way around the table toward Pollak. "Bye,

Charlie. Good-bye." The two men touched glasses, drank, set down the glasses, and embraced. The others, picking up their glasses as well, made their way toward Pollak.

Vandermark remained at Anne's side. They were the last in line. Anne had been visibly touched by McCagg's speech. Her expression was no longer so withdrawn; now she looked rather pensive.

"Is McCagg leaving?" she asked.

Vandermark nodded. "Today was his last day."

"And you?"

He was glad that he did not have to answer, not right away, for it was her turn to clink glasses with Pollak. Vandermark used the moment to exchange a glance with Gloria Lindsay, who was passing by him to return to her seat. During dinner they had not spoken a single word to each other, and even now they communicated only by a swift look.

The orchestra had added a few musicians and was beginning to play for dancing. Temperance C. Butler and Pollak were the first on the dance floor, and her light voice was singing along.

> *Linger longer, Lucy,*
> *Linger longer, Lu.*
> *How I love to linger, Lucy,*
> *Linger longer, you.*

"She's acting as though she were eighteen years old." Anne's face once more wore a stern, disparaging look, as if she were ashamed of her grandmother.

"The musicians love her," Vandermark said, "and whenever she's on board, they start out with her favorite."

"They have to, don't they? I'm sure she pays for it."

He shook his head but said nothing more. He was thinking of the conversation he had had with Temperance C. Butler three days earlier, in the little café on the boardwalk of Bar Harbor. She had sent him a letter—"Could we meet?" She had pulled out all the stops. He had never known her so charming, so cordial, so warm—"The two of us, we'd get along so well together." And when that had had no effect on him, she had tried practicality and realism—"I'll make you an offer." There had been talk of a house for Anne and him, of a monthly allowance, of a Boston shipping line where she would acquire a majority on the board and which he, Vandermark, could then head just as soon as his naturalization had been taken care of. . . .

But he admired most the way she had borne herself in accepting his refusal. She was a truly remarkable woman. She was eccentric, she was tyrannical, she was not easy to be with—but how much energy she possessed, how much warmth. She was one of those women whose strength feeds and nourishes whole families and who never get any thanks for it, for everyone accepts it as a matter of course, as one dips water from a well without thinking where it comes from.

"Shall we dance?" He turned to Anne.

"Captain's orders?" Her sudden smile was tinged with malice, making her resemble her grandmother.

"It is the custom on board."

"You're forgetting one thing—the older ladies take precedence." Her eyes went straight to Gloria Lindsay, who was chatting with Kuhn.

He laughed. "You do know your way around shipboard etiquette. Nevertheless, I'd like to dance with you now."

"Later I'd be happy to—after her." She turned from him and grabbed an astonished McCagg by the arm. In vain he pointed to his patent-leather pumps.

"You made a beautiful speech," she said.

He looked at her in surprise. "Really? But I can't talk at all. And dance even less, really, and my shoes are pinching. . . ."

"We'll see about that." Anne pulled him along energetically.

Vandermark hesitated for a moment, then went up to Gloria Lindsay. He bowed and, overriding Kuhn's protests, led her to the dance floor. The orchestra was playing a two-step. He took her in his arms, correctly and maintaining a proper distance. She smiled. "The older ladies first, right?"

"That's what Anne thought."

"She turned serious. "Aren't you expecting just a little too much of her?"

"I'm making every effort to be nice to her."

"That's a cruel word—*nice.* . . . Remember, it's the last night for her, not for me. We have many more in store for us."

"That sounds equally cruel."

"We both are."

He pulled her closer, he felt her body's suppleness, and for a moment he had only one desire—to be alone with her, to possess her. Streamers wound around their feet. Confetti rained down on them. Temperance C. Butler had climbed up on the orchestra platform, and from this vantage, laughing and giggling, she pelted the dancers with streamers and confetti. Charles Pollak held Edith Connors in his arms. Anne could barely follow McCagg's jumps and hops.

"I'll be disappearing soon," Gloria was saying softly by his ear, "without a lot of fuss. Just so that you know."

"All right."

"I want to leave Bar Harbor. The sale is closed. I only stayed because I promised Pollak I'd attend his dinner, but I'd really like to take the yacht out tonight. Did you talk to Pollak?"

The orchestra was playing a waltz. He led her to the edge of the dance floor. "There's been a change, quite suddenly. I've only known for a couple of hours. . . . We'll be leaving Bar Harbor."

"We?"

"The *Cecilie* is being transferred to Boston. For now only a few of us know about it. You shouldn't mention it to anyone. It will be hard enough to get the ship away from here, even at high tide, but if we have hundreds of boats on our tail, it will be impossible."

"That is a surprise."

"Not for Pollak, I suspect."

"And what does it mean for us?"

Vandermark looked over at Pollak. He was dancing tirelessly. On his head was perched a tiny red hat; the black rubber band that was holding it on cut deep into his cheek.

"You can't leave him alone on this particular trip," Gloria said thoughtfully, as if she had read his mind. "Is that it?"

"At first I thought I could. But then . . . it may be her last voyage."

"When will it happen?"

"Less than six hours from now."

"I understand. It's only a few days. . . . So I will set out tonight in any case. It's best that way. We'll meet again in Baltimore."

"Yes, in Baltimore."

"All right. When do you think you'll be in Boston?"

"As early as tomorrow night."

"I'll telephone Lyman to send someone about the formalities of naturalization. . . . That still stands, doesn't it?"

He nodded, but it was a matter he could not imagine at the moment; it seemed so far in the future.

"Does Anne know?"

"No."

"Maybe you should tell her. I'm sure it makes a difference to her that you're leaving Bar Harbor, not just with me, but with the ship. . . . Please take me back to the table now. I'll have a dance with Pollak, and then I'll go. . . . Come soon."

He led her back to her seat, bowed, kissed her hand. Suddenly he felt like an actor, and the worst of it was the feeling that he was playing his part too perfectly, with too much rehearsal. Yes, both of them were cruel. Both thought only of themselves and their secret goal. They were anything but a young couple in love. And yet—they loved each other. Did that fact excuse them? Only the future would tell.

The next half-hour passed for him like something unreal. But wasn't there something unreal about the whole party? At the center of the large saloon a few actors were performing a strange play. The stewards in the background were the extras. Only the audience was missing, and yet sometimes, when he glanced at the galleries, he felt that in the shadow of the pillars eyes were watching the goings-on.

He had danced with Temperance C. Butler, with Edith Connors. Now he became aware that Gloria was no longer at the party. She was not sitting at the table, and she was not on the dance floor. When had she taken leave of Pollak?

"I believe it's time that we were leaving too. Will you help me tear Grandmother away?" Anne was speaking to him. She had taken off her paper hat and was placing it on the table. She picked up the menu lying next to her plate and looked at him questioningly. "May I?"

"Of course." Was she still young enough to keep a scrapbook? Would she paste the menu in it? He felt that he was looking at her properly for the first time that night: the white dress cut low at the neck, the garnet choker, the earrings of the same stone glimmering through the light hair like red berries. And her scent . . . "Are you wearing a new perfume?"

She turned to him, and the movement increased the scent. "You've sat next to me all night, and you didn't notice until now?" A little evening purse lay in her lap, covered by the menu with Pollak's photograph. "Do you really want to know what the scent is? Or is that one of those questions you ask every woman?"

"I really want to know."

"I went specially to Bangor for it. A new dress and a new perfume. It hasn't done much good."

"Anne, please . . ."

"Anyway, I tried. I told myself, 'You need something that he'll remember long after he's forgotten everything else.'" Her eyes seemed to turn even darker. "Anne . . . that's a name to forget. Who, after years, can remember an Anne? But sometime, in ten, twenty years, a woman will walk past you, an unknown woman wearing the same perfume, and you will turn around, and suddenly you will remember: Surely there was something, years and years ago, a summer. . . ."

She rose so quickly that he could not even hold her chair for her. The orchestra had stopped playing. The guests were surrounding Charlie Pollak. At the back the stewards were already holding the ladies' coats.

Temperance C. Butler protested. "What's the rush? Charlie! It's only just midnight. Since when do your parties end so soon?"

Pollak waved to the stewards. They came, bringing the coats. "Captain McCagg is leaving us in the morning."

"But Charlie! Let those who want to leave, leave. Gloria Lindsay needs her beauty sleep, but me, Charlie, I don't have to worry about my beauty anymore. . . . One little game. Just a single game. I did so look forward to some poker. Dr. Fischer will surely join us. No high stakes. A dollar opens. Aren't you tempted? Maybe tonight you can win back every penny you lost to me over the years."

"The night wouldn't be long enough."

"All right, I can see that the party's over. It was an enchanting evening. I thank you, Charlie. I . . . any minute now I'll grow sentimental. . . . Meinert, my fur." The chief steward placed the floor-length sable around her shoulders. "My handbag, Meinert. . . . How many stewards are there?"

"Fifteen, madam."

"Fifteen, and the orchestra . . ." She opened her reticule, counted out notes unobtrusively, and just as unobtrusively lowered her right hand as a bundle of banknotes slid into the chief steward's hand. "This time the bills aren't torn, Meinert," she said. "I dare say there won't be a return crossing for me."

"I'm afraid not for any of us, madam."

The orchestra began to play again as Temperance C. Butler took Pollak's arm.

Linger longer, Lucy,
Linger longer, Lu.

Charlie Pollak and Temperance C. Butler led the procession of guests. The stewards formed a cordon to the left and the right. Two held open the folding doors.

How I love to linger, Lucy
Linger longer, you.

Vandermark, bringing up the rear at Anne's side, gave a last backward look into the dining saloon. At the farthest tables the lights were already extinguished. The old and white, luminous just a moment ago, turned dull; mirrors filled with darkness. The crushed streamers on the dance floor lost their bright colors. The festively set table resembled a ruined landscape. A steward reached for one of the glasses left half full and drained it quickly and covertly.

Outside on the deck it was cold and damp. The iron floor plates glistened.

"Be careful." He held on to Anne's arm. Her other hand clutched her evening purse and the menu. And her scent was on the air.

"Shall we see each other again?" she asked.

If he was going to tell her the truth, he would have to do it now. But what use was the truth?

"When do you go back to Boston?" he asked.

"Tomorrow, on the afternoon boat. We . . . we've stayed a long, long time this year. In Bar Harbor the summers aren't usually this long. . . . This is good-bye, isn't it?"

"Yes." Suddenly the memory was vivid: his first day in Bar Harbor, the evening, the ripe peaches along the espaliers of the Yellow House. They had the same scent as Anne's perfume. "We're leaving Bar Harbor tomorrow morning," he said, "very early, with the first tide."

"But . . ." She stopped. "Are you saying the *Cecilie* is leaving Frenchman Bay? And you're staying on board?"

"Yes. I'm staying on board." It was not a lie, but it was not the whole truth either. "It's peach, your perfume, isn't it?"

"It's called something else, but I think that on my skin it smells like the peaches against the Yellow House."

"Anne . . ."

"Yes?"

He groped for the words, but there were none. His eyes fell on the Baroness' ring on his little finger. He pulled it off and took her hand. "It should bring you luck." He placed the ring on her middle finger.

She looked at her hand. Then she stood on tiptoe and kissed him. "Lots of luck!" She ran off along the deck after the others.

Was it only relief that it was over, without tears, without promises that neither of them could believe? Or was it the sudden realization that he too was experiencing a loss? For a second he had the crazy feeling that he would have to run after her and bring her back. Her heels clattered on the planks. Something fluttered from her hand, fell to the ground—the menu. . . . A cabin boy emerged from the darkness. He bent down for the card, hesitated, and then quickly concealed it under his blue blouse.

Vandermark should have been at the gangway, but he remained on deck. He could not have borne Temperance Butler's cheerfulness at this moment. He heard the voices coming from below. They must be about to get into a boat. The motor started, and then, as if on cue, the trumpet signal resounded.

All ashore that's going ashore!

The white boat gained distance from the *Cecilie,* floated beyond the circle of light. Mist hung above the water. Bar Harbor lay in the dark; only a few lights on the shore were burning. Vandermark's eyes traveled across to the yacht basin. He saw a red and a green light moving away from the shore. Behind him he heard the voices of Pollak and Kuhn.

"Now they've had their party," Pollak was saying. His voice sounded sober, as if he had not had a single drop of wine. The paper hat was no longer perched on his head, the streamers around his neck had disappeared.

"Mrs. Butler would have liked to go on longer," Vandermark said.

"A party that ends at midnight is no party at all as far as Temperance Butler is concerned." Pollak looked out into the bay. He raised his hand and pointed to the white yacht outlined against the dark, the three masts, the directional lights.

"The *Nirvana*," Pollak said. "Did you know that she would be putting out to sea?"

Vandermark nodded silently. The noise of the engines increased, the yacht moved past the *Cecilie*.

"Did you work it out?" Pollak asked.

"Yes, sir."

"In such matters my navigational skills were usually insufficient." Pollak was breathing deeply, as if to clear his lungs. "You'll quit in Boston?"

"Yes, sir."

Pollak's hand descended to the railing, coming to rest there. It seemed to Vandermark that he was spying on the captain during an illicit caress.

"A lot of soldered steel. Unbelievable how attached one can become to it. . . . Vandermark."

"Sir?"

"I'm glad you stayed on board for this trip. But . . . I want to see you on the bridge with three stripes on your sleeve."

"I don't know, sir."

"The appointment is in my desk drawer. And Pommerenke is sure to come up with a piece of braid. . . . She's a good ship, Vandermark. And when she leaves here, she deserves to have a captain and a first officer on the bridge. I want her to have all the honors due her."

"Very well, sir."

Pollak looked at the sky, which was overcast except for a small segment to the north, where a few stars shone. "I think we'll have fair weather. . . . See to it that you get a couple of hours' sleep."

"I don't think I'll be able to sleep, sir."

Pollak nodded. "Who can sleep on such a night? Come along. I bet there's a bottle of Pommery left somewhere on board."

Chapter 34

*I*n the dark they had passed the light on Egg Rock, moving very slowly, yard for yard, so as not to overstep the narrow shipping channel between the shallows. As morning began to dawn, they had sailed past Baker Island, still carefully. Now the ship was out in the gulf.

Charles Pollak stood on the bridge and observed the changing color of the water. His hand shaded his eyes against the sun, which had just broken through the mist. The sea was spread out before him. He had seldom seen it so unruffled, so smooth—no wind, no waves.

He listened to the *Cecilie's* engines. They were still not at full power. Impatiently he noted the increasing speed, the onset of the noises he had missed for so long. Just a little more patience, and the *Cecilie* would find her familiar pace.

And yet something was different from earlier crossings. The glass wall before him reflected the bridge, the man. His crew was so attuned to him that there was no need of vocal commands. A gesture sufficed, a look from him; an occasional casual word. Furthermore, today nothing interrupted the procedures on the bridge—no pilots leaving the ship, no revenue inspection, no excited chief purser demanding that he, the captain, settle an argument about a luxury cabin that had been assigned to two different parties. Perhaps it was just this that annoyed him. Perhaps it was some other trivial matter. . . . He threw a glance at his black shoes. No, it couldn't be that; he was standing correctly, his heels on the red runner, the soles on the polished teak.

He signaled to the mate at the engine telegraph. The motor noise turned a shade deeper. The ship's vibration lessened. The tingling in the soles of his feet decreased a little. The rising and falling of the ship grew more even. But his uneasiness remained. He was surprised by the sound of his own voice as he gave the command: "Full speed ahead."

The door to the outside platform was pushed open. Fred Vandermark entered; the third stripe on the sleeve of his coat, freshly stitched on, was clearly distinguishable from the other two. "We're running too fast, sir. The destroyers have wired. They want us to slow down. They can't keep up with us."

Silence pervaded the bridge. The men were waiting for Pollak's answer. Pommerenke moved out of his corner. "Coffee, anyone?" No one paid him any attention. "Freshly made hot coffee? Nobody?" He tried once more and then retreated with the pot.

"Continue full speed ahead, sir?"

Pollak turned vehemently and stared at the mate. The captain's eyes grew hard, a vein stood out on his temple—then he had himself back under control. "No sense running away from them, is there?" He did not know whether his expression betrayed any of his emotion. "Vandermark."

"Yes, sir."

"Take over. Pommerenke . . . coffee." He stepped aside, his eyes still straight ahead.

He drank his coffee, holding the cup with both hands. He only half listened as Vandermark gave orders. One day, he thought, he would have made a good captain, not just in the dining saloon with the ladies, but also on the high seas. He knew it would never happen. A few days in Boston, and then . . . He, Pollak, had always looked on his first officers—all who had served under him—as his sons. It was an old dream of his: the North Atlantic crisscrossed by ships commanded by his "sons." Later, when he was retired, he would keep track of their departures and arrivals. Perhaps they would invite him on board now and then, when they were in the home port, decant a bottle for him, perhaps even uncork a magnum. . . .

Would it ever happen? He tried to force himself to believe it, but at the thought his heart contracted. And today's trip? Hadn't he hoped too much from it?

He was suddenly reminded of a time, many years ago, when he steered one of his ships, which had been put out of service, to the wreckers. According to an old seamen's tradition, some of the men of the original crew had come along; a few of the earlier passengers had also been on board to accompany the ship to its final resting place. Pollak had been so depressed by the voyage that he swore never again to guide a ship to the scrapyard.

And now? Was this journey any different? Boston? Dead, brackish water. Barely any tides. A ship graveyard. No, he would not think about it now.

The noise of the engines filled the ship. The *Cecilie's* pace had altered. The long wedge of green-tinted surf pushing in from the Atlantic was battling against the hull. The rise and fall of the bow transferred itself to Pollak's body. The *Cecilie* went, as she had always gone, her gentle, elegant way.

Once again he became aware of how much she meant to him. She was not just a ship he happened to command. She was his companion, and at this hour he felt as if she were trying to console him in her own way.

The man on the bridge smiled without knowing that he did so. The smile mingled happiness and sorrow. Perhaps he had no reason for grieving. Perhaps *she* was right. And yet he felt that something irrevocable had taken place. Nothing would ever again be as it had been. . . .

At that very hour in Bar Harbor many people shared the captain's emotion. They crowded along the shore and stared, disconcerted, out into the empty bay. The *Cecilie* was no longer there—they saw, and yet they could not believe. And so they stood and looked, as if by sheer persistence they might be able to recall the ship to her mooring.

Only a few had personally seen her put out to sea, a few fishermen and dock workers. The news had spread like wildfire, and all of Bar Harbor had run to the shore. It was too late; the ship was out of sight, and yet more people still came running.

The few who had observed the *Cecilie's* departure were bombarded with questions, but what did they have to tell? A ship with four smoking funnels, anchors being hauled up . . .

Basically it was just the same as the ship's sudden appearance one morning in Frenchman Bay. At that time no one knew where she had come from—now no one knew where she had gone.

More than an hour passed before the crowd began to disperse. Once more the shore grew empty and silent. Only a few isolated figures remained, wandering up and down the wharf, time and again staring out into the empty bay.

The first morning ferry came in, and life resumed its normal course. Somewhat later that morning there was another commotion in front of the display window of the local shipping line on Main Street. Children had discovered it first: in the window, on blue material draped in such a way as to represent waves, lay the icing model of the *Cecilie* that had won first prize at the Eden Fair.

July 1940

S he stood before the tall folding doors in the library of their house
and looked out at the terrace and the grounds. After two weeks
without a drop, it had finally begun to rain in the early morning. It was
a redemption, and the overcast sky promised that it would not end soon.

She seemed delicate, almost fragile, in her dress of dull red silk.
The cane on which she leaned further emphasized the slenderness of
her figure. But when she turned because she heard him enter, the impression was erased; only a very animated woman remained.

"Something wrong with me?" Her green eyes smiled at him, and
the eyes more than anything else made him forget her age.

He did not answer at once. The possession of a beautiful wife was
for him a large part of his good fortune. He had been given a great
deal, and he had always remained aware of the fact. Today, however,
there was an occasion that made him particularly receptive to his wife's
beauty, so that he took in every detail: the delicate form; the plainly cut
dress; the thin gold chain that seemed natural to her and yet somehow
had a dramatic effect; her pale, fine complexion; her reddish-blond
hair. . . . Only the way she wore her hair was different from other days.
It was combed away from her forehead and waved. Involuntarily his
eyes went to her portrait over the fireplace in the library.

"Don't be unfair," she said, smiling. "When that picture was
painted I was thirty-six."

"So?" He said. "The picture has aged, not you. . . . What I noticed, you're wearing your hair differently?"

"Yes," she said. "It's back in fashion. Like in the old Bar Harbor days. . . . Just tell me if you don't like it. Helen has already gone on record against it."

"Where is she anyway? I hardly ever see my daughter anymore."

"You'll be seeing her tonight. She's bringing someone; be prepared to have him ask for her hand."

"The naval cadet from Annapolis?"

"Oh, I know, it's hard for you to get used to the idea of giving your daughter away. It's lucky we have only one. I wouldn't want to be your son-in-law."

"My only question is, does it have to be a navy man?"

"Apparently Helen can't be serious about anyone else. Don't forget that she has inherited the weakness from both parents."

He would not be amused; his thoughts went further. The war in Europe—this time the United States would not stay out of it as long as last time, and their two sons—aged twenty-five and twenty-three—would be serving in the navy. It was a different time; there were no more Bar Harbor summers. . . .

He looked at the clock on the mantelpiece. "If we want to get to the auction on time, we ought to be leaving."

"I wish you'd go alone." She had put the cane aside, as always when she was not alone; her broken hip, with its inserted pin, robbed her movements of some of their agility. "It's still a little too soon for me to climb around old ships."

He looked at her and shook his head. It was not like her to sidestep the truth. "That's not your only reason, is it?"

"It occurred to me that perhaps you were only being polite when you asked me to come along and that you might prefer to go alone." She went over to him and pulled the white handkerchief a little farther out of the breast pocket of his dark suit. Her hands were the only feature consonant with her true age; they were heavily dotted with pigmentation, and the thin golden wedding ring clung loosely on the fourth finger of her left hand. "I can imagine how you must be feeling. To see the ship again after all these years . . . There are feelings we don't want to share with anyone."

Surely some of what she said was true. It had been something of a shock when he read that the *Cecilie* would be going on the auction block. He had not even known that she still existed and had been lying for years in Chesapeake Bay—practically in his front yard. One company had bought her for scrap, and other had assumed the chore of selling off whatever could be wrested from her innards before the welders did their work.

"Maybe you're right," he said. "She won't be a pretty sight." He picked up the auction catalogue lying on the table at the center of the room. "Did you find anything you want me to bid for?"

"Most of the stuff seems worthless. I can't imagine who is supposed to buy it. Maybe number two hundred forty-one. I might like to have that. You really ought to be leaving."

Giving him no time to check the catalogue, she walked with him into the hall. The driver and car were already waiting outside the door. Fred Vandermark placed his raincoat over his arm and kissed her.

"I like the way you're wearing your hair."

"You have money with you?"

"Money?"

"They don't accept checks, according to the auction rules, only cash."

It was typical of Gloria, he thought later in the back seat of the leather-upholstered Daimler, that she had reminded him of the money, but equally typical that she would not go with him to the auction. This was perhaps her best trait—an unfailing instinct for when it was best to leave him alone. She had always made sure that he had enough space to remain himself. Perhaps it was instinct, perhaps it was cleverness. He really had been lucky with her—and she with him. For if at the beginning some people in Baltimore had seen him only as the prince consort—and a German one to boot—they had quickly forgotten this attitude in the face of the yearly increasing returns and dividends of the shipyard and the shipping firm. Today L & V was the largest repair yard in Baltimore harbor, and the L & V lines carried more freight than any other in the East.

"To the office?"

The chauffeur's question wrenched him from his thoughts. "No, George. Head for Chesapeake Bay. The Iron and Metal Docks. I'll give you directions when we get there."

The driver's eyes appeared in the rearview mirror. "The place they call death row, sir?"

"Yes."

"I know the place. There's a lot of ghost ships there. Sad old skeletons. I used to work for a scrapper, and I can tell you—"

"If we want to be on time, you'll have to step on it."

He leaned back. The drive would take an hour, perhaps longer in the heavy rain. The seesaw of the windshield wipers, the hum of the motor, the patter of the rain on the roof—all had a soothing effect on him.

They had left the city behind. From time to time the road ran along the water, and through the veil of rain he saw the funnels of ships at sea. From Baltimore to the Atlantic it was ninety miles as the crow flies, but there were days when the ocean seemed closer. This was one of them.

He opened the catalogue, turned the pages. He did not really intend bidding on anything. He knew about such auctions. He also knew the kinds of buyers they attracted: shipfitters, directors of maritime museums, antiquarians, a multitude of small bidders hoping for bargains. He scanned most of the items. Sixteen lifeboats were being sold off, four pewter coffins, gymnasium equipment, a printing press, ten leather armchairs from the smoking saloon, a billiard table, the wood paneling from a first-class cabin, ten ice-making machines, twenty patented egg cookers, one dinner gong, a hundred fifty silver-plated fish forks and knives. . . . Other items attracted his attention: a Steinway grand piano from the ladies' saloon; red runners from the captain's cabin; a ship's bell; complete wood paneling from the verandah café, East Frisian style; the original lettering of the ship's name from the stern, in brass, estimated value $150; the equivalent lettering from starboard, three missing letters, estimated value $100. He passed the page including item number 241. He went back to it.

> Table service for twelve persons, rimmed
> in cornflower blue, decor representing eagle
> and crown; Royal Factory Berlin, presum-
> ably honoring the ship's patroness; minimal
> damage.

The final dinner on board the *Cecilie*, the night before they raised anchor from Bar Harbor. . . . He remembered the table, the confetti, the streamers. Why out of everything that was being offered had Gloria chosen this particular item? The estimated value was around seventy dollars. Had her unfailing instinct realized the true value? Was she buying a memory? Where would the dishes find room in their house? Might she use them for a dinner party? . . . He laid the catalogue aside. It was truly astonishing that after so many years so many of the old objects were left.

He glanced out the window. They had arrived at the waterfront. They passed a wharf. The outlines of a new building became visible, the spark-spewing purple light arcs of the welders. . .

"To the cooling sheds, then make a left turn," he said.

"I'll find the way."

The twenty-six years that had passed since Bar Harbor contracted. In early December 1914 the formalities had been completed. At Christmas he had married Gloria Lindsay. Charles Pollak came to Baltimore to be his best man and returned to Boston, to the *Cecilie*. Three years later the captain had been allowed to make the trip to Baltimore once more, for the christening of their second son, named Charles after Pollak; their first son, Nick, born in 1915, had been named for Gloria's father.

In these early years Vandermark still struggled against the feeling that he had abandoned Pollak and the ship. He tried to lure Pollak away from Boston with offers, perhaps only so as to assuage his own conscience. But then, when the war dragged on and on—1915, 1916—he felt that he had acted properly. In April 1917 America entered the war against Germany. Within a couple of hours the many German ships resting in American harbors had been seized as spoils of war, their crews interned. The *Cecilie* and its captain had been among them. Less than six months later the ship put out to sea again—under a different name, of course—covered with camouflage paint, the dining saloon transformed into a provisional field hospital, the decks stuffed from bottom to top with American soldiers.

In the years 1917 and 1918 the *Mount Vernon*—as the *Cecilie* was now called—plied her old Atlantic route, taking troops to western France, bringing back the wounded. Her times of departure and arrival were secret, but Vandermark learned of them through his contacts in the Navy Department.

Then he heard that in early September 1918 she had received a torpedo hit in the forward boiler room; thirty-six dead, two hundred sea miles outside of Brest. No one had believed she could make port.

He recalled discussing the incident with Pollak. It had been their last encounter, in New York, before Pollak's journey home to Germany after a long internment. Pollak had wasted no words on his own fate but had spoken only of the *Cecilie*, which had just returned, leaking and damaged. Vandermark could almost hear Pollak's voice, see the smile on his face as he said, "That's how she is—just put enough water under her keel, and she won't let you down. She'd make it across the Atlantic on crutches. She always was a lucky ship."

But she was not to be lucky after that. She was made fast, put in mothballs. Time and again there had been plans. Two American lines considered using her for passenger cruises. He himself had once thought of buying her and refitting her, but the mail contract fell through. None of the many projects became a reality, and as the years passed, he had forgotten them. Did she still exist? He had not even wondered any more until, a few days ago, he came across the notice that Iron and Metal had bought a ship named *Stars and Stripes*, formerly *Mount Vernon*, formerly *Kronprinzessin Cecilie*. Scrap value $178,300. His first reaction had been something like pride at the large figure. . . .

He realized that the car was slowing down. The wheels slithered over a siding. Scummy water splashed out of potholes. Then the car stopped.

"I can't drive any closer."

He got out, put on his raincoat, and picked up the catalogue. The drizzle was mingled with the mist of the bay. One could smell the nearness of the water, a mixture of iron, spilled oil, and fish.

"No umbrella?"

"No, thanks." He could see that he did not have a long way to go. They were parked in the front row of a lot reserved for visitors to the auction; a few private cars, many trucks, two buses which had brought the small bidders. Some of the cars were already being loaded with stuff garnered at the auction.

"There she lies."

He nodded silently. He had been prepared for a sorry sight, but what he saw was worse. The *Cecilie* was no more than a ghost of her former self, begrimed all over, her sides and stern scraped and dented, corroded by rust. No longer a ship, merely a helpless wreck, she lay there, listing slightly toward the dock. She seemed to him a colossal creature of the ocean that had been harpooned and dragged to land, there to be gutted. And still there remained a remnant of dignity, a composure preserved with difficulty, symbolized by the four powerful funnels and the three masts.

On the gangway leading to the ship, he had to step aside and wait while two men carried out a heavy bronze relief. He vaguely remembered that the carving had been set in the wall over the fireplace in the smoking saloon. Once on board, his feeling of being on a ghost ship grew stronger. Everything around him seemed strange and alien.

He did not follow the red arrows to the auction room. Suddenly he had a desire to seek out his own cabin. His steps on the bare iron, where once thick carpets had been laid, echoed in his ears. Wood paneling had been torn away, doors were missing. . . . Had this been his cabin? He stared into a burnt-out, blackened room, a hole. He knew what had happened. On beached ships rats gnaw at the rubber insulation around the electrical wires hidden behind the paneling, causing short circuits, starting fires.

He roamed aimlessly, as if he were on a ship he had never seen before, until finally he came across the red arrows again. In the distance he heard the voice of the auctioneer, monotonous and penetrating, only occasionally interrupted by the thud of the hammer. The voice was coming from the onetime first-class dining saloon.

The auctioneer stood on the platform where the orchestra used to play. The rows of chairs for the bidders had already begun to empty. On entering he had hesitated for an instant, overcome by the shock of recognition. The memory of the many brilliant parties he had attended here formed too drastic a contrast to the melancholy somberness pervading the hall. The men and women had kept on their damp raincoats, their wet hats. The smell of damp clothing filled the air.

A center aisle separated the rows of chairs. He walked to the front and found a seat on the aisle in the third row. The chair was upholstered in green leather.

"Number two hundred and seven. Three oil paintings, representing seascapes, signed J. Ohling, from the former ladies' saloon. I'm offered fifteen dollars. . . ."

He listened to the auctioneer's voice, the offers, the hammer thuds. He perceived the objects being carried in, held up, auctioned off, and carried out again. He was equally struck by the totality of his forgetting and by the precision of some memories. The chair on which he sat, for example—he could clearly see the place and the room where it used to stand. He had half closed his eyes. It was as if something were irresistibly drawing him back into times past. The room around him seemed to grow lighter. Stucco ornaments that had been chipped away were back in place. He saw a table set festively, he heard music, a particular tune. He heard laughter, he saw the streamers wriggling down upon the tables. And there was a unique, fresh scent. The illusion was complete. . . .

"Presumably dedicated to the ship's sponsor, damaged. I am offered seventy dollars. Will anyone bid higher? No other offers?"

He had almost missed the announcement of item number 241. Hastily he raised his hand. "Eighty dollars."

Someone in the front row outbid him. He raised again. The auctioneer's voice became more animated.

"A hundred and twenty dollars." The hammer pointed at him, then again at the front row. "A hundred and forty dollars."

Until now he had paid no attention to the other bidder. Leaning sideways, he saw that it was a woman. She wore a moss-green dress with black polka dots, on her head a veiled hat. Her hand, raised in bidding, sparkled with many rings. She too seemed to take an interest in her rival, for she turned around. The hair under the small black hat was white as snow, the face under the veil was old. A pair of dark eyes was turned on him, an expression of recognition, of surprise—and then a smile.

"Are you still in the bidding?" The auctioneer's voice sounded impatient. "The gentleman in the third row. Are you still in the running?"

Vandermark hesitated, then gestured his retreat.

"A hundred and forty dollars once, a hundred and forty dollars twice, a hundred and forty dollars . . . going, going, gone. Number two hundred and forty-two, four table lamps, candle-shaped, brass base . . ."

The woman in the front row got to her feet. She took money out of her purse. He could see her quickly counting out bills and handing them to a man in a brown chauffeur's uniform. Then she walked toward Vandermark. Her high-heeled pumps clattered on the parquet. Gold hoops glittered at her wrists. She lifted the veil from her face and opened her arms. But she did not speak. She, who had never lacked for the right word, remained silent.

Vandermark had been afraid that he would see the face of an aged woman, but the opposite was the case. Without the veil she appeared younger. The smooth, high forehead, the dark eyes—it was the face of a precocious, stubborn child. He leaned down, and she kissed him on both cheeks, all the while holding him by the arms.

"Thank you," she said. "Thank you for letting me have it."

How old would she be? He did some mental arithmetic. Eighty-nine? Had she grown a little shorter? A little smaller? Her posture was straight as an arrow, her eyes held the same glow, the same vitality as before. Vandermark could not find words.

"Of course, I would have preferred getting it for seventy dollars," she said.

"You still got a bargain."

"Don't let anyone hear you." She lowered her voice. "Fortunately no one here has any idea of its real value. Come along. One can never be sure that they pack things properly. I don't want to take home a crate of broken china."

"Temperance Butler," he said. "Temperance C. Butler . . . I can hardly believe it. And you came all the way from Boston to bid on the china?"

"There's only one set of this table service in the whole world. It's an oddity. And I've come from farther away than Boston—I've come from Bar Harbor. If I'd been in Boston, I probably would never have found out about the auction, but they reported it in our little Bar Harbor paper. People there still care about the *Cecilie*."

He could not help himself; he could not stop staring at her. "How old are you Temperance?"

"But Fred, what a question."

"You seem—"

"Not so very decrepit, is that what you mean? Someone who wants to live a long time can't afford to be sick." She took his arm. "All the same, I'll be glad to let you support me."

The distribution post was located in the former main lounge. Her chauffeur was standing by the table, supervising the packers.

"Keep an eye on them, Jenkins," she said.

"Jenkins?" Vandermark asked. "Jenkins, wasn't he . . ."

She smiled. "A few years have passed, after all. This is the son. I'm the one who is old. I like to surround myself with young people. It's enough having to stand by as one's old friends die off one by one, but one's staff—no."

"You haven't changed, dear lady."

"Should I have? Sometime or other I will change, perhaps in my next life. It's too late for this one, don't you agree?"

"Presumably. . . . And you've come from Bar Harbor? How is Anne?"

"Still the same, polite, proper Fred Vandermark who knows the right thing to say. Even then I liked that about you. Yes, Anne is well. You did know that she married Alec Butler the very same year? By now she's on her third husband. Her first two marriages weren't very happy, but now she seems to have found the right one. I don't see much of her during the year. They live in Chicago. But in the summer they come to Bar Harbor and stay with me."

"You still have the house?" What was the point of these questions? Anne? Edith Connors? He knew from the outset that he was only causing himself pain, and her as well.

"Oh, yes, there have been a lot of changes in Bar Harbor, but not everything has changed, not my house. . . . What is it, Jenkins? Did they really do a good job of packing? Better make two trips. And then wait for me in the car. Don't worry, Mr. Vandermark will see to it that I get off the ship safe and sound."

"You still go to Bar Harbor every summer?"

"Wouldn't that be a major revolution in the family, a summer without Bar Harbor! The Yellow House is filled to the rafters with grandchildren and great-grandchildren. I always thought, Once my children have left home, life will simmer down. But then the grand-children came, the great-grandchildren—and my first great-great-grandchild is already on the way."

Behind the folding doors the announcements and bids went on.

"No more trips to Europe?"

"No. I tried it once or twice after the war, but it wasn't the same. Do you like the new liners? I think they're horrible. The ships and the captains . . . Tell me"—her eyes, expressing aversion, wandered through the ugly space—"what became of Charlie Pollak?" She made a gesture. "Does he know about this?"

"Oh no, no . . ." Vandermark hesitated, and yet something drove him to put the question. "When did you see him last?"

"Charlie? In Boston, after that terrible business. . . . I don't think he ever felt easy in Boston, not through all those years. I tried every-thing in my power, but his heart was still in Bar Harbor. Somehow or other he regretted having left Frenchman Bay. He hid on his ship, cut himself off; you could hardly persuade him to accept an invitation. And then, of course, the public mood shifted after the sinking of the *Lusitania*; now they were the 'wicked Huns.' But for him the worst was when the *Cecilie* was seized in nineteen seventeen. They came marching up with more than a hundred policemen, and they herded the crew into the dining saloon. All the men were made to leave the ship in a matter of hours, and then they were kept sitting in the emigration halls. It took weeks before they were given decent quarters. No place was willing to harbor them, the 'wicked Huns.'"

"He never said a word about it," Vandermark said, "the last time I saw him, before he returned to Germany. Did you keep in touch with him?"

"No. He promised to write as soon as he was given another ship—"

"He was not given another ship. There were no more ships after the war. And by the time there were ships again, he was too old."

"What are you keeping from me, Fred?"

"Pollak is no longer alive."

"Charlie? If he did not have a ship . . . how could it have happened? Don't tell me he died in bed."

"What makes you say that?"

"I simply can't imagine it. Charlie Pollak dying of some ordinary disease—it doesn't suit him. Charlie . . . when did it happen?"

"Some . . . it must be over five years ago."

"Then he was . . . seventy-five. Am I right?" She lowered the veil of her hat.

"You do know that Pollak looked on all the first officers he trained as his sons? He was very proud of them. One of them later became the captain of the *Bremen,* the first major ship Lloyd built after the war; in nineteen twenty-nine she garnered the Blue Riband."

"Does that have to do with his death?"

Vandermark nodded. Suddenly he could no longer stand it. He took her arm and led her outside. "The captain of the *Bremen* was called Ziegenhain," he continued, "and whenever his ship made fast in Bremerhaven, Pollak visited him on board. You know, he was a familiar figure, the former captain of the *Cecilie,* looking up his 'sons.'. . . Charlie hadn't changed. These visits were the occasion for monumental binges. It was in November of nineteen thirty-four, the sixteenth of November. The *Bremen* was anchored at the Columbus

Dock, slated to put to sea the following day. There was the usual farewell drinking bout. Pollak left the ship around midnight. The man who saw him last was the quartermaster, who had the watch at the gangplank. The wharves in the channel area are very narrow. . . . Yes, he fell in the water and drowned."

Jenkins, the chauffeur, had waited for Temperance C. Butler at the dock. He opened the umbrella and held it over her head.

"My God," she said. "He went to sea for forty years, and then that had to happen."

"They did not find his body for three months; the water did not give him up until then."

"And he never went to sea again, you said . . . later, after the war?"

"No. He did all sorts of things, even social director at a spa on the North Sea, but he never went to sea again. Perhaps he didn't want to anymore, after the *Cecilie*."

She walked with short steps, carefully avoiding the larger puddles. The rain was coming down harder now, and she was eager to reach her car. It was a black Rolls-Royce, and Vandermark had it on the tip of his tongue to say something about her change of mind, but she was quicker off the mark. "Would you still claim that I haven't changed? To stop time altogether—even I can't do that. But in Bar Harbor I still keep two horses and an old victoria."

Jenkins was holding the door open for her.

"And now you haven't bought anything at all," she said to Vandermark. "And that is why you came, isn't it?"

"No, that wasn't the reason. . . . I'm glad to have seen you again."

She smiled. "When you say something, it sounds as if you mean it. Why don't you visit Bar Harbor?" She got into the back seat, rolled down the window. "It's been an eternity since I played four-handed piano."

"Perhaps." She had not asked about Gloria, his marriage, his children. Was the oversight intentional, or did she know everything she needed to know already?

She put out her hand. "You're probably right; what's done is done. But you know what makes me angry? I should have bought L and V stock in time. I should have known that it would go up. Good-bye, Fred."

He kissed her hand. She smiled under the veil. "Still some European remnants?"

She rolled up the window. The car jumped backward, went into gear. Her head appeared behind the pane of glass, she waved her hand, and although it was not possible, he thought he heard the clatter of her bracelets.

He turned around and looked back at the *Cecilie*. It was good that Pollak had not had a chance to see her again.

Only now did he realize that he had left the auction catalogue on the ship. Somehow he felt relieved that he had not acquired anything.

Very near him stood a man who, like himself, was looking over at the ship. His light gabardine coat was dark with rain at the shoulders. "Used to be a beautiful ship. . . . She was a real beauty."

The man had spoken without turning his head. He did not have any foreign accent, but his appearance had something that was not American—the gabardine coat perhaps, the shoes of pale buckskin. His hands held a small object.

"Did you get something at the auction?" Vandermark asked.

The man opened his hand and held it out. "Just this." His palm held a bottle opener. The handle was engraved in blue, "Viennese Café."

The man smiled. "I used to be a steward on the *Cecilie*—that used to be her name, *Kronprinzessin Cecilie*—and the Viennese Café was my station." He stared straight at Vandermark. "Say, do we know each other?"

Vandermark shook his head, although a vague recollection was stirring in him.

"Excuse me, I just thought . . ." The hand closed around the opener again.

Vandermark gave a final look at the *Cecilie*. He was searching for the bridge. Like the rest of the ship, it was covered with rust, a metal skeleton. But he saw something else: a resplendent facade of windows, and behind it the shadow of a gigantic figure. . . .

The man at his side was saying, "Nobody can understand . . . nobody who didn't sail on her."